大範圍、多情境練習╳最實用、超精闢解析，
語感好了，什麼英文考試都難不倒你，
聽得懂、看得快，高分自然輕鬆手到擒來！

使用說明

聽力測驗 🎧 Track 025

在學習英文的過程中,「聽」可能是最直接觸的第一線接觸,也可能是最需要快速習得的能力。現在,就讓我們來熟悉各種英文情境,提升自己的英文臨場感吧!

( ) 1. The passage is mainly about_____.
  (A) a photo　　　　(B) a painting
  (C) a newspaper　　(D) a studio

( ) 2. According to the text, the most intriguing part of the painting is Mona Lisa's_____.
  (A) eyes　　　(B) smile
  (C) hair　　　(D) face

( ) 3. The "Mona Lisa" painting is now exhibited in_____.
  (A) the Louvre Museum in Berlin
  (B) the Louvre Museum in Boston
  (C) the Louvre Museum in London
  (D) the Louvre Museum in Paris

( ) 4. Who's Mona Lisa?
  (A) Lisa del Giocondo.
  (B) Leonardo da Vinci.
  (C) Lillian Schwartz of Bell Labs.
  (D) There's no solid proof yet.

( ) 5. "Mona Lisa" is no doubt the most_____ painting in the world.
  (A) suspicious　　(B) dramatic
  (C) ridiculous　　(D) famous

🎧 聽力測驗 🎧 Track 025

在學習英文的過程中,「聽」可能要快速習得的能力。現在,就讓場感吧!

1. The passage is

⭐ Step 1. 聽力強化

「聽」是人類與生俱來的學習本能!先掃描QR code MP3(見封面),開始答題,透過耳朵來做第一時間的英語感知練習,看看你的英語反射神經有多快!

⭐ Step 2. 閱讀強化

聽力成績不理想?口音、語速等都可能是肇因,別太鑽牛角尖,改由閱讀方式來重新測驗,不僅可能有扳回一城的機會,也能回頭檢視聽力問題並且改進!

閱讀測驗

剛剛的聽力測驗是否因為答聽不順而感到讀懂?或是覺得自己有某些地方聽不夠好?現在就讓我們來自看!剛剛的聽力測驗,並透過後面的閱讀測驗來彌補聽力上的不足,同時考驗自己的閱讀能力吧!

Leonardo da Vinci's "Mona Lisa" is no doubt the most famous painting in the world. The paint was applied in thin layers, and this almost makes the painting **glow**. The most intriguing part of the painting is Mona Lisa's fleeting, knowing smile. It is depicted as one of the most **subtle** smiles in art history. But da Vinci did not accidentally capture this haunting and **mysterious** smile on his model. He intentionally wanted it that way. It is said that he had beautiful music played all through the sittings to make sure the smile wouldn't fade away.

The painting is now exhibited in the Louvre Museum in Paris and protected by **thick** glass to prevent damage.

Due to the bewildering smile, which has caused so much speculation and is like no other, "Mona Lisa" has been so loved and adored by the world. They say that da Vinci always wrote the records of model's sittings in his journal. No one, however, could find out any records about who the model of Mona Lisa was.

Some say that the model was Lisa del Giocondo, the wife of a Florentine **businessman**. But Dr. Lillian Schwartz of Bell Labs suggested that da Vinci appears to be the model of the Mona Lisa. She proved her opinion by analyzing the facial features of da Vinci's face and those of Mona Lisa's on the painting, and then used a computer to digitize both the self-portrait of da Vinci and the Mona Lisa painting and merge the two images together. What this results in is the fact that the features of the two faces lined up perfectly.

The truth is that no matter who the model of Mona Lisa was, da Vinci really successfully **captured** the character of his subject. So, who's Mona Lisa? What's your viewpoint?

☆ Step 3. 中譯輔助學習

在「聽完」和「看完」題目內容，並順利回答完題目後，本書每單元情境內容皆附中譯，鉅細靡遺，讓你不再孤軍奮戰！

☆ Step 4. 解析能力再提升

題題解析，幫助你找到破解聽力、閱讀的蛛絲馬跡，並養成具備一眼看穿題型和答案的能力，不只答得對、更答得快！

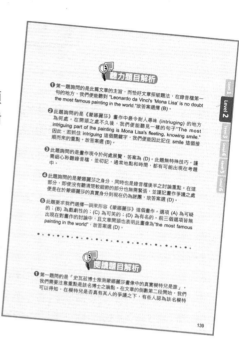

☆ Step 5. 暖心單字補充

為了讓你更高分，本書貼心彙整出常用單字，讓你一面用現有的英文實力挑戰聽力和閱讀題，同時又學到更多單字！

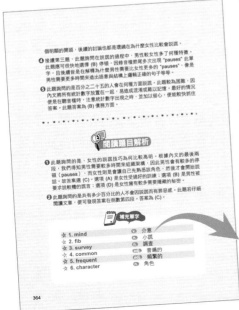

補充單字

1. mind	v.	介意
2. fib	n.	小謊
3. survey	n.	調查
4. common	adj.	普遍的
5. frequent	adj.	頻繁
character	n.	角色

Preface 前言

　　考試，美其名是在「檢視學習成果」，但實際上它大多數時候，都只有「扼殺學習樂趣」的功用。這並非指考試的存在一無是處，而是我認為它欠缺了除成績、分數以外，可以給學習者們主動參與、積極練習的「刺激與誘因」，如果能讓考試本身或它的準備過程變得更彈性靈活，會不會讓大家不會再這麼抗拒它？這個問題我思考許久後，便寫下了這本書。

　　雖然大家常把我當成是一名「英語教學者」，但事實上，我同樣是個「英語學習者」，每天都在這樣的環境下學到新東西。我特別喜歡從「教」和「學」兩種不同角度來看待英語，發覺其奇妙之處，並從此不斷發掘學習的樂趣，而其中覺得最無壓力的學習方式就是「多聽多看」——但不是硬是強迫自己去聽和看考試會考的文章，因為那實在是太枯燥乏味了，一點都不好玩，連我自己當學生時都痛苦不堪。相反地，從生活化的內容、或感興趣的議題去下手，才是我從小到大都願意持續學習的動力。

　　所以我開始思考，我自己的學習經驗有沒有辦法套用在教學上？我希望能將心比心，把我喜歡的方法分享給更多學習者，使他們自動自發學習，並且順利通過「考試」這個過程，從中強化自信心，建立起一個「快樂學習→取得高分→快樂學習→取得高分」的良性循環本書從各大英語考試都一定會有的「聽力題」和「閱讀題」著手，藉由先後順序的設計，讓你先從聽力部分開始習慣語感，接著在閱讀題型深刻思考，達成眼耳相通的雙感官連結，逐漸習慣英文考試的步調。當然，要想長時間不間斷的練習，題目的選擇就必須夠好玩才行，所以本書精選了共90篇不同情境，但都具備著生活下、有趣、不死板的短文，讓你可以省下買咖啡提神的動作，清醒地一篇接著一篇練習下去。

　　語言的學習絕對不是片段性的，應該是一種有邏輯的、全方面並且可以同步提昇各項能力的學習。我由衷希望這本書可以對於想要考到好成績，卻苦無好方法的你有所幫助，如果你因為這樣的學習方法而有所斬獲，我也將感到榮幸，並且更有動力去傳授我的經驗給更多想學好英文的人。

張慈庭

Contents

使用説明／002　　前言／004

基礎程度╳小試身手

01 螃蟹與媽媽／014

02 潘朵拉的盒子／019

03 狼與鶴／024

04 以德報怨／029

05 無價的狗／034

06 奧爾良的女英雄／039

07 公主的百寶箱／044

08 沉默是金／049

09 奇怪的訪客／054

10 花床的秘密／059

11 奇聞軼事／064

12 富有的國王和貧窮的農夫／069

13 阿基米德與金皇冠／074

14 神奇的魔法帽／079

15 致命傷／084

16 不當將軍的士兵不是好士兵？／089

17 別用笨方法思考！／094

18 貓有九條命／099

19 貧窮的音樂家／104

20 獅身人面的謎／109

循序漸進╳難度加強

01 麵包店老闆娘與她的貓／116

02 給人以魚不如授人以漁／121

03 三明治的由來／126

04 耶誕節的由來／131

05 蒙娜麗莎之謎／136

06 達摩克利斯之劍／141

07 永遠的兩姐妹／146

08 誠實的華盛頓／151

09 愚人節的電話你敢接嗎？／156

10 蘇格蘭男人的裙子／161

11 巴比倫的空中花園／166

12 連體嬰／171

13 伊莉莎白一世／176

14 美國第一千金──伊凡卡／181

15 世界上最高的人／186

16 金氏世界紀錄：世界最長壽的男性人瑞──
克里斯塔爾／191

17 老人與海／196

18 美國雇主與雇員之間的關係／201

19 《我就要你好好的》／206

20 《怪獸與牠們的產地》／211

Level 3

持續精進╳挑戰自我

01 英美待客的差異／218

02 女神卡卡／223

03 英國媒體／228

04 不同的飲食習慣／233

05 科技巨人：伊隆・馬斯克／238

06 英式足球與美式足球的區別／243

07 老少配會幸福嗎？／248

08 英國皇室新成員──梅根・馬克爾／253

09 外商公司對英文履歷的要求／258

10 英美文化的差異／263

11 智商測驗／268

12 美國人最忙的一天／273

13 巴黎風情 ／278

14 美國精神科醫生與牙醫的共同點 ／283

15 美國鄉村音樂 ／288

隨心所欲╳運用自如

01 十字軍東征 ／294

02 亞洲最受歡迎的手機通訊軟體之一：Line ／299

03 紀梵希的品牌創始人──紀梵希先生 ／304

04 世紀大發現──中國秦兵馬俑 ／309

05 什麼是內容農場？ ／314

06 擴增實境 ／318

07 神奇的極光 ／323

08 機器人醫生問世 ／328

09 英語的發展歷史 ／333

10 通往幸福之路 ／339

11 東西文化的差異 ／345

12 北美發現最古老靈長類化石 ／350

13 托福簡介 ／355

14 英國人最常撒的小謊 ／360

15 睡眠的重要性 ／365

Level 5

驚艷老外╳嘖嘖稱奇

01 職場成功小秘訣／372

02 美國高階主管的薪資／378

03 健康飲食有益健康／384

04 敘利亞內戰，和平遙遙無期？／389

05 複製羊的成敗關鍵／393

06 英國脫歐／399

07 2016里約奧運開幕式／404

08 潔淨能源帶來永續未來／409

09 紙與印刷的歷史／414

10 安寧照護／420

Level 6

頂尖高手╳滿分到手

01 成功的國際商務談判／426

02 白領階級現況／432

03 不可或缺的團隊合作／438

04 服務業的前景展望／444

05 企業外包的好與壞／449

06 直播經濟／454

07 人工智慧虛擬護理助理／459

08 美式英語與英式英語的主要差異／464

09 所謂的後現代主義／469

10 大數據與電子商務／474

CONNECTION
ANALYSIS
DATA
SEARCHING
VERIFICATION
CODING
SENDING

Level 1

基礎程度
×
小試身手

The Crab and His Mother
螃蟹與媽媽

Level 1 01

聽力測驗 🎧 Track 001

在學習英文的過程中，「聽」可能是最直接的第一線接觸，也可能是大家最想要快速習得的能力。現在，就讓我們來熟悉各種英文情境，提升自己的英文臨場感吧！

(　　) 1. The story is taken from _____.
　　(A) a Greek story　　　(B) Aesop's Fables
　　(C) a fairy tale　　　　(D) a novel

(　　) 2. What does the word "strangely" mean according to the article?
　　(A) happily　　　　　(B) beautifully
　　(C) crazily　　　　　(D) weirdly

(　　) 3. Choose the right statement.
　　(A) The crab can only walk to the right.
　　(B) The crab can only walk to the left.
　　(C) The crab walks in a one-sided way.

(　　) 4. Which is wrong according to the text?
　　(A) Crabs live in water.
　　(B) A mother crab used to walk straight.
　　(C) Every creature has its living way.
　　(D) Nature can not be changed easily.

(　　) 5. From the fable we know:
　　(A) Actions speak louder than words.
　　(B) Example is better than precept.
　　(C) Two heads are better than one.
　　(D) No pain, no gain.

 **閱讀測驗**

剛剛的聽力測驗是否因為答題不順而感到遺憾？或是覺得自己有某些地方掌握地不夠好？現在就讓我們來直接「看」剛剛的聽力測驗，並透過後面的閱讀測驗來補齊聽力上的不足，同時考驗自己的閱讀能力吧！

"The Crab and His Mother" is one of the most **famous**[1] Aesop's Fables, which every child, boy or girl, enjoys reading. Please read the fable carefully and try to understand the meaning of the story. It goes as follows:

One day, when the sun was going to rise and the weather was not so hot, a mother crab and her son were crawling together on the seashore. At first they talked happily. About ten minutes later, the mother crab suddenly noticed her son's strange walking. "My child, why do you walk so strangely – in a one-sided way?" she said to her son with surprise. "If you **wish**[2] to make a good appearance and look great, you should go straight forward instead of walking sideways as you do so constantly."

"I do wish to make a good appearance, Mamma," said the **young**[3] crab, "but I do not know the right way to walk. If you could show me how, I will try to walk straight forward."

"Like this, of course," said the mother, as she started off to the **right**[4]. "No, this is the way," said she, as she made another attempt to the left. But no matter how the mother crab tried, she could not walk straight forward even for half a minute. Then the mother crab gave up and walked in her usual way.

The little crab smiled and said, "Maybe you can teach me next time," and he went back to **play**[5] his game.

From the fable, we should learn the **lesson**[6]: "Example is better than precept." While parents usually wish their children the best, it is sometimes easier for children to learn by showing them real examples. In this way, both parents and children will know better about the right way to do a thing.

【 Question 】

(　　) 1. What was the weather like when they are walking on the seashore?
　　　(A) rainny　　　　　　(B) scorching hot
　　　(C) foggy　　　　　　(D) not so hot

(　　) 2. What is the mother crab's attitude toward her own failed attempts?
　　　(A) She was upset.
　　　(B) She blamed the young crab.
　　　(C) She went back to her normal way of walking.
　　　(D) She kept on trying.

【 文章中譯 】

每個孩子，不管男孩或女孩，都喜歡閱讀《伊索寓言》，而〈螃蟹與媽媽〉是伊索寓言裡最著名的其中一則。請仔細地閱讀這則寓言，試著瞭解故事的意義，故事如下：

有一天，當太陽正要升起，並且天氣不是那麼炎熱的時候，螃蟹媽媽和她的兒子在海濱一起爬行。起初他們愉快地交談著。大約過了十分鐘後，螃蟹媽媽突然注意到了兒子奇怪的走路方式。她驚訝地對她的孩子說：「我的孩子，你為什麼走起路來這麼笨拙？如果你想留給別人一個好印象，看上去更好一點，就應該筆直地向前走，而不是像你這樣經常倒向一邊走。」

「我確實想留給別人一個好印象。」小螃蟹說。「但我不知道正確的走路方式。如果妳能教我怎麼走，我就會儘量筆直地往前走。」

「當然就像這個樣子走。」螃蟹媽媽邊說邊開始向右走。「不對，是這個樣子走才對。」她邊說邊又試了一次，這次向左走。但是無論螃蟹媽媽如何努力嘗試，都無法筆直地向前走個至少半分鐘。於是螃蟹媽媽只得放棄，並重回她原本的走路方式。

小螃蟹笑了笑說：「也許你可以下次再教我。」說完，他又自己去玩了。

從這個寓言中，我們懂了一個道理──「身教勝過言教。」儘管父母大多都是為孩子好，有時向孩子們展現真實例子才會讓他們學習得更快更好。如此一來，父母與孩子便能更加清楚如何正確地去做一件事情。

Level 1

Level 2

Level 3

Level 4

Level 5

Level 6

❶ 此題詢問的是故事的來源，我們在錄音檔第一句便能聽見，故答案選 (B)。

❷ 此題詢問「strangely」一字之意。此單字出現在螃蟹媽媽要求小螃蟹改變走路姿勢之時，隨後小螃蟹便開始嘗試筆直地走，代表此單字有負面之意。故答案選 (D) 奇怪地。選項 (A) 為開心地；選項 (B) 為漂亮地；選項 (C) 為瘋狂地。

❸ 此題要求我們選出正確的陳述。選項 (A) 為螃蟹只能向右走路；選項 (B) 為螃蟹只能向左走路；選項 (C) 為螃蟹以單向行走。根據錄音檔的描述，螃蟹並沒有特定只有向左或向右走，而是 "in a one-sided way"，故答案選 (C)。

❹ 此題詢問的是針對故事錯誤的描述。選項 (A) 為螃蟹住在水裡；選項 (B) 為螃蟹媽媽曾經是筆直地走路；選項 (C) 為每個物種都有其生存方式；選項 (D) 為大自然無法被輕易地改變。根據寓言故事的內容，螃蟹媽媽無法向小螃蟹示範如何筆直地走路，且沒有提及螃蟹媽媽以前能否這麼做，故答案選 (B)。選項 (A) 可以 seashore 此單字作為提示。本題為理解題，仔細聽並注意細節即可。

❺ 此題詢問的是我們從這個寓言故事中得知了哪些訊息。若仔細聽錄音檔，我們可以發現答案就在錄音檔的最後一句；若因大意忽略掉訊息，我們也能從故事中得知，螃蟹媽媽本身便無法示範給小螃蟹看如何筆直地走路，因此重點便是「身教勝過言教」。答案選 (B)。選項 (A) 為坐而言不如起而行；選項 (C) 為三個臭皮匠，勝過一個諸葛亮；選項 (D) 為一分耕耘一分收穫。

閱讀題目解析

❶ 此題詢問的是當牠們在海灘上走路時,天氣的狀況如何。答案可見內文第二段,太陽正要升起,且天氣不那麼炎熱,故答案選則 (D)。選項 (A) 為下雨的;選項 (B) 為非常熾熱;選項 (C) 為多霧的。

❷ 此題詢問的是螃蟹媽媽在自身的嘗試失敗後態度為何。答案可見內文倒數第三段,螃蟹媽媽最後只得放棄,並重回她原本走路的方式。故選 (C)。選項 (A) 為她很生氣;選項 (B) 為她責罵小螃蟹;選項 (D) 為她繼續嘗試。

補充單字

☆ 1. famous	adj.	著名的
☆ 2. wish	v.	希望
☆ 3. young	adj.	年輕的、年幼的
☆ 4. right	adj.	正確的、右邊的
☆ 5. play	v.	玩、做遊戲
☆ 6. lesson	n.	課

Level 1 02 — Pandora's Box 潘朵拉的盒子

聽力測驗 Track 002

在學習英文的過程中，「聽」可能是最直接的第一線接觸，也可能是大家最想要快速習得的能力。現在，就讓我們來熟悉各種英文情境，提升自己的英文臨場感吧！

( ) 1. Pandora was the_____woman made by Zeus according to the story.
    (A) first   (B) second
    (C) third   (D) last

( ) 2. What did Venus give Pandora?
    (A) beauty   (B) persuasion
    (C) music   (D) sun

( ) 3. Who gave Pandora the box?
    (A) Prometheus
    (B) Prometheus' brother
    (C) She made it herself.
    (D) the Gods

( ) 4. What made Pandora open the box?
    (A) her illness   (B) her happiness
    (C) her curiosity   (D) her fear

( ) 5. What is the only thing that is left in the box?
    (A) hunger   (B) war
    (C) hope   (D) violence

閱讀測驗

剛剛的聽力測驗是否因為答題不順而感到遺憾？或是覺得自己有某些地方掌握地不夠好？現在就讓我們來直接「看」剛剛的聽力測驗，並透過後面的閱讀測驗來補齊聽力上的不足，同時考驗自己的閱讀能力吧！

Pandora, who was the first woman made by Zeus, was sent to Prometheus and his brother to punish them for caring so much about human beings. She was made in heaven. Every god gave her something to make her perfect. Venus gave her **beauty**[1], Mercury persuasion, Apollo music, and so on. All Gods gave her gifts, and that was why they called her Pandora, which means "all-gifted."

The last gift was a box, in which there was supposed to be a great treasure, but Pandora was ordered never to open it. Then the Messenger took the girl and **brought**[2] her to a man named Epimetheus, who was Prometheus' brother.

Epimetheus had been warned never to **receive**[3] any gift from Zeus, but he was a stupid person and Pandora was very lovely. He accepted her. For a while they got married and lived together in happiness. In the end, however, Pandora's curiosity got the better of her, and she was determined to see for herself what treasure it was that the Gods had given her.

One day when she was alone, she went over to the corner, where her box lay, and with **care**[4] she lifted the lid to have a quick look. The lid flew up out of her hands and knocked her aside, while before her frightened eyes, shadowy shapes flew out of the box in an endless stream.

They were hunger, disease, war, greed, anger, jealousy, labor, and all the griefs and hardships from which man from that day has been suffering. At last the stream became weak, and Pandora, with fear and horror, found strength to shut her box.

Level 1

Level 2
Level 3
Level 4
Level 5
Level 6

The only thing **left**[5] in it now, however, was the only good gift the Gods had put in among the evil ones. It was **hope**[6], and from that time, the hope that is in man's heart is the only thing that has made them able to stand the sorrows that Pandora brought upon them.

【Question】

(　　) 1. What can we infer from the description of Epimethues?
(A) He is a very clever guy.
(B) He was brought to Prometheus.
(C) He was afraid to marry Pandora.
(D) He still accepted a gift from Zeus.

(　　) 2. What word can we use to describe the things coming out of the box?
(A) dark　　　　　　(B) shiny
(C) white　　　　　　(D) bright

【文章中譯】

天神宙斯創造的第一個女人，潘朵拉，被送給了普羅米修斯和他的兄弟，以懲罰他們對人類過分的關心。她是在天上被創造出來的，每個神都給了她一些東西讓她變得完美。維納斯給了她美麗，水神給了她勸服的本領，太陽神阿波羅給她音樂等等。所有的神都給了她禮物，也因此他們叫她潘朵拉，意思是「諸神的禮物」。

最後的禮物是一個盒子，其中按理應是個珍貴的寶物，但潘朵拉卻被警告絕對不能打開它。然後，信使把這個女孩帶到普羅米修斯的兄弟那裡，他的兄弟名叫艾皮米修斯。

艾皮米修斯曾被警告絕對不要收宙斯送的禮物，但他是一個沒有頭腦的人，而潘朵拉又很可愛。他接受了她。過了一段時間他們結了婚，並且很幸福地生活在一起了。然而，最後潘朵拉受好奇心的驅使，她決定親自看一看盒子裡面是什麼寶物。

有一天，當她獨自一人的時候，她走到角落放置盒子的地方，小心翼翼地打開蓋子快速地看了一眼。蓋子飛出她的手，把她打在一邊，她非常害怕，在她面前不斷有可怕、陰暗的奇形怪狀從盒子裡飛出來。

這些是饑餓、疾病、戰爭、貪婪、憤怒、嫉妒、勞碌，和人類從那天起一直在忍受的所有憂患和苦難。最後，潘朵拉儘管非常害怕，還是鼓起勇氣和力量把盒子蓋上了蓋子。

然而，唯一留在盒子裡的，是諸神放在諸多邪惡之中的唯一一個好禮物——希望。至今，它一直是人類生活動力的來源，因為它帶給人類無窮的「希望」，不管遭遇何種困境，它是人類一切不幸中唯一的安慰。

聽力題目解析

❶ 此題詢問的是根據故事，潘朵拉為宙斯之何種女人。根據錄音檔的一開始，我們便能得知，潘朵拉為宙斯所造的第一個女人，故答案選 (A)，此題僅需把握文章的破題手法。選項 (B) 為第二的；選項 (C) 為第三的；選項 (D) 為最後的。

❷ 此題詢問的是維納斯給了潘朵拉什麼禮物。這部分只能仔細聽，並注意關鍵字 "Venus"，故答案選 (A) 美貌。選項 (B) 為勸服；選項 (C) 為音樂；選項 (D) 為太陽。

❸ 此題詢問的是，是誰給了潘朵拉那個盒子。根據錄音檔，我們可以得知潘朵拉被送至普羅米修斯和其兄弟那作為懲罰。後來，其他的天神便送給潘朵拉許多禮物，其中包括那個盒子。故答案選 (D)。

❹ 此題詢問的是，是什麼促使了潘朵拉打開盒子。根據錄音檔中段，我們可以聽見潘朵拉被警告絕不能打開盒子，但好奇心戰勝了她，故答案選 (C)。選項 (A) 為她的疾病；選項 (B) 為她的快樂；選項 (D) 為她的恐懼。此題僅需特別注意潘朵拉在接收到警告之後的後續反應，應能找到關鍵字 "curiosity"。

Level 1
Level 2
Level 3
Level 4
Level 5
Level 6

❺ 此題詢問的是在盒子內的僅剩之物為何。根據錄音檔的後段部分,我們可以聽到在眾多邪惡之物被釋放出來之後,唯一被留在盒子內的是 "hope",即「希望」,故答案選 (C),此題只需注意聽即可。選項 (A) 為饑荒;選項 (D) 為戰爭;選項 (D) 為暴力。

閱讀題目解析

❶ 此題詢問的是,我們可以從針對艾皮米修斯的描述之中推測出何者。選項 (A)為他是個非常聰明的男人;選項 (B) 為他被帶到普羅米修斯那裡;選項 (C) 為他害怕和潘朵拉結婚;選項 (D) 為他仍然接受了來自宙斯的禮物。此題可見內文第二到第三段,潘朵拉被帶至普羅米修斯那,而艾皮米修斯因愚昧和抵擋不了潘朵拉的可愛,便無視警告,仍接受了禮物,故答案選 (D)。

❷ 此題詢問的是選項中何字可以拿來形容從盒子內跑出來的東西。答案可見內文倒數第二段,一旦掌握了 "shadowy"(陰暗的)這個關鍵字,便能選出 (A) 黑暗的作為答案。選項 (B) 為閃亮的;選項 (C) 為白色的;選項 (D) 為明亮的。

補充單字

☆ 1. beauty	n.	美貌
☆ 2. bring	v.	帶來
☆ 3. receive	v.	收到
☆ 4. care	n.	小心
☆ 5. leave	v.	留下
☆ 6. hope	n.	希望

Level 1
03
The Wolf and the Crane
狼與鶴

在學習英文的過程中，「聽」可能是最直接的第一線接觸，也可能是大家最想要快速習得的能力。現在，就讓我們來熟悉各種英文情境，提升自己的英文臨場感吧！

(   ) 1. Many children like reading the story because _____.
     (A) it is a lousy story.
     (B) it is an interesting and meaningful story.
     (C) it is a foreign story
     (D) it is a short story

(   ) 2. Why did the crow and the squirrel not offer their help? Because _____.
     (A) they were not so tall.
     (B) they were busy looking for food at that time.
     (C) they didn't believe the wolf's words and wanted to teach him a lesson.
     (D) they were playing together.

(   ) 3. What does the last word the wolf said to the crane mean?
     (A) The wolf didn't have anything to give the crane.
     (B) He didn't want to give him anything as a reward.
     (C) If the crane had not helped save his life, he would have swallowed the crane.

(   ) 4. What is the main idea of the story?
     (A) We should help people in trouble.
     (B) A greedy person will never appreciate others' help.
     (C) Be a helpful man.

 **閱讀測驗**

剛剛的聽力測驗是否因為答題不順而感到遺憾？或是覺得自己有某些地方掌握地不夠好？現在就讓我們來直接「看」剛剛的聽力測驗，並透過後面的閱讀測驗來補齊聽力上的不足，同時考驗自己的閱讀能力吧！

Level 1
Level 2
Level 3
Level 4
Level 5
Level 6

There is a very interesting and meaningful **story**[1] that children all over the world like to listen to or read. It is called "The Wolf and the Crane." One hot day, when a wolf was eating an animal at the foot of the hill near a river, a small bone from the meat got stuck in his throat. He could not swallow it, so he felt a terrible pain. "Ouch! Ouch!" he tried to shout out painfully.

He ran up and down the hill and along the river and tried to find something to relieve the pain.

He tried to persuade others to remove the bone. "I would give anything you want," he said, "if you would take it out." "I promise, please help!"

At first he saw a crow which was also looking for some food. He begged the crow for help. The crow rolled her eyes and then answered, "No." then she flew away.

The wolf was so sad that he sat on the ground. Looking up, he **found**[2] a squirrel playing in a **tree**[3] near the river. The wolf turned to him, saying, "Will you please be so kind as to help me get the bone out? I will give you everything I have." Hearing this, the squirrel **laughed**[4] and said, "You deserve it!"

At last, the wolf met the crane and he **agreed**[5] to have a try. He told the wolf to open his mouth, and then put his long neck down the wolf's throat.

The crane loosened the bone with its beak, and finally got it out.

"Will you kindly give me the reward?" asked the crane.

The wolf showed his teeth, and said, "Be content; you have put your head into a wolf's mouth and taken it out again safe and sound. That is the **greatest**[6] reward for you."

【Question】

(   ) 1. What can we infer from the crow and squirrel's attitude toward the wolf?
(A) The wolf did not behave in a nice way before.
(B) The crow was excited to help the wolf.
(C) The squirrel only paid attention to look for food.

(   ) 2. What word can be used to describe the relationship among the animals?
(A) fresh   (B) not so well
(C) funny   (D) friendly

【文章中譯】

有一個古老的故事,全世界的孩子們都喜歡聽或讀,那就是《狼與鶴》。在一個很熱的日子,狼在山腳下的小河邊吃著死掉的動物時,不幸地,肉裡的一小塊骨頭卡在牠的喉嚨裡。牠吞不下去,覺得很疼。「唉唷!唉唷!」狼痛苦地叫著。

他沿著山丘、河流四處奔走,想找個辦法減輕痛苦。

牠試圖說服別人幫他取出骨頭。「如果能取出這塊骨頭,」他說:「要我付出什麼都可以。」「我承諾一定會做到,請幫幫我!」

首先他遇到了一隻正在覓食的烏鴉。他向烏鴉求助。烏鴉轉轉她的眼珠說:「不要。」然後她飛走了。

狼很傷心地坐在地上。他抬頭一望,發現河邊的樹上有一隻松鼠正在玩遊戲。於是狼向他求助,說道:「你能好心點幫我把嘴裡的骨頭取出來嗎?

我可以把我的一切給你。」聽到這裡，松鼠笑著說：「你活該！」

最後，狼遇到鶴，鶴同意試試看。他叫狼張大嘴巴，然後將長長的脖子伸進狼的喉嚨。鶴用尖嘴弄鬆骨頭，終於把骨頭叼出來了。

鶴問：「你要給我什麼報酬呢？」狼露出他的狼牙，說：「喂，朋友，你能從狼嘴裡平安無事地把頭收回來，這就是最好的報酬。你該滿足啦！」

聽力題目解析

❶ 此題詢問的是許多孩子喜歡讀這個故事的原因為何。選項 (A) 為這是一個很爛的故事；選項 (B) 為這是一個有趣且有意義的故事；選項 (C) 為這是一個異國的故事；選項 (D) 為這是一個簡短的故事。根據錄音檔第一句，我們可馬上選出 (B) 作為答案。

❷ 此題詢問的是烏鴉和松鼠不願幫助狼的原因。選項 (A) 為牠們不夠高；選項 (B) 為牠們當時太忙著找食物；選項 (C) 為牠們不相信狼的話且想要給牠的教訓；選項 (D) 為牠們當時正在一起玩。根據錄音檔中烏鴉和松鼠的反應，我們可以得知牠們對狼的態度堅決，且無其他拒絕的原因。故答案選 (C)。此題需注意烏鴉和松鼠與狼之間的互動模式。

❸ 此題詢問的是在最後一段狼對鶴說的話的真正意義為何。選項 (A) 為狼沒有東西可以給鶴；選項 (B) 為狼不想要給鶴任何獎賞；選項 (C) 為如果鶴沒有幫助狼，狼可能會吞掉鶴。根據錄音檔，最後狼說：「你該滿足了。你能從狼嘴裡平安無事地把頭收回來，這就是最好的報酬。」意即，狼認為他沒有把鶴吃掉就是最大的獎賞。故答案選 (C)。

❹ 此題詢問的是故事的主旨為何。選項 (A) 為我們應該幫助有難之人；選項 (B) 為一個貪婪的人絕不會感激他人的幫助；選項 (C) 為當一個樂於助人的人。根據錄音檔的結尾，我們可以從狼的態度轉變得知牠的貪婪本性，故答案選 (B)。

閱讀題目解析

❶ 此題詢問的是，我們可以從烏鴉和松鼠對狼的態度中得知何事。選項 (A) 為狼以前的行事作風並不好；選項 (B) 為烏鴉很興奮可以幫助狼；選項 (C) 為松鼠只把注意力放在覓食上面。答案可見內文第四及第五段，烏鴉的斷然回絕和松鼠的嘲笑，皆表示狼以前曾做過另他們感到不快的事，才會在狼的苦苦哀求下仍拒絕幫忙。故答案選 (A)。

❷ 此題詢問的是選項中有哪一個字可以拿來形容文中動物們之間的關係。答案應能同樣從烏鴉的回絕和松鼠的訕笑中得知，故答案選 (B) 不太好的。選項 (A) 為新鮮的；選項 (C) 為有趣的；選項 (D) 為友善的。若難以選擇，我們也可按照刪去法，將正面的形容詞刪去，便可得 (B) 作為解答。

補充單字

☆ 1. story	n.	故事
☆ 2. find	v.	發現、找到
☆ 3. tree	n.	樹
☆ 4. laugh	v.	大笑
☆ 5. agree	v.	同意
☆ 6. great	adj.	大量的、很好的

Good for Evil
以德報怨

聽力測驗 🎧 Track 004

在學習英文的過程中，「聽」可能是最直接的第一線接觸，也可能是大家最想要快速習得的能力。現在，就讓我們來熟悉各種英文情境，提升自己的英文臨場感吧！

( ) 1. Where did the story happen?
    (A) in the river   (B) in the street
    (C) in the forest   (D) in the city

( ) 2. Why did the Indian come to the settler's door?
    (A) Because the settler was his good friend.
    (B) Because he was tired and hungry and wanted to ask for help.
    (C) Because he wanted to live in his house.
    (D) Because a wolf was running after him.

( ) 3.Did the settler feel ashamed of what he had done?
    (A) Yes, he did.   (B) No, he didn't.
    (C) We don't know.   (D) The passage doesn't tell us.

( ) 4. What is the Indian's advice?
    (A) be rude to a stranger. (B) be kind to others.
    (C) be honest.   (D) be brave.

( ) 5. Which is wrong according to the story?
    (A) The settler was rough at first.
    (B) The settler gave the Indian nothing.
    (C) The settler was kind to the Indian.
    (D) The settler lost his way in the forest.

 **閱讀測驗**

剛剛的聽力測驗是否因為答題不順而感到遺憾？或是覺得自己有某些地方掌握地不夠好？現在就讓我們來直接「看」剛剛的聽力測驗，並透過後面的閱讀測驗來補齊聽力上的不足，同時考驗自己的閱讀能力吧！

One evening, a settler was resting at his house. An Indian, tired and hungry, came to **ask**[1] him for something to eat. The settler said, "I have nothing for you." The Indian then asked for a glass of milk, and the settler again refused. The Indian then begged for a little cold water, but the settler only answered in rough words, "Go away, you Indian dog!" After looking at the settler for a moment, the Indian turned away.

A few days later, the same settler went hunting and lost his way in the forest. By and by it grew dark. He saw a dim light through the trees, which came from the fire in a hut, whose owner was the very Indian.

But the settler didn't recognize him and went up to ask the way to his home. But the Indian said: "It is a long way from here, and it is dark now. You cannot get **home**[2] tonight. If you wander about in the woods, you will fall into a trap. But if you don't **mind**[3] **staying**[4] with me for the **night**[5], you may."

Of course the settler gladly accepted the kind offer. And the Indian baked some cake for him and gave him clear water to drink, and then prepared a warm bed for him to sleep on. Early the next morning the Indian showed the settler his way home.

They had traveled for many miles, when the Indian turned to the hunter saying, "Do you know me?" "I think I have seen you **before**[6]," said the hunter.

"Yes, you have seen me at your own door," said the Indian. "And now, I'll give you a piece of advice. When a poor Indian, hungry and thirsty, asks you again for a little food or drink, do not say to him—go away, you Indian dog!"

The settler felt very ashamed of what he had done, and begged the Indian to forgive him. Later he became a wiser man.

【 Question 】

(　　) 1. What didn't the Indian ask from the settler?
   (A) a glass of milk
   (B) something to eat
   (C) a little cold water
   (D) a bed to sleep

(　　) 2. What is the main reason why the settler felt ashamed?
   (A) The Indian forced him to feel ashamed.
   (B) The Indian helped him while he treated the Indian badly at first.
   (C) The Indian baked better cakes than him.
   (D) The Indian had warmer house to rest.

【 文章中譯 】

有一天晚上，一位移民者在他的房子內休息。一名又累又餓印第安人來向他要點東西吃。移民者說：「我沒有東西給你。」印第安人接著向他要一杯牛奶，但移民者再次拒絕。印第安人接著乞求一點冷水，但移民者的回答非常粗魯，他說：「走開，你這個印第安狗！」印第安人看著移民者一會兒後，便轉身走了。

幾天後，同一個移民者去打獵，他在森林中迷路了。不久天色漸漸暗了下來。他看到一縷微光從樹林中隱隱傳來，光線來自一間小屋的火光，小屋的主人正是那名印第安人。

但是移民者沒認出他，便上前詢問回家的路。但是那名印第安人說：「從這裡回去的路程太遠了，而且現在天已經黑了。今晚你沒辦法回家。如果你在樹林裡徘徊，你會落入陷阱。如果你不介意，你可以留在我這過夜。」

移民者當然愉快地接受了幫助。印第安人烤了蛋糕給他吃，並給了他乾淨的水喝，還有溫暖的床供他休息。第二天一早，印第安人帶移民者走向回家的路。

他們向前走了許多英里，印第安人轉身問獵人：「你認識我嗎？」移民者回答：「我想我以前見過你。」「是啊，你在自己家的門口見過我。」印地安人說。「現在，我給你一點忠告。當再有饑餓、口渴的可憐印第安人懇求你給點吃的、喝的，不要對他說——走開，印第安狗！」

移民者為他的所作所為感到非常羞愧，並懇求印第安人原諒他。後來，他成為一個更明智的人。

聽力題目解析

❶ 此題詢問的是故事發生的地點。根據錄音檔，我們可得知該名移民者到森林中打獵 (hunting)，後續才發生他與印地安人之間的故事。故答案選 (C)。選項 (A) 為河流；選項 (B) 為街上；選項 (D) 為城市中。若此題沒有聽見 "forest"，我們也可以移民者的遭遇來做地點上的判斷，並用刪去法得到 (C)。

❷ 此題詢問的是印地安人到移民者門前的理由。選項 (A) 為因為移民者是他的好朋友；選項 (B) 為因為印地安人很疲倦且需要幫助；選項 (C) 為因為印地安人想要住在移民者家中；選項 (D) 為因為一隻狼正在追逐著他。在錄音檔的一開始，我們便能聽見該名印地安人 "tired and hungry, came to ask him for something to eat"，故答案選 (B)。其於的選項皆沒有在音檔中提及。

❸ 此題詢問的是移民者是否有因為他本身的作為而覺得羞愧。根據錄音檔的末段，我們可以清楚地聽見 "The settler felt very ashamed of what he had done." 故答案選 (A)。

❹ 此題詢問的是印地安人的忠告為何。選項 (A) 為對陌生人要粗魯；選項 (B) 為對他人要友善；選項 (C) 為要誠實；選項 (D) 為要勇敢。根據錄音檔後段，印地安人在幫助移民者後，對他說 "When a poor Indian, hungry and thirsty, asks you again for a little food or drink, do not say to him－go away, you Indian dog!" 故答案為 (B)。

Level 1

Level 2

Level 3

Level 4

Level 5

Level 6

❺ 此題詢問的是根據故事而做出之錯誤陳述。選項 (A) 為移民者在一開始很粗魯；選項 (B) 為移民者沒有給印地安人任何東西；選項 (C) 為移民者對印地安人很好；選項 (D) 為移民者在森林中迷了路。根據錄音檔，我們可以得知這是一個移民者在印地安人身上學習的故事，從一開始的不友善，到最後因迷路接收了幫助，成為一名更有智慧的人。故答案選 (C)。此題需注意聆聽細節。

閱讀題目解析

❶ 此題詢問的是印地安人沒有向移民者身上要什麼。選項 (A) 為一杯牛奶；選項 (B) 為一些能吃的東西；選項 (C) 為一點冷水；選項 (D) 為一張可以睡覺的床。答案可見內文第一二段，選 (D)。

❷ 此題詢問的是移民者感到羞愧的主要原因。選項 (A) 為印地安人迫使他覺得羞愧；選項 (B) 為印地安人幫助了他，儘管他在一開始用很糟糕的方式對待印地安人；選項 (C) 為印地安人烤的蛋糕比他好吃；選項 (D) 為印地安人的家比較溫暖。此題應注意到在內文中，移民者態度的轉變是出現在印地安人幫助了他並揭示自己的身分之後，故答案選 (B)。

補充單字

☆ 1. ask	v.	要求
☆ 2. home	n.	家
☆ 3. mind	v.	介意
☆ 4. stay	v.	停留；留下
☆ 5. night	n.	夜晚
☆ 6. before	adv.	先前；之前

The Priceless Dog
無價的狗

聽力測驗 🎧 Track 005

在學習英文的過程中，「聽」可能是最直接的第一線接觸，也可能是大家最想要快速習得的能力。現在，就讓我們來熟悉各種英文情境，提升自己的英文臨場感吧！

(　　) 1. We can infer that the apron is something that _____.
　　　　(A) the baby was playing with.
　　　　(B) the baby was wearing.
　　　　(C) is like an umbrella.
　　　　(D) is like a toy machine.

(　　) 2. We can see all about the dog except _____.
　　　　(A) the dog was brave and clever.
　　　　(B) the dog wanted to have a swim.
　　　　(C) the dog was a trained one.
　　　　(D) the dog wouldn't part with his maste

(　　) 3. Which is true according to the story?
　　　　(A) The mother let the maid drop her child.
　　　　(B) The gentleman made the maid do it.
　　　　(C) The baby jumped out of the maid's arms without warning.
　　　　(D) The baby was afraid of the gentleman's dog.

(　　) 4. What do you think would happen later?
　　　　(A) The dog jumped into the water again.
　　　　(B) The lady gave the gentleman a lot of money.
　　　　(C) The gentleman asked the lady for a lot of money.
　　　　(D) The gentleman left without asking for a reward from the lady.

 **閱讀測驗**

剛剛的聽力測驗是否因為答題不順而感到遺憾？或是覺得自己有某些地方掌握地不夠好？現在就讓我們來直接「看」剛剛的聽力測驗，並透過後面的閱讀測驗來補齊聽力上的不足，同時考驗自己的閱讀能力吧！

A French lady was going aboard a ship from a city to another in America with her maid, who was **carrying**[1] the lady's child in her arms.

As the ship came near to the seashore, it began to slow down. The maid walked to the side of the ship to look over, when suddenly the child sprang out of her arms and into the water below.

The mother was frightened and nearly mad. The sailors began to lower a boat. The baby was drowning! What was to be done? Hearing the cries of the mother, a gentleman who was reading in another part of the **ship**[2] came quickly forward and said, "Can you give me something the child has worn?" The maid gave him a tiny apron, which had been left in her hands as she tried to save the child from **falling**[3]. The gentleman turned to a dog that **stood**[4] near, looking up into his face. He pointed first to the apron, and then to the spot where the child had sunk.

Very quickly the noble dog sprang into the river. Soon the dog was seen far away with something in his mouth. Bravely he swam **against**[5] the strong stream, but it was feared that his strength would soon give way. People on board cried for joy as the boat **reached**[6] him and the sailors drew the child and the dog from the water.

When they were brought on board, the mother was happy to see that her baby was alive, saying, "Oh, sir, I must have this dog! I will give anything for the dog that has saved my darling's life!" The gentleman smiled, "I am very glad, madam, that Hector has been of service to you, but I would not part with him for anything in the world." And meanwhile, the dog gave his sides a shake and lay down at his master's feet, as if saying, "No, master, nothing shall part us!"

【 Question 】

(　　) 1. What can we infer from the story?
(A) The lady knows the dog's name at the very beginning.
(B) The dog is eager to go with the lady.
(C) The gentleman was willing to help the lady.
(D) The maid was happy.

(　　) 2. What was the gentleman doing when the baby was drowing?
(A) swimming　　　　　(B) sleeping
(C) reading　　　　　　(D) shopping

【 文章中譯 】

一位法國女士正乘船從美國的一個城市前往另外一個城市，她的女僕懷裡抱著她的孩子。

當船要靠岸時，速度慢了下來。當女僕走到船邊看看時，孩子突然從她的懷裡蹦出來掉入水中。

孩子的母親嚇得幾乎要發瘋，此時水手們放下一條小船。孩子快淹死了！怎麼辦？聽到孩子的母親哭喊著，正在船的另一處看書的一位先生很快地走上前説：「妳能給我一件孩子穿過的衣服嗎？」女僕便給了他一條當時為了救回掉落的孩子卻遺留在手上的小圍兜。這位先生轉身面向一隻站在附近的狗，那隻狗也正望著他。他先指了指圍兜，又指了指孩子掉下去的地方。

這條英勇的狗迅速跳入水中，沒多久就看到他在遠處嘴裡叼著個東西。狗勇敢地同激流搏鬥著，但是人們擔心他會筋疲力盡。當小船靠近狗時，人們非常高興，把小孩和狗從水中救了上來。

當他們被帶上岸時，孩子的母親看到孩子還活著非常高興，她對那位先生説：「喔，先生，我必須要擁有這條狗，我願意付出一切！」。那位先生説：「夫人，很高興赫克特能為您效勞；但無論給我什麼，我都不會與他分離的。」這時，狗兒搖晃著身子，躺在主人跟前，好像在説：「是的，主人，什麼也不能把我們分離！」

聽力題目解析

❶ 此題詢問關於圍兜的相關陳述。選項 (A) 為孩子正在玩弄之物；選項 (B) 為孩子穿戴之物；選項 (C) 意為圍兜就像一把雨傘；選項 (D) 意為圍兜就像一個玩具機。根據錄音檔，該名紳士問 "Can you give me something that child has worn?" 故選 (B)，以 "worn" 作為關鍵字。

❷ 此題要求我們選擇與狗狗相關的正確陳述。選項 (A) 為狗狗很勇敢且聰明；選項 (B) 為狗狗想要游泳；選項 (C) 為狗狗是受過訓練的；選項 (D) 為狗狗不想要與主人分離。根據錄音檔，狗狗透過圍兜便前往救落水的孩子，且最後我們也聽見 "No, master, nothing shall part us!" 意即狗狗不想與主人分開，故答案選 (B)。此提為理解題，需專注聆聽理解整起事件。

❸ 此題詢問的是根據故事的推論何者為真。選項 (A) 為媽媽讓女僕丟棄孩子；選項 (B) 為紳士叫女僕丟棄孩子；選項 (C) 為孩子從女僕手中毫無預警地跳出來掉入水中；選項 (D) 為孩子害怕紳士的狗。根據錄音檔，我們可以在一開始得知，孩子是自己從女僕手上跳出（"suddenly the child sprang up"），且該名紳士為救援者（"came quickly"），同時媽媽也相當緊張，故答案應選 (C)。選項 (D) 音檔中為提及。此題需仔細聆聽注意細節。

❹ 此題詢問的是我們認為接下來會發生何事。選項 (A) 為狗狗再度跳入水裡；選項 (B) 為女士給了紳士許多錢；選項 (C) 為紳士向女士要求了一大筆金錢；選項 (D) 為紳士離去且沒有向女士拿取任何獎賞。根據錄音檔的結尾，我們可以推測紳士無意與狗狗分離，且沒有進一步討論到獎賞，故答案 (D) 最為可能。

閱讀題目解析

❶ 此題詢問的是我們可以從故事中推測何事。選項 (A) 為該名女士在一開始便知道狗狗的名字為何;選項 (B) 為狗狗渴望和女士一起離去;選項 (C) 為紳士願意幫助那名女士;選項 (D) 為女僕很開心。答案可見內文第三段,紳士原本正在讀書,聽見呼叫後便前往查看,最後讓狗狗幫忙拯救孩子。故選 (C)。

❷ 此題詢問的是當孩子溺水時,紳士正在從事何種活動。選項 (A) 為游泳;選項 (B) 為睡覺;選項 (C) 為閱讀;選項 (D)為購物。答案同樣可見內文第三段,故選 (C)。

補充單字

☆ 1. carry	v.	搬運
☆ 2. ship	n.	大船,海船
☆ 3. fall	v.	倒下、落下
☆ 4. stand	v.	站起、立起
☆ 5. against	prep.	反對
☆ 6. reach	v.	到達

A Heroine of Orleans
奧爾良的女英雄

聽力測驗 Track 006

在學習英文的過程中，「聽」可能是最直接的第一線接觸，也可能是大家最想要快速習得的能力。現在，就讓我們來熟悉各種英文情境，提升自己的英文臨場感吧！

(   ) 1. Why did the French soldiers want to give up at first?
     (A) Because Joan was not there.
     (B) Because they were defeated many times by the English army.
     (C) Because they had no interest in the war.
     (D) Because they were tired of the war.

(   ) 2. When did Joan hear the voices?
     (A) when she was staying at home
     (B) when she was studying at school
     (C) when she was climbing the hill
     (D) when she was watching her sheep in the fields

(   ) 3. Choose the right statement according to the story.
     (A) The war happened in 1600.
     (B) The French army invaded England
     (C) Joan was a goddess.
     (D) Joan was caught by the English army.

(   ) 4. Which is true?
     (A) Joan wanted to be an army officer, so she went to war.
     (B) The commander did not listen to her at all.
     (C) Joan led the French army later.
     (D) At last the French soldiers were not so brave.

閱讀測驗

剛剛的聽力測驗是否因為答題不順而感到遺憾？或是覺得自己有某些地方掌握地不夠好？現在就讓我們來直接「看」剛剛的聽力測驗，並透過後面的閱讀測驗來補齊聽力上的不足，同時考驗自己的閱讀能力吧！

Have you ever heard of the story about Joan of Arc? It is a true story about a real heroine.

About six hundred years ago, a great war **broke out**[1] between the two countries— France and England. At that time, England was a rather powerful country, so it often had wars with other countries. One year France became his aim of attack. And so the story began.

The English army invaded France and won one battle after another, and the French army was **driven**[2] back again and again. The French soldiers were so discouraged that they were almost ready to **give up**[3]. But things soon changed.

At that time there lived a poor peasant girl named Joan of Arc. One day while she was in the field looking after her sheep, she heard voices coming to her. They told her that she must go to the French army and lead it against the English. She **believed**[4] that the voices came from Heaven and she fell on her knees and prayed.

The next day she left her home and went to the Commander of the French army and told him the story of the voices. The Commander listened to her and believed her. He gave her a beautiful white horse and suit of white armor.

When the soldiers saw her and heard her story, they followed her willingly to help the city of Orleans, which had been surrounded by the English army for some months and was on the point of giving in. But the French army **fought**[5] so bravely that the English were **beaten**[6] back.

After that, Joan was called the Maid of Orleans. Not long after that, Joan was taken prisoner by the English and burned at Rouen (a French city). She lived and died bravely, and the entire world honors her to this day.

【Question】

(   ) 1. What can be inferred from the soldiers' attitude after Joan told them about the voice?
　　　　(A) They belived that the voices came from Heaven too.
　　　　(B) They did not like Joan.
　　　　(C) They were forced to follow Joan.
　　　　(D) They wanted Joan to die for them in the war.

(   ) 2. Where was Joan captured by the English?
　　　　(A) Toulouse　　　　(B) Lyon
　　　　(C) Paris　　　　　　(D) Rouen

Level 1
Level 2
Level 3
Level 4
Level 5
Level 6

【文章中譯】

你聽過聖女貞德的故事嗎？這是關於一個真正女英雄的真實故事。

大約六百年前，一場大戰在法國和英國之間爆發了。那時，英國是一個相當強大的國家，因此經常與其他國家戰爭。有一年，法國成為其攻擊的目標。故事就這樣展開了。

英國軍隊入侵法國，贏得一場又一場戰役，法國軍隊一次又一次地被擊退。法國士兵洩氣得幾乎準備要放棄。但事情很快發生了變化。

當時，那裡住著一個貧苦的農民女孩，名叫貞德。一天，當她在田野照看她的綿羊時，她聽見一道道聲音傳過來，告訴她必須加入法國軍隊並帶領他們對抗英國。她相信這聲音來自天堂，並跪下來祈禱。

第二天，她離開家，去找法國軍隊的指揮官，並告訴他聽到聲音的經過。指揮官聽了並相信她。他給了她一匹美麗的白馬和白色的鎧甲。

士兵看見她並聽了她的經歷，都願意跟隨她幫助奧爾良，而此時的奧爾良還被英國圍攻了幾個月並眼看要屈服了，但是法國軍隊英勇地戰鬥，最後擊退了英國人。

之後，貞德被稱為奧爾良的女英雄。此後不久，貞德被英國俘虜並在盧昂（法國城市）被焚燒而死。她生得勇敢、死得不屈，全世界都非常景仰她。

聽力題目解析

❶ 此題詢問的是法軍為何在一開始想要放棄。選項 (A) 為因為貞德沒有與他們同在；選項 (B) 為因為他們被英軍打敗太多次；選項 (C) 為因為他們對戰爭沒有興趣；選項 (D) 為因為他們對戰爭感到疲乏。如上題，我們在故事開始後得知英國在當時為大國，先抓住 "powerful" 這個關鍵字，後來我們也接著得知法軍節節敗退（driven back again and again），故答案選 (B)。

❷ 此題詢問的是貞德聽見聲音的時間。選項 (A) 為當她在家的時後；選項 (B) 為當她在學校上課的時後；選項 (C) 為當她在爬山的時後；選項 (D) 為當她在田原裡看守羊群的時候。此題僅需專注聆聽故事，便可得知出身貧苦的貞德是在選項 (D) 之時聽見來自上天的聲音。

❸ 此題要求我們選出關於故事的正確陳述。選項 (A) 為戰爭發生在西元 1600 年；選項 (B) 為法國軍隊入侵英國；選項 (C) 為貞德是名女神；選項 (D) 為貞德被英國軍隊俘虜。根據錄音檔，在故事開始前，我們便得知戰爭是發生在 600 年前，且英國經常攻掠他國，後來出身貧苦的農民女孩貞德出現了，並在帶領軍隊後被英軍俘虜焚燒致死，故答案選 (D)。此題需注意聆聽細節，誤被數字混淆。

❹ 此題詢問的是選項中的陳述何者正確。選項 (A) 為貞德想要當士官長，所以她才從軍；選項 (B) 為指揮官並沒有聽進貞德的說法；選項 (C) 為

貞德不久後便帶領法軍；選項 (D) 為最後法軍並不驍勇善戰。此題僅需聆聽故事重點，抓住關鍵字即可。若大意疏忽細節，也可先將較不可能的選項 (B)、(D) 刪去，最後依照較合故事走向的策略選擇 (C)。

· ·

閱讀題目解析

❶ 此題詢問的是我們可以從法軍的態度中得知何事。選項 (A) 為他們也相信貞德聽見的聲音來自天堂；選項 (B) 為他們不喜歡貞德；選項 (C) 為他們被強迫跟隨貞德；選項 (D) 為他們希望貞德替他們戰死。答案可從內文倒數第二段推測，法軍自願跟隨貞德，表示他們認同貞德的敘述，故答案選 (A)。

❷ 此題詢問的是最後英軍將貞德俘虜至哪個城市。答案可見內文最後一段，故選 (D)。

補充單字

☆ 1. break out	v.-phrase	爆發
☆ 2. drive	v.	驅趕
☆ 3. give up	v.-phrase	放棄
☆ 4. believe	v.	相信
☆ 5. fight	v.	戰鬥
☆ 6. beat	v.	擊打、打敗

The Treasure Box of the Princess

Level 1 07

公主的百寶箱

聽力測驗 🎧Track 007

在學習英文的過程中,「聽」可能是最直接的第一線接觸,也可能是大家最想要快速習得的能力。現在,就讓我們來熟悉各種英文情境,提升自己的英文臨場感吧!

( ) 1. Who saved the prince from the monster?
    (A) the prince herself   (B) the king
    (C) one of the ministers   (D) her friend One-Inch

( ) 2. What treasure was mentioned in the box?
    (A) a magic hat   (B) a magic hammer
    (C) a magic gun   (D) a magic shoe

( ) 3. Who took away the princess's treasure box?
    (A) the young man   (B) the king
    (C) the monster   (D) the princess's maid

( ) 4. Which is wrong according to the story?
    (A) The monster was killed immediately.
    (B) One-Inch man was very brave.
    (C) The king loved his daughter very much.
    (D) The hammer was magic.

( ) 5. Choose the right statement.
    (A) The monster was a black one.
    (B) The monster was a red one.
    (C) The monster was a green one.
    (D) The monster was a brown one.

剛剛的聽力測驗是否因為答題不順而感到遺憾？或是覺得自己有些地方掌握地不夠好？現在就讓我們來直接「看」剛剛的聽力測驗，並透過後面的閱讀測驗來補齊聽力上的不足，同時考驗自己的閱讀能力吧！

Level 1

Level 2 Level 3 Level 4 Level 5 Level 6

A long time ago, there was a princess, who is greatly loved by the king. The king gave her a "treasure"－a treasure box. The magic box can not only help her when she is in **danger**[1], but also help kind people with the completion of their wishes. Unfortunately, on one day, when she was in the garden, playing with her old friend called One-Inch, a red monster **took**[2] the advantage, **appeared**[3] in her bedroom, and tried to steal the treasure chest.

When princess returned to her room with One-Inch no long after, the red monster roared and tried to attack them. The princess cried out with fear, and the monster dragged her off and attempted to take her away. One-Inch, who knew martial art, pulled out his sword and fought back the monster. He struck the monster many times. At the end, the monster couldn't bar the pain and ran away, dropping the treasure chest.

The treasure chest works in the way that if a man shook the magic hammer and made a **wish**[4], the wish would come true. So, when the princess asked One-Inch for his wish after he saved her, he replied, "I should like to become as tall and strong as an ordinary man."

The princess shook the hammer and, in a flash, little One-Inch became a big and noble young man. Together they went to the **palace**[5] to tell the king about One-Inch's victory over the monster.

"I thank you from the bottom of my **heart**[6]," said the king. "What can I give you in return for your brave act?"

"I would like to marry your daughter. I really adore her," he said.

The king laughed and he asked if the princess felt the same toward One-Inch. The princess replied with a yes, shyly. Therefore, One-Inch married the beautiful princess and lived happily ever after.

【Question】

(　　) 1. Where was the treasure box when the monster stole it?
(A) in the garden
(B) in the princess's bedroom
(C) in the palace
(D) in One-Inch's hands

(　　) 2. What was One-Inch's reward for saving the princess?
(A) a lot of money
(B) the kingdom
(C) the monster
(D) the marriage with the princess

【文章中譯】

很久以前，有一位公主， 她非常受國王的喜愛。國王給了她一件「寶貝」——一個百寶箱。這個神奇的箱子不僅在危難的時候可以幫助她，還可以完成人們的心願。不幸的是，有一天，當公主在和她名為小不點的朋友於花園玩時，一隻紅色的怪物趁她不在時，出現在她的寢室裡，並且試著把她的百寶箱偷走。

當公主和小不點不久之後回到房間時，紅怪獸對著他們狂吼並試著攻擊他們。公主害怕地哭了起來，且怪物開始拖著她，想把她帶走。會武功的小不點拔出他的劍，將怪物擊退。他擊中怪物好幾次，最後怪物無法忍受疼痛便逃跑了，留下了百寶箱。

這個百寶箱是這麼運作的，如果有人搖一搖這支魔鎚並許個願，他的願望就會實現。所以，當公主問小不點想許什麼願時，小不點回答道：「我想變得和正常人一樣高大。」

她搖了搖魔鎚，隨著一道亮光，小不點變成了一個高大、優雅的年輕人。他們後來一起到皇宮裡，把小不點打敗怪物的消息告訴了國王。

Level 1
Level 2
Level 3
Level 4
Level 5
Level 6

「我打從心底裡感謝你。」國王說。「我能給你什麼作為你英勇行為的獎賞呢?」

「我想要和您的女兒結婚。我喜歡她很久了」他說。

君主笑了笑,便詢問公主是否對小不點有同樣的感受。公主害羞地給了肯定的回覆。於是小不點便和美麗的公主結婚了,從此幸福快樂地住在一起。

聽力題目解析

❶ 此題詢問的是誰將公主從怪物的手中拯救出來。選項 (A) 為公主自己;選項 (B) 為國王;選項 (C) 為其中一位大臣;選項 (D) 為她的好友小不點。此題僅需專心聆聽故事即可,答案選 (D)。

❷ 此題詢問的是何者寶物曾被提及出現在百寶箱裡面。選項 (A) 為魔法帽;選項 (B) 為魔鎚;選項 (C) 魔法槍;選項 (D) 為魔法鞋。根據錄音檔,在小不點擊退怪獸之後,公主便利用遺落的魔鎚 (magic hammer) 將小不點便成成人大小。故答案選 (B)。

❸ 此題詢問的是何者拿走了公主的百寶箱。選項 (A) 為一位年輕人:選項 (B) 為國王;選項 (C) 為怪物;選項 (D) 為公主的女僕。此題同上,僅需仔細聆聽即可,答案選 (C)。

❹ 此題詢問的是根據故事何者的陳述為錯誤的。選項 (A) 為怪物被馬上殺死了;選項 (B) 為小不點非常勇敢;選項 (C) 為國王非常愛他的女兒;選項 (D) 為那個鎚子是具有魔法的。根據錄音檔,我們可以得知小不點和怪物經歷了一番搏鬥,怪物才逃跑,最後遺落了魔鎚。此題可以把握 "ran away" 和 "dropping his treasure chest" 為關鍵字,答案選 (A)。

❺ 此題要求我們選出正確的陳述。選項 (A) 為怪物是黑色的;選項 (B)為怪物是紅色的;選項 (C) 為怪物是綠色的;選項 (D) 為怪物是棕色的。

此題只能注意聆聽，"red" 共出現過兩次，建議先看過題目及選項，以免錯失機會，選擇 (B)。

閱讀題目解析

❶ 此題詢問的是當怪物偷走百寶箱的時候，百寶箱的位置是在哪裡。答案可見內文第一段，僅需注意是公主在花園，不是百寶箱，選項 (A) 為陷阱，故選 (B)。

❷ 此題詢問的是小不點得到了什麼獎賞。答案可見內文倒數第三段至最後一段，選擇 (D)。

☆ 1. danger	n.	危險
☆ 2. take	v.	拿、取
☆ 3. appear	v.	出現
☆ 4. wish	v.&n.	願望
☆ 5. palace	n.	宮殿
☆ 6. heart	n.	心臟

Level 1

Level 2

Level 3

Level 4

Level 5

Level 6

Level 1
08 Silence Is Golden
沉默是金

聽力測驗 🎧 Track 008

在學習英文的過程中，「聽」可能是最直接的第一線接觸，也可能是大家最想要快速習得的能力。現在，就讓我們來熟悉各種英文情境，提升自己的英文臨場感吧！

( ) 1. There are two main characters in the story. They may be _____.
    (A) two Indians
    (B) two Americans
    (C) one Indian and one American
    (D) one American and one with an unknown nationality

( ) 2. Who bought the elephant?
    (A) an American   (B) a Frenchman
    (C) an Italian   (D) It isn't mentioned in the story.

( ) 3. Which of the following statements is correct?
    (A) The elephant had blemish on the left foreleg.
    (B) The elephant had blemish on the right foreleg.
    (C) The elephant was blind in the right eye.
    (D) The elephant was blind in the left eye.

( ) 4. Choose the right statement according to the story.
    (A) The American wanted to buy the elephant.
    (B) The American just wanted to know more about the elephant.
    (C) The American was also a merchant.
    (D) The American took the money that the merchant offered.

 **閱讀測驗**

剛剛的聽力測驗是否因為答題不順而感到遺憾？或是覺得自己有某些地方掌握地不夠好？現在就讓我們來直接「看」剛剛的聽力測驗，並透過後面的閱讀測驗來補齊聽力上的不足，同時考驗自己的閱讀能力吧！

Today we are going to read a very interesting story, but there is some truth in it. "Silence is golden" is now a very useful expression. Sometimes if you keep silent over something, it may prevent you from getting involved in trouble, which of course does good to you. As a student, in class, you may often hear your teacher say to you, "Keep quiet and put your heart into your study and you may make progress." In a certain degree, we may say, keeping silent may bring good luck or fortune. Here is how the story goes.

At an Indian fair there was a merchant who had an elephant for **sale**[1] He saw an American, who was examining it with very great care, walking round and round it, putting his head on one side, and taking in everything. The merchant felt very **strange**[2]. "He might have found out the blemish!" he thought to himself, so he went up to the American, and said, "Don't say anything about the elephant till I have sold it, and I will give you a present."

"All right," agreed the American, **surprised**[3].

After the elephant was sold, the merchant gave him one-tenth of the **price**[4] he had got for it, and said: "Now tell me how you found out that blemish on the left foreleg of the elephant. I thought it was quite concealed, and nobody would find it out."

"Blemish?!" said the American, surprised again. "I never found any blemish on it."

"Then, why did you **examine**[5] the elephant so closely?" asked the merchant.

"Because I had never seen an elephant before, and I wanted very much to see what it was like," said the American. What facial expression do you think the merchant would have when he heard the American's words?

【Question】

(   ) 1. What can be inferred from the story?
(A) Silence is good for greedy person.
(B) They trade animals in the fair.
(C) The American did it on purpose.

(   ) 2. What may be the final facial expression of the merchant?
(A) sad
(B) surprised
(C) happy

【文章中譯】

今天我們來讀一個非常有趣、並且有一些道理在其中的故事。「沉默是金」現在是一個非常有用的表達方式。有時候，如果你對某事保持沉默，也許能使你不捲入麻煩，當然對你有好處。作為一個學生，在課堂上，你可以經常聽到你的老師對你說：「保持安靜，用心學習，你就會取得進展。」在一定程度上，我們可以說，保持沉默可能會帶來好運或財富。故事是這樣發生的。

在印第安市集，有個商人要賣一頭大象。他看見了一個美國人非常仔細地觀察這頭大象。商人感到非常奇怪。「他也許已經發現了傷疤！」他思忖著，因此他走到美國人面前說：「直到我把大象賣出之前，不要說出關於大象的任何事情，我將給您一個禮物。」

「好吧。」美國人同意，但是感到很驚訝。

在大象被賣出後，商家給了他十分之一的賣價，並說：「現在告訴我你是如何發現大象的左前腿有傷疤的。我以為那相當隱蔽，應該沒有人會發現。」

「傷疤？！」美國人說，再度感到訝異。「我未曾發現有傷疤啊。」

「那麼，您為什麼那麼仔細地檢查大象呢？」商人問道。

「因為我從未見過大象，我很想看看牠長得什麼樣子。」美國人說。當商人聽見了美國人的話後，您認為他會有什麼樣的表情呢？

聽力題目解析

❶ 此題詢問的是故事的兩大主角為何。選項 (A) 為兩名印第安人；選項 (B) 為兩名美國人；選項 (C) 為一名印第安人及一名美國人；選項 (D) 為一名美國人及一名無法得知其國籍的人。根據錄音檔，我們可以得知主角是一位商人及一位美國人，兩人相遇的地點是在印第安市集，商人的國籍並未加以解說，因此很有可能被 "Indian market" 而誤導，但若仔細聆聽再加上刪去法便能選出答案為選項 (D)。

❷ 此題詢問是誰買了大象。選項 (A) 為一名美國人；選項 (B) 為一名法國人；選項 (C) 為一名義大利人；選項 (D) 為故事中未提及。根據錄音檔，在商人向美國人進一步質問前，我們僅能得知大象已被賣出（"after the elephant was sold"），故答案選 (D)。

❸ 此題詢問的是選項中的陳述何者正確。選項 (A) 為大象的左前腳有傷疤；選項 (B) 為大象的右前腳有傷疤；選項 (C) 為大象的右眼失明；選項 (D) 為大象的左眼失明。根據商人的描述，大象的左前腳有傷疤，故選 (A)。此題僅需仔細聆聽主角的對話。

❹ 此題要求我們選擇關於故事的正確的描述。選項 (A) 為美國人想要買那頭大象；選項 (B) 為美國人只想要多了解一下大象；選項 (C) 為美國人也是名商人；選項 (D) 為美國人拿了商人提供的錢。根據錄音檔，我們可以從對話中得知，在商人給美國人獎賞之後，美國人表示以前從未看過大象，他只是想要多觀察，故答案選則 (B)。

閱讀題目解析

❶ 此題詢問的是我們可以從故事推斷出什麼。選項 (A) 為沉默對貪心的人來說是好的；選項 (B) 為這個市集會交易動物；選項 (C) 為美國人是故意這麼做的。答案可見內文第二段，選 (B)。選項 (A) 、(C) 為錯誤答案，因美國人在聽到商人提出的交易之後是感到驚訝的。

❷ 此題詢問的是商人最後可能的表情為何。選項 (A) 為悲傷的；選項 (B) 為驚訝的；選項 (C) 為開心的。此題可從故事結尾推敲，商人最後發現他的想法和美國人真實的意圖並不一樣，且商人還給了美國人錢，故選 (B)。

 補充單字

☆ 1. sale	n.	銷售
☆ 2. strange	a.	奇怪的、陌生的
☆ 3. surprise	v.	使驚奇
☆ 4. price	n.	價格
☆ 5. examine	v.	檢查

Level 1
Level 2
Level 3
Level 4
Level 5
Level 6

A Strange Visitor
奇怪的訪客

聽力測驗 🎧Track 009

在學習英文的過程中，「聽」可能是最直接的第一線接觸，也可能是大家最想要快速習得的能力。現在，就讓我們來熟悉各種英文情境，提升自己的英文臨場感吧！

(   ) 1. The story happened _____.
         (A) at a bus station   (B) at a taxi stand
         (C) in a book store   (D) at a railway station

(   ) 2. The clerk did not notice anything else, because _____.
         (A) he was blind in both eyes.
         (B) he was nearsighted.
         (C) he was fixing his attention on his letter.
         (D) he was sleeping then.

(   ) 3. What did the Englishman want to do?
         (A) to steal something
         (B) to have a rest
         (C) to make a telephone call
         (D) to buy a ticket

(   ) 4. What does the word "monster" represent in the article?
         (A) the tiger   (B) the clerk
         (C) the Englishman   (D) the ticket

(   ) 5. The clerk turned around and what did he find?
         (A) a wolf   (B) a tiger
         (C) a cat   (D) a monkey

 **閱讀測驗**

剛剛的聽力測驗是否因為答題不順而感到遺憾？或是覺得自己有某些地方掌握地不夠好？現在就讓我們來直接「看」剛剛的聽力測驗，並透過後面的閱讀測驗來補齊聽力上的不足，同時考驗自己的閱讀能力吧！

The story **happened**[1] in a railroad station in a far inland part of India. The railroad passed through a wild jungle full of wild birds and beasts.

One morning, Harry Simpson, a **ticket**[2] clerk at that railroad station, arrived at the station. He found that his **watch**[3] was too fast, and he had come half an hour too early. So he sat down at his desk to write to his mother and soon he was too buried in his letter to **notice**[4] anything else. However, he heard a sound and turned around, and found the office door, which had been left unlocked, pushed open, and found himself face to face with none other than the largest tiger he had ever seen in his life!

He tried to stay calm and came up with a good idea—to jump into a small closet and to shut the door after him. Harry would have liked to lock the door, but the key was left outside. So he could only try to hold to the handle of the door. But the tiger was trying to **force**[5] the door open. Unluckily, the door of the house had **shut**[6] itself behind him, and the window was guarded by strong iron bars. Mr. Tiger found that he was caught in a trap. His anger changed into fear and he tried to seek for some ways of escape, but found none. He spied the ticket-window, and with his paw, succeeded in pushing it open. There outside an old English merchant with a red face saw the tiger's face just in front of his own! He knew what had happened. He opened his gun-case in a hurry, and got out his rifle. He loaded his rifle in an instant, and soon shot the monster through the head, dead.

"Many thanks for your timely rescue." said Harry Simpson, coming out of the closet. "Don't mention it." said the Merchant. "Give me my ticket at once."

【Question】

(　　) 1. How did the tiger end up being shot?
   (A) It attacked the old English merchant.
   (B) The old English merchant saw it when it pushed the ticket-window open.
   (C) Simpson asked the old English merchant to shoot it.

(　　) 2. What can we infer from the attitude of the old English merchant at the end?
   (A) He just wanted to get a ticket as quickly as possible and leave.
   (B) He did not want to help Simpson.
   (C) He felt sad after killing the tiger.

【文章中譯】

故事發生在印度內陸區的一個火車站，鐵路通過一個充滿野生鳥類和野獸的荒野叢林。

有一天清晨，火車站的票務員——哈利‧辛普生——抵達了火車站，他發現他的手錶走快了，使他提早到了半小時，於是他便索性坐在書桌前寫信給他的母親。由於他太過專心了，以至於他沒注意到其他事物。然而，他聽見了聲響，隨後轉過身子，發現原本沒上鎖的辦公室門被推開了，而他正面對著他此生見過最大的老虎。

他設法保持冷靜，並想出一個好主意一跳進小壁櫥裡把門關上。哈利希望把門鎖上，但是鑰匙被留在外面。因此他只能設法握住門把柄。但是老虎試圖強行推開門。不幸地，房子的門自行關上了，窗戶外圍著堅固的鐵欄杆。這時虎先生發現自己掉入陷阱。他的憤怒變成恐懼，接著試著尋找逃命的方法但是卻徒勞無功。。他接著看見了賣票窗口，使用他的爪子，成功把賣票窗口推開。一位面色紅潤的老英國商人看見了老虎就在自己前面！他知道發生什麼事了。他急忙打開了他的槍盒，並且取出他的步槍。他立即裝上子彈並發射，這個龐然大物的頭即被子彈穿透，死了。

「非常感謝您的救命之恩。」辛普生說著，一面從壁櫥裡出來。「不用謝。」商人說。「趕快賣我車票。」

聽力題目解析

❶ 此題詢問的是故事發生的地點。選項 (A) 為公車站；選項 (B) 為計程車招呼站；選項 (C) 為書店；選項 (D) 為火車站。根據錄音檔的最一開始，我們即可得知故事是發生在印度內陸區的一個火車站。故選 (D)。

❷ 此題詢問的是票務員並沒有注意到周遭事物的原因。選項 (A) 為他的雙眼失明；選項 (B) 為他近視；選項 (C) 為他正專著在信件上；選項 (D) 為他在睡覺。根據錄音檔，該名票務員提早到了火車站，因此他便開始寫信給他的母親，並因太專注而沒注意到其他事情（"to write to his mother andsoon he was too buried in his letter to notice anything else"），故選 (C)。此題需注意聆聽。

❸ 此題詢問的是那名英國人想做什麼。選項 (A) 為偷東西；選項 (B) 為休息；選項 (C) 為打電話；選項 (D) 為買票。答案出現在音檔最後的對話中：Give me my ticket at once. (趕快賣我車票)，故選 (D)。

❹ 此題詢問的是在故事中的 "monster" 意指何物。選項 (A) 為老虎；選項 (B) 為票務員；選項 (C) 為英國人；選項 (D) 為票。根據錄音檔，一隻老虎闖入了票務員所在之處，且故事中只有出現老虎這隻動物，故最適合之答案為 (A)。

❺ 此題詢問的是在票務員轉過身後，他發現了何物。選項 (A) 為一隻狼；選項 (B) 為一隻老虎；選項 (C) 為一隻貓；選項 (D) 為一隻猴子。同上述，答案為 (B)。

閱讀題目解析

❶ 此題詢問的是老虎為何會被槍殺致死。選項 (A) 為老虎攻擊了那名老英國商人；選項 (B) 為那名英國老商人看見老虎從票務窗爬出來；選項 (C) 為辛普生要求那名英國老商人開槍射殺老虎。答案可見內文倒數第二段，選 (B)。

❷ 此題詢問我們可以從那名英國老商人最後的態度推測出什麼。選項 (A) 為他想要趕緊買票離開；選項 (B) 為他並不想要幫助辛普生；選項 (C) 為他在殺了老虎之後感到很難過。答案可從內文最後一段推敲，當辛普生出來致謝，那名英國老商人說了不客氣之後，便要求辛普生趕緊把票賣給他，故選 (A)。

補充單字

☆ 1. happen	v.	發生	
☆ 2. ticket	n.	票	
☆ 3. watch	n.	手錶	
☆ 4. notice	v.	注意到	
☆ 5. force	v.	迫使	
☆ 6. shut	v.	關上	

The Secret of the Flowerbed
花床的秘密

Level 1 10

Level 1
Level 2
Level 3
Level 4
Level 5
Level 6

聽力測驗 🎧 Track 010

在學習英文的過程中,「聽」可能是最直接的第一線接觸,也可能是大家最想要快速習得的能力。現在,就讓我們來熟悉各種英文情境,提升自己的英文臨場感吧!

(　　) 1. How many people are mentioned in the story?
   (A) one   (B) two
   (C) three   (D) four

(　　) 2. Who made the king's son happy at last?
   (A) the king   (B) Sir Arthur
   (C) the prince himself (D) the queen

(　　) 3. The secret to be happy according to the text is _____.
   (A) to work hard
   (B) to play
   (C) to do good to someone every day
   (D) to quarrel with people every day

(　　) 4. Why did the king give his son all things?
   (A) He wanted to make his son happy
   (B) They were useless.
   (C) The queen let him do so.
   (D) His father did not like the things.

(　　) 5. What should we learn from the story?
   (A) No pain, no gain.
   (B) Do good to others and you will be happy.
   (C) Mind your own business.
   (D) Two heads are better than one.

 **閱讀測驗**

剛剛的聽力測驗是否因為答題不順而感到遺憾？或是覺得自己有某些地方掌握地不夠好？現在就讓我們來直接「看」剛剛的聽力測驗，並透過後面的閱讀測驗來補齊聽力上的不足，同時考驗自己的閱讀能力吧！

Henry, whose father was the English King, was loved deeply and made **happy**[1] by his father in every **possible**[2] way.

The King gave the prince everything. However, Prince Henry was not happy. The King gave the boy a pony, also a boat, and so on. Yet, for all that, the young prince was still not happy. All the time he was **wishing for**[3] something that he did not have.

One summer day, Sir Arthur was sitting at the King's table when Prince Henry came into the room, with an unsatisfied face as usual. Seeing the frown on the Prince's face, Sir Arthur **turned to**[4] the King, saying, "The prince seems unhappy, but I can make him happy. If you will let him live with me, I will change him." "Good," said the King. "Please take him with you, and do as you like." That very day Prince Henry went into the country with Sir Arthur. "I have a flowerbed in my **garden**[5] that can talk, which is very strange," said Sir Arthur to the Prince. "It has a secret," said Sir Arthur, "and it tells its secret only to people who watch it everyday. If you **learn**[6] the secret, you will be happy every day."

"I'd like to see it," said Prince Henry. "It is right under your very eyes," said Sir Arthur. The Prince looked and saw a newly made flowerbed. But there was no flower, not even a leaf, upon it. "Come and watch it every day, and soon it will tell you its secret," said Sir Arthur.

Prince Henry did as told. But, many days later, he did not hear it talk at all. The flowerbed was watered, and the warm sun shone upon it. At last, one fine morning, he saw tiny plants coming up. And he saw that these plants made lines, and formed such letters as spelling:

DO SOME GOOD   TO SOMEONE   EVERY DAY.

Prince Henry realized that he had been selfish because he only cares about himself. He then understood why his father and Sir Arthur were always so happy: they helped other people. Prince Henry decided to do the same, and he felt he was the most grateful person in the world ever.

【Question】

(　　) 1. What word can not be used to describe the King?
    (A) loving　　　　(B) caring
    (C) worried　　　(D) angry

(　　) 2. What can we say about Sir Arthur's attitude toward Prince Henry?
    (A) He tried to help Prince Henry.
    (B) He wanted to take Prince Henry away.
    (C) He was angry with Prince Henry's attitude.

【文章中譯】

亨利的父親是英國國王，他深深地疼愛著亨利，他用盡一切可能的方法使他快樂。

國王給了王子一切。 然而，亨利王子並不快樂。國王給了王子一匹小馬、一艘小船等等。儘管如此，年輕王子仍然不快樂。他總是想要他所沒有的東西。

一個夏日，亞瑟爵士坐在國王的桌前，亨利王子帶著一臉不滿足的表情走進屋內。看見王子皺眉的面孔，亞瑟爵士轉身對國王説：「王子似乎不快樂，但是我可以使他快樂。如果您願意讓他與我住在一起，我可以改變他。「太好了！」國王説。「請帶走他，你要怎麼做都可以。」就在當天，亨利王子進入亞瑟爵士的住處。「我有一個會説話的花床，很奇怪吧。」亞瑟爵士對王子説。「它有一個秘密，」亞瑟爵士説：「並且只將它的秘密告訴每天留心它的人。如果您知道了它的秘密，您每天都會很開心。」

「我想看看它。」亨利王子説。「它就在您的眼下。」亞瑟爵士説。王子看了看並且看到了一個新做的花床。但是沒有花，上面甚至連葉子都沒有。「每天來看它，很快地它將會告訴您它的秘密。」亞瑟爵士説。

亨利王子照他說的話做了。但是，許多天之後，花床仍然沒說一句話。花床被澆灌了，溫暖的太陽照射著它。最後，在一個美好的早晨，他看到了微小的植物冒出頭來。並且他看見這些植物連成許多條線，形成了這樣拼寫的幾個字：

每天　　對別人　　做點好事。

後來，亨利王子理解了，原來他一直以來都是自私的，因為他只想到自己。這就是為什麼他永遠感到不滿足。他明白了為什麼他的父親和亞瑟爵士總是那麼開心：他們幫助他人。亨利王子決定也要開始做同樣的事，而且從此覺得他是世界上最快樂的人

聽力題目解析

❶ 此題詢問的是故事共提及了多少人。根據錄音檔，我們在一開始可以聽見主角亨利和他的父親，不久接著也出現亞瑟爵士。故仔細聽便能選 (C) 作為答案。

❷ 此題詢問的是，是誰最後讓國王的兒子開心起來。選項 (A) 為國王；選項 (B) 為亞瑟爵士；選項 (C) 為王子自己；選項 (D) 為皇后。根據錄音檔，我們可以得知，亞瑟爵士最後帶著王子到一個花圃，後來從無到有，出現排著字型的小花朵時，王子才開心了起來。此題把握最後一句即可。答案選 (B)。

❸ 此題詢問的是根據故事，快樂的秘訣為何。選項 (A) 為努力工作；選項 (B) 為玩樂；選項 (C) 為每天對別人做點好事；選項 (D) 為每天與別人吵架。根據錄音檔的末段，我們可以得知小花朵所排出的字型為「每天對別人做點好事」，故答案選擇 (C)。

❹ 此題詢問的是為什麼國王要把所有的事物都給王子。選項 (A) 為他想要讓他的兒子快樂；選項 (B) 為那些事物都沒有用處；選項 (C) 為皇后指使國王這麼做；選項 (D) 為他的父親不喜歡那些事物。根據錄音檔的一開始，我們即可得知，國王用盡一切可能的方法使王子快樂，此部分有

把握到 "made happy"、"In every possible way"，以及 "gave the prince everything" 的話，應能快速選出 (A)。

❺ 此題詢問的是我們可以從這個故事學習到什麼。選項 (A) 為一分耕耘，一分收穫；選項 (B) 為向他人做好事便會感到開心；選項 (C) 為管好自己的事；選項 (D) 為三個臭皮匠，勝過一個諸葛亮。根據錄音檔，我們可以得知王子最後得到的訊息便是「每天對別人做點好事」，故選 (B)。

閱讀題目解析

❶ 此題詢問的是選項中哪個單字無法拿來形容國王。選項 (A) 為關愛的；選項 (B) 為關心的；選項 (C) 為擔憂的；選項 (D) 為生氣的。答案可見內文第一至二段，國王自始至終皆無特別表現出生氣的態，故選 (D)。

❷ 此題詢問的是我們可以如何形容亞瑟爵士對亨利王子的態度。選項 (A) 為他試著幫住亨利王子；選項 (B) 為他想要把亨利王子帶走；選項 (C) 為他對亨利王子的態度感到生氣。答案可從內文第三段推敲，亞瑟爵士自行向國王提出改變亨利王子的意見，並說他可以幫助亨利王子，故答案選 (A)。

補充單字

☆	1. happy	**adj.**	愉快
☆	2. possible	**adj.**	可能的
☆	3. wish for	**v-phrase.**	希望得到
☆	4. turned to	**v-phrase.**	轉向、向……求助
☆	5. garden	**n.**	花園
☆	6. learn	**v.**	學會、得知

Stories and Anecdotes
奇聞軼事

Level 1
11

聽力測驗 🎧 Track 011

在學習英文的過程中，「聽」可能是最直接的第一線接觸，也可能是大家最想要快速習得的能力。現在，就讓我們來熟悉各種英文情境，提升自己的英文臨場感吧！

( ) 1. Where did the story take place?
　　(A) North Carolina　　　(B) South Carolina
　　(C) Philadelphia　　　　(D) Alabama

( ) 2. How old was the infant?
　　(A) 7 years old.　　　　(B) 1 month old.
　　(C) 7 months old.　　　(D) 10 months old.

( ) 3. What happened to Finn?
　　(A) He was abused by the babysitter.
　　(B) He was well taken care of by the babysitter.
　　(C) He became aggressive towards the babysitter.
　　(D) He slapped the babysitter.

( ) 4. How did the Jordans find out what happened to Finn?
　　(A) They hired a private investigator.
　　(B) They were told by their neighbors.
　　(C) They were told by the police.
　　(D) They used a cell phone to record what happened.

( ) 5. Who alerted the Jordans that their child was abused?
　　(A) Their parents.　　　(B) Their dog.
　　(C) Their housekeeper.　(D) Their employer.

 閱讀測驗

剛剛的聽力測驗是否因為答題不順而感到遺憾？或是覺得自己有某些地方掌握地不夠好？現在就讓我們來直接「看」剛剛的聽力測驗，並透過後面的閱讀測驗來補齊聽力上的不足，同時考驗自己的閱讀能力吧！

It is said that dogs are man's best friends. In South Carolina, Benjamin and Hope Jordan hired a 22-year-old babysitter to look after their 7-month-old son, Finn, while they were off to work. After about five months of employment, they started to notice that their dog became very **aggressive**[1] towards the babysitter. There were times when they even had to **restrain**[2] their dog from attacking the babysitter.

Suspicious[3] of their dog's changes, the Jordans decided to place an iPhone under the couch to record what happened when the babysitter and their son were alone. What they found was extremely shocking and **disturbing**[4]—they heard the babysitter swearing and slapping the infant as the child's cries changed to a distressful and painful cry. "Had our dog not alerted us to the trouble, had my wife's **instincts**[5] not said we need to do something about the dog's abnormal behavior, it could have been Finn that was killed by the babysitter. You never know," said Mr. Jordan.

Apparently, the dog knew early on about the abuse and became protective of the child. The babysitter confessed to the abuse and was sentenced to one to three years in prison. She has also been placed on a child abuse registry, which means that she will never be allowed to work with children again. The family credited their dog with saving their child, and probably many other children from further abuse.

【Question】

( ) 1. Which of the following is false?
   (A) Finn didn't survive the abuse.
   (B) After the incident, the babysitter has been put on the child abuse registry.
   (C) The Jordans will definitely be more careful when hiring their babysitter.
   (D) The family dog was aware of the child abuse.

( ) 2. Since when did the family dog become aggressive to the babysitter?
   (A) After two months of her employment.
   (B) After three months of her employment.
   (C) After four months of her employment.
   (D) After five months of her employment.

【文章中譯】

我們經常說狗狗是人類最好的朋友。在南卡羅萊納州，班傑明和荷普·喬登這對夫妻雇用了一名 22 歲的保姆，讓她在他們上班時可以來家裡照顧他們 7 個月大的兒子費恩。保姆工作約 5 個月左右時，他們發現家裡的狗狗對保姆非常具攻擊性，他們甚至好幾次必須制止牠攻擊保姆。

他們對於狗狗的性情驟變開始起疑，於是決定放一支蘋果手機在沙發底下，打算記錄保姆和兒子獨處的情況。結果他們發現極為驚人並令人心碎的事實，他們聽到保姆對兒子飆罵髒話，並聽到一陣耳光聲，夾雜著兒子不安與痛苦的哭聲。「要不是我們的狗狗提醒我們有麻煩，若不是我妻子的直覺告訴我們應該採取行動，說不定費恩會被這個保姆虐待致死。你真的無法預測。」喬登先生說。

顯然地，狗狗一開始就察覺到小孩受虐的事，因此變得很保護他。這個保姆坦承虐童，並面臨 1 到 3 年的徒刑，她也被列入虐童資料系統裡，終身不得從事兒童照護的相關工作。這家人也因此十分感謝他們的狗狗救了自家人，甚至更多人家的小孩。

聽力題目解析

Level 1

Level 2

Level 3

Level 4

Level 5

Level 6

❶ 此題詢問的是故事的發生地點。選項 (A) 為北卡羅萊納州；選項 (B) 為南卡羅來納州；選項 (C) 為費城；選項 (D) 為阿拉巴馬。在錄音檔開頭，我們便能聽到 "In South Carolina, Benjamin and Hope Jordan hired a ..." 故答案選擇 (B)。

❷ 此題詢問的是嬰兒的年齡。同上，答案也在 "… hired a 22-year-old babysitter to look after their 7-month-old son Finn while they were at work." 此題無特殊技巧，謹需細心聆聽錄音檔，並切記，通常地點和時間，都有可能出現在考題中，故答案選擇 (C)。

❸ 此題詢問的幼兒費恩發生了何事。選項 (A) 為他被保姆虐待；選項 (B) 為他受到保姆極好的照顧；選項 (C) 為他對保母的態度開始具攻擊性；選項 (D) 為他打了保母耳光。在錄音檔的中後段，我們可以聽見費恩的父母已經開始起疑，因此當我們聽到他們決定利用手機錄影時，我們便注意，並把握住 "the babysiiter swearing and slapping the infant" 以及 "the child's cries" 等關鍵字，此種題型建議先看過題目與選項以便掌握，答案選擇 (A)。

❹ 此題詢問的是喬登夫婦是如何發現發生在費恩身上的事。選項 (A) 為他們請了一個私家偵探；選項 (B) 為他們的鄰居告訴他們的；選項 (C) 為警方告知他們的；選項 (D) 為他們用手機錄下整個過程。在錄音檔的中間，我們可以先得知喬登夫婦已經開始起疑，接著我們便可掌握 "place an iPhone" 和 "to record what happened" 等關鍵字，故答案選擇 (D)。

❺ 此題詢問的是誰提醒喬登一家孩子受虐。選項 (A) 為他們的父母；選項 (B) 為他們的狗；選項 (C) 為他們的管家；選項 (D) 為他們的雇主。"Suspicious of their dog's changes" 可以說是關鍵字，因為在此之後便是喬登夫婦開始採取行動，最後發現保姆的作為。故答案選擇 (B)。

閱讀題目解析

❶ 此題詢問的是何者為錯誤之選項。選項 (A) 為費恩並未從受虐中存活下來；選項 (B) 為事發後，保姆被列入虐童資料系統裡；選項 (C) 為喬登一家未來在雇用保姆時，會更加謹慎小心；選項 (D) 為喬登一家的狗狗有注意到孩子受虐的事。答案可見內文最後一句 "The family credited their dog with saving their child, and probably many other children from further abuse." 可知孩子費恩因狗狗的警覺而獲救，故答案選 (A)。

❷ 此題詢問的是喬登一家的狗狗何時開始對保姆具攻擊性。選項 (A) 為保姆工作 2 個月以後；選項 (B) 為保姆工作 3 個月以後；選項 (C) 為保姆工作 4 個月以後；選項 (D) 為保姆工作5個月以後。答案可見內文第一段 "After about five months of employment, they started to noticed …" 故答案選 (D)。

補充單字

☆ 1. aggressive	**adj.**	攻擊性的
☆ 2. restrain	**v.**	遏制；控制
☆ 3. suspicious	**adj.**	可疑的，有蹊蹺的
☆ 4. disturbing	**adj.**	令人不安的；令人憂心的
☆ 5. instinct	**n.**	直覺

Level 1
12 A Rich King and Poor Farmers

富有的國王和貧窮的農夫

聽力測驗 Track 012

在學習英文的過程中，「聽」可能是最直接的第一線接觸，也可能是大家最想要快速習得的能力。現在，就讓我們來熟悉各種英文情境，提升自己的英文臨場感吧！

( ) 1. Why did the king have to go down under the water?
　　(A) Because there was something wrong with his arms.
　　(B) Because there was something wrong with his face.
　　(C) Because something went wrong with one of his legs.
　　(D) Because something went wrong with his heart.

( ) 2. Which is wrong according to the story?
　　(A) Before the farmer jumped into the water, he didn't know the man was the king.
　　(B) He didn't want others to know he had saved the king.
　　(C) The farmer was very brave.
　　(D) The farmer asked the king for a lot of money.

( ) 3. Choose the right statement.
　　(A) The king was cruel to his men.
　　(B) The king was kind to his men.
　　(C) People loved the king very much.
　　(D) The king liked fishing very much.

( ) 4. Which sentence has the same meaning as "he had not got any game"?
　　(A) He hadn't played any sport.

(B) He didn't like games.

(C) Hunting is a good game.

(D) He hadn't hunted any animals.

 **閱讀測驗**

剛剛的聽力測驗是否因為答題不順而感到遺憾？或是覺得自己有某些地方掌握地不夠好？現在就讓我們來直接「看」剛剛的聽力測驗，並透過後面的閱讀測驗來補齊聽力上的不足，同時考驗自己的閱讀能力吧！

A long, long time ago there lived a king. The king was a big tyrant. His people all **hated**[1] him.

One summer day, the king went to the river to have a **bath**[2]. But while the king was happy playing with water in the river, he had a sudden cramp in the leg. So he had no choice but to sink under the water. "Help! Help!" he cried. Just at that very **moment**[3], a farmer passed by and heard his shout. Without hesitation the farmer jumped into the river to rescue him. After the farmer **pulled**[4] the drowning man out of the river to the shore, he found out that the man he just **saved**[5] was the king. This farmer felt very much afraid. At this moment, the king was very happy, saying to him, "You have saved my life, and if you want anything, I will give it to you!" The farmer thought for a while, and then said, "I beg you not to tell others that it was I that saved your life."

Another summer morning, the king and two other ministers went hunting in the forest. But somehow, the king got separated from the ministers. So the king got lost in the forest. He walked for a long time, tired and hungry. Because he had not got any game, the king had an empty feeling in his stomach. Nearly at noon, the king managed to get out of the forest and arrived at a farmer's home. He wanted two eggs from the farmer and ate them. After finishing eating, the king pulled out the moneybag and asked the farmer how much he should **pay**[6] for the eggs.

"My dear king, each egg costs five pounds!"

"Really? You have few eggs here, don't you?"

"No! We have a lot of eggs here, but there is only one king."

【Question】

(　　) 1. What season and time was it when the King got lost in the forest?
(A) winter afternoon
(B) summer morning
(C) autumn evening
(D) spring midnight

(　　) 2. How much do two eggs cost in the story?
(A) 10 pounds　　　　(B) 5 pounds
(C) 1 pound　　　　(D) 2 pounds

【文章中譯】

很久以前，有一個國王。這個國王是個大暴君，他的臣民們都恨他。

一個夏日，國王去河裡泡澡。正當國王開心地在河裡玩水時，他的腿突然抽筋了。於是他被迫沉到水底，眼看要淹死了。「救命啊！救命！」他大喊。恰好一個農夫路過聽到他的叫聲。農夫毫不猶豫地跳進河裡救了他。等到農民把人拖到岸上，他才知道他救的人是國王。這個農民感到非常害怕。此時，國王很高興地對他說：「你救了我的命，你要什麼東西我都答應你！」農民考慮了一會兒後說：「我請求您不要告訴別人是我救了您。」

另一個夏日早晨，這個國王和另外兩名大臣到森林裡打獵。在打獵途中，國王與另外兩名大臣不知不覺走散了，於是國王在森林裡迷了路。他一個人走了好久，又餓又渴。由於沒獵到獵物，他的肚子很餓。快到中午時，國王總算走出了森林來到一個農民家中。他向農民要了兩個雞蛋吃，吃完後他掏出錢袋，問農民這些雞蛋多少錢。

「尊敬的國王，每個雞蛋要五磅！」

「啊？是因為你們這裡的雞蛋很少吧？」

「不！我們這裡的雞蛋很多，但國王只有一個。」

聽力題目解析

❶ 此題詢問的是國王沉入水裡的原因。選項 (A) 為因為國王的手臂出了問題；選項 (B) 為因為國王的臉出了問題；選項 (C) 為因為國王的腳出了狀況；選項 (D) 為國王的心臟出了狀況。根據錄音檔，我們可以掌握住 cramp (抽筋)這個關鍵字，故選 (C)。

❷ 此題詢問的是關於故事的陳述何者是錯誤的。選項 (A) 為在農夫跳入水中之前，他並不知道水中之人是國王；選項 (B) 為農夫並不希望別人知道是他救了國王；選項 (C) 為農夫非常勇敢；選項 (D) 為農夫向國王要求一大筆錢。根據錄音檔，農夫在救起國王之後，僅是表示不希望別人知道是他救了國王，接著便接續到另一個國王的遭遇，故 (D) 是錯的。

❸ 此題要求我們選出正確的陳述。選項 (A) 為國王對他的子民很殘酷；選項 (B) 為國王對他的子民很友善；選項 (C) 為國王很受人民愛戴；選項 (D) 為國王非常喜歡釣魚。根據錄音檔的內容，我們可以從兩個國王的遭遇中得知，他的子民和國王並沒有維持一個友善的關係，故選 (A)。選項 (D) 並未在故事中提及。

❹ 此題詢問的是選項中哪個句子和 "he had not got any game" 的意思一樣。選項 (A) 為他尚未參與任何運動活動；選項 (B) 為他不喜歡玩遊戲；選項 (C) 為打獵是個不錯的遊戲；選項 (D) 為他沒有獵到任何動物。根據錄音檔，此句是出現在 "the king had an empty feeling in his stomach"（他的肚子很餓）之前，故選 (D)。"game" 在這裡指的即是狩獵到的物品。

閱讀題目解析

❶ 此題詢問的是當國王在森林迷路時，當時正值什麼季節。選項 (A) 為冬天下午；選項 (B) 為夏天早晨；選項 (C) 為秋天晚上；選項 (D) 為春天凌晨。答案可見內文第三段的開頭，仔細閱讀文本即可，答案選 (B)。

❷ 此題詢問的是在故事中兩顆雞蛋的價格多少。答案可從內文倒數第三段開始理解，先找出一顆雞蛋為五磅這個資訊，再算出兩顆雞蛋為十磅，故答案為 (A)。此題需先把題目看清楚。

補充單字

☆	1. hate	v.	憎恨
☆	2. bath	n.	洗澡
☆	3. moment	n.	時刻
☆	4. pull	v.	拉、扯
☆	5. save	v.	挽救、節省
☆	6. pay	v.	付錢

Level 1
13 Archimedes and the Gold Crown

阿基米德與金皇冠

聽力測驗 🎧Track 013

在學習英文的過程中，「聽」可能是最直接的第一線接觸，也可能是大家最想要快速習得的能力。現在，就讓我們來熟悉各種英文情境，提升自己的英文臨場感吧！

( ) 1. Archimedes was a famous _____ scientist.
  (A) American   (B) Greek
  (C) German   (D) Roman

( ) 2. According to the story, the king lived on _____.
  (A) the island of Sicily   (B) the island of St. Helena
  (C) the long island   (D) the island of Corfu

( ) 3. Why did Archimedes run naked into the street?
  (A) Because he was forgetful.
  (B) Because he was mad.
  (C) Because he was hungry.
  (D) Because he was excited.

( ) 4. Which of the following statements is true?
  (A) Archimedes was a minister
  (B) Archimedes was the son of the king.
  (C) Archimedes was a famous scientist.
  (D) Archimedes was a goldsmith.

( ) 5. What can we learn from the story?
  (A) Gold Crown Principle   (B) Silver Crown Principle
  (C) Archimedes' Principle   (D) Bathtub Principle

 **閱讀測驗**

剛剛的聽力測驗是否因為答題不順而感到遺憾？或是覺得自己有某些地方掌握地不夠好？現在就讓我們來直接「看」剛剛的聽力測驗，並透過後面的閱讀測驗來補齊聽力上的不足，同時考驗自己的閱讀能力吧！

Archimedes was a famous Greek scientist. He is regarded as one of the leading scientists in classical era. He was also a great inventor and is given credit for many **inventions**[1] and discoveries. One of his best-known contributions to science is Archimedes' Principle. There's an interesting story behind it. The tale goes as follows.

Over two thousand years ago, on the island of Sicily lived a rich king called Heron. The king had a golden crown which was supposed to be made of **pure**[2] gold. But the king had a suspicion that the crown contained some cheaper metals like silver. To prove his suspicion, the king asked Archimedes to check the golden crown to see if it was really made of pure gold, but the crown could not be **harmed**[3] or damaged in any way.

As Archimedes contemplated this difficult problem in his house, his servant prepared a bath for him. The bathtub was filled with water to the very brim and Archimedes stepped into his bath. As he sat down into the tub fully, he noticed water **spilling**[4] over the edge of the tub. He suddenly discovered the relation between the water that had fallen out and the weight of his body, and knew the method to solve the crown problem. Archimedes was so excited with his discovery that he jumped out of the bath and ran naked into the street, yelling "Eureka!" (Greek word for "I've found it!")

Archimedes realized that the space his body occupied in the tub discharged the same weight of water from it. All he had to do is put the gold crown into a vessel with water to the very brim. If the overflow of water was **equal**[5] to the volume of an equal mass of pure gold, the crown would be made of pure gold. If not, the crown might contain some cheaper materials. And after the **experiment**[6], it was clear that the crown indeed contained some cheaper metals. This is where Archimedes' Principle comes from.

【Question】

(　　) 1. What is the origin of the word Eureka?
　　　(A) Greek　　　　　　(B) Italy
　　　(C) Roman　　　　　　(D) America

(　　) 2. What was the water condition of the bathtub before Archimedes stepped into the water?
　　　(A) half full　　　　　　(B) filled with water to the brim
　　　(C) almost empty　　　　(D) overflowing

【文章中譯】

阿基米德是一個有名的希臘科學家。他被認為是上古時代主要的科學家之一。他也是一個偉大的發明家，有許多備受讚揚的發明和發現。其中一個對科學上最知名的貢獻就是「阿基米德定律」。這個定律背後有一個有趣的故事如下：

兩千多年前，在西西里島上住著一位名叫希羅的富有國王。國王有一個金皇冠。照理金皇冠應該是純金打造的，但是國王懷疑裡面摻雜了例如銀這種便宜的金屬。為了證明他的懷疑，國王要求阿基米德想辦法檢查這個皇冠，看看它是否真的是純金打造，但是皇冠不能以任何方式被破壞。

當阿基米德正在苦思這個難題時，他的僕人幫他準備了一缸洗澡水。浴缸裡的水加得滿滿的，阿基米德就站進了洗澡水裡。當他整個人坐進浴缸裡時，他注意到水越過了浴缸邊緣溢了出去。他忽然發現了溢出去的水與身體重量之間的關連，也知道了解決皇冠問題的方法。阿基米德對於自己的發現非常興奮，於是跳出浴缸、光著身子跑到大街上，一面喊著：「Eureka！」（希臘文，意為「我發現了！」）

阿基米德明白了佔據著浴缸空間的身體把同樣重量的水量排了出去。他只要將金皇冠放進裝滿水的容器就可以解決問題了。如果溢出的水與同樣份量的純金塊一樣多，則金皇冠就是純金打造的。如果不一樣多，則皇冠可能摻雜了便宜的材料。實驗後發現，皇冠果然摻了便宜的金屬。這就是「阿基米德定律」的由來。

聽力題目解析

❶ 此題詢問的是阿基米德是為來自哪個國家的有名科學家。選項 (A)為美國人；選項　(B) 為希臘人；選項 (C) 為德國人；選項 (D) 為羅馬人。根據錄音檔的一開始，我們便能得知阿基米德是一位有名的希臘科學家。故答案選 (B)。

❷ 此題詢問的是根據故事，國王住在何處。選項 (A) 為西西里島；選項 (B) 為聖赫倫那島；選項 (C) 為長島；選項 (D) 為科孚島。此題同上題，在故事開始前便提供資訊，故仔細聆聽即可，答案選擇 (A)。

❸ 此題詢問的是為什麼阿基米德要赤裸地跑上街。選項 (A) 為因為他健忘；選項 (B) 為因為他發瘋了；選項 (C) 為因為他餓了；選項 (D) 為因為他很興奮。根據錄音檔，阿基米德在赤裸地跑到街上後，便大喊：「我知道了！」由此可推測答案為 (D)。

❹ 此題詢問的是選項的陳述何者為真。選項 (A) 為阿基米德是位大臣；選項 (B) 為阿基米德是國王的兒子；選項 (C) 為阿基米德是一位有名的科學家；選項 (D) 為阿基米德是位金匠。在錄音檔的一開始，我們就能得知阿基米德是一個有名的希臘科學家，故答案選 (C)。

❺ 此題詢問的是我們能從故事中學習到什麼。選項 (A) 為金黃冠定律；選項 (B) 為銀皇冠定律；選項 (C) 為阿基米德定律；選項 (D) 為浴缸定律。錄音檔的一開始即提及此篇故事的主旨，也就是阿基米德定律的由來，若疏忽此重點，也可把握錄音檔最後一句。答案選 (C)。

閱讀題目解析

❶ 此題詢問的是 Eureka 的字源為何。選項 (A) 為希臘;選項 (B) 為義大利;選項 (C) 為羅馬;選項 (D) 為美國。答案可見內文倒數第二段的最後一句。

❷ 此題詢問的是在阿基米德踏入浴缸前,浴缸的水量狀態為何。選項 (A) 為半滿;選項 (B) 為加得滿滿的;選項 (C) 為幾乎是空的;選項 (D) 為滿了出來。答案可同樣查見內文倒數第二段的開頭,答案應選 (B)。

補充單字

☆ 1.	invention	**n.**	發明
☆ 2.	pure	**adj.**	純粹的
☆ 3.	harm	**v.**	傷害
☆ 4.	spill	**v.**	使濺出
☆ 5.	equal	**adj.**	相等的
☆ 6.	experiment	**n.**	實驗

A Hat with Magic Power
神奇的魔法帽

Level 1
Level 2
Level 3
Level 4
Level 5
Level 6

聽力測驗 🎧 Track 014

在學習英文的過程中，「聽」可能是最直接的第一線接觸，也可能是大家最想要快速習得的能力。現在，就讓我們來熟悉各種英文情境，提升自己的英文臨場感吧！

( ) 1. What kind of school did the writer graduate from?
    (A) medical   (B) law
    (C) wizardry   (D) music

( ) 2. When he left the school, what did his master give him?
    (A) a magic stick   (B) a magic hat
    (C) a magic cap   (D) a magic cat

( ) 3. Which is wrong according to the story?
    (A) The writer first asked for some money.
    (B) The hat gave him seven dollars at first.
    (C) The hat could meet the writer's needs.
    (D) The writer did a good thing for the villagers.

( ) 4. Why were the villagers happy?
    (A) They needn't work any more.
    (B) The writer helped them a lot.
    (C) The writer gave the hat to the villagers.
    (D) The writer became their head.

( ) 5. What can we learn from the story?
    (A) There's no shortcut to learning.
    (B) Nothing is impossible.
    (C) Doing good things is very important

剛剛的聽力測驗是否因為答題不順而感到遺憾？或是覺得自己有某些地方掌握地不夠好？現在就讓我們來直接「看」剛剛的聽力測驗，並透過後面的閱讀測驗來補齊聽力上的不足，同時考驗自己的閱讀能力吧！

Last fall, I graduated from a wizardry school. On leaving, my master gave me a magic hat and taught me how to use it. "Oh, my magic hat! Everything I want will arrive! GO!" Then my **master**[1] said these words to me repeatedly, "My child, the black magic hat may meet your need, but, you must **remember**[2] its power is limited. But if you use it for everybody's happiness, its power will revive!"

I did not care about the last few words. I had just learned the incantation, and then my master disappeared. I walked down the street, thinking of how to make the black magic hat work.

A few minutes later, I was a little **hungry**[3]. I began to say the incantation,"...Give me several dollars!" Immediately, I put my hand into the hat and there really were ten dollars in it. It was really magical! I would use it to get everything I needed then.

Then I repeated the magic words, and then everything came－an automobile, a house, a swimming pool, an **airplane**[4] and so on. I took a walk freely in the sky and sea. I was enjoying all the magic hat had brought me.

Suddenly, the hat gave out a fizz. I did not know what was wrong, so I called out, "...Please let the black magic hat speak!" The black magic hat replied sadly, "My master, you use me to the utmost; my **power**[5] is in short supply."

I regretted. "Why don't I use it to do something meaningful? I must certainly make the most of the final power!"

I **discovered**[6] a place, where people were very poor and they were often hungry. So I said the incantation, "Let the villagers get rich!" The black magic hat did immediately provide money, houses and clothing. The villagers jumped cheerfully. A grandpa said excitedly, "Good child, our village will remember you forever!" My magic hat's power was also revived.

I was very proud of what I did!

【Question】

(　　) 1. When was the turn of the events regarding the writer's use of the hat?
(A) when the writer got rich
(B) when the hat gave out a fizz
(C) when the villagers asked for help

(　　) 2. What emotion did the magic hat give out when it spoke to the writer?
(A) angry 　　　　　(B) sad
(C) glad 　　　　　(D) no emotions

【文章中譯】

去年秋天，我從魔法學校畢業了，臨別時，大師送給我一頂魔法帽，並且教會我使用魔法帽的咒語：「魔法帽，魔法到，變！」教完咒語，大師再三囑咐我說：「孩子，你只要一唸這個咒語，魔法帽就可以滿足你的需求，但是，你要記住它的法力有限。但如果你是為了大家的幸福而使用它，它的法力會回復！」

我並不在意大師最後說的那些話。我才剛剛學會了咒語，大師就不見了。我沿著大街走著，想著如何讓魔法帽滿足我的需求。

走了一會，我覺得肚子有點餓了，我就唸起了咒語：「……給我幾塊錢！」我用手一摸，帽子裡立即有了十塊錢。我覺得這個魔法帽實在太神奇了，我就讓它給我我所需要的東西吧！我重複唸著咒語，變出汽車、房子、游泳池、飛機等等。於是我在天空、海洋中悠閒地散步，享受著魔法帽帶給我的一切。

突然，魔法帽發出了嘶嘶聲。我不知道是怎麼回事，就叫道：「……請讓魔法帽說話吧！」魔法帽傷心地說：「主人，你到處利用我做事，我的法力不夠了。」

我後悔了：「我何不用它做有意義的事情呢？我一定要把最後的法力用得有意義、有價值！」

我發現一個地方，那裡的人們非常窮苦，常常挨餓。於是我唸了唸咒語，說道：「讓村民們富有起來吧！」魔法帽立刻變出錢、房子和衣物。村民們歡呼跳躍起來。一位老爺爺激動地說：「好孩子，我們村子會永遠記得你的！」這時，魔法帽的法力回復了。

我為我所做的這件事而感到自豪！

聽力題目解析

❶ 此題詢問的是作者在去年秋天從何種學校畢業。選項 (A) 為醫學；選項 (B) 為法律；選項 (C) 為魔法；選項 (D)為音樂。根據錄音檔的開始，我們便能得知魔法學校為正解（Last fall, I graduated from a wizardry school.）。

❷ 此題詢問的是當作者離開學校時，大師送了他什麼。選項 (A) 為魔法杖；選項 (B) 為魔法帽；選項 (C) 為魔法鴨舌帽；選項 (D) 為魔法貓。同上題，只要注意聽，便能從錄音檔的開頭得知，大師送了他一頂魔法帽（a magic hat），故答案為 (B)。

❸ 此題要求我們選出與故事相關的錯誤陳述。選項 (A) 為作者首先要了一些錢；選項 (B) 為帽子在一開始給了他七元；選項 (C) 為帽子可以滿足作者的需求；選項 (D) 為作者替村民們做了一件好事。根據錄音檔，我們可以得知帽子在一開始給了他十塊錢，故選項 (B) 的陳述是錯誤的。此題僅需仔細聆聽細節。

❹ 此題詢問的是村民們快樂的原因。選項 (A) 為他們再也不需要工作；選項 (B) 為作者幫了他們很多；選項 (C) 為作者把帽子給了村民們；選項 (D) 為作者成為他們的領袖。在錄音檔的最後，我們可以得知作者最後想要做一件有意義的事，因此用帽子變了許多錢和物資給貧苦的村民，故答案選 (B)。

❺ 此題詢問的是我們可以從這個故事中學習到什麼。選項 (A) 為學習沒有捷徑；選項 (B) 為任何事情都是有可能的；選項 (C) 為做好事很重要。根據錄音檔的結尾，作者利用了魔法帽使村民們的生活好了起來，作者不僅為自己感到自豪，魔法帽也恢復了法力，故答案選 (C)。

• •

閱讀題目解析

❶ 此題詢問的是作者使用魔法帽的方式是在什麼時候出現了轉變。選項 (A) 為當作者變得有錢時；選項 (B) 為當那頂帽子發出了嘶嘶聲時；選項 (C) 為村民們向他求助時。答案可見內文倒數第四段至倒數第三段，作者感到後悔，並改變了他以往揮霍的做法，故答案選 (B)。

❷ 此題詢問的是當魔法帽向作者說話時，它的情緒為何。選項 (A) 為生氣的；選項 (B) 為難過的；選項 (C) 為開心的；選項 (D) 為沒有情緒。答案可見內文倒數第四段。答案選 (B)。

補充單字

☆	1. master	**n.**	大師
☆	2. remember	**v.**	記住
☆	3. hungry	**adj.**	饑餓的
☆	4. airplane	**n.**	飛機
☆	5. power	**n.**	能量
☆	6. discover	**v.**	發現

Level 1
15
Achilles' Heel
致命傷

在學習英文的過程中，「聽」可能是最直接的第一線接觸，也可能是大家最想要快速習得的能力。現在，就讓我們來熟悉各種英文情境，提升自己的英文臨場感吧！

(   ) 1. Where does the idiom Achilles' heel come from?
       (A) The Arabian nights   (B) Aesop fables
       (C) The Iliad   (D) A Chinese history

(   ) 2. Where did Achilles' mother put him to make him bulletproof?
       (A) in the swimming-pool
       (B) in the river
       (C) in the bathtub
       (D) in oil

(   ) 3. Which part of Achilles' body was his weakness?
       (A) his head   (B) his belly
       (C) his stomach   (D) his heel

(   ) 4. Why was his heel the weakest part?
       (A) He couldn't walk.
       (B) There was something wrong with his feet.
       (C) It didn't touch the river.

(   ) 5. What can we learn from the story?
       (A) We should be brave in a battle.
       (B) Everyone has his or her merits.
       (C) Everyone has his or her weak points.

閱讀測驗

剛剛的聽力測驗是否因為答題不順而感到遺憾？或是覺得自己有某些地方掌握地不夠好？現在就讓我們來直接「看」剛剛的聽力測驗，並透過後面的閱讀測驗來補齊聽力上的不足，同時考驗自己的閱讀能力吧！

Achilles' heel has a story of itself. The literary quotation comes from Homer's epic, The Iliad. In the Trojan War, the Myrmidons, the **bravest**[1] and the most skillful in battle, were under the command of Achilles. His mother, Thetis, had done Achilles peculiar treatment when he was born, and therefore, he was invulnerable.

Thetis was a goddess of the sea. Both Poseidon, the god of the sea, and Zeus, the king of the gods, were **interested**[2] in her, but neither of them dared to marry her because her future son was doomed to be more capable than his father. Finally, she married a mortal King Peleus and gave **birth**[3] to Achilles. After Achilles was born, she carried him to the River Styx and held him in the water to make him invulnerable. However, the water did not touch his heel, so his heel became his only weakness.

The first of the fifty princes of Troy was called Hector, who protected Troy from being brought down. He was brave, but in the **final**[4] decisive battle with Achilles, he was still **chased**[5] a good many laps around the city walls. In the folk drama, Hector is often described as a role of boast, and therefore, in the English language, the word "hectoring" is employed to express "to boast" and "to talk big".

Achilles, who **killed**[6] Hector in the battle, was also killed by Prince Paris of Troy with an arrow shot in his heel. Since then, "Achilles' heel" has been used to refer to a man's small but fatal weakness.

Level 1

Level 2

Level 3

Level 4

Level 5

Level 6

(　　) 1. What was the reason why neither of Poseidon and Zeus dared
to marry Thetis?
(A) She was too pretty.
(B) She was too smart.
(C) Her son was fated to outdo his father.
(D) Her life was coming to an end.

(　　) 2. How many princes were there in the city of Troy?
(A) 10　　　　　　　(B) 50
(C) 30　　　　　　　(D) 20

【 文章中譯 】

阿基里斯的腳踝（致命傷）的典故出自荷馬史詩《伊里亞德》（The Iliad）。特洛伊戰爭中，最驍勇善戰的一支軍隊「邁爾彌頓人」是由阿基里斯率領的。阿基里斯出生時，他的母親忒提斯替他做過特殊處理，因此全身刀槍不入。

忒提斯是海洋女神，天神宙斯和海神波賽頓對她都有意思，可是都不敢娶她，因為命運註定她所生的兒子會比父親更厲害。最後她下嫁凡人珀琉斯國王，生下阿基里斯之後，抱著他來到冥河邊泡水，使他刀槍不入。可是因為手捏著他的腳踝沒泡到水，因而他的腳踝成了唯一的弱點。

特洛伊城五十個王子之首的赫克托是維持特洛伊不倒的人物。他雖勇敢，可是最後面對阿基里斯決戰時，仍被追著繞了城牆好幾圈才敢停下來作戰。在民間戲劇中，往往把赫克托描繪成愛吹牛的角色，所以英文中有 hectoring 一詞表示「大吹大擂」、「說大話」。

阿基里斯殺死赫克托之後，亦被特洛伊城的帕里斯王子（Paris）一箭射中腳踝而陣亡。後人即以Achilles' heel 表示「罩門、致命傷、最大的弱點」。

❶ 此題詢問的是「阿基里斯的腳踝」這個俗諺的來源為何。選項 (A) 為一千零一夜;選項 (B) 為伊索寓言;選項 (C) 為伊里亞德;選項 (D) 為中國歷史。根據錄音檔的開頭,我們能立即得知「阿基里斯的腳踝」的典故是出自荷馬史詩《伊里亞德》(The Iliad),故答案選 (C)。

❷ 此題詢問的阿基里斯的媽媽將他放在何處使他刀槍不入。選項 (A) 為游泳池裡;選項 (B) 為河裡;選項 (C) 為浴缸裡;選項 (D) 為油裡。根據錄音檔,我們可以得知阿基里斯的媽媽帶他到 "the River Styx",故只需把握住 "river" 此關鍵字即可,答案選 (B)。

❸ 此題詢問的是阿基里斯身體的何處為其弱點。選項 (A) 為他的頭;選項 (B) 為他的腹部;選項 (C) 為他的胃;選項 (D) 為他的腳踝。根據錄音檔的描述,因為阿基里斯媽媽的手捏著他的腳踝所以沒泡到水,因而他的腳踝成了唯一的弱點。若沒有把握到此內容,也可直接從此文的標題來得知,答案選 (D)。

❹ 此題詢問的是為什麼他的腳踝是弱點。選項 (A) 為他無法走路;選項 (B) 為他的腳有問題;選項 (C) 為他的腳踝沒有碰到河水。同上題,答案選 (C),此題僅仔細注意故事細節即可。

❺ 此題詢問的是我們可以從故事中學習到什麼。選項 (A) 為我們應在戰爭中表現勇敢;選項 (B) 為每個人都有其價值;選項 (C) 為每個人都有其弱點。根據故事內容,我們可以得知阿基里斯雖然刀槍不入,但最後仍因腳踝中箭而死,故可推論出 (C) 為最佳解答。

閱讀題目解析

❶ 此題詢問的是為什麼波賽頓和宙斯都不敢娶忒提斯。選項 (A) 為她太美麗；選項 (B) 為她太聰明；選項 (C) 為她的兒子註定會勝過父親；選項 (D) 為她的生命快要走到終點。答案可見內文第二段，答案應選 (C)。

❷ 此題詢問的是特洛伊城共有幾個王子。答案可查找內文第三段的開頭，只要注意細節便能快速選出 (B) 作為答案。

補充單字

☆ 1. brave	**adj.**	勇敢的
☆ 2. interest	**v.**	使……有興趣
☆ 3. birth	**n.**	出生、出身
☆ 4. final	**adj.**	最後的
☆ 5. chase	**v.**	追逐
☆ 6. kill	**v.**	殺害

A Soldier Who Doesn't Want to be a General Isn't a Good Soldier?

不當將軍的士兵不是好士兵？

聽力測驗 🎧 Track 016

在學習英文的過程中，「聽」可能是最直接的第一線接觸，也可能是大家最想要快速習得的能力。現在，就讓我們來熟悉各種英文情境，提升自己的英文臨場感吧！

(　　) 1. Who said the first sentence of this story?
    (A) Edison　　　　　　(B) Newton
    (C) Gauss　　　　　　 (D) Napoleon

(　　) 2. When did the French general say that?
    (A) In the wartime　　　(B) 20 years ago
    (C) 50 years ago　　　 (D) At the present time

(　　) 3. What is right about a good soldier according to the text?
    (A) A good soldier wants to be a general.
    (B) A good soldier wants to be a leader.
    (C) A good soldier tries to do his work well.
    (D) A good soldier likes to fight with others.

(　　) 4. Choose the right statement.
    (A) Napoleon was not a good general.
    (B) Napoleon was not a good soldier.
    (C) Napoleon served in the army at that time.
    (D) Napoleon was not right to say that.

(　　) 5. Which is wrong?
    (A) No matter what you are, you should try your best.

Level 1

Level 2
Level 3
Level 4
Level 5
Level 6

(B) We only need scientists.

(C) Everybody should do his or her job well.

(D) People should trust each other.

 閱讀測驗

剛剛的聽力測驗是否因為答題不順而感到遺憾？或是覺得自己有某些地方掌握地不夠好？現在就讓我們來直接「看」剛剛的聽力測驗，並透過後面的閱讀測驗來補齊聽力上的不足，同時考驗自己的閱讀能力吧！

" A soldier who does not want to work as a general is not a good soldier." These words were once said by Napoleon, the famous French general. At that time, these words **sounded**[1] very reasonable. But, in modern society, is it right to say these words? Is it often the case? In my opinion, a soldier who does not want to work as a general can still be a good soldier.

In the wartime, these words were treated as the truth by many people. However, in modern society, I don't think these words prove right. First, if everybody wants to **become**[2] that dazzling star, that is simply inconceivable. There are not that many chances in the world, and not every place offers chances to people. We know chances only favor those who are well prepared. Also, If everyone were a **star**[3], what difference would it make between a **common**[4] person and a star? A soldier who does not want to work as a general can still be a good soldier. If everybody wants to become a man with great power, the world will become unable to withstand chaos. People will not trust each other, and all people may become **greedy**[5]. If each person wants to work as a county magistrate, a governor, or a state cadre, there will be the struggle for power everywhere.

Most of important of all, not everyone is suitable to be a general, and not every general is really good at being a general. It depends on each person's personality, skills, knowledge, and ways to deal with things to decide if he or she should be a general or soldier. So, of course a soldier can have no wish to be a general. Being a good solider is better than being a not-so-good general. As long as it is what he or she wants

Level 1

Level 2

Level 3

Level 4

Level 5

Level 6

or desires, choosing to be a soldier doesn't make him/her less than a human. We just need to find where our passion is and do things well.

Yes, we need not refuse to say that we need generals and cadres, but we need good soldiers, and scientists and people of all walks of life. Therefore, we say, "A soldier who does not want to work as a general can be a good soldier."

【 Question 】

(　　) 1. Which of the following is not mentioned as the factor to choose what one wants to do in the article?
　　　　(A) skills　　　　　　　(B) personality
　　　　(C) knowledge　　　　 (D) money

(　　) 2. What does "doesn't make him/herless than a human" mean in the article?
　　　　(A) to be like an animal
　　　　(B) to be a human as everybody else
　　　　(C) to be a human but everyone else is not
　　　　(D) to be more like a human

【 文章中譯 】

「不想當將軍的士兵不是好士兵。」這句話是拿破崙説的。在當時,這句話似乎是很有道理。可是,在當今社會,這句話還有道理嗎?情況真的如此嗎?依我看不想當將軍的士兵也可以是好士兵。

在那個動盪的年代,這句話被很多人當作至理名言。然而,在當今社會,我無法苟同這句話。首先,假若人人都想成為那一顆耀眼的明星,那簡直無法想像。世界不可能充滿機會也不是每個地方都有機會,更不可能人人都如此幸運,我們都了解機會是留給準備好的人。如果大家都是閃耀的明星,那麼明星與平民有什麼差別呢?不想當將軍的士兵也可以是好士兵。假若人人都想成為大人物,那麼,世界將變得混亂不堪,互不信任,人們的貪心就會被引誘出來。對於一個國家來說,如果每個人都想當縣長、省長、州長,那麼到處將充滿權力的鬥爭。

最重要的是，並不是每個人都適合當將軍，也不是每個將軍都真的擅長當將軍。它取決於每個人的個性、技能、知識，以及處事方法，進而才能決定他或她應該要當將軍還是士兵。所以，一個士兵當然可以不想要當一名將軍。當一名好士兵比當一名不好的將軍還來的好。只要這是他或她想要或渴望的，選擇當一名士兵並不會減損其身為人的價值只要我們找出熱情所在並把分內事做好。

是的，毋庸諱言，我們需要將軍，也需要州長，但更需要好的士兵，也同樣需要科學家和各行各業的人才。所以，我們說：「不想當將軍的士兵也可以是好士兵。」

聽力題目解析

❶ 此題詢問的是錄音檔中的第一句話為何人所說。選項 (A) 為愛迪生；選項 (B) 為牛頓；選項 (C) 為高斯；選項 (D) 為拿破崙。錄音檔在一開始即告訴我們答案，選擇 (D)。

❷ 此題詢問的是這位法國將軍是在何時說這句話。選項 (A) 為戰爭時；選項 (B) 為二十年前；選項 (C) 為五十年前；選項 (D) 為現今。在作者提出反問之後，我們接著可以聽到關鍵字 "in the wartime ... these words ...”，後面的 "these words" 指的即是前面拿破崙所說的話，故掌握好時間點即可，選擇 (A)。

❸ 此題詢問的是根據內文，何者針對一名好士兵的陳述是正確的。選項 (A) 為一名好士兵會想要當一名好將軍；選項 (B) 為一名好士兵會想要領導人；選項 (C) 為一名好士兵會試著把份內的事做好；選項 (D) 為一名好士兵喜歡和別人博鬥。在作者的言論中，我們可以先知道作者並不認同拿破崙的說法，因此選項 (A) 和 (B) 可以快速刪去，接著我們可以聽見 "We just need to find where our passion is and do things well." 由此連接士兵與將軍這個題目，故選 (C)。

❹ 此題要求我們選出正確的陳述。選項 (A) 為拿破崙並不是一名好將軍；選項 (B) 為拿破崙並不是一位好士兵；選項 (C) 為拿破崙當時正在軍隊中工作；選項 (D) 為拿破崙這麼說是不對的。答案為 (C)，因其是唯一

有在內文中提及的選項，其餘的 (A)、(B)、(D) 我們皆無法根據內文做出推測。

❺ 此題要求我們選出錯誤的陳述。選項 (A) 為無論如何，你應盡全力；選項 (B) 為我們只需要科學家；選項 (C) 為每個人都應該把事情做好；選項 (D) 為人們應信任對方。在錄音檔後段，我們可以得知 "... we need good soldiers, and scientists and people of all walks of life." 這裡就算不熟悉 "all walks of life" 作為「各行各業」的用法，也可以從前面出現的 soldiers 來推判，故 (B) 是錯的。

閱讀題目解析

❶ 此題詢問的是選項何者並沒有在內文中被提及作為選擇志向的要素之一。選項 (A) 為技能；選項 (B) 為個性；選項 (C) 為知識；選項 (D) 為金錢。答案可見內文倒數第二段第二句，選 (D)。

❷ 此題詢問的是 "doesn't make him/her less than a human" 之意。選項 (A) 為變得像動物；選項 (B) 和大家一樣都是人；選項 (C) 為自身為人但其餘人不是；選項 (D) 為變得更像個人。這邊我們可以注意到 "less" 本來是負面的「更少的」之意，但是前面有出現否定的 "does not"，因此兩個負面詞語相互抵消，不多也不少，留下「同樣為人」之意，故選 (B)。

補充單字

☆ 1. sound	**v.**	聽
☆ 2. become	**v.**	變得；變成
☆ 3. star	**n.**	星星；明星
☆ 4. common	**adj.**	平凡的
☆ 5. greedy	**adj.**	貪心的

Level 1
17
Don't Think the Way a Donkey or a Bee Does!

別用笨方法思考！

聽力測驗 🎧 Track 017

在學習英文的過程中，「聽」可能是最直接的第一線接觸，也可能是大家最想要快速習得的能力。現在，就讓我們來熟悉各種英文情境，提升自己的英文臨場感吧！

(   ) 1. Who wrote Donkey of Guizhou Province?
      (A) Su Dongpo   (B) Han Yu
      (C) Liu Zong-yuan   (D) Du Fu

(   ) 2. Which is right according to the story?
      (A) The donkey kicked the tiger to death.
      (B) The tiger was afraid to run away forever.
      (C) The tiger ate the donkey at last
      (D) The donkey was very clever.

(   ) 3. Where were the bees and flies put in the experiment?
      (A) in a box   (B) in a paper bag
      (C) in the water   (D) in a bottle

(   ) 4. Choose the right statement.
      (A) At last the bees ran away.
      (B) At last the flies ran away.
      (C) Both the bees and flies ran away.
      (D) Neither the bees nor the flies ran away.

(   ) 5. What should we learn from the story?
      (A) We should work hard.

(B) We should be strict in our work.
(C) We should be kind to others.
(D) We should be creative in our work.

 閱讀測驗

剛剛的聽力測驗是否因為答題不順而感到遺憾？或是覺得自己有某些地方掌握
地不夠好？現在就讓我們來直接「看」剛剛的聽力測驗，並透過後面的閱讀測
驗來補齊聽力上的不足，同時考驗自己的閱讀能力吧！

You must have read "A Donkey in Guizhou Province," written by the famous ancient Chinese writer Liu Zongyuan, right? The **tiger**[1] knew how the donkey would think and do, so he ate the donkey at the end. There is another famous experiment of this kind as follows.

Put[2] six honeybees and six **flies**[3] into a glass bottle, and keep the bottle lied flat with the bottom facing the window.

What will **happen**[4] to the honeybees and the flies?

You'll see that the honeybees won't stop looking for the exit on the bottom of the bottle until their strength gives out and they die or starve to **death**[5]; but the flies, in less than two minutes, will pass through the other end of the bottle and run away.

Why is that? Because the honeybees like sunlight, they think the exit must be in the **brightest**[6] place. Therefore, they will keep trying to escape from the brightest side and then fail in the end. The way honeybees think is what causes their death.

But on the other hand, these flies are not attracted to the sunlight, and they fly in every possible direction. Finally, luck comes to them. It is the place where the honeybees die but all the six flies escape from death.

People who live or work in a certain environment will gradually form a fixed pattern of thinking. It will lead people to see things from a fixed

Level 1
Level 2
Level 3
Level 4
Level 5
Level 6

angle. It is the natural enemy of creative thinking. Therefore, we must learn to take a risk, think creatively and play it by ear, and then the sky is the limit!

【Question】

(　　) 1. What attracted the honeybees in the experiment?
      (A) the smell
      (B) the sound
      (C) the light

(　　) 2. In the experiment, how many insectes were in the bottle?
      (A) 6
      (B) 20
      (C) 12

【文章中譯】

你一定讀過中國古代著名作家柳宗元的《黔之驢》吧？老虎抓住了驢子的行為規律，最終把驢子吃掉。還有下列這樣一個著名的類似實驗。

把六隻蜜蜂和六隻蒼蠅裝進一個玻璃瓶中；然後將瓶子平放，讓瓶底朝著窗戶。

結果發生了什麼情況？

你會看到，蜜蜂不停地想在瓶底上找到出口，一直到它們力竭而死或餓死；而蒼蠅則會在不到兩分鐘之內，穿過另一端的瓶頸全部逃出來。

為什麼會這樣？由於蜜蜂對光亮的喜愛，牠們以為瓶子的出口必然在光線最明亮的地方，牠們因此不停地試圖從最亮的地方逃跑，但最終失敗。蜜蜂的思考模式造成牠們的死亡。

然而，另一方面，那些蒼蠅則全然不顧亮光的吸引，四下亂飛，結果碰上了好運氣，這些蒼蠅在蜜蜂消亡的地方反而順利得救，重獲新生。

人們在一定的環境中工作和生活，久而久之就會形成一種固定的思維模式，使人們習慣於從固定的角度來觀察、思考事物。它是創新思維的天敵。因此，我們必須學會冒險、學會創意思考、學會應變，只有這樣做，才能發揮無限潛能！

聽力題目解析

❶ 此題詢問是誰寫了《黔之驢》。在錄音檔的開頭我們即可快速得知答案為 (C)。

❷ 此題詢問的是選項中針對故事的描述何者正確。選項 (A) 為驢把老虎踢死了；選項 (B) 為老虎害怕一輩子都需要逃跑；選項 (C) 為老虎最終吃掉了驢；選項 (D) 為驢非常聰明。根據錄音檔，我們可以在一開始便得知老虎抓住了驢子的行為規律，最終把驢子吃掉（ "so he finally ate the donkey" ），故答案選 (C)。

❸ 此題詢問的是在實驗中蜜蜂和蒼蠅被放置在何處。選項 (A) 為一個盒子裡；選項 (B) 為一個紙袋裡；選項 (C) 為水裡；選項 (D) 為一個瓶子裡。此題僅需注意聽，錄音檔在一開始有提及 "were put into a glass bottle"，故選 (D)。

❹ 此題要求我們從選項中選出正確的陳述。選項 (A) 為蜜蜂最後飛走了；選項 (B) 為蒼蠅最後飛走了；選項 (C) 為蜜蜂和蒼蠅都飛走了；選項 (D) 為蜜蜂和蒼蠅都沒有飛走。根據錄音檔，我們可以得知最後只剩蒼蠅活著飛走。若一開始在聆聽時沒有把握到，也可以透過末段分析蒼蠅的內容來判斷答案為 (B)。

❺ 此題詢問的是我們可以從故事中學習到什麼。選項 (A) 為我們應該努力工作；選項 (B) 為我們應嚴謹地工作；選項 (C) 為我們應對他人友善；選項 (D) 我們在工作中應具有創造力。根據錄音檔的末段，我們可以聽見 "think creatively"，故選項 (D) 應最符合本篇故事主旨。

閱讀題目解析

❶ 此題詢問的是在實驗中是什麼吸引了蜜蜂。選項 (A) 為氣味；選項 (B) 為聲音；選項 (C) 為光線。答案可見內文第五段 "the honeybees like sunlight"（蜜蜂對光亮的喜愛），故答案選 (C)。

❷ 此題詢問的是在實驗中瓶子裡共有多少隻昆蟲。答案可見內文第二段，我們得知共有六隻蜜蜂和六隻蒼蠅，故總共加起來為十二隻，答案選 (C)，此題需注意答案應選蜜蜂和蒼蠅的總數。

補充單字

☆ 1. tiger	n.	老虎
☆ 2. fly	n.	蒼蠅
☆ 3. put	v.	放、放置
☆ 4. happen	v.	發生
☆ 5. death	n.	死、死亡
☆ 6. bright	adj.	明亮的

A Cat has Nine Lives
貓有九條命

Level 1
Level 2
Level 3
Level 4
Level 5
Level 6

聽力測驗 Track 018

在學習英文的過程中，「聽」可能是最直接的第一線接觸，也可能是大家最想要快速習得的能力。現在，就讓我們來熟悉各種英文情境，提升自己的英文臨場感吧！

(　　) 1. What animal does the passage mainly talk about?
(A) a cat　　　　　　(B) a dog
(C) a wolf

(　　) 2. What does "a cat has nine lives" really mean?
(A) A cat can live in nine houses.
(B) A cat can catch a lot of rats.
(C) A cat can't be killed by anything.
(D) A cat can get better soon by itself after it is injured.

(　　) 3. "It is raining cats and dogs." means＿＿＿＿.
(A) The cats and dogs are crying out.
(B) The cats and dogs are fighting.
(C) It is raining heavily.
(D) The cats and dogs are swimming.

(　　) 4. Which is wrong according to the story?
(A) The dogs have fewer lives than the cats.
(B) The cats have more lives than the dogs.
(C) The dogs can climb up a tall tree easily.
(D) The cats can climb up a tall tree easily.

(　　) 5. Which of the following is not mentioned in the text?
(A) cats　　　　　　(B) dogs
(C) scientists　　　　(D) doctors

 閱讀測驗

剛剛的聽力測驗是否因為答題不順而感到遺憾？或是覺得自己有某些地方掌握地不夠好？現在就讓我們來直接「看」剛剛的聽力測驗，並透過後面的閱讀測驗來補齊聽力上的不足，同時考驗自己的閱讀能力吧！

As is well known, **animals**[1] make English language rich and colorful. The **cat**[2], for example, has given English many useful expressions. When we talk about a heavy rain, we say: "It rains cats and dogs." There is another saying: "The rats will play while the cat is away." Today we will learn why a cat has nine lives.

When having a rest, cats will purr. Some people think that the cat is only snoring, but the American scientists have discovered that this is one way how cats heal themselves. People say that a cat has nine lives, which has a lot to do with the purring sound that cats make. The scientists pointed out that after being injured, a cat will expose itself to the purring sound and it will help repair the wound.

Scientists also discovered that a human body could be treated in a similar way. The manager of the Animal Communication Research Center in North Carolina indicated that because the cat may take advantage of the sound sent out by itself to cure its wound. Therefore, the **idea**[3] of a cat having nine lives is by no means ridiculous.

As a kind of domestic animal, cats' **climbing**[4] ability is second to none. It is easy for a cat to climb up to the roof of a house. Sometimes cats can even climb up to the top of a very tall tree. When cats are **under**[5] attack, they always crawl rapidly to a high place, where the enemy cannot reach. We saw frequently that a cat can fall from a very high place without getting hurt. But **if**[6] a dog jumps off a high place, it will be either dead or wounded. So people often say, "A cat has nine lives."

【Question】

(   ) 1. Which city did the research mentioned in the article come from?
          (A) North Carolina   (B) North California
          (C) North Coast   (D) North Korea

(   ) 2. What may happen if a dog falls from a high place according to the article?
          (A) It will be safe and sound.
          (B) It may be badly injured.
          (C) It may be stuck in the tree.
          (D) Its tail will protect its body.

【文章中譯】

眾所周知，動物豐富了英語這個語言，使其增添色彩。就貓而言，就有許多的習慣表達方式，例如，當我們說下大雨時，我們用「It rains cats and dogs.」來形容。另一個用語為：「老貓不在家，老鼠鬧翻天。」（The rats will play while the cat is away.）今天我們要來研究一下，為什麼貓有九條命（A cat has nine lives.）。

貓在休息時，常會發出呼嚕聲。有人認為這是貓在打呼，但美國科學家卻發現這是貓自療的方式之一。人們之所以稱貓有九條命，與貓休息時的呼嚕聲有密不可分的關係。科學家指出，貓在受傷後，會把自己處於呼嚕聲中，且呼嚕聲有助於療傷。

科學家從人類實驗中也發現，將人體暴露於如同貓咪呼嚕聲的聲波下，有助於改善體質。美國北卡羅萊納州區系動物溝通研究所所長表示，由於貓可藉自己發出的聲波療傷，因此「九命怪貓」的傳說並非荒誕不經。

貓的爬高本領在家畜中可謂首屈一指。爬上屋頂對貓來說是輕而易舉之事，有時甚至能爬到很高的大樹上去。貓在遭到追擊時，總是會迅速地爬到敵人無法觸及的高處。我們經常看到貓從很高的地方掉下來，而身體卻不會有絲毫損傷。然而狗要是從同樣高度掉下來，非死即傷，這就是人們常說的「貓有九條命」的由來。

Level 1
Level 2
Level 3
Level 4
Level 5
Level 6

聽力題目解析

❶ 此題詢問文章主要在講述何種動物。選項 (A) 為貓;選項 (B) 為狗;選項 (C) 為狼。根據錄音檔的開頭,我們可以得知許多關於貓的俗諺,且接下來舉出了貓咪呼嚕聲的研究,故答案選 (A)。

❷ 此題詢問的是「貓有九條命」的真正意義為何。選項 (A) 為貓可以住在九間房子裡;選項 (B) 為貓可以抓許多老鼠;選項 (C) 為貓無法被任何東西殺死;選項 (D) 為貓可以在受傷後快速地自我修復。在錄音檔開頭不久之後,我們即能聽見關鍵字 "purr",即貓會發出呼嚕聲,後續便是在討論此種行為的真正意義,把握住 "heal themselves"(療癒自己)即可。答案選擇 (D)。

❸ 此題詢問的是「下了許多貓和狗」的意思為何。選項 (A) 為貓和狗正在嚎叫;選項 (B) 為貓和狗正在打架;選項 (C) 為雨勢正大;選項 (D) 為貓和狗正在游泳。根據錄音檔的開頭,我們可以立即得知此俗諺被拿來形容 "a heavy rain",意即大雨,故選 (C)。

❹ 此題詢問的是何者關於內文的描述錯誤。選項 (A) 為狗的性命數量比貓少;選項 (B) 為貓的性命數量比狗多;選項 (C) 為狗可以輕易地爬上高樹;選項 (D) 為貓可以輕易替爬上高樹。根據錄音檔,我們可以得知貓被形容為有九條命,主要是因一開始提及的呼嚕聲,以及末段時提到的攀爬高處之能力,且後者有和狗進行比較,故答案選 (C),此題需注意選項 (A) 及 (B) 可能會造成誤導。

❺ 此題詢問的是哪一個選項的陳述並未在文章中提及。選項 (A) 為貓;選項 (B) 為狗;選項 (C) 為科學家;選項 (D) 為醫生。答案為 (D),我們在錄音檔中並未聽見任何關於醫生的描述,選項 (C) 在討論呼嚕聲的治癒能力時有被提及。

閱讀題目解析

Level 1
Level 2
Level 3
Level 4
Level 5
Level 6

❶ 此題詢問的是內文中所提及的研究是來自於哪座城市。答案可見文章的
第三段,僅需注意誤被選項 (B) 誤導,答案選 (A)。

❷ 此題詢問的是根據內文,如果狗從高處墜落可能會發生何種狀況。選項
(A) 為牠會安全墜地;選項 (B) 為牠可能會受重傷;選項 (C) 為牠可能
會被卡在樹上;選項 (D) 為牠的尾巴會保護牠的身體。答案可詳見內文
最後一段,我們可以得知狗並不具有像貓咪那樣的爬高本領,且無法毫
髮無傷地從高處躍下,故答案選 (B)。

補充單字

☆ 1. animal	n.	動物
☆ 2. cat	n.	貓、貓科動物
☆ 3. idea	n.	想法
☆ 4. climb	v.	攀登
☆ 5. under	prep.&v.	在⋯⋯下
☆ 6. if	conj.	如果

A Poor Musician
貧窮的音樂家

聽力測驗 🎧 Track 019

在學習英文的過程中，「聽」可能是最直接的第一線接觸，也可能是大家最想要快速習得的能力。現在，就讓我們來熟悉各種英文情境，提升自己的英文臨場感吧！

(   ) 1. Who is the main character in the story?
      (A) Xian Xing-hai   (B) Hua Yan-jun
      (C) Nie-Er   (D) Hua Xue-mei

(   ) 2. When was Ah Bing born?
      (A) in June, 1389   (B) in July, 1983
      (C) in July, 1893   (D) in June, 1983

(   ) 3. Who did Ah Bing learn music from?
      (A) himself   (B) his mother
      (C) his father   (D) his friends

(   ) 4. How did Ah Bing earn his living?
      (A) by selling newspapers
      (B) by begging
      (C) by singing and playing
      (D) by stealing

(   ) 5. In which eye was Ah Bing blind?
      (A) in the right eye
      (B) in the left eye
      (C) in both eyes
      (D) in neither of the eyes

 **閱讀測驗**

剛剛的聽力測驗是否因為答題不順而感到遺憾？或是覺得自己有某些地方掌握地不夠好？現在就讓我們來直接「看」剛剛的聽力測驗，並透過後面的閱讀測驗來補齊聽力上的不足，同時考驗自己的閱讀能力吧！

Level 1
Level 2
Level 3
Level 4
Level 5
Level 6

Hua Yan-jun, also **called**[1] Ah Bing, was a great Chinese musician. He was born in July, 1893 and **died**[2] in December, 1950. When Ah Bing was in his twenties, he contracted eye disease, and worse still, his father passed away. He was so poor that he could not afford the medicine, and therefore he became blind soon in both eyes. From then on, people called him Ah Bing the Blind.

Ah Bing **studied**[3] **music**[4] since his childhood with his father Hua Xue-mei, who was a Taoist. He was so outstanding that the local Taoism music world recognized him. Ah Bing mainly based his musicianship on Taoism music. Moreover, he was deeply affected by his dear father. Taoism music mainly belongs to religious folk music, including many folk song melodies.

Being blind in both eye, he was not popular with rich people, so he had to **leave**[5] to take to singing for a living. In the city of Wuxi, people often saw a person **wearing**[6] sunglasses, carrying some musical instruments like the sheng, the flute, and the pipa, and playing the Chinese violin while walking in the street. The very person is Ah Bing.

Ah Bing earned his living by singing and playing musical instruments. He never begged other people for food or money. He struggled for dozens of years in the darkness and lived with illness and poverty. He expressed and reflected his feelings about life through his music. Poor as he was, he did not give in to his fate. On the contrary, his music expressed his love for the lower-working people. "Erquan Yingyue" became his immortal work. After liberation, when the people's government sent people to care about him and recognize his music work, he was actually unable to hope for anything and died of spitting blood.

【Question】

(　　) 1. What was the religion Ah Bing and his father believed in?
           (A) Christian   (B) Taoism
           (C) Islam   (D) Buddhism

(　　) 2. How did Ah Bing pass away?
           (A) fever   (B) car accident
           (C) spitting blood   (D) suicide

【文章中譯】

阿炳，原名華彥鈞（阿炳是他的小名），是一個偉大的中國音樂家。生於 1893年 7 月，卒於 1950 年 12 月。阿炳二十多歲時，患了眼疾，更不幸的是，父親又過世。他貧病交加，眼疾惡化，雙眼相繼失明，從此，人家便叫他瞎子阿炳。

阿炳從童年起就同他父親華雪梅學習音樂。華雪梅是一位道士，是當地道教音樂界所公認的技藝傑出的人才。阿炳的音樂修養主要的基礎出於道家音樂，而且，是出於家傳。道家音樂大部分是屬於宗教性的民俗音樂，其中有許多是毫未更動的民謠旋律。

阿炳雙目失明後得不到有錢人的歡迎，只能離開，開始以賣唱為生。在無錫市裡，一位戴著墨鏡，胸前背上掛著笙、笛、琵琶等樂器，拉著胡琴，在街頭上行走著，這人便是阿炳。

阿炳純粹靠演唱及演奏樂器來維持生活，他從來沒有向人乞討食物或金錢。他在黑暗、貧病中掙扎了幾十年，他對痛苦生活的感受，透過他的音樂反映出來。他沒有因為生活艱難困苦而潦倒，相反地，他的音樂表達出他對底層人民的關愛。阿炳用他的生命凝成了《二泉映月》等不朽作品。在解放後，當人民政府派人去關心他時，表揚他的音樂作品，他卻無法了願，突然吐血病死了。

聽力題目解析

❶ 此題詢問的是故事中的主角為何人。我們在錄音檔的一開始即可得知答案，注意聽即可，答案為 (B)。

❷ 此題詢問的是阿炳出生的年份。此題同上，可在一開始得知，建議先快速看過題目，便可把握關鍵字。答案為 (C)。

❸ 此題詢問的是阿炳向何人學習音樂。根據錄音檔，我們在聆聽阿炳的身世時，可以直接聽見阿炳的父親是阿炳學習音樂的對象，且其父也為道教音樂中的傑出人才，故答案選 (C)。

❹ 此題詢問的是阿炳如何養活自己。選項 (A) 為賣報紙；選項 (B) 為乞討；選項 (C) 為唱歌和彈奏樂器；選項 (D) 為偷竊。根據錄音檔，我們可以掌握到關鍵字 "earned his living"，意即餬口，接著便是 "singing and playing musical instruments"， 故答案應選 (C)。

❺ 此題詢問的是阿炳的哪一隻眼睛失明。根據錄音檔的內容，我們可以在開始不久便聽見 "became blind soon in both eyes"，意即雙眼失明，故答案為 (C)，此題需在得知阿炳患眼疾後仔細聆聽。

閱讀題目解析

❶ 此題詢問的是阿炳及其父所信仰的宗教為何。選項 (A) 為基督教；選項 (B) 為道教；選項 (C) 為伊斯蘭教；選項 (D) 為佛教。答案可在內文第二段中得知，掌握細節即可，答案選擇 (B)。

❷ 此題詢問的是阿炳如何離世。選項 (A) 為發燒；選項 (B) 為車禍；選項 (C) 為吐血；選項 (D) 為自盡。答案可詳見於內文最後一句，選擇 (C)。

補充單字

☆ 1. call	**v.**	叫喊、取名
☆ 2. die	**v.**	死
☆ 3. study	**v.**	學習、研究
☆ 4. music	**n.**	音樂
☆ 5. leave	**v.**	離開
☆ 6. wear	**v.**	穿戴

The Riddle of the Sphinx
獅身人面的謎

聽力測驗 Track 020

在學習英文的過程中，「聽」可能是最直接的第一線接觸，也可能是大家最想要快速習得的能力。現在，就讓我們來熟悉各種英文情境，提升自己的英文臨場感吧！

(　　) 1. What is the sphinx?
   (A) a real person
   (B) a human being
   (C) a lion
   (D) a statue made of rock

(　　) 2. Where did the sphinx live?
   (A) in the river
   (B) in the city
   (C) on a high rock outside the city
   (D) in the mountain

(　　) 3. The answer to the riddle is _____.
   (A) man　　　　　　(B) animal
   (C) rock　　　　　　(D) lion

(　　) 4. What is the old man's third foot?
   (A) a rock　　　　　(B) a walking stick
   (C) a sword　　　　　(D) a gun

(　　) 5. Why was the kind of creature used to guard their temples and tombs?
   (A) It was kind.　　　(B) It was strong.
   (C) It was brave.　　　(D) It was wise.

Level 1
Level 2
Level 3
Level 4
Level 5
Level 6

109

 **閱讀測驗**

剛剛的聽力測驗是否因為答題不順而感到遺憾？或是覺得自己有某些地方掌握
地不夠好？現在就讓我們來直接「看」剛剛的聽力測驗，並透過後面的閱讀測
驗來補齊聽力上的不足，同時考驗自己的閱讀能力吧！

The people who lived in ancient Egypt, Greece, and the Near East all had legends about invented/imaginary creatures with the **head**[1] of a man and the body of an animal. These people thought that this kind of creature was very brave, so they built statues of these creatures, which were called sphinxes, to defend their temples and tombs. The sphinx in Greek legends had the head of a woman and the body of a lion. People say that she had lived on a high rock outside the ancient city of Thebes (in Greece) and **stopped**[2] all travelers from **passing**[3] by to ask them the following riddle, which is known to many people today.

What goes on four feet in the morning, on two feet at noon, and on three feet in the evening?

Anyone who couldn't solve the riddle was eaten by the sphinx. For many, many years, lots of travelers were said to have suffered from the same fate.

Finally, a young man named Oedipus, who was then the prince of Thebes, brought the sphinx's evil doings to an end by giving the correct answer. Thus, the sphinx was so enraged that she **jumped**[4] from the mountainside to her death.

The answer to the sphinx's riddle is man. In the morning, which means in his babyhood, he goes on four feet (he crawls); at noon ,which means the man has become an adult, he goes on two feet (he walks); and in the evening (in his old age) he uses a walking stick as his third foot!

But unluckily, Oedipus, Prince of Thebes, who had cracked the puzzle of the monster (Sphinx), murdered his father and **married**[5] his mother. When he discovered his guilt, he pierced his **own**[6] eyes and died in the street.

【 Question 】

(　　) 1. Which of the following areas may not have the legends of invented creatures according to the article?
　　　(A) Egypt　　　　　　　(B) North Korea
　　　(C) Greece　　　　　　(D) Near East

(　　) 2. Why did Oedipus pierce his own eyes?
　　　(A) He realized what he had done.
　　　(B) He did not solve the puzzle.
　　　(C) The sphinx asked him to do so.

【 文章中譯 】

在古老埃及希臘和近東居住的人民之間，全都流傳著關於虛構的生物長著人頭和動物身體的傳說。這些人認為這種生物是非常勇敢的，因此他們塑造了這些生物雕像，稱為獅身人面，來保衛他們的寺廟和墳墓。

在希臘傳說裡的獅身人面像有婦女的頭和獅子的身體。人們說她居住在古希臘底比斯城的一塊高岩石上，且她停下了所有由此通過的旅客，並要求他們回答以下的謎語，這個謎語今天為許多人所知。

什麼東西早晨四條腿走路，中午兩條腿走路，晚上三條腿走路？

任何解不開謎語的人就會被獅身人面像吃掉。很長時間有許多旅客都遭受了同一種命運。

終於，有一個年輕人，名字叫伊底帕斯，是當時底比斯的王子，他正確地解開了謎語，結束了獅身人面像的邪惡之舉。因此，獅身人面被觸怒，她從山腰跳了下來，最後死亡。

獅身人面像的謎底是人。早晨，意指嬰兒時期，人使用四隻腳（即，爬行）；在中午，意指成人時期，人使用兩隻腳（即，行走）；在晚上（指晚年時期），人用拐杖作為他的第三隻腳！

不幸的是，破解了這個怪獸（獅身人面像）謎題的底比斯王子，伊底帕斯，謀殺了他的父親，並且與他的母親結了婚。發現了自己的過錯後，他刺瞎自己的眼睛，流落街頭而死。

聽力題目解析

❶ 此題詢問的是獅身人面為何物。選項 (A) 為真人；選項 (B) 為人類；選項 (C) 為獅子；選項 (D) 為一顆石製雕像。根據錄音檔的一開始，我們即能得知這些物種（creature）會被製作為雕像來保護人們的寺廟，因此掌握住 statue 此關鍵字即可，答案選擇 (D)。

❷ 此題詢問的是獅身人面的居住地。選項 (A) 為水裡；選項 (B) 為城市裡；選項 (C) 為在城市外的高石上；選項 (D) 為山裡。根據錄音檔，我們可以在開頭對於獅身人面的介紹之後，得知人們認為其住在 "a high rock outside the ancient city of Thebes"，故答案為 (C)，此題需仔細聆聽。

❸ 此題詢問的是謎題的正確解答為何。根據錄音檔，我們可以得知伊底帕斯最後給出了正確的答案，因此在聆聽的過程中，我們便需注意伊底帕斯給了什麼解答。答案為 (A)。

❹ 此題詢問的是老人的第三隻腳為何。選項 (A) 為石頭；選項 (B) 為拐杖；選項 (C) 為劍；選項 (D) 為槍。根據錄音檔，我們最後可以得知解答為人的原因在於，在晚上（指晚年時期），人用拐杖作為他的第三隻腳。故答案選 (B)。

❺ 此題詢問的是獅身人面被用於守護寺廟和墳墓的原因為何。選項 (A) 為因為它很友善；選項 (B) 為因為它很強壯；選項 (C) 為因為它很勇敢；選項 (D) 為因為它很睿智。根據錄音檔的開頭，我們可以立即得知答案為 (C)，此題建議在聆聽前先看過題目及選項，便能快速掌握關鍵字 "brave"。

閱讀題目解析

❶ 此題詢問的是根據內文，選項中何地可能不會有被創造出來的物種。答案可詳見內文第一句，應能快速選擇 (B) 作為答案。

❷ 此題詢問的是為什麼伊底帕司要刺瞎自己的眼睛。選項 (A) 為他發現了他的所作所為；選項 (B) 為他沒有給出正確解答；選項 (C) 為獅身人面要求他刺瞎自己的眼睛。答案可從內文最後一段中得知，伊底帕斯謀殺了他的父親，並且與他的母親結了婚，在發現此真相後他便刺瞎了自己的眼睛，最後流落街頭而死，故答案選 (A)。

補充單字

☆ 1. head	n.	腦袋、首領
☆ 2. stop	v.	停止
☆ 3. pass	v.	通過
☆ 4. jump	v.	跳躍
☆ 5. marry	v.	結婚
☆ 6. own	adj.	自己的

Level 2

循序漸進 × 難度加強

The Bakery Lady and Her Cat

麵包店老闆娘與她的貓

聽力測驗

在學習英文的過程中，「聽」可能是最直接的第一線接觸，也可能是大家最想要快速習得的能力。現在，就讓我們來熟悉各種英文情境，提升自己的英文臨場感吧！

(　　) 1. The story is mainly about _____.
      (A) a cat   (B) a chick
      (C) a rat   (D) a hat

(　　) 2. When the cat kept himself warm by the stove, what happened to him?
      (A) His body became smaller and smaller.
      (B) His body became bigger and bigger.
      (C) He disappeared.
      (D) He fainted.

(　　) 3. What did the cat like doing?
      (A) He liked swimming.
      (B) He liked fishing and eating fish.
      (C) He liked sleeping.

(　　) 4. What did the mayor give the cat after he saved the town?
      (A) a gold medal   (B) a silver medal
      (C) a bronze medal   (D) a silk ribbon

(　　) 5. What does a bakery mainly sell?
      (A) ice cream   (B) bread
      (C) pizza   (D) meat

 **閱讀測驗**

剛剛的聽力測驗是否因為答題不順而感到遺憾？或是覺得自己有某些地方掌握地不夠好？現在就讓我們來直接「看」剛剛的聽力測驗，並透過後面的閱讀測驗來補齊聽力上的不足，同時考驗自己的閱讀能力吧！

Level 1
Level 2
Level 3
Level 4
Level 5
Level 6

Ms. Jones ran a bakery. She got up early every day. People in her **neighborhood**[1] liked her bread very much. Ms. Jones had a cat named Morgue. Morgue also got up very early. He drove all the mice out of the bakery and went fishing in the river every day.

One day, it rained heavily, so Morgue caught a cold. Ms. Jones dried him with a towel and gave him some hot milk, allowing him to sit by the stove. When Morgue fell asleep, Ms. Jones took an **umbrella**[2] and went out shopping, leaving her cat at home alone.

What happened to the cat then? Morgue's body became bigger and bigger when keeping himself **warm**[3] by the stove. His body became as big as a big hippopotamus and nearly broke Ms. Jones's house. When Ms. Jones arrived home, she looked at her house and cried in fear, "Oh, boy! What happened to my house?" The house looked like a disaster.

Her neighbors took pity on Ms. Jones and invited her to stay at their houses. But they did not let Morgue stay. Poor Morgue had been driven off and Ms. Jones felt very sad. Morgue went into a valley and his body was as big as a whale. As he ran up to the river to seize the fish, his huge body stopped up the river water. The rain was even heavier now. Morgue heard a terrible sound from above the mountain valley and saw a wall of water flooded towards him.

"If I don't block the water, the delicious fish in the river will be washed away." Morgue, therefore, sat down at once in the mountain valley, and the water formed a great lake behind him without flooding. At the same time, people in the neighborhood began to **fix**[4] the dam. Having fixed the dam, Mayor said, "Morgue is a brave cat. He stopped the flood and saved our neighborhood. Now he may come back and live with Mrs. Jones again."

The mayor took out a silver medal and hung it on Morgue's **neck**[5]. The medal reads, "Morgue has **saved**[6] our town."

【Question】

(　　) 1. How did Morgue stop the flood?
　　　(A) He sat down in the mountain valley.
　　　(B) He cursed at the heavy rain.
　　　(C) The rain stopped itself.

(　　) 2. What can we infer from the article?
　　　(A) The mayor wanted to help Morgue at first.
　　　(B) Morgue mainly wanted to stop the fish in the river from being washed away.
　　　(C) The neighbor asked Ms. Jones to go away with Morgue.

【文章中譯】

鐘斯太太開了一家麵包店。她每天都很早起床。小鎮上的人都很喜歡她做的麵包。鐘斯太太養了一隻貓，名叫莫格。莫格也起得很早。他每天都會把所有的老鼠趕出麵包店，然後到河裡去抓魚吃。

一天，雨下得很大，莫格著涼了。鐘斯太太用毛巾把莫格擦乾，給他喝了些熱牛奶，讓他在火爐邊坐著取暖。等到莫格睡著了，鐘斯太太把莫格獨自留在家裡，自己打著傘出去買東西。

但貓發生了什麼事呢？莫格在火爐邊取暖時，身子脹得越來越大。他脹大得像一頭大河馬，快把鐘斯太太的房子擠破了。鐘斯太太回家一看，害怕地叫了起來：「天哪！我的房子怎麼了？」只見整座房子歪七扭八的。

鐘斯太太的鄰居很同情她，要她搬到他們家住。但是他們不讓莫格去住。可憐的莫格被趕走了。鐘斯太太傷心極了。莫格走進山谷，他的身體幾乎有鯨魚那麼大了。他跑到河裡去捉魚，巨大的身體把河水堵住了。雨越下越大，莫格突然聽到山谷上面傳來一聲巨響，他看到洪水像巨大的牆向它撲來。

「我要是不把水攔住,那麼河裡好吃的魚就會被沖走。」莫格立刻坐在山谷中間,河水沒有氾濫,反而在他身後形成一個大湖。同時,鎮上的人開始修理堤壩。修好水壩後,鎮長說:「莫格是一隻了不起的貓,他阻止河水氾濫,救了我們這個地區。現在,他可以回來住在這裡,重回鐘斯太太身邊。」

鎮長還拿出銀獎章,給莫格掛在脖子上。獎章上刻著:「莫格拯救了我們的鎮。」

聽力題目解析

❶ 此題詢問的是故事的主角為何。選項 (A) 為一隻貓;選項 (B) 為一隻雞;選項 (C) 為一隻老鼠;選項 (D) 為一頂帽子。根據錄音檔,我們可以得知這是一個關於一隻名叫 Morgue 的貓之故事。故選 (A)。

❷ 此題詢問的是當貓在爐邊取暖時,發生了什麼事。選項 (A) 為牠的身體變得越來越小;選項 (B) 為牠的身體變得越來越大;選項 (C) 為牠消失了;選項 (D) 為牠暈倒了。根據錄音檔,我們可以得知答案為 (B),此題僅需仔細聆聽。

❸ 此題詢問的是貓喜歡從事什麼活動。選項 (A) 為牠喜歡游泳;選項 (B) 為牠喜歡抓魚和吃魚;選項 (C) 為牠喜歡睡覺。根據錄音檔一開始,我們可以特別把握住說出貓的名字後之後續介紹,此為常見模式,故答案為 (B)。

❹ 此題詢問的是鎮長在貓咪救了小鎮之後給了牠什麼。選項 (A) 為一面金獎章;選項 (B) 為一面銀獎章;選項 (C) 為一面銅獎章;選項 (D) 為一個絲帶。跟句錄音檔的末段,我們可以得知鎮長拿出銀獎章,給莫格掛在脖子上。故答案選 (B),此題建議先看題目,即可掌握重點。

❺ 此題詢問的是麵包店裡主要賣的東西為何。選項 (A) 為冰淇淋;選項 (B) 為麵包;選項 (C) 為披薩;選項 (D) 為肉。根據錄音檔的一開始,我們可以得知鎮上的人都很喜歡她做的麵包 (bread),故答案選則 (B)。

❶ 此題詢問的是莫格是如何防止洪水氾濫的。選項 (A) 為牠坐在山谷中；選項 (B) 為牠對著大雨咒罵；選項 (C) 為雨自己停了。答案可詳見內文倒數第二段，選 (A)。

❷ 此題詢問的是我們可以從文章中做出何種推斷。選項 (A) 為鎮長一開始便想要幫助莫格；選項 (B) 為莫格主要是不想讓河流中的魚被沖走；選項 (C) 為鄰居要求鐘斯太太和莫格一起離開。根據內文倒數第二段，我們可以看見莫格對自己説的話 ("If I don't block the water, the delicious fish in the river will be washed away.")，意即幫助小鎮屬意外的發展。選項 (A) 及 (C) 為錯誤之選項，可見內文第四段 ("Her neighbors took pity on Ms. Jones" 及 "they did not let Morgue stay")，故答案選 (B)。

補充單字

☆	1. neighborhood	n.	鄰里
☆	2. umbrella	n.	雨傘
☆	3. warm	adj.	溫暖的
☆	4. fix	v.	修理
☆	5. neck	n.	脖子
☆	6. save	v.	拯救

To Give a Fish or to Teach How to Fish

給人以魚不如授人以漁

Level 1
Level 2
Level 3
Level 4
Level 5
Level 6

聽力測驗 🎧 Track 022

在學習英文的過程中，「聽」可能是最直接的第一線接觸，也可能是大家最想要快速習得的能力。現在，就讓我們來熟悉各種英文情境，提升自己的英文臨場感吧！

( ) 1. According to the text, the learner graduated from high school and did not pass _____.
    (A) the college entrance exam
    (B) the graduate school exam
    (C) the government exam

( ) 2. It is _____ that helps him learn new skills.
    (A) the P.E training program
    (B) the vocational training program
    (C) the dancing training program
    (D) the farming training program

( ) 3. The man gave his fish to neighbors _____.
    (A) for money
    (B) for food
    (C) for nothing

( ) 4. According to the text, _____.
    (A) there is no poverty in the world now
    (B) everyone in the U.S.A. is very rich
    (C) you can ask other people for everything
    (D) a lot of people need help throughout the world

(　　) 5. We can draw a conclusion from the story that ＿＿＿＿.
     (A) it is better to teach how to fish than to give fish
     (B) it is better to give fish than to teach how to fish
     (C) it is stupid to share things with others

 閱讀測驗

剛剛的聽力測驗是否因為答題不順而感到遺憾？或是覺得自己有某些地方掌握地不夠好？現在就讓我們來直接「看」剛剛的聽力測驗，並透過後面的閱讀測驗來補齊聽力上的不足，同時考驗自己的閱讀能力吧！

"I'm grateful to the government for providing such a good training program and giving a subsidy to help us live well. I certainly will study hard and learn the **skills**[1] to solve my family difficulties and contribute to the society," a learner on the vocational training program said excitedly. His grandfather is nearly 80 yeas old, and his mother suffers from several diseases. So his father, who is a farmer, is the main support of the family. The family is in poverty. The learner **graduated**[2] from high school and did not pass the college **entrance**[3] exam. It is the vocational training program that helps him learn the skills he'll need in the workplace.

The story reminds me of another story. It goes like this:

Once upon a time, there was a man who liked fishing very much, and therefore, he caught lots of fish every day. The man was a kind-hearted person, so he always shared his fish with his neighbors who did not know how to fish. One day, he thought that it would be great if he taught them how to fish. So he gathered his neighbors around him and showed them how to fish. Everybody was very happy that they could eat the fish they themselves caught. This is a famous story about teaching others how to fish instead of just giving them fish.

At present, there is **poverty**[4] throughout the world. But it's not going to **solve**[5] any problems if we give only financial assistance to them instead of giving them an opportunity to learn new skills. Therefore, a technical training is very important to people in need, and they will learn the ability

to make money. On a vocational training program, people can gain the skills they need in the workplace, and what they learn can **pave**[6] their way for employment.

Level 1
Level 2
Level 3
Level 4
Level 5
Level 6

【 Question 】

(   ) 1. What can we know from the ancient story mentioned in the article?
(A) There was a man who liked eating fish.
(B) The neighbors finally knew how to fish.
(C) The man was very mean and selfish.
(D) The neighbors only wanted to eat the fish the man caught.

(   ) 2. Which of the following statement is correct according to the article?
(A) Financial assistance is the most important thing to help people.
(B) A technical training gives more help to people in need than money.
(C) Money paves way for people's employment better.
(D) Only people who did not pass the college entrance exam need a vocational training program.

【 文章中譯 】

「感謝政府提供了我一個這麼好的學習機會,每年還補貼生活費。我一定會努力學習, 學好一技之長來解決家庭困難和回報社會。」一名參加技職訓練計畫的學生激動地說。他的爺爺年近八旬,母親重病纏身,全家靠父親種田艱難度日,家庭很貧困。他高中畢業,未能考入大學,政府技職訓練計畫讓他學習職業技能。

這讓我想起一個故事,大概是這樣的:

古時候,有一個人喜歡釣魚,所以他每天都釣到許多魚。他是一個心地善良的人,他把釣來的魚分給鄰居吃。而別人都不會釣魚。有一天他想,要是他教會他們釣魚，這豈不是一件快樂的事。他召集大家，講解如何釣魚，大家非常高興能夠吃到自己親手釣到的魚。這就是給人以魚，不如授之以漁的故事。

目前，在全世界各地還是存在著貧困，需要多方面的資助。但是單靠資助而不給他們學習新技能的機會，是解決不了根本問題的。所以對這些貧苦的人進行技術培訓，掌握賺錢的本領是一個很好的辦法。因此各級政府辦了技能培訓班，他們將在這裡學習各項技能，為自己將來的就業鋪路。

聽力題目解析

❶ 此題詢問的是根據內文，這些學生從高中畢業但是並無通過何種考試。選項 (A) 為大學入學考試；選項 (B) 為研究所考試；選項 (C) 為政府考試。在錄音檔開頭不久後，我們便可得知關於職業訓練計畫的相關資訊，也就是 "graduated from high school and did not pass the college entrance exam"，故答案為 (A)。

❷ 此題詢問的是何者幫助了作者學習新技能。選項 (A) 為體育訓練計畫；選項 (B) 為職業訓練計畫；選項 (C) 為跳舞訓練計畫；選項 (D) 為農業訓練計畫。此題同上，答案為 (B)，若疏忽掉此細節，我們也可以用 "learn the skills"（學好一技之長）等關鍵字來答題。

❸ 此題詢問的是那個人用魚換取鄰居得何物。選項 (A) 為錢；選項 (B) 為食物；選項 (C) 為不換取任何事物。在故事開始之後，我們即可得知 "he always shared his fish with his neighbors who did not know how to fish"，且故事並沒有提及任何物質交換之資訊，故選 (C)。

❹ 此題要求我們選出根據內文做出的正確陳述。選項 (A) 為當前世界中不存有貧窮；選項 (B) 為在美國的每個人都很富有；選項 (C) 為你可以向他人要求任何事情；選項 (D) 為在這個世界中許多人都需要幫助。根據錄音檔的末段，我們可以推斷出答案為 (D)，且根據故事之邏輯和職業訓練的重要性，我們也可以以刪去法作答。

❺ 此題要求我們選出根據內文的正確結論。選項 (A) 為給人以魚不如授人以漁;選項 (B) 為給魚比教人釣魚來得好;選項 (C) 為和他人分享事物是很愚蠢的。我們可以根據故事內容迅速地將選項 (B) 和 (C) 刪去,並選與題目相應的 (A)。

• •

閱讀題目解析

❶ 此題詢問的是我們可以從內文中的古代故事裡得知何事。選項 (A) 為從前有個男人喜歡吃魚;選項 (B) 為那些鄰居最後習得如何補魚;選項 (C) 為那名男人非常壞心且自私;選項 (D) 為那些鄰居只想要吃男人補的魚。答案可詳見內文中完整的第三段,答案應選 (B)。

❷ 此題詢問的是根據文章何者選項正確。選項 (A) 為金錢資助是幫助人時最重要的事;選項 (B) 為比起金錢,技能培訓給予需要的人更多幫助;選項 (C) 為金錢能更好地幫人們的就業鋪路;選項 (D) 為只有沒有通過大學入學測驗的人才需要技能培訓計畫。根據內文最後一段,我們可以得知單靠金錢資助是無法幫助人們解決問題的,故可刪去選項 (A) 和 (C),並選擇 (B) 作為答案。內文中並沒有詳述技能培訓計畫的身份限制,故 (D) 為錯誤之選項。

補充單字

☆ 1. skill	n.	技能
☆ 2. graduate	v.	畢業
☆ 3. entrance	n.	進入
☆ 4. poverty	n.	貧困
☆ 5. solve	v.	解決
☆ 6. pave	v.	鋪、築(路)

Level 2 03

The Origin of Sandwich
三明治的由來

聽力測驗 🎧 Track 023

在學習英文的過程中，「聽」可能是最直接的第一線接觸，也可能是大家最想要快速習得的能力。現在，就讓我們來熟悉各種英文情境，提升自己的英文臨場感吧！

( ) 1. What does the passage talk about?
    (A) a kind of ice cream   (B) a kind of cloth
    (C) a kind of food   (D) a kind of drink

( ) 2. Sandwich was possibly named after_____.
    (A) a person's title   (B) an animal
    (C) a kind of fruit   (D) a gambling game

( ) 3. Sandwich was first invented by an_____.
    (A) Earl's scientist   (B) Earl's cook
    (C) Earl's mother   (D) Earl's friend

( ) 4. Which is not true according to the text?
    (A) There are many kinds of sandwich now.
    (B) People do not like sandwich any longer.
    (C) It is very simple and easy to eat sandwich.
    (D) John Montague was very fond of playing cards.

( ) 5. B.L.T means_____.
    (A) bacon, lettuce, tomato
    (B) bagel, latte, toppings
    (C) beverage, lemon, tofu
    (D) big, large, tall

Level 1
Level 2
Level 3
Level 4
Level 5
Level 6

 閱讀測驗

剛剛的聽力測驗是否因為答題不順而感到遺憾？或是覺得自己有某些地方掌握地不夠好？現在就讓我們來直接「看」剛剛的聽力測驗，並透過後面的閱讀測驗來補齊聽力上的不足，同時考驗自己的閱讀能力吧！

The word "sandwich" for an item of food is said to have **originated**[1] over two thousand years ago. It was possibly named after John Montague, the 4th Earl of Sandwich. In 1762, the 4th Earl of Sandwich, who is an English nobleman as well as a **notorious**[2] gambler, got hungry during a marathon gambling game. Even though he was hungry, he was too **busy**[3] gambling to stop for a meal. He asked the cook to get him something to eat that wouldn't interrupt the game. The cook got an idea and put slices of roasted meat between two pieces of bread. This way, the Earl could eat a good meal with one hand and still be able to play the card game with the other hand.

Sandwiches in all its forms are most popular with world-wide eaters. Generally, everyone get a sandwich at least once a week. Some people even eat it **daily**[4]. I'm a sandwich eater. Club Sandwich is my favorite thing to eat. It is made with 3 slices of bread, bacon, tomato and green leaf lettuce. Classic B.L.T. sandwich made with bacon, crisp lettuce and finely cut tomato also can't be beat. (B.L.T means bacon, lettuce, tomato). I know some people who like to eat B.L.T. without mayonnaise. But I think eating a B.L.T. without mayonnaise is like having a hamburger without ketchup. I can't even **swallow**[5] it. But every man has his taste. Who knows? Maybe you'll love that **flavor**[6].

There are other flavors of sandwiches, such as chicken sandwich, tuna sandwich, turkey sandwich, seafood sandwich and so on. And you cannot miss "Finger Sandwich" for a snack! Usually I get to choose the bread for my sandwich. Rye bread and whole wheat are my favorite. I always call ahead to order my sandwich, so the store can have it ready when I arrive. It saves me a lot of time. Are you hungry for some food now? Go pick up your phone and order a sandwich!

【Question】

(　　) 1. Which of the following sandwich flavor is not mentioned in the article?
(A) chicken　　　　　(B) seafood
(C) tuna　　　　　　(D) peanut

(　　) 2. Which of the following statement is wrong according to the article?
(A) The word "sandwich" is said to have originated over two hundred years ago.
(B) The writer prefers to eat a B.L.T. with mayonnaise.
(C) The writer thinks that calling ahead to order himself a sandwich is a good idea.
(D) The cook of the Earl satisfied his master.

【文章中譯】

據說「三明治」這個食品名稱是起源於兩千多年前，可能是根據第四代的三明治伯爵，約翰‧孟塔古的頭銜所命名。在 1762 年時，身為一名英國貴族兼惡名昭彰的賭徒，第四代三明治伯爵在一場馬拉松式的賭局裡肚子餓了。但是即使他餓了，他仍忙著賭博而無法停下來用餐。他要求他的廚師幫他弄點不會干擾賭局的食物來吃。他的廚師想出了一個點子。他把烤過的肉片放在兩片麵包中間。如此一來，伯爵就可以一手拿著吃，另一手仍舊可以玩牌。

各種型式的三明治是最受到全世界的食客歡迎的食物。一般來說，每個人一週最少會吃一次三明治，有些人甚至每天吃呢。我自己就是個三明治的愛好者。包含三片麵包、培根、蕃茄和綠葉萵苣的總匯三明治是我的最愛。經典的 B.L.T 三明治（B.L.T 代表培根、萵苣、蕃茄）也是好吃得不得了。我知道有些人吃 B.L.T 三明治不加美乃滋。可是我覺得吃 B.L.T 不加美乃滋就像吃漢堡不加蕃茄醬一樣，令我食不下嚥。不過人各有所好。誰知道呢？搞不好你會愛上那樣的口味。

現在還有許多口味的三明治，例如雞肉三明治、鮪魚三明治、火雞肉三明治、海鮮三明治等等。而你絕對不能錯過當點心吃的「一口吃三明治」！通常我可以選擇三明治麵包的種類。裸麥麵包和全麥麵包是我的最愛。我總是先打電話訂我要的三明治，然後店家在我到達時就會準備好了。這樣節省了我很多時間。你現在餓了嗎？想吃點好吃的嗎？趕快拿起電話，訂購一個三明治吧！

Level 1
Level 2
Level 3
Level 4
Level 5
Level 6

聽力題目解析

❶ 此題詢問的是內文的主旨。選項 (A) 為一種冰淇淋；選項 (B) 為一種服飾；選項 (C) 為一種食物；選項 (D) 為一種飲料。根據錄音檔的破題式開頭，我們可以快速選出 (C) 作為答案。

❷ 此題詢問的是三明治可能是由何種人事物來命名。選項 (A) 為一個人的頭銜；選項 (B) 為一種動物；選項 (C) 為一種水果；選項 (D) 為一種賭博遊戲。在開頭的部分，我們可以立即聽見三明治可能是根據第四代的三明治伯爵(約翰·孟塔古)的頭銜所命名，故答案選 (A)，此題僅需注意細節，建議先看過題目及選項。

❸ 此題詢問的是三明治最一開始是由何人發明。選項 (A) 為伯爵的科學家；選項 (B) 為伯爵的廚師；選項 (C) 為伯爵的母親；選項 (D) 為伯爵的朋友。在介紹伯爵的時候，我們得知伯爵嗜賭，且 "asked the cook to get him something to eat that wouldn't interrupt the game"，故答案選 (B)。

❹ 此題詢問的是根據內文所做之錯誤的陳述。選項 (A) 為現今有非常多種三明治；選項 (B) 為人們不再喜歡吃三明治；選項 (C) 為三明治簡單又方便食用；選項 (D) 為約翰·孟塔古非常喜歡玩牌。根據錄音檔末段，我們可以聽見許多針對三明治的介紹，包括其多元樣式和受歡迎的程度，故選項 (A) 及 (C) 可刪去；而在錄音檔一開始時，我們也能得知伯爵非常熱愛 gambling (賭博)，故最後答案應選擇 (B)。

❺ 此題詢問的是 "B. L. T." 代表的三個單字為何。選項 (A) 為培根、萵苣、番茄；選項 (B) 為貝果、拿鐵、配料；選項 (C) 為飲料、檸檬、豆腐；選項 (D) 為大的、巨大的、高的。 根據錄音檔，我們可以得知此單字代表 bacon、lettuce，以及tomato。此題僅需注意細節，建議先看過題目及選項。

閱讀題目解析

❶ 此題詢問的是選項中哪一個三明治口味沒有在內文中出現。答案可見內文最後一段，答案選 (D)。

❷ 此題詢問的是何種根據內文所做之選項是錯誤的。選項 (A) 為三明治這個名稱據傳是起源於兩百多年前；選項 (B) 為作者喜歡吃 B.L.T 三明治加美乃茲；選項 (C) 為作者認為替自己打電話訂三明治是個很好的主意；選項 (D) 為伯爵的廚師讓伯爵很滿意。答案可見內文第一段第一句，名稱應是起源於兩千多年前，故選 (A)。

補充單字

☆ 1. originate	**v.**	起源於
☆ 2. notorious	**adj.**	惡名昭彰的
☆ 3. busy	**adj.**	忙碌的
☆ 4. daily	**adj.**	每天的
☆ 5. swallow	**v.**	吞嚥
☆ 6. flavor	**n.**	口味

The History of Christmas
耶誕節的由來

聽力測驗 🎧 Track 024

在學習英文的過程中，「聽」可能是最直接的第一線接觸，也可能是大家最想要快速習得的能力。現在，就讓我們來熟悉各種英文情境，提升自己的英文臨場感吧！

( ) 1. What does the passage talk about?
    (A) The Spring Festival
    (B) The Valentine's Day
    (C) The Dragon Boat Festival
    (D) The Christmas holiday

( ) 2. The origin of Christmas began in the land that is now Israel where the birth of _____ took place.
    (A) God's son   (B) Jesus
    (C) Christ   (D) all of the above

( ) 3. It is said that Jesus was born to Joseph and Mary in a _____.
    (A) manger
    (B) hotel
    (C) hospital

( ) 4. Mary and Joseph were on the way to _____ when Mary was about to give birth.
    (A) Bethlehem   (B) Vietnam   (C) Seoul

( ) 5. _____ is the real reason why we celebrate Christmas
    (A) Sophie   (B) Jesus Christ   (C) Magi

Level 1
Level 2
Level 3
Level 4
Level 5
Level 6

 **閱讀測驗**

剛剛的聽力測驗是否因為答題不順而感到遺憾？或是覺得自己有某些地方掌握地不夠好？現在就讓我們來直接「看」剛剛的聽力測驗，並透過後面的閱讀測驗來補齊聽力上的不足，同時考驗自己的閱讀能力吧！

Most people think of cards, **presents**[1] and Santa Claus when they think of Christmas. But these things are not the real **meaning**[2] of Christmas. The origin of the holiday began over two thousand years ago in the land that is now Israel where the birth of Jesus Christ took place. It is said that Jesus was born to Joseph and Mary in a manger. The baby, actually, is not Joseph's. But Joseph did not divorce Mary because God had told him that Mary was pregnant by the power of the Holy Spirit and the baby was the Son of God. He came to the world to spread the message of God.

By the time Mary was about to have the baby, Mary and Joseph were on the way back to Bethlehem. But they couldn't find anywhere to stay when they arrived. Fortunately, an inn owner **allowed**[3] them to stay in his stable. That night, the baby was born, and they named him Jesus and laid him in the **manger**[4]. The story also mentions that a star guided the three Magi who traveled from the East to send gifts to baby Jesus. According to the biblical scholars, Jesus was a real, historical person and lived within 200 miles of his birthplace all his life. Yet he has influenced the world deeply.

With the **spread**[5] of Christianity, Christmas also got spread all over the world. Now the holiday of Christmas is celebrated in different countries around the world. When we say "Merry Christmas," it's not just about cards, gifts, vacation or family members gathering together. It's about Jesus coming to the world to give people love, peace and joy. So Jesus is the real reason why we **celebrate**[6] Christmas.

【Question】

(　　) 1. Where did the three Magi come from according to the article?
        (A) the East   (B) the South
        (C) the North   (D) the West

(　　) 2. What can we infer from the article?
        (A) Presents and gifts are the true orgin of Christmas.
        (B) Jesus was a real person.
        (C) The three Magi followed the moon.
        (D) Jesus only influenced the people lived near him.

Level 1
Level 2
Level 3
Level 4
Level 5
Level 6

【文章中譯】

多數人一想到聖誕節，就會聯想到卡片、禮物及聖誕老人。但這些東西都不是聖誕節的真正意義。這個節日起源於兩千多年前以色列目前所在的位置，那裡是耶穌基督出生的地方。據說耶穌是約瑟和瑪麗在馬槽出生的孩子。其實小孩不是約瑟的。但是約瑟沒有跟瑪麗解除婚約，因為上帝告訴他瑪麗是經由聖靈的力量受孕的，而寶寶是上帝的兒子，到世間來傳上帝的福音。

就在瑪麗快要生小孩時，瑪麗和約瑟正在回伯利恆的路上。但是當他們抵達時，卻找不到地方可住。所幸，一位客棧老闆允許他們住在馬廄裡。當晚，寶寶出生了，他們將他取名為耶穌，並把他放置在馬槽裡。故事還提到一個星星引領東方三賢人帶著禮物來給剛誕生的耶穌。根據研究聖經的學者所說，耶穌是真有其人的歷史人物。他一生住在不超過他出生地兩百英里的地方。然而，他已深深影響了世人。

隨著基督教的傳播，聖誕節傳遍全世界。現今，世界各國都在慶祝聖誕節這個節日。當我們說「聖誕快樂」時，並不僅僅是指卡片、禮物、假期或家人團聚，而是指耶穌降臨世間，帶給人們愛、和平與歡樂。所以耶穌是我們慶祝聖誕節的真正理由。

聽力題目解析

❶ 此題詢問的是內文主旨。選項 (A) 為春節；選項 (B) 為情人節；選項 (C) 為端午節；選項 (D) 為聖誕節。錄音檔的開頭即破題，告訴我們文章探討的主旨，故答案選 (D)。

❷ 此題詢問的是聖誕節的由來是使於現今為以色列的土地，且為何人的初生之地。選項 (A) 為上帝之子；選項 (B) 為耶穌；選項 (C) 為基督；選項 (D) 為上述皆是。在錄音檔開始不久後，我們便可得知這個節日始於 "the land that is now Israel where the birth of Jesus Christ took place"，接著後面提及瑪莉是因聖靈的力量受孕的，因此寶寶是 "the Son of God"，故答案為 (D)。

❸ 此題詢問的是約瑟和瑪莉在何處迎接耶穌的誕生。選項 (A) 為馬槽；選項 (B) 為旅館；選項 (C) 為醫院。根據錄音檔的內容，我們可以在 "the baby was born" 之後，聽見 manger (馬槽)此關鍵字，故選 (A)。

❹ 此題詢問的是當瑪莉準備要臨盆時，他們正準備前往何處。選項 (A) 為伯利恆；選項 (B) 為越南；選項 (C) 為首爾。根據錄音檔的內容，我們可聽見幾乎與題目一樣之句子，故選 (A)。

❺ 此題詢問的是選項何者為我們慶祝聖誕節的真正原因。選項 (A) 為索菲；選項 (B) 為耶穌基督；選項 (C) 為賢人。根據錄音檔，我們得知卡片及禮物等等並不是聖誕節的真正意義，在此開頭之後，內文再繼續探討何者為聖誕節的真正意義，因此按照此邏輯及故事內容，我們可以選擇 (B) 作為答案。

閱讀題目解析

❶ 此題詢問的是三賢人是從哪個地區而來。選項 (A) 為東方；選項 (B) 為南方；選項 (C) 為北方；選項 (D) 為西方。答案可見內文第二段之末段，故選 (A)。

❷ 此題詢問的是我們可以從文章中推斷出下列哪個選項。選項 (A) 為禮物和卡片是聖誕節的真正由來；選項 (B) 為耶穌是真有其人的；選項 (C) 為三賢人跟隨著月亮；選項 (D) 為耶穌只影響住在他周圍的人。答案可見內文第二段之末段，選 (B)。

補充單字

☆ 1. present	n.	禮物
☆ 2. meaning	n.	意義
☆ 3. allow	v.	允許
☆ 4. manger	n.	馬槽
☆ 5. spread	n.	散播
☆ 6. celebrate	v.	慶祝

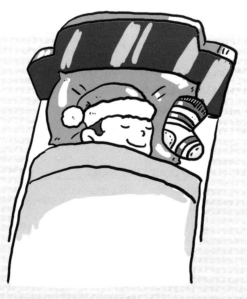

Level 2
05
Who's Mona Lisa?
蒙娜麗莎之謎

聽力測驗 🎧 Track 025

在學習英文的過程中,「聽」可能是最直接的第一線接觸,也可能是大家最想要快速習得的能力。現在,就讓我們來熟悉各種英文情境,提升自己的英文臨場感吧!

( ) 1. The passage is mainly about _____.
    (A) a photo   (B) a painting
    (C) a newspaper   (D) a studio

( ) 2. According to the text, the most intriguing part of the painting is Mona Lisa's _____.
    (A) eyes   (B) smile
    (C) hair   (D) face

( ) 3. The "Mona Lisa" painting is now exhibited in _____.
    (A) the Louvre Museum in Berlin
    (B) the Louvre Museum in Boston
    (C) the Louvre Museum in London
    (D) the Louvre Museum in Paris

( ) 4. Who's Mona Lisa?
    (A) Lisa del Giocondo.
    (B) Leonardo da Vinci.
    (C) Lillian Schwartz of Bell Labs.
    (D) There's no solid proof yet.

( ) 5. "Mona Lisa" is no doubt the most _____ painting in the world.
    (A) suspicious   (B) dramatic
    (C) ridiculous   (D) famous

閱讀測驗

剛剛的聽力測驗是否因為答題不順而感到遺憾？或是覺得自己有某些地方掌握地不夠好？現在就讓我們來直接「看」剛剛的聽力測驗，並透過後面的閱讀測驗來補齊聽力上的不足，同時考驗自己的閱讀能力吧！

Level 1

Level 2

Level 3

Level 4

Level 5

Level 6

Leonardo da Vinci's "Mona Lisa" is no doubt the most famous painting in the world. The paint was applied in thin layers, and this almost makes the painting **glow**[1].The most intriguing part of the painting is Mona Lisa's fleeting, knowing smile. It is depicted as one of the most **subtle**[2] smiles in art history. But da Vinci did not accidentally capture this haunting and **mysterious**[3] smile on his model. He intentionally wanted it that way. It is said that he had beautiful music played all through the sittings to make sure the smile wouldn't fade away.

The painting is now exhibited in the Louvre Museum in Paris and protected by **thick**[4] glass to prevent damage.

Due to the bewildering smile, which has caused so much speculation and is like no other, "Mona Lisa" has been so loved and adored by the world. They say that da Vinci always wrote the records of model's sittings in his journal. No one, however, could find out any records about who the model of Mona Lisa was.

Some say that the model was Lisa del Giocondo, the wife of a Florentine **businessman**[5]. But Dr. Lillian Schwartz of Bell Labs suggested that da Vinci appears to be the model of the Mona Lisa. She proved her opinion by analyzing the facial features of da Vinci's face and those of Mona Lisa's on the painting, and then used a computer to digitize both the self-portrait of da Vinci and the Mona Lisa painting and merge the two images together. What this results in is the fact that the features of the two faces lined up perfectly.

The truth is that no matter who the model of Mona Lisa was, da Vinci really successfully **captured**[6] the character of his subject. So, who's Mona Lisa? What's your viewpoint?

【Question】

(　　) 1. Who does Dr. Lilian Schwartz suggest to be the model of Mona Lisa to be?
　　　　(A) Lisa del Giocondo
　　　　(B) Mona Lisa
　　　　(C) da Vinci himself
　　　　(D) the wife of a Forentine businessman

(　　) 2. What material is employed to protect the painting of Mona Lisa?
　　　　(A) Ceramics　　　　　(B) Thick glass
　　　　(C) Papers　　　　　　(D) China

【文章中譯】

李奧納多・達文西的《蒙娜麗莎》無疑是世界上最有名的畫作。薄透的層層顏料幾乎讓這幅畫看起來閃閃發光。這幅畫最迷人的部分就是蒙娜麗莎那瞬間會心的微笑。這微笑是藝術史上最神秘難解的微笑之一。但是達文西可不是無意間才捕捉到模特兒這扣人心弦的神秘微笑。他其實是故意這樣要求的。據說為了確保這抹微笑不會消失，他在模特兒擺姿勢時全程播放優美的音樂呢。

這幅畫現在在法國羅浮宮裡展示，用厚厚的玻璃保護著以避免損害。

由於這抹引起諸多臆測且獨一無二的奇異微笑，《蒙娜麗莎》始終受到全世界的愛慕。據說達文西總是會將每幅畫作的模特兒資訊記錄在手扎裡。但是卻沒有人找到任何關於誰是蒙娜麗莎的紀錄。

有些人說蒙娜麗莎其實是一個佛羅倫斯商人的老婆，名叫麗莎・德爾喬康多。但是在貝爾實驗室工作的史華茲博士主張《蒙娜麗莎》似乎是達文西的自畫像。她利用電腦分析達文西與畫作裡蒙娜麗莎的五官，然後利用電腦將達文西的一張自畫像和《蒙娜麗莎》畫作數位化，再結合兩者的影像來證明她的觀點。結果顯示，兩張臉的五官完美地對在一起。

其實，無論誰是蒙娜麗莎的模特兒，達文西都成功地捕捉了人物的特性。因此，關於蒙娜麗莎之謎，你的觀點為何呢？

聽力題目解析

❶ 第一題詢問的是此篇文章的主旨，而恰好文章採破題法，在錄音檔第一句的地方，我們便能聽到 "Leonardo da Vinci's 'Mona Lisa' is no doubt the most famous painting in the world."故答案選擇 (B)。

❷ 此題詢問的是《蒙娜麗莎》畫作中最令耐人尋味 (intriuging) 的地方為何處。在開頭之處不久後，我們便能聽見一樣的句子"The most intriguing part of the painting is Mona Lisa's fleeting, knowing smile." 因此，若抓住 intriguing 這個關鍵字，我們便能因此記住 smile 這個接順而來的重點。故答案選 (B)。

❸ 此題詢問的是畫作現今於何處展覽，答案為 (D)。此題無特殊技巧，謹需細心聆聽錄音檔，並切記，通常地點和時間，都有可能出現在考題中。

❹ 此題詢問的是蒙娜麗莎之身分，同時也是錄音檔後半之討論重點。在這部分，即使沒有聽清楚較細節的部分也無需緊張，並謹記畫作爭議之處便是在於蒙娜麗莎的真實身分到現在仍為謎團，故答案選 (D)。

❺ 此題要求我們選擇一詞來形容《蒙娜麗莎》這個畫作。選項 (A) 為可疑的；(B) 為戲劇性的；(C) 為可笑的；(D) 為有名的。前三個選項皆無出現在對畫作的討論中，且文章開頭也表明此畫像為"the most famous painting in the world"，故答案選 (D)。

· ·

閱讀題目解析

❶ 第一題問的是史瓦茲博士推測蒙娜麗莎畫像中的真實模特兒是誰。我們需要注意重點是該名博士之論點。在文章的倒數第二段開始，我們可以得知，在模特兒是否真有其人的爭議之下，有些人認為該名模特兒叫作

Lisa del Giocondo，她同時是一位佛羅倫斯商人的妻子，在此處，史瓦茲博士的推測尚未出現，因此選項 (A) 和 (D) 可先刪除。接下來，作者才提出史瓦茲博士的推論，史瓦茲博士認為"da Vinci appears to be the model of the Mona Lisa"，因為在實驗之下，達文西和畫像中的蒙娜麗莎之輪廓完全相符。因此答案應選 (C)。

❷ 第二題詢問的是《蒙娜麗莎》被何種材質所保護。答案可見內文第二段之結尾，畫作現今有"thick glass" 厚玻璃所保護，故答案選 (B)。選項 (A) 為陶瓷；選項 (C) 為紙張；選項 (D) 為瓷器。

 補充單字

☆	1. glow	**v.**	發光
☆	2. subtle	**adj.**	微妙的、難捉摸的
☆	3. mysterious	**adj.**	神秘的
☆	4. thick	**adj.**	厚的
☆	5. businessman	**n.**	商人
☆	6. capture	**v.**	捕捉

The Sword of Damocles 達摩克利斯之劍

🔊 **聽力測驗** 🎧 Track 026

在學習英文的過程中，「聽」可能是最直接的第一線接觸，也可能是大家最想要快速習得的能力。現在，就讓我們來熟悉各種英文情境，提升自己的英文臨場感吧！

(   ) 1. This is a _____ legend.
       (A) Chinese   (B) Japanese
       (C) Greek   (D) German

(   ) 2. Who was Damocles?
       (A) He was one of the king's ministers.
       (B) He was the prince.
       (C) He was a doctor in the palace.
       (D) He was one of the king's friends.

(   ) 3. What was hanging from the ceiling of the palace?
       (A) a gun   (B) a picture
       (C) a rope   (D) a sword

(   ) 4. Why did Damocles want to escape from the palace? Because
       _____.
       (A) He didn't enjoy the dishes.
       (B) The king didn't like him anymore.
       (C) The king was tired of him.
       (D) He was afraid of the hanging sword.

(   ) 5. How many characters are mentioned in the story?
       (A) one   (B) two
       (C) three

Level 1
Level 2
Level 3
Level 4
Level 5
Level 6

剛剛的聽力測驗是否因為答題不順而感到遺憾？或是覺得自己有某些地方掌握地不夠好？現在就讓我們來直接「看」剛剛的聽力測驗，並透過後面的閱讀測驗來補齊聽力上的不足，同時考驗自己的閱讀能力吧！

According to a Greek legend, there once was a king called Dionysius. He was very rich and lived in a beautiful **palace**[1] where there was plenty of beautiful and costly treasure. Every day he was waited upon by a group of servants. The King had a friend named Damocles, who often said to the king, "You are so lucky that you have everything that any man could wish. You must be the happiest man in the whole world."

One day, the King became **tired**[2] of such words, saying to Damocles, "Do you really think that I am happier than others? Then I am **willing**[3] to trade places with you." Damocles, therefore, put on the king's gown and the royal crown, sitting at a table in the banquet hall. All the **delicious**[4] foods were placed before him. With everything he wanted at hand, he felt that he was the happiest man in the world.

When he was to hold up the wine glass, he suddenly saw a sharp sword hanging from the ceiling upside down, nearly touching his head. Damocles' smiling face disappeared. He was pale and shaking with fear. He did not want to eat or drink anymore. All he wanted to do was to escape－the farther the better.

The King said, "Oh, my friend. What is the matter? You feared that the sword might fall? I see it daily. It hangs over my head all the time. Perhaps someone would cut off that fine lace that holds the sword. Perhaps a certain minister wants to kill me for my power. Perhaps our neighboring country will send troops to take my throne. If you want to be the king, you must **risk**[5] losing your life."

Damocles said, "I see, besides the wealth and the honor, you also have many worries. Please **return**[6] to your throne, and I will go home." After that, Damocles treasured his life and never wanted to be rich again.

Level 1
Level 2
Level 3
Level 4
Level 5
Level 6

【Question】

(　　) 1. What color did Domacles's face turn when he saw the sword?
(A) red (B) black
(C) blue (D) white

(　　) 2. What can we say about Domacles based on the story?
(A) He was happy at first when the King trade places with him.
(B) He continued to live in the palace.
(C) He fought with the King.
(D) He stole the sword.

【文章中譯】

此典故出於希臘的一個傳說故事。從前有一個國王名叫狄奧尼修斯，他非常富有。他住在一座美麗的官殿裡，裡面有無數美麗絕倫、價值連城的寶藏，每天都有一大群的侍從伺候著他。國王有個朋友名叫達摩克利斯，他時常對國王說：「您真是幸運啊，擁有人們想要的一切，您一定是世界上最幸福的人。」

有一天，國王聽膩了這樣的話，便對達摩克利斯說：「你真的認為我比別人幸福嗎？那麼我願意跟你交換位置。」於是，達摩克利斯穿上了王袍，戴上了王冠，坐在宴會廳的桌邊，面前擺滿了美味佳餚。他想擁有的一切都隨手可得，他覺得自己是世界上最幸福的人。

當他正要舉起酒杯時，他突然發現天花板上倒懸著一把鋒利的寶劍，尖端差點觸到了自己的頭。他的笑容消失了，臉色因害怕而發白，全身顫抖不已。他不想吃也不想喝了，只想逃出王宮，越遠越好。

國王說：「噢，怎麼了，我的朋友？你怕那把隨時可能會掉下來的劍嗎？我天天看著它，它一直懸在我的頭上，說不定什麼時候有人會斬斷那根撐著劍的細線；或許哪個大臣垂涎我的權力想殺死我；或許鄰國的國王會派兵奪取我的王位。如果你想當國王，你就必須冒著失去生命的風險。」

達摩克利斯說：「我明白了，除了財富和榮耀之外，您還有很多憂慮。請您回到您的寶座上去吧，我會回家去。」從那次之後，達摩克利斯非常珍惜自己的生活，再也不想當個有錢人了。

聽力題目解析

❶ 此題詢問的是內文為何國的傳說。選項 (A) 為中國；選項 (B) 為日本；選項 (C) 為希臘；選項 (D) 為德國。根據錄音檔的一開始，我們便能聽見這是一個 Greek legend，故答案選擇 (C)。

❷ 此題詢問的是何人為達摩克利斯。選項 (A) 為他是國王的臣子之一；選項 (B) 為他是王子；選項 (C) 為他是皇宮中的醫生；選項 (D) 為他是國王的朋友之一。根據錄音檔的一開始，在國王短暫出場後，我們便能聽見 "The King had a friend named Damocles."，故答選擇 (D)。

❸ 此題詢問的是何物懸吊在皇宮的天花板上。選項 (A) 為一把槍；選項 (B) 為一張圖畫；選項 (C) 為一把繩子；選項 (D) 為一把劍。根據故事內容，我們可以得知在達摩克利斯開心地舉起酒杯時，他看見 a sharp sword hanging from the ceiling upside down，且後來當他逃離皇宮後，國王也主動提起 the sword，故答案選擇 (D)。

❹ 此題詢問的是達摩克利斯逃離皇宮的原因。選項 (A) 為他不享受那些美食；選項 (B) 為國王不再喜歡他了；選項 (C) 為國王對他感到厭煩；選項 (D) 為他害怕那把懸吊的劍。此題同上，把握住 sword 此關鍵字即可，選 (D)。

❺ 此題詢問的是故事中總共提及了幾個角色。在錄音檔中，我們只聽見國王和達摩克利斯兩人之間的互動內容，故答案選 (B) 兩個。

閱讀題目解析

❶ 此題詢問的是當達摩克利斯看見那把劍時，他的臉變成何種顏色。選項 (A) 為紅色；選項 (B) 為黑色；選項 (C) 為藍色；選項 (D) 為白色。答案可見內文第三段，並選出與 pale (發白的；蒼白的) 的單字，故 (D) 為正解。

❷ 此題詢問的是選項何者為針對達摩克利斯的正確陳述。選項 (A) 為一開始國王和他將交換身份的時候，他很開心；選項 (B) 為他繼續住在皇宮裡面；選項 (C) 為他與國王爭鬥；選項 (D) 為他偷走了劍。答案可詳見內文第二段，達摩克利斯覺得他是世界上最快樂的人，故選擇 (A)。其於選項可依照最後一段做推論。

補充單字

☆ 1. palace	n.	宮殿
☆ 2. tired	adj.	疲累的、膩煩的
☆ 3. willing	adj.	願意的
☆ 4. delicious	adj.	美味的
☆ 5. risk	v.	冒險
☆ 6. return	v.	返回

Forever Sisters
永遠的兩姐妹

聽力測驗 🎧Track 027

在學習英文的過程中,「聽」可能是最直接的第一線接觸,也可能是大家最想要快速習得的能力。現在,就讓我們來熟悉各種英文情境,提升自己的英文臨場感吧!

(　　) 1. The story is mainly about _____.
　　　　(A) two brothers
　　　　(B) one brother and one sister
　　　　(C) two sisters
　　　　(D) one father and his only daughter

(　　) 2. What did the two sisters' father like doing? He liked _____.
　　　　(A) nothing　　　　　　(B) staying at home
　　　　(C) stealing　　　　　　(D) gambling

(　　) 3. Why did the two sisters stay at a friend's house? Because _____.
　　　　(A) their own house was burned down in a big fire
　　　　(B) their house was destroyed in the earthquake
　　　　(C) their house was too big
　　　　(D) they had no house to live

(　　) 4. Which of the following statements is true?
　　　　(A) The mother left the two sisters a lot of money when she died.
　　　　(B) The two sisters are very rich now.
　　　　(C) Many kind-hearted people offered help.
　　　　(D) Their house got their house back.

(   ) 5. Where is his father now?

        (A) He is in prison.

        (B) He is on his way back home.

        (C) Nobody knows where he is.

 閱讀測驗

剛剛的聽力測驗是否因為答題不順而感到遺憾？或是覺得自己有某些地方掌握
地不夠好？現在就讓我們來直接「看」剛剛的聽力測驗，並透過後面的閱讀測
驗來補齊聽力上的不足，同時考驗自己的閱讀能力吧！

Today we are reading a story about two sisters. Their names were Sandy and Candy. They were very **lonely**[1]. When their mother **died**[2], Sandy was only a junior high student, and Candy was an elementary school student. Their father was a gambler. He gambled nights and days and finally ended up in high debt. So, to avoid repaying the money, he ran away and left the two sisters behind.

At that time their mother had been dead for five years. After their father walked out on them, the two sisters could only stay at a friend's house because their own house was given away to **repay**[3] their father's debt. But the two sisters never feared hardship and did not lose **hope**[4] for a better life. They lived their lives happily and actively.

The two sisters were both very hardworking. After school, Sandy, the elder sister, did everything she could to **support**[5] the family. She sold newspapers and sometimes worked as a tutor to earn extra money. And Candy, the younger sister, prepared meals and did all the chores at home. Though the younger sister was little, she could manage money very well. The two sisters cared for each other. And their school grades were excellent.

Now, the two sisters are still in poverty. But their stories have touched a lot of people, and they help the two sisters in anyway they can. The landlord, the bathhouse keeper, the shop owners, their schoolmates and teachers in the same **neighborhood**[6] are all looking after them. Poor as they are, they say they are the happiest persons in the world because they can be with each other every day.

【Question】

(   ) 1. How many years had their mother been dead when their father ran away?
(A) ten years   (B) five years
(C) nine years   (D) one year

(   ) 2. Which of the following job had Sandy taken to support the family?
(A) cooking   (B) singing
(C) selling newspaper (D) begging

【文章中譯】

今天我們來讀一個關於兩姊妹的故事。兩姊妹的名字叫珊珊與糖糖。她們非常寂寞。當她們的母親去世時，珊珊還只個是中學生，而糖糖只是一個小學生。她們的父親是一個賭徒，從早到晚只知道賭博，最後落得債臺高築，所以為了逃避賭債，他丟下兩姊妹跑掉了。

那時母親也已經去世五年了。父親遺棄她們後，兩姐妹只能住在朋友家，因為自家的房子已經拿去抵債了。但兩姐妹不害怕艱辛，仍然對未來抱持著美好的希望，開朗快樂地過著每一天。

兩姊妹都非常勤奮。珊珊利用課餘時間打工賺錢養家。她送報紙，有時兼家教賺錢。妹妹糖糖在家負責做飯及掃除等一切家事，她年紀雖小，卻能好好掌管金錢。兩姐妹互相關心彼此，兩人在學校的成績都很突出。

如今， 她們依然貧困但她們的故事感動了許多人，大家紛紛在各方面幫助她們。住在同一區的房東、管澡堂的婆婆、商店街的店家們以及她們的同學和老師，都照顧著她們兩人。雖然生活貧困艱辛，但對兩人來說，姐姐妹妹能每天在一起就是最大的幸福。

① 此題詢問的是故事的主要對象為何。選項 (A) 為兩位兄弟；選項 (B) 為一位哥哥 (或弟弟) 及一位姐姐 (或妹妹)；選項 (C) 為兩位姊妹；選項 (D) 為一位父親及其獨生女。在錄音檔的一開始，我們便可以聽見 "a story about two sisters"，故答案選 (C)。

② 此題詢問的是這對姊妹的父親喜歡從事什麼活動。選項 (A) 為無所事事；選項 (B) 為待在家中；選項 (C) 為偷竊；選項 (D) 為賭博。根據錄音檔，我們可以聽見女孩們的父親是個 gambler，也出現了動詞 gamble，故答案選 (D)。

③ 此題詢問的是這對姊妹待在朋友家中的原因。選項 (A) 為她們的房子在一場大火中燃燒殆盡；選項 (B) 為她們的房子被地震摧毀；選項 (C) 為她們的房子太大了；選項 (D) 為她們沒有房子可以住。接續上題，我們接著得知女孩們的家已經被拿去抵債了。故選 (D)。

④ 此題詢問的是選項中何者為正確的陳述。選項 (A) 為那名母親在離世之後留了一大筆錢給這對姊妹；選項 (B) 為這對姊妹現在非常富有；選項 (C) 為許多善心人士出手相救；選項 (D) 為她們把房子拿了回來。根據錄音檔的末段，我們可以得知這對姊妹的故事感動了很多人，現在她們仍生活貧困，所以許多人 help the two sisters in anyway they can (大家紛紛在各方面幫助她們)，故選 (C)。

⑤ 此題詢問的是她們的父親現今位於何處。選項 (A) 為監獄；選項 (B) 為正在回家的路上；選項 (C) 為沒有人知道他在哪裡。在錄音檔中，我們能得知 "he ran away and left the two sisters behind"（他丟下兩姊妹跑掉了），故選 (C)。

❶ 此題詢問的是當她們的父親跑走時，她們的母親已經去逝多少年。選項 (A) 為十年；選項 (B) 為五年；選項 (C) 為九年；選項 (D) 為一年。答案可見內文第二段第一行，故選 (B)。

❷ 此題詢問的是珊珊曾做過何種工作來賺錢養家。選項 (A) 為下廚；選項 (B) 為唱歌；選項 (C) 為賣報紙；選項 (D) 為乞討。答案可見內文第三段之開頭，故選 (C)，其餘選項皆沒有出現在文章中。

補充單字

☆ 1. lonely	adj.	寂寞的
☆ 2. die	v.	死
☆ 3. repay	v.	償還
☆ 4. hope	n.	希望
☆ 5. support	v.	支撐
☆ 6. neighborhood	n.	鄰近地區

George Washington and the Cherry Tree

誠實的華盛頓

聽力測驗 🎧 Track 028

在學習英文的過程中，「聽」可能是最直接的第一線接觸，也可能是大家最想要快速習得的能力。現在，就讓我們來熟悉各種英文情境，提升自己的英文臨場感吧！

(　　) 1. The passage is mainly about _____.
    (A) hard work   (B) wisdom
    (C) bravery   (D) honesty

(　　) 2. Who is the hero in the story?
    (A) Edison   (B) Franklin
    (C) Washington   (D) Ali

(　　) 3. What did Washington want to be when he grew up？
    (A) a soldier
    (B) a scientist
    (C) a president
    (D) a film star

(　　) 4. What did the father do after Little Washington had cut down the cherry tree?
    (A) He punished his son.
    (B) He scolded his son.
    (C) He listened to his son and was happy about his honesty.
    (D) He got angry with his son and ordered him to plant another one.

(   ) 5. What can we learn from the story?

        (A) We should learn to share.

        (B) We should learn to depend on ourselves.

        (C) We should learn to be honest.

        (D) We should learn to tolerate.

 閱讀測驗

剛剛的聽力測驗是否因為答題不順而感到遺憾？或是覺得自己有某些地方掌握地不夠好？現在就讓我們來直接「看」剛剛的聽力測驗，並透過後面的閱讀測驗來補齊聽力上的不足，同時考驗自己的閱讀能力吧！

George Washington wanted to be a **hero**[1] when he was young. When he saw his elder brother wear the army uniform, he envied him. One day, after dinner, he ran to his father and said, "Daddy, when I grow up, I want to be a soldier like Big Brother."

"Very good, my dear!" the father replied happily. "But, do you know what kind of person can become a brave **soldier**[2]?" Washington thought about it for a while and replied, "An honest person can become a brave soldier. Am I right?" Hearing this, his father was very **pleased**[3].

There was a small cherry tree on the farm. The cherry tree had been **planted**[4] in honor of the birth of George Washington. Since George Washington wanted to be a brave soldier, he planned to make a small wooden gun. Becasue his father was very busy with his work all day long, instead of asking him for help, George Washington decided to make one on his own.

He took the saw and the axe and walked towards the farm. When he saw a small cherry tree there, he began to cut it. His father came home after work and knew somebody cut the tree and became very angry. He wanted to know who did that. Washington hid himself in his room, very afraid. But he thought it over and then came out to face the music. He said, "Daddy, you always tell me about being a honest person. So I am here to tell you the truth. It was me who cut the tree."

Hearing his son's words, the father realized that the child's good **quality**[5] is more precious than his beloved cherry tree. He patted George Washington on the shoulder, saying, "I forgive you, Son. Admitting your **mistake**[6] is a heroic behavior, more valuable than 1000 cherry trees."

【Question】

(　　) 1. What was the reaosn why the cherry tree was planted?
(A) in honor of the birth of George Washington
(B) in memory of George Washington's mother
(C) simply for a beautiful view

(　　) 2. Which of the following tool was used by George Washingto to cut the cherry tree?
(A) a wooden gun　　(B) an axe
(C) a spoon　　(D) a bowl

Level 1
Level 2
Level 3
Level 4
Level 5
Level 6

【文章中譯】

喬治‧華盛頓自小就想當個英雄人物。當他看到哥哥穿著軍裝,他羨慕極了。一天吃過晚飯,他急忙跑去告訴父親:「爸爸,我長大了也要像大哥那樣,當一個勇敢的軍人。」

「好極了, 親愛的孩子!」父親高興地回答。「可是,你知道什麼樣的人才能成為勇敢的軍人嗎?」華盛頓想了一下,然後回答道:「誠實的人才能成為一個勇敢的軍人,我說的對嗎?」聽到這樣的回答,華盛頓的父親非常高興。

在父親農場裡,有一顆小櫻桃樹,那是父親為紀念華盛頓的誕生而栽種的。因為華盛頓一心想長大做一名勇敢的軍人,所以他打算做一把小木槍。他看到父親忙於工作,沒有時間,於是決定自己動手做。

小華盛頓拿起鋸子、斧頭,走到農場裡,看到了一棵小櫻桃樹,就把它鋸倒了。父親回來,知道了這件事後大發脾氣,問是誰做的。華盛頓躲在房間裡，非常害怕。他後來想了想，最後還是勇敢地出來接受懲罰。他說：「爸爸，您常常跟我說做人要誠實，所以我在這裡告訴您實話，櫻桃樹是我砍的。」

聽兒子這麼一說，父親了解到孩子良好的素質，要比自己心愛的櫻桃樹還要珍貴。他拍拍華盛頓的肩膀，說：「兒子，爸爸原諒你。承認錯誤是英雄行為，要比一千棵櫻桃樹還有價值。」

聽力題目解析

❶ 此題詢問的是文章主旨。選項 (A) 為努力工作；選項 (B) 為智慧；選項 (C) 為勇敢；選項 (D) 為誠實。錄音檔的開頭提及，父親對於「誠實」這個答案很滿意，而在結尾時，華盛頓的父親也認為華盛頓坦白以告是很珍貴的人格特質，故答案選 (D)。

❷ 此題詢問的是誰為故事中的英雄。選項 (A) 為愛迪生；選項 (B) 為法蘭克林；選項 (C) 為華盛頓；選項 (D) 為阿里。錄音檔的開頭即提供了答案，故選 (C)。

❸ 此題詢問的是華盛頓長大之後想要當什麼人物。選項 (A) 為軍人；選項 (B) 為科學家；選項 (C) 為總統；選項 (D) 為電影明星。根據錄音檔的開頭，我們可以得知華盛頓很羨慕 (envied) 他的哥哥，並和他的爸爸說 "I want to be a soldier."，故選 (A)。

❹ 此題詢問的是在小華盛頓砍倒了櫻桃樹之後，他的父親做了什麼。選項 (A) 為他誠罰了他的兒子；選項 (B) 為他責罵了他的兒子；選項 (C) 為他聆聽他的兒子並對他的誠實感到開

Level 1

Level 2

Level 3

Level 4

Level 5

Level 6

心;選項 (D) 為他對他的兒子感到生氣並要求他種新的一顆。根據錄音檔的結尾,我們可以得知,華盛頓的父親很欣賞兒子的坦誠,並認為 "the child's good quality is more precious than his beloved cherry tree" (孩子良好的素質要比心愛的櫻桃樹還要珍貴),故選擇 (C)。

⑤ 此題詢問的是我們可以在故事中學習到何事。選項 (A) 為我們應學著分享;選項 (B) 為我們應學著依靠自己;選項 (C) 為我們應學著誠實;選項 (D) 為我們應學著容忍。同上題,選擇 (C)。

閱讀題目解析

❶ 此題詢問的是櫻桃樹被栽種的原因。選項 (A) 為紀念華盛頓的誕生;選項 (B) 為緬懷華盛頓的母親;選項 (C) 為單純想要有個美景。答案可見內文第三段,選擇 (A)。

❷ 此題詢問的是選項中的哪個工具被華盛頓用來砍櫻桃樹。選項 (A) 為木槍;選項 (B) 為斧頭;選項 (C) 為湯匙;選項 (D) 為碗。答案可查見內文第四段第一行,故選 (B)。

補充單字

☆ 1. hero	n.	英雄
☆ 2. soldier	n.	軍人
☆ 3. pleased	a.	感到滿意的
☆ 4. plan	v.	計劃
☆ 5. quality	n.	品質
☆ 6. mistake	n.	錯誤

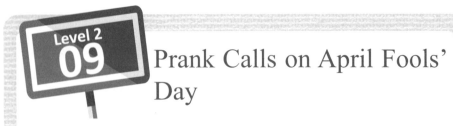

Level 2
09 Prank Calls on April Fools' Day

愚人節的電話你敢接嗎？

聽力測驗 🎧 Track 029

在學習英文的過程中，「聽」可能是最直接的第一線接觸，也可能是大家最想要快速習得的能力。現在，就讓我們來熟悉各種英文情境，提升自己的英文臨場感吧！

(   ) 1. The passage is about _____.
         (A) the Spring Festival   (B) the National Day
         (C) the Earth Day   (D) April Fools' Day

(   ) 2. In which country did April Fools' Day start?
         (A) America   (B) England
         (C) France   (D) Canada

(   ) 3. Which is true according to the passage?
         (A) The Day started in Asia.
         (B) You can play a joke on others on the Day.
         (C) You can fool "110."
         (D) You can make a joke on "119."

(   ) 4. On which day did people in France first celebrate the New Year?
         (A) May 5   (B) March 15
         (C) March 25   (D) May 25

(   ) 5. According to the text, the rescue center received a _____.
         (A) prank call   (B) emergency call
         (C) birthday call   (D) Christmas call

閱讀測驗

剛剛的聽力測驗是否因為答題不順而感到遺憾？或是覺得自己有某些地方掌握地不夠好？現在就讓我們來直接「看」剛剛的聽力測驗，並透過後面的閱讀測驗來補齊聽力上的不足，同時考驗自己的閱讀能力吧！

In the 16th century in France, people changed the date of New Year's Day from March 25 to April 1. In the mid-1560s, King Charles IX changed it again from March 25 to January 1. But some people still celebrated it on April 1. Others called them April Fools. For a long time, April Fools' Day has been a day to **play**[1] jokes on others. You can play any joke on others to fool them. It was originally a western festival, but now it has spread across the world to any country.

With the development of modern science and technology, the ways of fooling others on April Fools' Day have changed quite a bit. Last year on the very day, my brother picked up the phone and called one of his friends. He said to him, "Hi, Paul, I have two movie tickets for tonight, and I'd like you to go to the movies with me. Can you come?" "Of course!" His friend was very pleased to hear that.

That night, his friend got to the movie theater and **waited**[2] for my brother. He waited and waited, and suddenly found out that the movie theater was actually closed on that day, and my brother didn't even show up. He thought for a moment and remembered that day was April Fools' Day.

Today I saw a piece of news in the newspaper and it says that the rescue center **received**[3] a prank call at seven o'clock this morning. A young man called the rescue center saying that one of his family members committed suicide and bled heavily. So he needed an ambulance immediately. But the phone number and **address**[4] that he told the rescue center was different from those shown on the center's computer. To make sure of the real address, the rescue center asked the young man to repeat his location again. But the young man was **laughing**[5] hard on the phone, saying "Happy April Fools' Day, you fool!" And then he hung up the phone.

Level 1
Level 2
Level 3
Level 4
Level 5
Level 6

157

Prank calls of all levels occur on the April Fools' Day. While it is more acceptable to joke around on this day, we need to keep in mind that the calls should not cause troubles to other people, especially when life and death is involved. After all, we need to put ourselves into others' shoes so that pranks don't end up as disasters.

【Question】

(　　) 1. Who changed the date of New Year from March 25 to January 1 according to the article?
　　　(A) Charles X
　　　(B) Charles IX
　　　(C) Charles XI

(　　) 2. What can we infer from the article?
　　　(A) The development of technology has changed the ways of fooling others.
　　　(B) The two prank calls in the article are the best examples to learn from.
　　　(C) People in the 16th-century France did not want to celebrate New Year.

【文章中譯】

在16世紀的法國，人們把慶祝新年的時間從3月25日改到4月1日。在16世紀60年代中期，國王查理斯九室又把它從3月25日改到1月1日。但是某些人仍然在4月1日慶祝，因此其他人稱他們為四月愚人。長期以來，愚人節是對別人開玩笑的一天。只要不太過分，你可以對他人開任何玩笑。它最初是西方的節日，但是它現在傳播到世界所有國家。

隨著現代科學技術的發展，在愚人節那天，作弄別人的方式已大大改變。去年的愚人節，我哥哥拿起電話打給他的朋友說：「嗨！保羅，我有二張今晚的電影票，我想要你跟我一起去看電影。你可以來嗎？」

「當然！」他的朋友聽到時非常高興。

那夜，朋友到電影院赴約，等待我哥哥的到來。他等著等著，赫然發現那天電影院根本停止營業，而我哥哥連一個影子也沒看見。他想了想，這才記起那天是愚人節。

今天我看到一則報紙新聞說，救護中心上午七點接到一通愚人節的惡作劇電話。一名年輕男子打進救護中心說家裡有人自殺，流血不止，急需一輛救護車。但是他報出的地址及電話，與急救中心的電腦上秀出來的不一致。為了確定其具體地址，救護人員再次向其確定位置，沒想到只聽電話裡年輕男子一陣哄笑，說道，「愚人節快樂，笨蛋！」隨即就把電話掛掉了。

在愚人節這天上，各種程度的惡作劇電話都會發生。不過，雖然大家在這天會比較能夠接受這些惡作劇，我們仍需要謹記，這些惡作劇電話不應該造成別人的麻煩，尤其是牽涉到人命的時候。畢竟，我們需要換個立場思考，這樣惡作劇才不會到最後變成災難。

聽力題目解析

❶ 此題詢問的是內文的討論對象為何。選項 (A) 為春節；選項 (B) 為國慶日；選項 (C) 為地球日；選項 (D) 為愚人節。錄音檔的開頭給了我們法國慶祝新年的時間更動，後來便導入主題 "April Fools"，故選擇 (D)。

❷ 此項題目詢問得是愚人節的起始之國為何。選項 (A) 為美國；選項 (B) 為英國；選項 (C) 為法國；選項 (D) 為加拿大。錄音檔的開頭即告訴我們法國慶祝新年的日期更動，故選擇 (C)，此題注意聆聽即可。

❸ 此題要求我們選出正確的選項。選項 (A) 為這個節日使於亞洲；選項 (B) 為我們可以在這個節日對別人開玩笑；選項 (C) 為我們可以打 110 愚弄別人；選項 (D) 為我們可以打 119 開玩笑。我們在一開始便依照上述說法，得知唯一歐洲國家，故選項 (A) 不對；接著，在音檔後段，我們可以聽見兩則惡作劇電話，最後一則是玩笑開過了頭，故選項 (C) 及 (D) 不對，應選 (B)。

❹ 此題詢問的是法國最一開始在哪一天慶祝新年。選項 (A) 為五月五日；選項 (B) 為三月十五日；選項 (C) 為三月二十五日；選項 (D) 為五月二十五日。音檔在一開始即告訴我們，法國人一開始是在三月二十五日慶祝新年，故答案選 (C)。建議先看過題目，以掌握此種類型的細節題。

❺ 此題詢問的是急救中心收到何物。選項 (A) 為一通惡作劇電話；選項 (B) 為一通急救電話；選項 (C) 為一通生日祝賀電話；選項 (D) 為一通聖誕節祝福電話。根據音檔最後，我們可以聽見男子說 "Happy April Fools' Day, you fool!"（愚人節快樂，笨蛋！），故答案為 (A)。

閱讀題目解析

❶ 此題詢問的是根據內文，何人將新年日期從 3 月 25 日改至 1 月 1 日。答案可見內文第一段第二句，選 (B)，注意勿將數字混淆。

❷ 此題詢問的是我們可以從文章中推論出何事。選項 (A) 為科技的發展讓作弄別人的方式大大改變；選項 (B) 為文章中的兩通惡作劇電話是很好的學習範本；選項 (C) 為 16 世紀的法國人並不想要慶祝新年。答案可見內文第二段第一行，故選 (A)；內文中的案例皆稍微過火，故選項 (B) 為錯誤之答案；選項 (C) 則可查見內文第一段。

補充單字

☆ 1. play	v.	玩耍
☆ 2. wait	v.	等待
☆ 3. receive	v.	收到
☆ 4. address	n.	地址
☆ 5. laugh	v.	笑

Scottish Men's Skirt
蘇格蘭男人的裙子

聽力測驗 🎧Track 030

在學習英文的過程中，「聽」可能是最直接的第一線接觸，也可能是大家最想要快速習得的能力。現在，就讓我們來熟悉各種英文情境，提升自己的英文臨場感吧！

( ) 1. The subject of the passage is _____.
    (A) food
    (B) clothing
    (C) means of transportation
    (D) ways of life.

( ) 2. The Scots wear the kilts because _____.
    (A) they have been ordered to do that
    (B) the law makes it so
    (C) it shows their love for freedom
    (D) they have nothing else to wear

( ) 3. In which year did they win their own right to wear the kilts?
    (A) in 1745   (B) in 1782
    (C) in 1792   (D) in 1715

( ) 4. Which of the following statements is true?
    (A) Only Scotsmen wear the kilts.
    (B) Only the Americans wear it.
    (C) Only the Irish wear it.
    (D) Anyone could wear a kilt if they like.

( ) 5. In which year did Scotland and England join together?
    (A) before 1700   (B) in 1707
    (C) in 1701   (D) Before 1071

 **閱讀測驗**

剛剛的聽力測驗是否因為答題不順而感到遺憾？或是覺得自己有某些地方掌握地不夠好？現在就讓我們來直接「看」剛剛的聽力測驗，並透過後面的閱讀測驗來補齊聽力上的不足，同時考驗自己的閱讀能力吧！

When you see this **topic**[1], you may feel strange. Why do Scottish men **wear**[2] skirts while in Europe men don't usually wear skirts? The Scottish men's skirt comes from a kind of ancient clothing called a "kilt." This is a knee-length garment with tartan pattern on it. For Scots, a "kilt" is not only a national dress they are fond of wearing, but also a cultural symbol. Even though Scotland and England became one country in 1707, the "kilt" was still kept alive as Scotland's national dress. They wore this kind of skirt clothing to express that they were against the rule of the English and that they wanted independence very much.

In 1745, after the Scottish uprising was put down by Britain during the Hannover Dynasty, the British passed a law that no Scots were allowed to wear the kilt. So anyone who violated this law would be put into jail or exiled. The Scots launched a 30-year struggle for this law, and finally, in 1782, they **forced**[3] the Hannover Dynasty to cancel the law and won their own right to wear kilts.

Scots are very **proud**[4] of their country and **history**[5]. They feel that the kilt is part of their history. Now kilts have become normal wear for formal occasions. Also, they have increasingly become more and more common around the world for casual wear. So, it's not rare at all to see kilts making an appearance at pubs. However, it is now not **common**[6] to see them in the workplace. Scots used to have kilts in several colors. But nowadays, each family only chooses the colors they like best to represent the part of their family history.

Level 1
Level 2
Level 3
Level 4
Level 5
Level 6

【 Question 】

(　　) 1. Which dynasty was in power when the Scottish uprising happened?
(A) Windsor
(B) Stuart
(C) Lionheart
(D) Hannover

(　　) 2. Approximately how many years did it take for the Scots to win back the lawful right to wear kilts?
(A) 10 years
(B) 30 years
(C) 20 years
(D) 5 years

【 文章中譯 】

當你看到這個標題時，可能會感到奇怪。歐洲男人通常不穿裙子的，為什麼蘇格蘭的男人穿裙子呢？蘇格蘭方格裙起源於一種叫「基爾特」的古老服裝。這是一種及膝的服飾，布面有方格圖樣。在蘇格蘭人看來，「基爾特」不僅是他們愛穿的民族服裝，而且是蘇格蘭文化的標誌。1707年蘇格蘭與英格蘭合併後，「基爾特」作為蘇格蘭的民族服裝被保留下來。蘇格蘭人穿著這種裙服，表示他們對英格蘭人統治的反抗和要求獨立的強烈願望。

1745年，英國漢諾威王朝鎮壓了蘇格蘭人的武裝起義後，下令禁止蘇格蘭人穿裙子，違背者將被處以監禁或放逐。蘇格蘭人為此展開了長達30多年的鬥爭，最後於1782年迫使漢諾威王朝取消了「禁裙令」，為自己贏得了穿裙子的權利。

蘇格蘭人對他們的國家與歷史非常自豪。他們覺得蘇格蘭方格裙是其歷史的一部份。現今蘇格蘭方格裙已成為正式場合的正常穿戴。而且，蘇格蘭短裙也逐漸變成全球化的便裝，因此在酒吧看見蘇格蘭方格裙也是稀鬆平常的事。然而，在工作場所就比較少見了。蘇格蘭人一向擁有多種顏色的蘇格蘭方格裙。但如今,每個家庭僅會選擇他們最喜歡的顏色來代表其家族的歷史。

聽力題目解析

❶ 此題詢問的是內文的探討對象。選項 (A) 為食物;選項 (B) 為服飾;選項 (C) 為運輸方式;選項 (D) 為生活方式。錄音檔的一開始,我們即可聽到 "skirt"(裙子)此關鍵字,故答案選 (B)。

❷ 此題詢問的是蘇格蘭人穿著基爾特的原因為何。選項 (A) 為他們被命令穿著基爾特;選項 (B) 為法律規定;選項 (C) 為基爾特展現了他們對自由的熱愛;選項 (D) 為他們沒有其他的衣服可以穿。根據錄音檔的描述,我們可以把握兩個關鍵字 "against the rule" 以及 "independence",也就是反抗統治及獨立,故答案選 (C)。

❸ 此題詢問的是在哪一年他們贏得了穿著基爾特的權力。答案為 (B),此題只能仔細聆聽注意細節,建議先快速看過和題目及選項。本文年份較多,需小心。

❹ 此題詢問的是選項中何者陳述是正確的。選項 (A) 為只有蘇格蘭男人會穿基爾特;選項 (B) 為只有美國人會穿基爾特;選項 (C) 為只有愛爾蘭人會穿基爾特;選項 (D) 為任何人只要想要都可以穿基爾特。根據錄音檔的內容,我們可以得知基爾特現今仍為蘇格蘭人所穿,且我們沒有聽見任何對於此穿著的身份限制,故答案選 (D)。

❺ 此題詢問的是在哪一年蘇格蘭和英格蘭合併在一起。答案為 (B),此題同第三題,只能仔細聆聽注意細節,建議先快速看過和題目及選項。

閱讀題目解析

❶ 此題詢問的是蘇格蘭人武裝起義發生之時正值什麼朝代。選項 (A) 為威塞克斯；選項 (B) 為斯圖亞特；選項 (C) 為獅心；選項 (D) 為漢諾威。答案可見內文第二段第二句，選擇 (D)。

❷ 此題詢問的是蘇格蘭人花了多少年才將穿著基爾特的法定權力奪回來。答案可見內文第二段之結尾，選擇 (B)。

 **補充單字**

☆ **1. topic**	**n.**	主題
☆ **2. wear**	**v.**	穿戴
☆ **3. force**	**v.**	逼迫
☆ **4. history**	**n.**	歷史
☆ **5. proud**	**adj.**	驕傲的
☆ **6. common**	**adj.**	普遍的

Level 1
Level 2
Level 3
Level 4
Level 5
Level 6

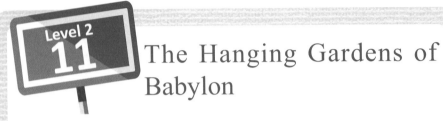

Level 2
11 The Hanging Gardens of Babylon

巴比倫的空中花園

聽力測驗 🎧 Track 031

在學習英文的過程中，「聽」可能是最直接的第一線接觸，也可能是大家最想要快速習得的能力。現在，就讓我們來熟悉各種英文情境，提升自己的英文臨場感吧！

(　　) 1. The location of Babylon was along the east bank of _____?
    (A) Euphrates River　　(B) Red Sea
    (C) Sun Moon Lake　　(D) Nile

(　　) 2. In order to alleviate his wife's _____, Nebuchadnezzar II decided to build the Hanging Gardens.
    (A) seasickness　　(B) cancer
    (C) homesickness　　(D) bad cold

(　　) 3. It is said that the Hanging Gardens were destroyed by several _____ after the 2nd century B.C.
    (A) earthquakes　　(B) battles
    (C) wars　　(D) floods

(　　) 4. The gardens were being watered by a _____ watering system.
    (A) simple　　(B) complicated
    (C) strange

(　　) 5. The existence of the Hanging Gardens of Babylon is still a _____.
    (A) tragedy　　(B) mystery
    (C) truth

Level 1
Level 2
Level 3
Level 4
Level 5
Level 6

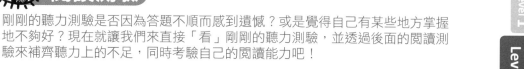

閱讀測驗

剛剛的聽力測驗是否因為答題不順而感到遺憾？或是覺得自己有某些地方掌握
地不夠好？現在就讓我們來直接「看」剛剛的聽力測驗，並透過後面的閱讀測
驗來補齊聽力上的不足，同時考驗自己的閱讀能力吧！

The location of Babylon was along the east bank of Euphrates River. Its central **location**[1] made the city one of the main trading points of the **ancient**[2] world. It is also home to one of the Seven Wonders of the World, The Hanging Gardens of Babylon. They were built by Nebuchadnezzar II around 600 B.C. (the 7th century B.C.) It is said that Nebuchadnezzar II, the most important king of Neo-Babylonian Empire, constructed the gardens to cheer his wife, Amytis of Media, who desperately **missed**[3] the lush and mountainous land she came from. She longed for the trees and flowering plants of her homeland, and found Babylon's flat and barren landscape depressing.

In order to alleviate his wife's homesickness, Nebuchadnezzar II decided to re-create her homeland by constructing an artificial terraced hill with rooftop gardens. Some stories have it that the Hanging Gardens towered hundreds of feet into the air, but **archaeological**[4] explorations have proved it wrong. The gardens were being watered by a complicated watering system; the water was from the Euphrates River. However, getting the water to the top and also preventing the foundation from **collapsing**[5] were a more challenging job. Special care had to be taken while watering the gardens because the gardens ran the risk of falling apart if the foundation supporting the gardens took in too much water.

It is said that the Hanging Gardens were destroyed by several earthquakes after the 2nd century B.C. As a matter of fact, there are no solid records of the Hanging Gardens from the time Nebuchadnezzar II ruled. They were never referred to on any of the many clay tablets excavated in the region of the ancient Babylonia, except for some tablets describing the palace, the city of Babylon, and the walls. So did the Hanging Gardens of Babylon really **exist**[6]? Thousands of years have passed, but it is still an insolvable mystery.

【Question】

(   ) 1. Which part of Euphrates River made Babylon one of the main trading points in the past?
         (A) the central location
         (B) the front part
         (C) the tail end

(   ) 2. Which of the following statement is incorrect according to the article?
         (A) There are proofs that the Hanging Garden truly exists.
         (B) It is said that the Hanging Garden soared into the air, while the truth may be the opposite.
         (C) The mystery of the Hanging Garden may remain temporarily unsolved.

【文章中譯】

巴比倫的地點位在幼發拉底河的東岸。它的中心位置使它成為古老世界的貿易樞紐之一。它也是世界七大奇觀之一——巴比倫空中花園——的發源地。空中花園是尼布甲尼撒二世在大約西元前六百年（西元前七世紀）時建造的。據說，新巴比倫帝國最重要的國王－尼布甲尼撒二世，是為了要討好他嚴重思念家鄉青翠山地的王妃－米底亞人阿密斯提，而建造的空中花園。阿密斯提很想念家鄉的花草樹木，而對巴比倫平坦又貧瘠的景象感到失望。

為了緩解王妃的思鄉病，尼布甲尼撒二世決定建造一座人工的花園，將花園建在幾層平台的頂端。傳說空中花園高聳入雲，有幾百英尺高，但考古學上的探究證明這樣的說法不正確。這座花園有一套複雜的灌溉系統；水是從幼發拉底河引過來的。然而，要將水引置頂端、又要防止灌溉時地基崩塌更是難上加難。灌溉花園時要採取特別的措施，因為若支撐花園的地基吸入過多的水，則花園會有倒塌的危險。

據說空中花園在西元前二世紀時被幾次的地震摧毀。事實上，空中花園在尼布甲尼撒二世統治時代並沒有有力的文獻記載，古巴比倫帝國所在地所挖掘出的泥板文獻除了有一些描述宮殿、巴比倫這個城市及城牆之外，也沒有其他的記載。所以，巴比倫的空中花園真的存在嗎？經過了幾千年，這依然是一個難解的謎。

聽力題目解析

❶ 此題詢問的是巴比倫的位置是在何處的東岸。選項 (A) 為幼發拉底河；選項 (B) 為紅海；選項 (C) 為日月潭；選項 (D) 為尼羅河。錄音檔在一開始即告訴我們此題的答案為 (A)，仔細聆聽即可。

❷ 此題詢問的是為了緩解尼布甲尼撒二世之妻的何種症狀，尼布甲尼撒二世決定建造空中花園。選項 (A) 為暈船；選項 (B) 為癌症；選項 (C) 為思鄉病；選項 (D) 為嚴重的感冒。根據錄音檔，我們可以得知尼布甲尼撒二世之妻非常想念其家鄉的青翠山地，接著我們也可以直接掌握到關鍵字 "homesickness"，故答案為 (C)。

❸ 此題詢問的是空中花園據傳曾被何種現象毀壞。選項 (A) 為地震；選項 (B) 為打鬥；選項 (C) 為戰爭；選項 (D) 為水災。在錄音檔的結尾部分，我們可以聽見 "destroyed by several earthquakes"（被幾次的地震摧毀），故答案選 (A)。

❹ 此題詢問的是這些花園是使用何種灌溉系統。選項 (A) 為簡單的；選項 (B) 為複雜的；選項 (C) 為奇怪的。在聆聽音檔的過程中，我們可以略知這個空中花園的建造相當困難，既需將水引至頂端，又需顧慮地基吸水過多，故選擇 (B)。

❺ 此題詢問的是巴比倫空中花園的存在至今仍是何物。選項 (A) 為悲劇；選項 (B) 為神秘之謎；選項 (C) 為真相。錄音檔的結尾直接給了我們 "mystery" 作為第五題之答案，仔細聆聽即可。

閱讀題目解析

❶ 此題詢問的是幼發拉底河的哪個位置讓巴比倫成為古老世界的貿易樞紐之一。選項 (A) 為中間位置；選項 (B) 為前端；選項 (C) 為末端。答案可見內文第一段第二句，故答案選則 (A)。

❷ 此題詢問的是哪一個選項為針對文章所做之錯誤陳述。選項 (A) 為有許多證據指出空中花園確實存在；選項 (B) 為據傳空中花園高聳入雲，而事實也可能是相反的；選項 (C)為空中花園之謎可能會暫時沒有解答。答案可見內文最後一段第二句，故 (A) 為錯誤之選項。選項 (B) 可見內文第二段第二句；選項 (C) 可見內文最後一段。

補充單字

☆ 1. location	n.	地點
☆ 2. ancient	adj.	古老的
☆ 3. miss	v.	想念
☆ 4. archaeological	adj.	考古學的
☆ 5. collapse	v.	倒塌
☆ 6. exist	v.	存在

Level 1
Level 2
Level 3
Level 4
Level 5
Level 6

Level 2
12 Conjoined Twins
連體嬰

聽力測驗 🎧 Track 032

在學習英文的過程中，「聽」可能是最直接的第一線接觸，也可能是大家最想要快速習得的能力。現在，就讓我們來熟悉各種英文情境，提升自己的英文臨場感吧！

( ) 1. This passage is about _____.
 (A) normal people
 (B) the blind
 (C) doctors
 (D) conjoined twins

( ) 2. Conjoined twins are genetically identical twins with _____ sex.
 (A) the same (B) different
 (C) female

( ) 3. The case of Mary and Jodie, the conjoined twins, was a very controversial issue in_____.
 (A) 2000 (B) 2008
 (C) 1900

( ) 4. A _____ twin means he or she is literally living off of the other twin.
 (A) parasitic (B) plastic
 (C) pantry

( ) 5. For some unknown reason, _____ conjoined twins appear to have a better chance for survival than _____ conjoined twins.
 (A) female, male (B) male, female
 (C) black, white

 閱讀測驗

剛剛的聽力測驗是否因為答題不順而感到遺憾？或是覺得自己有某些地方掌握
地不夠好？現在就讓我們來直接「看」剛剛的聽力測驗，並透過後面的閱讀測
驗來補齊聽力上的不足，同時考驗自己的閱讀能力吧！

Conjoined twins are genetically identical twins with the same sex whose bodies, including skin and perhaps internal organs, are joined together. The case of Mary and Jodie, the conjoined twins, was a very **controversial**[1] issue in 2000. The twins were conjoined, and Mary was a "parasitic" twin, which means she was literally living off of Jodie. This began to wear Jodie's heart down and in the end they might both die. In order to save maybe one of the twins, courts in England judged that the twins should be **separated**[2]. At that time no one knew if this separation surgery would be totally **successful**[3].

A group of doctors separated the twins. Jodie survived, but Mary died. This result has brought up many moral issues and questions. Is it a correct thing to **sacrifice**[4] one baby in order for the other to live on? Were they meant to be conjoined? Is surgical separation the most **logical**[5] solution? I think an issue like this one can be debated until the end of time. I do not know whether I would make the same decision if Mary and Jodie were my kids. I would find it a very difficult decision to make.

For some unknown reason, female conjoined twins appear to have a better chance for survival than male conjoined twins. The overall survival rate of conjoined twins is somewhere between five percent and twenty-five percent. If the twins have separate sets of organs, chances for separation surgery and survival are greater than if they share the same organs. Over the years, **survival**[6] rates have improved a lot.

Level 1
Level 2
Level 3
Level 4
Level 5
Level 6

【Question】

(　　) 1. What was the writer's attitude toward the surgical separation?
      (A) firm
      (B) understanding
      (C) hesitant

(　　) 2. How has the survival rate of the conjoined twins been over the years?
      (A) declining
      (B) improving
      (C) still

【文章中譯】

連體嬰在遺傳學上是身體與皮膚相連（或許體內器官也會相連）的同卵雙胞胎，一般都為同樣性別。連體嬰「瑪麗和茱蒂」這個案件在2000年是個極富爭議性的議題。這對連體嬰裡的瑪麗是寄生的一方，也就是說她是寄生在茱蒂身上存活的。這樣下來，造成了茱蒂心臟的衰弱，最終兩個嬰兒都將會死去。為了讓其中一個存活下來，英國法院判決這對連體嬰應該被切割開來。在當時，沒有人知道切割手術是否會完全成功。

一群醫生做了這項切割手術。結果茱蒂存活下來了，而瑪麗卻死了。這個結果引起了許多道德上的爭議。為了救活連體嬰中的其中一個而犧牲另一個是正確的作法嗎？她們是命中註定連在一起的嗎？切割手術是合理的解決方式嗎？像這樣的議題，我想一直爭辯到世界末日都不會有結果。我不知道我是否會做出同樣的決定，如果瑪麗和茱蒂是我的小孩。我想那會是一個非常難的抉擇。

由於某種未知的原因，女性連體嬰的存活率似乎比男性的連體嬰高。連體嬰的整體存活率大約在百分之五到二十五之間。如果連體嬰的器官是分開的，切割手術成功及存活的機率會比器官相連的連體嬰高出許多。這幾年下來，存活率已經大大的提升了。

聽力題目解析

❶ 此題詢問的是文章的探討對象。選項 (A) 為正常人；選項 (B) 為失明之人；選項 (C) 為醫生；選項 (D) 為連體嬰。錄音檔在一開始即告訴我們答案為 (D)。

❷ 此題詢問的是連體嬰是何種性別的同卵雙胞胎。選項 (A) 為同性；選項 (B) 為不同性；選項 (C) 為女性。在錄音檔的一開始，我們便能聽見連體嬰是 "genetically identical twins with the same sex"，故答案為 (A)，此題需仔細聆聽。

❸ 此題詢問的是瑪莉與茱蒂是發生於哪一年的爭議事件。錄音檔不久後即告訴我們瑪莉與茱蒂在 2000 是極富爭議的案例，答案選 (A)。

❹ 此題詢問的是一對何種的雙胞胎代表其中一方式依靠著另一方生存。選項 (A) 為寄生的；選項 (B) 為塑膠的；選項 (C) 為儲藏室。在聆聽的過程中，我們需注意為什麼瑪莉與茱蒂為一爭議性的案例，而音檔開頭不久後，我們也可快速掌握到 "parasitic"（寄生性）此單字，表示瑪麗是寄生在茱蒂身上存活的一方，故答案選 (A)。

❺ 此題詢問的是基於不明原因，何種連體嬰會比何種連體嬰的存活率還要高。選項 (A) 為女性，男性；選項 (B) 為男性，女性；選項 (C) 為黑皮膚，白皮膚。在錄音檔的結尾部分，我們可以聽到與題目相近的開頭，故需趁機把握，仔細聆聽，選出 (A) 作為答案。

閱讀題目解析

❶ 此題詢問的是作者對於切割手術的態度為何。選項 (A) 為堅定的；選項 (B) 為理解的；選項 (C) 為猶豫的。答案可見內文第二段，選擇 (C)。

❷ 此題詢問的是近年來連體嬰的存活率為何。選項 (A) 為下降的；選項
   (B) 為進步的；選項 (C) 為靜止的。答案詳見內文最後一段的最後一
   句，選擇 (B)。

補充單字

☆ 1. controversial	**adj.**	有爭議性的
☆ 2. separate	**n.**	分開
☆ 3. sacrifice	**v.**	犧牲
☆ 4. successful	**adj.**	成功的
☆ 5. logical	**adj.**	合理的
☆ 6. survival	**n.**	存活

Queen Elizabeth I
伊莉莎白一世

聽力測驗 🎧 Track 033

在學習英文的過程中，「聽」可能是最直接的第一線接觸，也可能是大家最想要快速習得的能力。現在，就讓我們來熟悉各種英文情境，提升自己的英文臨場感吧！

( ) 1. The first Queen Elizabeth was born in _____.
  (A) 1588   (B) 1558
  (C) 1533   (D) 1603

( ) 2. Queen Elizabeth I never married and had _____ children.
  (A) 1   (B) 2
  (C) 3   (D) no

( ) 3. Elizabeth I came to the throne of England at the age of _____.
  (A) 20   (B) 23
  (C) 25   (D) 28

( ) 4. England defeated the _____ Armada in 1588.
  (A) Spanish
  (B) French
  (C) American
  (D) Ireland

( ) 5 Queen Elizabeth I was the last monarch of _____ dynasty.
  (A) Tudor
  (B) Windsor
  (C) Haus Hannover
  (D) Stuart

閱讀測驗

剛剛的聽力測驗是否因為答題不順而感到遺憾？或是覺得自己有某些地方掌握地不夠好？現在就讓我們來直接「看」剛剛的聽力測驗，並透過後面的閱讀測驗來補齊聽力上的不足，同時考驗自己的閱讀能力吧！

Queen Elizabeth I is considered one of the greatest **monarchs**[1] that England ever had. She was born on September 7, 1533, the only child of Henry VIII and his second wife, Anne Boleyn. She was born in Greenwich Palace, but much of her youth was spent in Hatfield Palace in Hertfordshire. She was well educated and **fluent**[2] in six languages. One of her tutors, Roger Ascham, once wrote about her, "When she writes Greek and Latin, nothing is more beautiful than her handwriting."

She came to the **throne**[3] of England at the age of twenty-five after the death of her half sister, Queen Mary I. When she first came to the throne, England was in a difficult position. But later during her reign, England became one of the most powerful and **prosperous**[4] countries in the world.

The reign of Queen Elizabeth I is often considered as the Golden Age, where arts and English literature flourished. This was the age of William Shakespeare, while Francis Bacon, who once said, "Knowledge is power," was one of the greatest minds of the day. Also, great explorers toured the world in the name of Queen Elizabeth I.

Spain was the greatest sea power in the 16th century Europe. Therefore, leading her country in **defeating**[5] the Spanish Armada in 1588 was arguably one of Queen Elizabeth I's greatest achievements. In politics, she chose capable people to assist her. She listened to their advice and would change a policy if it was unpopular.

Queen Elizabeth I never married or had children. She is often called as the "Virgin Queen." However, she often used the possibility of marriage as a **political**[6] tool to help with diplomatic relations. Elizabeth I was the last monarch of Tudor dynasty and the last queen of England. She died on March 24, 1603, aged 69, and was buried in Westminster Abbey.

Level 1
Level 2
Level 3
Level 4
Level 5
Level 6

【Question】

(　　) 1. Where did Queen Elizabeth I spent most of her youth?
- (A) Hatfield Palace
- (B) Royal Palace
- (C) Charles Bridge Palace
- (D) Hilton Palace

(　　) 2. How many languages was Queen Elizabeth I fluent in?
- (A) 5
- (B) 4
- (C) 3
- (D) 6

【文章中譯】

伊莉莎白一世被認為是英格蘭有史以來最偉大的君主之一。她生於1533年9月7日，是亨利八世與他的第二任妻子安妮・博林的獨生女。她出生於格林威治宮，但大部分的青少年時光都在赫特福德郡的哈特菲爾德宮度過。她受過良好的教育，精通六國語言。她的一位教師，羅傑・阿斯坎，曾經這麼描寫她：「當她書寫希臘文與拉丁文時，再沒有什麼比她的字跡更美麗的了。」

在同父異母的姊姊瑪麗一世去世後，她二十五歲時被加冕為女王。她初登基時，英格蘭正處於艱難的情勢。但之後在她統治的期間，英格蘭已成為世界上最強大富庶的國家之一。

伊莉莎白一世的統治期被認為是「黃金年代」，藝術與英格蘭文學皆蓬勃發展。那是莎士比亞的時代，而曾說過「知識就是力量」的法蘭西斯・培根也是當時最偉大的思想家之一。另外，偉大的探險家們以伊莉莎白女王一世之名，遊歷了全世界。

西班牙在十六世紀的歐洲是最強大的海權國家。因此，在1588年率領她的國家打敗西班牙無敵艦隊一役，無疑是伊莉莎白一世最偉大的成就。在政治上，她選擇有才幹的人士輔佐她，傾聽他們的建言，也會改變不得人心的政策。

Level 1

Level 2

Level 3

Level 4

Level 5

Level 6

伊莉莎白一世從未結婚，亦無子女。她常被稱為「童貞女王」。然而，她卻常運用婚姻作為外交策略與政治手段。伊莉莎白一世是都鐸王朝最後一位君主，也是英格蘭最後一個女王。她死於1603年3月24日，享年69歲，被安葬於西敏寺。

聽力題目解析

❶ 此題詢問的是伊莉莎白一世的出生年份。根據錄音檔的開頭，我們可以快速得知答案為 (C)。此種題型建議先看過題目，以把握數字型的資訊。

❷ 此題詢問的是伊莉莎白一世沒有結婚而有幾個小孩。在錄音檔的結尾部分，我們可以得知伊莉莎白一世沒有結婚，亦無子女，也因此被稱為 "Virgin Queen"（童貞女王），故答案選則 (D)。

❸ 此題詢問的是伊莉莎白一世在幾歲登基。答案為 (C)；同第一題，此種題型建議先看過題目，以把握數字型的資訊。

❹ 此題詢問的是英國在 1588 年擊敗了何國的無敵艦隊。選項 (A) 為西班牙；選項 (B) 為法國；選項 (C) 為美國；選項 (D) 為愛爾蘭。在聆聽完伊莉莎白一世時期的文豪之後，我們接著得知西班牙是十六世紀的歐洲強大海權國家，而伊莉莎白一世因領導有方，打敗了西班牙無敵艦隊，故答案選 (A)。此題目和陳述之句子相似，故可先看過題目以便在聆聽時把握關鍵字。

❺ 此題詢問的伊莉莎白一世是哪一個王朝的最後一位君主。選項 (A) 為都鐸王朝；選項 (B) 為溫莎王朝；選項 (C) 為漢斯漢諾威王朝；選項 (D) 為斯圖爾特王朝。音檔最後告訴我們伊莉莎白一世 "was the last monarch of Tudor dynasty"，故答案選擇 (A)。

❶ 此題詢問的是伊莉莎白一世在何處渡過其大部分的年少時光。選項 (A) 為哈特菲爾德宮;選項 (B) 為皇家宮殿;選項 (C) 為查爾斯喬皇宮;選項 (D) 為希爾頓宮殿。答案可見內文第一段,選擇 (A)。

❷ 此題詢問的是伊莉莎白一世精通幾國語言。答案可見內文第一段倒數第二句,選擇 (D)。

補充單字

☆ 1. monarch	n.	君主
☆ 2. fluent	adj.	流利的
☆ 3. throne	n.	王位
☆ 4. prosperous	adj.	繁榮的
☆ 5. defeat	v.	打敗
☆ 6. political	adj.	政治(上)的

America's First Daughter— Ivanka Trump

美國第一千金──伊凡卡

聽力測驗 🎧 Track 034

在學習英文的過程中,「聽」可能是最直接的第一線接觸,也可能是大家最想要快速習得的能力。現在,就讓我們來熟悉各種英文情境,提升自己的英文臨場感吧!

( ) 1. Which of the following has Ivanka Trump never tried to be?
　　 (A) a fashion designer 　　　　(B) a model
　　 (C) a career woman 　　　　　(D) a singer

( ) 2. Who was considered the Trump card that helped Donald Trump win the US presidential election?
　　 (A) Ivanka 　　　　　　　　　(B) Eric
　　 (C) Tiffany 　　　　　　　　　(D) Barron

( ) 3. What do many people think about Ivanka's speech about her father in 2016?
　　 (A) terrible 　　　　　　　　　(B) biased
　　 (C) very good 　　　　　　　　(D) disastrous

( ) 4. Did Ivanka Trump have any political experience before her father ran for president?
　　 (A) yes 　　　　　　　　　　 (B) temporarily
　　 (C) a little 　　　　　　　　　(D) never

( ) 5. What does Ivanka do now?
　　 (A) Vice President 　　　　　　(B) Advisor to the President
　　 (C) Secretary of Defense 　　　(D) Attorney General

 閱讀測驗

剛剛的聽力測驗是否因為答題不順而感到遺憾？或是覺得自己有某些地方掌握地不夠好？現在就讓我們來直接「看」剛剛的聽力測驗，並透過後面的閱讀測驗來補齊聽力上的不足，同時考驗自己的閱讀能力吧！

Never has a first daughter been quite like her before. She was a runway[1] model, a fashion designer, a successful businesswoman, and a popular reality TV personality. She is Ivanka Trump, the daughter of the 45th president of the United States, Donald Trump.

Many believe she was the **Trump card**[2] that helped Trump get elected. Indeed, she had appeared by her father's side on the campaign trail to support him and defend him. Her speech about her father at the 2016 Republican National Convention was widely viewed and **well-received**[3]. After her father's election victory, she was **appointed**[4] Advisor to the President on March 29, 2017.

With no previous political experience, Ivanka represented her father on diplomatic missions and sits side by side with the President at meetings with Russian and Turkish presidents, German chancellor, Angela Merkel, and British Prime Minister, Theresa May. She was also given a key role in drafting Trump's childcare policies, which included paid **maternity**[5] leave. Now, some credit her with pushing the President for better deals for working women. Some says if there is going to be a female president of the U.S. anytime soon, it will be Ivanka Trump.

【Question】

(   ) 1. What has Ivanka NOT done for her father?
       (A) running for president herself
       (B) meeting foreign leaders
       (C) drafting childcare policies
       (D) going on foreign trips

(　　) 2. What can be inferred from the article?
　　　 (A) Ivanka didn't support her father's campaign.
　　　 (B) The Trump family is falling apart.
　　　 (C) Donald Trump trusts his daughter Ivanka.
　　　 (D) Ivanka doesn't want to get involved in politics.

Level 1
Level 2
Level 3
Level 4
Level 5
Level 6

【文章中譯】

過去從來沒有出現過像她這樣的第一千金。她是伸展台上的模特兒、時尚設計師、成功的商界女強人，還是受歡迎的電視實境秀明星。她是美國第 45 任總統唐納‧川普的千金伊凡卡‧川普。

許多人認為她是幫助川普當選的王牌，她也的確於父親競選期間一路陪在他的身邊支持他、捍衛他。她於 2016 年共和黨全國代表大會中發表有關父親的演說獲得許多人觀看並廣受好評。在父親勝選後，她也於 2017 年 3 月 29 日被指派擔任總統顧問一職。

儘管無從政經驗，伊凡卡仍代表父親出訪各國，並與擔任總統的父親會晤俄羅斯總統、土耳其總統、德國總理梅克爾，以及英國首相梅伊。她也擔任了草擬帶薪育嬰假的兒童照護政策之重要角色。現在，有人稱讚她是協助川普為職業婦女爭取更好權益的重要推手，也有人認為若美國未來選出第一位女性總統，那個人將會是伊凡卡‧川普。

聽力題目解析

❶ 此題詢問的是伊凡卡從未從事過的領域。選項 (A) 為時尚設計師；選項 (B)為模特兒；選項 (C) 為職業婦女；選項 (D) 為歌手。錄音檔的開頭即描述伊凡卡曾是 "runway model, a fashion designer, a successful businesswoman, and a popular reality TV personality"，僅無當過歌手，此題仔細聆聽即可，故答案選(D)。

❷ 此題詢問的是誰被許多人認為是幫助川普贏得總統大選的王牌，選項 (A) 為伊凡卡；選項 (B) 為艾利克；選項 (C) 為蒂芬妮；選項 (D) 為拜倫。在錄音檔中段即點名 "Many believe she was the Trump card that helped Trump get elected." 這句及全文都在談伊凡卡，因此可確定she指的是伊凡卡，故答案選 (A)。
（註：艾利克、蒂芬妮、拜倫都是川普總統的子女，但外界普遍認為伊凡卡才是助川普當選的最重要推手。）

❸ 此題詢問的是多數人怎麼看待伊凡卡在2016年發表有關父親的演講。選項 (A)為很糟；選項 (B) 為帶有偏見；選項 (C) 為非常好；選項 (D) 為形同一場災難。在錄音檔中段提到該場演說廣受好評 "Her speech ... was widely viewed and well-received." 故答案選 (C)。

❹ 此題詢問的是伊凡卡在父親參選總統以前，是否曾有從政經驗。選項 (A) 為是的；選項 (B) 為短暫地；選項 (C) 為一點點；選項 (D) 為未曾過。錄音檔中後段提到 "With no political experience, Ivanka ..."，可知伊凡卡過去從未曾參政，故答案選(D)。

❺ 此題詢問的是伊凡卡目前的職務。選項 (A) 為副總統；選項 (B) 為總統顧問；選項 (C) 為國防部長；選項 (D) 為司法部長。錄音檔中後段提到 "... she was appointed Advisor to the President on March 29, 2017." 故答案選(B)。

閱讀題目解析

❶ 此題詢問的是伊凡卡還沒替父親執行過何事。選項 (A) 為參選總統；選項 (B) 為會晤外國領袖；選項 (C) 為草擬兒童照護法政策；選項 (D) 為出訪。答案可見內文第三段，伊凡卡曾代表父親出訪、會晤外國領袖，也協助草擬兒童照護法政策，全文未提到應父親要求參選總統，故答案選 (A)。

❷ 此題詢問的是我們可以從內文推論出何者。選項 (A) 為伊凡卡不支持父親競選；選項 (B) 為川普家族四分五裂；選項 (C) 為唐納‧川普信任女兒伊凡卡；選項 (D) 為伊凡卡並不想介入政治。答案可見內文第二段，指川普當選總統後，伊凡卡被指派擔任總統顧問一職，可見對她信任之深，故答案為(C)。

補充單字

☆ 1. runway	n.	伸展台
☆ 2. Trump card	n.	王牌
☆ 3. well-received	adj.	廣獲好評的
☆ 4. appoint	v.	指派
☆ 5. maternity	n.	產婦；母親身份

The Tallest Man in the World
世界上最高的人

Level 2
15

在學習英文的過程中,「聽」可能是最直接的第一線接觸,也可能是大家最想要快速習得的能力。現在,就讓我們來熟悉各種英文情境,提升自己的英文臨場感吧!

( ) 1. How old was Bao Xishun according to the text?
　　(A) 20　　　　　　　　(B) 55
　　(C) 15　　　　　　　　(D) 35

( ) 2. Bao is _____.
　　(A) Guinness
　　(B) a woman
　　(C) a Mongolian
　　(D) a baby

( ) 3. His height is _____.
　　(A) 2.36 metres
　　(B) 2.63 metres
　　(C) 1.80 metres
　　(D) 2.1 metres

( ) 4. His legs are _____ metres.
　　(A) 2.1　　　　　　　　(B) 1.8
　　(C) 2.36　　　　　　　(D) 1.5

( ) 5. He and Xia Shujuan married in _____, 2007.
　　(A) April　　　　　　　(B) May
　　(C) June　　　　　　　(D) July

閱讀測驗

剛剛的聽力測驗是否因為答題不順而感到遺憾？或是覺得自己有某些地方掌握地不夠好？現在就讓我們來直接「看」剛剛的聽力測驗，並透過後面的閱讀測驗來補齊聽力上的不足，同時考驗自己的閱讀能力吧！

Bao Xishun, a 55-year-old **Mongolian**[1], is 236 centimeters tall. He was lucky to be listed in the Guinness Book of World Records for the world's tallest man **alive**[2].

He was born in the Inner Mongolia Autonomous Region in 1951. He has 5 siblings, and they all have normal height. He **grew**[3] normally until he was 15 years old. At the age of 15, he began to grow quickly and reached 189 centimeters. And when he was 20 years old, he reached about 210 centimeters. Now he is 165 kilograms in weight and his legs are 150 centimeters long. His feet are 38 centimeters long, and he has to wear the clothes made of more than 5 meters cloth.

A comprehensive medical check-up was done by The Second Affiliated Hospital of China Medical University and found his cardiorespiratory function and pituitary secretion are normal. Experts believe that his height was of natural growth.

In July 2007, He and Xia Shujuan **married**[4] and they live happily now. He said that he was satisfied with his **current**[5] life, and he wanted to have a child of his own. If he put his hand together, they are bigger than a baby. On November 3, 2008, his big palms could be used at last. He cradled his child in his palms until his child fell asleep. He often said, "Look at my son. He is **particularly**[6] strong. Only one month and a day after he was born, he is able to raise his neck. Few children can do that!" Bao Xishun said to the reporters proudly and happily on November 3, at his home in Chifeng , Inner Mongolia.

Level 1
Level 2
Level 3
Level 4
Level 5
Level 6

【Question】

(　　) 1. At what age did Bao start to grow quickly?
(A) 15　　　　　　　　(B) 17
(C) 20　　　　　　　　(D) 25

(　　) 2. Why did Bao grow so quickly according to the medical check-up?
(A) due to a genetic disease
(B) due to natural growth
(C) due to different eating habits
(D) due to exercises

【文章中譯】

五十五歲的蒙古族男子鮑喜順以兩百三十六公分的身高，成為金氏世界紀錄中「世界上長得最高的活人」。

鮑喜順於一九五一年出生於內蒙古自治區，有五名兄弟姐妹，他們的身高都正常。鮑喜順童年時發育正常，但從十五歲開始突然快速長高，那時已長到了一百八十九公分，到了二十歲時更高達兩百一十公分左右。現在鮑喜順的體重是一百六十五公斤，雙腿長一百五十公分，腳長三十八公分，做一身衣服要五米多的布才夠。

中國醫科大學附屬第二醫院曾為鮑喜順做過全身健康檢查，發現其心肺功能及腦垂體分泌均屬正常。專家認為他的身高屬於自然生長而成。

2007年七月，鮑喜順與夏淑娟結婚，婚後生活非常美滿。鮑喜順說，他對自己目前的生活很滿意，但他還有一個心願，就是想生個孩子。巨人鮑喜順的兩隻大手合起來要比一個小嬰兒還大。2008年十一月三日，他的這雙大手終於派上了用場，孩子要睡覺時，他就用這雙大手托著、搖晃著，孩子就睡著了。他說：「看看我的兒子，他長得特別結實。才一個月零一天，他的脖子就能立起來了。有幾個孩子能這樣啊？肯定不多見！」十一月三日，鮑喜順在內蒙古赤峰的家中抱著自己的兒子驕傲而幸福地對記者說。

聽力題目解析

❶ 此題詢問的是鮑喜順的年紀。錄音檔在一開始便給了我們答案,為 55 歲。此種數字型題目建議先快速看過題目,以便掌握聆聽的內容。

❷ 此題詢問的是鮑喜順的身份。選項 (A) 為金氏;選項 (B) 為一名女子;選項 (C) 為一名蒙古人;選項 (D) 為一名嬰兒。根據錄音檔,鮑喜順為一名五十五歲的蒙古族男子,故答案選則 (C)。

❸ 此題詢問的是鮑喜順的身高為何。錄音檔在一開始便給了我們答案,為 236公分,故選擇 (A)。同上,此種數字型題目建議先快速看過題目,以便掌握聆聽的內容。

❹ 此題詢問的是鮑喜順的腿長為何。答案為 (D),此種數字型題目建議先快速看過題目,以便掌握聆聽的內容,尤其此題的答案出現在一連串的數字之中。

❺ 此題詢問的是鮑喜順和夏淑娟在 2007 年的幾月結婚。選項 (A) 為四月;選項 (B) 為五月;選項 (C) 為六月;選項 (D) 為七月。答案為 (D),此題僅需仔細聆聽音檔注意細節即可。

閱讀題目解析

❶ 此題詢問的是鮑喜順在幾歲開始快速長高。答案可見內文第二段,選 (A)。

❷ 此題詢問的是在健康檢查過後,鮑喜順快速長高的原因為何。選項 (A) 為起因於一種基因疾病;選項 (B) 為起因於自然生長;選項 (C) 為由不同的飲食習慣所導致;選項 (D) 為因為運動的緣故。答案可見內文第三段最後一句,選 (B)。

補充單字

☆ 1. Mongolian	**adj.**	蒙古(人)的
☆ 2. alive	**n.**	活著的
☆ 3. growth	**n.**	成長
☆ 4. marry	**v.**	結婚
☆ 5. current	**adj.**	現在的,現行的
☆ 6. particularly	**adv.**	特別,尤其

The World's Oldest Man — Yisrael Kristal

金氏世界紀錄：世界最長壽的男性人瑞——克里斯塔爾

Level 1
Level 2
Level 3
Level 4
Level 5
Level 6

聽力測驗 🎧 Track 036

在學習英文的過程中，「聽」可能是最直接的第一線接觸，也可能是大家最想要快速習得的能力。現在，就讓我們來熟悉各種英文情境，提升自己的英文臨場感吧！

(　　) 1. What happened to Yisrael Kristal when the Nazi Germany invaded Poland?
(A) He was sent to the Auschwitz.
(B) He fled to the United States.
(C) He was killed.
(D) He was safe from any harm.

(　　) 2. How much did Kristal weigh when he was rescued by the Red Army?
(A) 47 kilograms　　　(B) 40 kilograms
(C) 35 kilograms　　　(D) 37 kilograms

(　　) 3. Which country did Kristal and his second wife move to after the Holocaust?
(A) Israel　　　　　　(B) United States
(C) United Kingdom　　(D) Hungary

Guinness World Records

(   ) 4. What did Kristal do for a living?
             (A) tailor   (B) bus driver
             (C) candy business   (D) writer

(   ) 5. How old was Kristal when he passed away?
             (A) 111   (B) 112
             (C) 113   (D) 114

 閱讀測驗

剛剛的聽力測驗是否因為答題不順而感到遺憾？或是覺得自己有某些地方掌握地不夠好？現在就讓我們來直接「看」剛剛的聽力測驗，並透過後面的閱讀測驗來補齊聽力上的不足，同時考驗自己的閱讀能力吧！

Yisrael Kristal, a **Holocaust**[1] survivor, was recognized as the world's oldest man by the Guinness Book of Records in March 2016. Born in 1903 in a Polish village, Kristal lost his parents during World War One. He later moved to Lodz to start his own family and opened a candy factory.

After the **invasion**[2] of Poland by Nazi Germany in 1939, Kristal was **deported**[3] to Auschwitz in 1940 and lost his first wife and two children in the Holocaust. When he was liberated by the Red Army in 1945, he weighed only 37 kilograms. The only survivor from his family, Kristal met his second wife and they **emigrated**[4] to Israel, where he continued running his **confectionery**[5] business until his retirement. The couple had a son and a daughter.

Kristal seldom talked about his experience in the Holocaust. "Two books could be written about a single day there," he said in a rare interview. Asked about the secret to a long life, Kristal said, "There have been smarter, stronger, and better-looking men than me who are no longer alive." He passed away at the age of 113, a month before his 114th birthday.

【**Question**】

(　　) 1. Did Kristal talk a lot about his experience in the Holocaust?
   (A) often   (B) seldom
   (C) never   (D) always

(　　) 2. What was Kristal's secret to a long life?
   (A) He didn't have a secret to a long life.
   (B) He was smarter.
   (C) He ran faster.
   (D) He was better-looking.

【文章中譯】

伊斯雷爾‧克里斯塔爾是大屠殺的倖存者，在 2016 年 3 月被金氏世界紀錄列為全球最長壽的男性人瑞。他於 1903 年出生於一個波蘭小鎮，在第一次世界大戰時失去了雙親，後來他搬到波蘭的羅茲城市娶妻生子，並開了一家糖果工廠。

1939 年納粹德國攻佔波蘭，克里斯塔爾於次年被送到奧斯威辛集中營，並在大屠殺中失去第一任妻子和 2 位摯愛的孩子。在 1945 年他被蘇聯紅軍救出時，體重只剩下37公斤。他是家族唯一的存活者，後來遇到第二任妻子並移居到以色列，兩人育有一子一女，並繼續靠著經營糖果生意一直到他退休為止。

克里斯塔爾很少談論他在大屠殺的經歷，「集中營裡一天內發生的事情就足以寫成兩本書」，他難得受訪時這麼表示。問到長壽的秘訣，克里斯塔爾說：「世界上有許多更聰明、健壯、英俊的男人，但他們都已經離開人世了。」他於 113 歲時辭世，只差一個月就年滿 114 歲了。

聽力題目解析

❶ 此題詢問的是納粹德國攻佔波蘭時，伊斯雷爾‧克里斯塔爾發生了什麼事。選項 (A) 為他被送進了奧斯威辛集中營；選項 (B) 為他逃到美國了；選項 (C) 為他遇害喪命；選項 (D) 為他平安無事。在錄音檔的中間部分，我們可以聽見描述 "After the invasion … Kristal was deported to Auschwitz in 1940." 此種題型只要在出現時間點的關鍵字把握即可，故答案選 (A)。

❷ 此題詢問的是克里斯塔爾被蘇聯紅軍救出時，他當時只有幾公斤。選項 (A) 為47公斤；選項 (B) 為 40公斤；選項 (C) 為 35公斤；選項 (D) 為37公斤。在錄音檔中段部分即有説 "… he weighed only 37 kilograms." 故答案選 (D)。

❸ 此題詢問的是大屠殺後，克里斯塔爾和第二任妻子移居到哪個國家。選項 (A) 為以色列；選項 (B) 為美國；選項 (C) 為英國；選項 (D) 為匈牙利。在錄音檔中段提到在大屠殺中，克里斯塔爾是家族中唯一的存活者，接著"Kristal met his second wife and they emigrated to Israel" 此種題型建議先看過題目及選項，答案選 (A)。

❹ 此題詢問的是克里斯塔爾靠什麼樣的方式謀生。選項 (A) 為裁縫；選項 (B) 為巴士司機；選項 (C) 為糖果生意；選項 (D) 為作家。錄音檔前段提到他在第一次世界大戰時失去雙親，後來娶妻生子，並開了一家糖果工廠 "opened a candy factory"，後來和第二任妻子移居以色列後 "… continued running his confectionery business."可知他是名糖果師傅，故答案選 (C)。此題若不懂 confectionary 的意思，仍可藉由 "candy factory" 和 "continue" 來推論。

❺ 此題詢問克里斯塔爾過世時是幾歲。選項 (A) 為111歲；選項 (B) 為112歲；選項 (C) 為 113歲；選項 (D) 為114歲。錄音檔最後一句提到 "He passed away at the age of 113, a month before his 114th birthday."，而「只差一個月就年滿114歲了」是補充説明，但可能造成混淆，是考生應小心的陷阱題，故答案選 (C)。

❶ 此題詢問的是克里斯塔爾是否常常談論他在大屠殺的經歷。選項 (A) 為經常；選項 (B) 為很少；選項 (C) 為從不；選項 (D) 為總是。答案可見內文第三段第一句 "Kristal seldom talked about his experience in the Holocaust." 故答案選 (B)。

❷ 此題詢問的是克里斯塔爾長壽的秘訣為何。選項 (A) 為他沒有長壽的秘訣；選項 (B) 為他比較聰明；選項 (C) 為他跑得比較快；選項 (D) 為他長得比較英俊。答案可見 "There have been smarter, stronger, and better-looking men than me who are no longer alive." 可推斷他並沒有什麼保持長壽的秘訣，故答案為 (A)。

補充單字

☆ 1. Holocaust	n.	大屠殺
☆ 2. invasion	n.	侵略
☆ 3. deport	v.	放逐
☆ 4. emigrate	v.	移居外國
☆ 5. confectionery	n.	糖果糕點店

The Old Man and the Sea
老人與海

Level 2 17

聽力測驗 🎧 Track 037

在學習英文的過程中，「聽」可能是最直接的第一線接觸，也可能是大家最想要快速習得的能力。現在，就讓我們來熟悉各種英文情境，提升自己的英文臨場感吧！

(　) 1. Who is the author of this novel?
    (A) Earnest Hemingway
    (B) V. C. Andrews
    (C) Scott Fitzgerald
    (D) Isaac Newton

(　) 2. What did the author win in 1954?
    (A) The Nobel Prize for Science
    (B) The Nobel Prize for Literature
    (C) The Pulitzer Prize for Fiction
    (D) The Pulitzer Prize for Poetry

(　) 3. The Old Man and the Sea is _____?
    (A) a epic poem   (B) a novella
    (C) a long story   (D) difficult to read

(　) 4. What is the name of the old man in the story?
    (A) Marlin   (B) Santiago
    (C) Hemingway   (D) Harry

(　) 5. What is the old man in the story?
    (A) a fisherman   (B) a worker
    (C) a farmer   (D) a writer

閱讀測驗

剛剛的聽力測驗是否因為答題不順而感到遺憾？或是覺得自己有某些地方掌握地不夠好？現在就讓我們來直接「看」剛剛的聽力測驗，並透過後面的閱讀測驗來補齊聽力上的不足，同時考驗自己的閱讀能力吧！

The Old Man and the Sea is one of Ernest Hemingway's most **remarkable**[1] achievements. Told in an extremely simple way, it is a story about **courage**[2]. It tells the story of an old Cuban fisherman named Santiago, who is experiencing misfortune, but whose spirit is as strong and determined as anything in nature.

Santiago has not caught a fish for eighty-four days. On the eighty-fifth day, he goes far out to sea in his small wooden boat all alone. The small boy who always fished with him in the past does not accompany him because the boy's parents prevent him from doing so. They think that Santiago is down on his luck.

Santiago hooks a **gigantic**[3] marlin. It is the kind of fish that fishermen only dream of catching. And after a fierce battle for three days, Santiago kills the marlin. He uses rope to tie the marlin alongside his wooden boat and sails for home, only to have it attacked and gorged on by the sharks, leaving only a skeleton.

The whole story is rich in symbolism. All of the symbols have an increased effect on the basic theme that life is an eternal struggle with unreal rewards. A man must show patience, courage, intelligence and optimism during the **struggle**[4]. Then, even though the prize is lost, the man has won the battle, **proving**[5] that he has the ability to retain grace under pressure.

The novella, The Old Man and the Sea, was the last work Ernest Hemingway published. It proved one of the timeless works of American fiction and made Hemingway one of the best-known authors of the twentieth century. And it was for this novella that Earnest Hemingway won the Nobel Prize for literature in 1954. The book has continued to greatly **affect**[6] readers of all ages and never been out of print.

【Question】

(　　) 1. Which of the following statement about the marlin in the story is incorrect?
(A) Santiago killed it at the end.
(B) It attacked the sharks.
(C) It was tied alongside the wooden boat.
(D) It was gorged on by sharks.

(　　) 2. What can we infer from the article?
(A) The novella is about courage, intelligence, and the mystery of forests.
(B) The novella has worldwide effects.
(C) The novella shows that reward is the most important thing after each struggle.

【文章中譯】

「老人與海」是海明威最著名的成就之一。這是一個以非常簡單的方式敘述著勇氣的故事。故事是關於一個名叫聖地亞哥的古巴漁夫，他歷經了厄運，但他的精神卻跟自然界中任何的一草一木一樣堅強與堅定。

聖地亞哥已經八十四天沒有釣到一條魚了。他在第八十五天，獨自乘坐他的小木船出海去捕魚。過去總是跟著他一起釣魚的小男孩被父母阻止而不能陪他出海，因為男孩的父母認為聖地亞哥正處於厄運之中。

聖地亞哥釣到了一條巨大的馬林魚。那是一條漁夫們都夢想釣到的魚。在經過三天激烈的奮戰後，聖地亞哥終於殺死了這條馬林魚。他利用繩子將馬林魚綁在他的木船邊，然後往家的方向行駛，卻沒想到馬林魚被一群鯊魚攻擊並吃得精光，僅剩下一具魚骨頭。

這整個故事裡充滿象徵主義。所有象徵的事物都更加凸顯基本的主旨，即生命是一場永無止盡的掙扎，即使得到了獎賞，也是虛幻的。人必須在掙扎當中表現出耐心、勇氣、睿智與樂觀。這樣，即使失去了獎賞，還是贏得了這場奮戰，證明了在壓力之下仍舊能保持優雅的應對進退的能力。

「老人與海」這部中篇小說是海明威生前最後出版的作品。這部小說證明是美國小說的經典作品，使海明威成為二十世紀最知名的作家。也是因為這部中篇小說，海明威在一九五四年贏得了諾貝爾文學獎。這本書已持續並廣大地影響各個年齡層的讀者，並且從未絕版過。

聽力題目解析

❶ 此題詢問的是《老人與海》的作者。錄音檔在一開始即給了我們答案，選 (A)。

❷ 此題詢問的是小說作者在 1954 年得了什麼講座。選項 (A) 為諾貝爾科學獎；選項 (B) 為諾貝爾文學獎；選項 (C) 為普立茲小說獎；選項 (D) 為普立茲詩歌獎。在錄音檔結尾，我們可以聽到 "Earnest Hemingway won the Nobel Prize for literature in 1954."，故答案選 (B)。此題聆聽前先看過題目及選項會較好把握。

❸ 此題詢問的是《老人與海》為何種作品。選項 (A) 為一首史詩；選項 (B) 為一本小說；選項 (C) 為一個長篇故事；選項 (D) 為難以閱讀的作品。答案選擇 (B)，且在錄音檔中並未出現與其他選項相關之單字。

❹ 此題詢問的是老人在故事中的名字為何。答案為 (B)，在講述故事的一開始，我們即可聽見老人的名字為 Santiago。

❺ 此題詢問的是老人在故事中的職業為何。選項 (A) 為一名漁夫；選項 (B) 為一名工人；選項 (C) 為一名農夫；選項 (D) 為一名作家。答案為 (A)，此題和上題出現在同樣的地方，仔細聆聽注意細節即可。

Level 1
Level 2
Level 3
Level 4
Level 5
Level 6

閱讀題目解析

❶ 此題詢問的是根據故事中馬林魚的描述何者為錯。選項 (A) 為聖地亞哥最終殺了它；選項 (B) 為它攻擊了鯊魚；選項 (C) 為它被綁在木船邊；選項 (D) 為它被鯊魚吃得精光。答案可見內文第三段全部，選擇 (B)。

❷ 此題詢問的是我們可以從內文推斷出何者。選項 (A) 為這本小說是一個有關勇敢、智識，以及森林的神秘之故事；選項 (B) 為這本小說影響了全球；選項 (C) 為這本小說展示出在每個掙扎過後，獎賞是最重要的。答案可見內文最後一段，選擇 (B)；選項 (A) 不符，因小說場景式設定在海洋。

補充單字

☆ 1. remarkable	adj.	最著名的
☆ 2. courage	n.	勇氣
☆ 3. gigantic	adj.	巨大的
☆ 4. struggle	n.	掙扎
☆ 5. prove	v.	證明
☆ 6. affect	v.	影響

Level 2
18 The Connection Between Employers and Employees in the U.S.

美國雇主與雇員之間的關係

Level 1
Level 2
Level 3
Level 4
Level 5
Level 6

聽力測驗 🎧 Track 038

在學習英文的過程中，「聽」可能是最直接的第一線接觸，也可能是大家最想要快速習得的能力。現在，就讓我們來熟悉各種英文情境，提升自己的英文臨場感吧！

(　　) 1. Americans have _____ basic avenues for making friends.
    (A) three   (B) four
    (C) several

(　　) 2. Americans make friends _____.
    (A) through a family or friend's connection
    (B) at work
    (C) at school
    (D) all of the above

(　　) 3. Americans employees normally _____ such social gatherings.
    (A) reject   (B) refuse
    (C) don't refuse   (D) dislike

(　　) 4. American companies have at least one major activity annually, usually during _____.
    (A) New year time   (B) Christmastime
    (C) Springtime

(　　) 5. The host will prepare _____ for everyone who comes to their home.
    (A) refreshments   (B) movies
    (C) nothing   (D) books

剛剛的聽力測驗是否因為答題不順而感到遺憾？或是覺得自己有某些地方掌握地不夠好？現在就讓我們來直接「看」剛剛的聽力測驗，並透過後面的閱讀測驗來補齊聽力上的不足，同時考驗自己的閱讀能力吧！

People in the United States like to make new friends at work, at school, via **hobbies**[1] or through a family or friend's connection. These are very common avenues for making friends. For most Americans, their job is more than just the work that goes from 9 a.m. to 5 p.m. every day. Their job is an **important**[2] socializing activity. A lot of housewives **prefer**[3] to have a job of their own so they can be free and independent in everyday life as well as in finance.

Top administrators in American **companies**[4] often hold social get-togethers in their own houses. Some social gatherings could be picnics in the backyard or at anyplace suitable. It's all depending on how large the employer's house is and how many employees there are. Some employers will **invite**[5] his employees to visit his home. They will chat or play cards with other guests or family members.

The host will have drinks or refreshments **available**[6] for everyone who comes to their home. People could come and go during the hours. Normally, employees don't refuse such social gatherings unless they have some urgent matter or have an excellent reason or have something much more important to do.

Corporations in the United States hold at least one major activity every year, usually Christmastime. Many employers arrange company gatherings at a local restaurant or in their house. Lots of companies have annual summer picnics where employees and administrators can play sports, such as basketball, baseball or volleyball.

Most American employers realize the importance of business social potential and will try their best to build a family atmosphere on the job so that the employees will feel cozy and secure in the work environment, which is good for the employees themselves, their family, the company and the whole society.

【Question】

( ) 1. What may be the reason why a lot of housewives in the U. S. prefer to have a job based on the article?
(A) They want to get away from house chores.
(B) They dislike being a parent.
(C) They can be independent financially and personally.
(D) They have more fun in the workplace than at home.

( ) 2. Which of the following word can not be used in place of the other three words?
(A) a socializing activity
(B) a social get-together
(C) a social gathering
(D) a social community

Level 1
Level 2
Level 3
Level 4
Level 5
Level 6

【文章中譯】

美國人喜歡在工作中、在學校、透過嗜好，或者經由家人或朋友牽線來交朋友。這是非常常見的四種交友管道。對大部分的美國人而言，工作不僅僅是每天朝九晚五的工作，而是一項重大的社交活動。許多家庭主婦希望能夠有一份工作，以求在日常生活中及財務上得到自由和獨立。

美國的高階主管時常在自己的家裡舉行社交聚會。根據雇主住家的大小以及員工的數量，這些社交聚會可能是辦在後院的野餐，或任何合適的地方。有些雇主會邀請其雇員到他的家拜訪，與其他客人和其他家人聊天或玩玩牌。

主人會準備點心飲料給所有來的人吃。人們可以自由地來去。對於這種社交聚會，雇員一般都不會拒絕邀請，除非他們遇到緊急事件，或有一個很好的理由，或有更重要的事情要辦。

美國公司每年至少會有一個主要的活動，通常是在耶誕節。一些雇主會在當地餐廳或在自家安排公司聯歡會。許多企業每年夏季會野餐，員工和主管可以參加運動項目，如籃球、棒球或排球。

大部分的美國雇主體認到商業社交的潛力，都會盡量建立一個有家庭氣氛的工作氛圍，使員工對工作環境感到更加舒適且安全，這對雇員本身、其家族成員、公司和整個社會都會帶來好處。

聽力題目解析

❶ 此題詢問的是美國人有擁有多少基本的社交場合。錄音檔的一開始即給我們答案，為 (B)。

❷ 此題詢問的是美國人是在何處交到朋友。選項 (A) 為透過家人或朋友的牽線；選項 (B) 為在職場上；選項 (C) 為在學校內；選項 (D) 為以上皆是。同上，我們在一開始即可聽見make new friends at work, at school, via hobbies, or through a family or friend's connection，故答案為 (D)。

❸ 此題詢問的是美國員工通常會對社交聚會的邀約表達何種反應。選項 (A) 為拒絕；選項 (B) 為拒絕；選項 (C) 為不拒絕；選項 (D) 為不喜歡。在接近錄音檔的後半部分，我們可以得知employees don't refuse such social gatherings，而選項 (A) 和 選項 (B) 同意，故可一起刪除，答案選擇 (C)。

❹ 此題詢問的是美國公司擁有至少一個年度重要聚會，且通常是在何時。選項 (A) 為新年期間；選項 (B) 為聖誕節期間；選項 (C) 為春節期間。答案為 (B)，此題建議先在錄音檔開始前快速看過選項，以便抓住關鍵字。

❺ 此題詢問的是主人通常會準備何物給到訪家中的客人。選項 (A) 為點心；選項 (B) 為電影；選項 (C) 為不準備任何東西；選項 (D) 為書。答案為 (A)，此題同上，且在聆聽的過程中，留意 "host" 此單字。

閱讀題目解析

❶ 此題詢問的是美國家庭主婦希望能夠有一份工作的可能原因為何。選項 (A) 為他們想要遠離家務；選項 (B) 為他們不喜歡為人母；選項 (C) 為他們可以在個人和經濟上獨立；選項 (D) 為他們在職場上比在家中更快樂。答案可見內文第一段最後一句，選擇 (C)。

❷ 此題詢問的是選項中的哪個單字無法與其他單字相互替換。選項 (A) 為社交活動；選項 (B) 為社交聚會；選項 (C) 為社交集會；選項 (D) 為社群。答案為 (D)。可以注意到此篇文章利用了許多稍微不同的字來傳達一樣的意思。

補充單字

☆ 1. hobby	n.	嗜好
☆ 2. important	adj.	重要的
☆ 3. prefer	v.	更喜歡
☆ 4. company	n.	公司
☆ 5. invite	v.	邀請
☆ 6. available	adj.	可得到的

Me Before You
《我就要你好好的》

聽力測驗 🎧 Track 039

在學習英文的過程中，「聽」可能是最直接的第一線接觸，也可能是大家最想要快速習得的能力。現在，就讓我們來熟悉各種英文情境，提升自己的英文臨場感吧！

( ) 1. Who is the writer of *Me Before You*?
    (A) Louisa Clark   (B) Will Traynor
    (C) Jojo Moyes   (D) New York Times

( ) 2. Does the book *Me Before You* sell well?
    (A) Yes.   (B) No.
    (C) So-so.   (D) Poorly.

( ) 3. What happened to Will after a traffic accident?
    (A) He recovered well.
    (B) He developed quadriplegia.
    (C) He became very active.
    (D) He got married.

( ) 4. Why did Louisa take Will on outings?
    (A) to have free meals
    (B) to obey Will's mother
    (C) to use up his money
    (D) to show him that his life was still worth living

( ) 5. What was Will's final wish for Louisa?
    (A) to pursue her dreams
    (B) to forgive him
    (C) to continue being a caretaker
    (D) to forget him

Level 1
Level 2
Level 3
Level 4
Level 5
Level 6

 **閱讀測驗**

剛剛的聽力測驗是否因為答題不順而感到遺憾？或是覺得自己有某些地方掌握地不夠好？現在就讓我們來直接「看」剛剛的聽力測驗，並透過後面的閱讀測驗來補齊聽力上的不足，同時考驗自己的閱讀能力吧！

Me me Before You is a romance novel written by Jojo Moyes, an English novelist and screenwriter. The book was first published in the UK and became a *New York Times* **bestseller**[1] in 2016. In the book, the twenty-six-year-old girl, Louisa Clark, is an Average Jane from a small town in England. She worked at a local cafe until its owner **abruptly**[2] shut the place down. Bummed, she goes to the Job Centre until she lands a job as a caretaker for Will Traynor, a wealthy and charming young man who developed **quadriplegia**[3] after he was hit by a motorcycle while crossing the street two years ago.

At first, Will is a total jerk, and he makes Louisa's job a difficult task. As time goes by, he becomes more open-minded to Louisa, and their relationship grows closer and closer. Later, she **overhears**[4] Will's mother and sister talking about his attempted suicide. To show him that life is still worth living, Louisa begins to take Will out on outings. They travel to Mauritius, a small island off the coast of Africa. On the final night before returning home, Louisa declares her love for him. Although he also loves her, he tells her that he will follow through with his plans—traveling to Dignitas, which is a facility in Switzerland that provides assisted suicide.

Furious and hurt, Louisa ignores Will when they return home, and she resigns as his caretaker. Eventually, Louisa **relents**[5] and makes it in time to share Will's final moments with him at Dignitas. Will leaves Louisa a considerable amount of money so she can go back to school and pursue her dreams.

【Question】

(   ) 1. At first, what was Will's attitude towards Louisa?
         (A) friendly   (B) bitter
         (C) considerate   (D) affectionate

(   ) 2. In the end, how did Louisa respond to Will's choice?
         (A) She could never forgive him.
         (B) She couldn't let go.
         (C) She respected his decision.
         (D) She hated him forever.

【文章中譯】

《我就要你好好的》是英國小說家兼電影編劇家喬喬‧莫伊絲的浪漫小說，該書在英國首度出版，於 2016 年登上《紐約時報》的暢銷書。在書中，26 歲的露易莎‧克拉克是來自英格蘭小鎮的平凡姑娘，她本來在當地的小餐館工作，直到老闆突然結束了營業。失望之於，她前往就業中心，並找到了看護威爾‧崔納的工作。威爾是個富有、迷人的年輕人，他在 2 年前過馬路時遭到機車撞上而成全身癱瘓。

一開始，威爾對露易莎的態度很差，讓她工作得很痛苦。隨著日子一天天過去，他的心門逐漸敞開，兩人的關係也越來越親近。隨後，露易莎無意間聽到威爾的母親和妹妹討論到他曾經企圖自殺。為了讓威爾感受他仍值得活下去，露易莎開始帶他出遊。他們到了非洲離岸的小島模里西斯，在旅程的最後一天，露易莎也向威爾表達了愛意。不過，雖然威爾也愛著她，但他告訴露易莎他仍將按照原訂計畫，前往瑞士名為「尊嚴」的安樂死機構。

露易莎既生氣又受傷，回程對威爾不予理會，並辭去了看護的工作。最終，露易莎態度軟化了，她及時趕到「尊嚴」，並陪伴威爾度過死前的時刻。威爾最後留下一筆龐大的錢給露易莎，讓她能回到校園進修，追尋她的夢想。

註：自殺不能解決問題，勇敢求救並非弱者。安心專線（0800-788-995）

聽力題目解析

❶ 此題詢問的是《我就要你好好的》的作者是誰。選項 (A) 為露易莎‧克拉克；選項 (B) 為威爾‧崔納；選項 (C) 為喬喬‧莫伊絲；選項 (D) 為《紐約時報》。在錄音檔的第一句即開宗明義指出 *"Me Before You is ... written by Jojo Moyes."* 故答案選(C)。另外，選項 (A)、(B) 分別為小說中的女、男主角，而選項 (D) 是本部小說有登上《紐約時報》的暢銷書排行榜，需注意陷阱。

❷ 此題詢問的是《我就要你好好的》的銷售是否良好。選項 (A) 為是；選項 (B) 為否；選項 (C) 為很普通；選項 (D) 為賣得很差。在錄音檔前段部分即有說 "The book .. became a *New York Times* bestseller in 2016." 本題考的是考生是否知道bestseller暢銷書這個單字的意思，故答案選 (A)。

❸ 此題詢問的是威爾在交通意外後，發生了什麼事。選項 (A) 為他復原良好；選項 (B) 為他全身癱瘓；選項 (C) 為他變得很活躍；選項 (D) 為他結婚了。在錄音檔中前段，我們能聽見 "Will Traynor... developed quadriplegia after he was hit by a motorcycle while crossing the street two years earlier." 本題考的是考生是否知道quadriplegia四肢癱瘓這個單字的意思（quadri-字首是「四」的意思；-plegia字根是「癱瘓」的意思），故答案選(B)。此題也可透過完整內文的理解來排除其它選項。

❹ 此題詢問的是為什麼露易莎要帶威爾出遊。選項 (A) 是為了要吃免費餐點；選項 (B) 是為了遵守威爾媽媽的指示；選項 (C) 是為了用掉威爾的錢；選項 (D) 是為了讓威爾感受他的生命仍值得活下去。錄音檔中段提到露易莎無意間聽說威爾曾企圖自殺，因此 "To show him that life is still worth living, Louisa begins to take Will out on outings." 故答案選 (D)。

❺ 此題詢問威爾對露易莎最終的願望是什麼。選項 (A) 為追尋她的夢想；選項 (B) 為他希望她能饒恕他；選項 (C) 為希望她繼續從事看護工作；

選項 (D) 為希望她忘了他。在錄音檔最後，我們可以得知 "Will leaves Louisa a considerable amount of money so she can go back to school and pursue her dreams." 故答案選(A)，此題可以把握「為什麼」威爾要留一大比錢給她，注意到關鍵 "so" 即可。

閱讀題目解析

❶ 此題詢問的是威爾剛開始對露易莎的態度如何。選項 (A) 為很友善；選項 (B) 為很帶刺；選項 (C) 為很體貼；選項 (D) 為充滿愛意。答案可見內文第二段第一句 "At first, Will is a total jerk, and he makes Louisa's job a difficult task."本題考的是考生是否知道jerk這個單字的意思是混蛋，故答案選 (B)。

❷ 此題詢問的是露易莎最終對威爾的選擇的反應如何。選項 (A) 為她永遠都無法原諒他；選項 (B) 為她對他的選擇無法釋懷；選項 (C) 為她尊重他的決定；選項 (D) 為她永遠都恨他。答案可見文章第三段 "Eventually, Lousia relents and makes it in time to share Will's final moments with him at Dignitas." 可知露易莎最終態度軟化，前去陪他走完最後一程，故答案為 (C)。

補充單字

☆ 1. bestseller	n.	暢銷書
☆ 2. abruptly	adv.	突然地
☆ 3. quadriplegia	n.	全身癱瘓
☆ 4. overhear	v.	無意中聽到
☆ 5. relent	v.	軟化；緩和
☆ 6. lesson	n.	課

Fantastic Beasts and Where to Find Them

《怪獸與牠們的產地》

Level 1
Level 2
Level 3
Level 4
Level 5
Level 6

聽力測驗 🎧 Track 040

在學習英文的過程中，「聽」可能是最直接的第一線接觸，也可能是大家最想要快速習得的能力。現在，就讓我們來熟悉各種英文情境，提升自己的英文臨場感吧！

( ) 1. Who is the target audience of *Fantastic Beasts and Where to Find Them*?
    (A) teenagers   (B) toddlers
    (C) children   (D) adults

( ) 2. Who is the screenwriter of the movie?
    (A) J.R.R. Tolkien   (B) J. K. Rowling
    (C) C. S. Lewis   (D) Charles Dickens

( ) 3. To which city did the wizard Newt Scamander travel?
    (A) New York City   (B) Oklahoma City
    (C) Houston   (D) Phoenix

( ) 4. What's the real identity of the Director of Magical Security?
    (A) an ordinary person   (B) a police officer
    (C) a dangerous Dark Wizard   (D) a baker

( ) 5. What did Newt Scamander promise Tina?
    (A) He will never travel in the US.
    (B) He will return to New York City.
    (C) He will not see her again.
    (D) He will miss her.

 **閱讀測驗**

剛剛的聽力測驗是否因為答題不順而感到遺憾？或是覺得自己有某些地方掌握地不夠好？現在就讓我們來直接「看」剛剛的聽力測驗，並透過後面的閱讀測驗來補齊聽力上的不足，同時考驗自己的閱讀能力吧！

Fantastic Beasts and Where to Find Them, a screenplay by J. K. Rowling, is a **prequel**[1] to the *Harry Potter* movies. Unlike the *Potter* movies which target mainly at a younger audience, *Fantastic Beasts* is for adult audience.

The story begins with the arrival of wizard Newt Scamander in the 1926 New York. After getting through customs and immigration, he travels through New York City, unaware that he is being secretly investigated by a witch, Tina, who has been dismissed from her position. Meanwhile, when a Niffler escapes from Newt's magically-expanded suitcase, he meets Jacob, an **aspiring**[2] baker. They **unwittingly**[3] swap suitcases, resulting in the escape of several of the beasts that Newt contains in his suitcase.

Credence, an abused child pressured by his foster mother to be "normal," is pushed to a breaking point that leads him to **manifest**[4] an Obscurus, which causes **massive**[5] destruction throughout the city. Newt and the Director of Magical Security both pursue Obscurus and try to control it, but the director turns out to be Gellert Grindelwald, a powerful and dangerous Dark Wizard. Over a turn of events, these characters bond with each other in different ways. The story ends with Grindelwald being taken away, and Newt gets on a boat, promising to return to give Tina a copy of his book on beasts in person.

【Question】

(　　) 1. What happened after Newt and Jacob unwittingly swap each other's suitcases?
　　　(A) Newt was arrested.
　　　(B) Jacob got a lot of money from Newt's suitcase.

(C) Tina coveted Newt's suitcase.

(D) Several of the beasts that Newt conceals in his suitcase escaped.

( ) 2. What do we know about Credence's foster mother?

(A) She is abusive.

(B) She is kind.

(C) She is open-minded.

(D) She is quiet.

【文章中譯】

《怪獸與牠們的產地》是 J.K. 羅琳所撰寫的電影劇本，它是哈利 · 波特系列電影的前傳。哈利 · 波特電影主要是鎖定年輕的觀眾，《怪物》的觀眾群是成人。

英國巫師紐特 · 斯卡曼德於 1926 年來到紐約市，在通過海關後，他在紐約市旅遊，全然不知自己已被一位遭撤職的正氣師（黑巫師獵人）蒂娜所監視。同時，當他的玻璃獸從魔法皮箱逃出來時，他遇見了立志當麵包師傅的雅各。他們在不知情的情況下互換了皮箱，導致許多紐特藏在皮箱裡的怪獸跑了出來。

魁登斯是名受虐兒，被養母要求應表現得「正常」，導致他情緒壓抑到爆發點，盛怒下釋放出了闇黑怨靈，並造成紐約市大規模的破壞。紐特和魔法安全部主任都在追緝闇黑怨靈並試圖控制它，但魔法安全部主任的真實身分居然是極為強大又危險的黑魔王蓋瑞 · 葛林戴華德。在一連串的事件之後，這些角色在不同層面上產生了連結，故事的結局是葛林戴華德最後被拘捕，而紐特則登上船，並承諾未來將親自送給蒂娜他所寫有關怪獸的著作。

聽力題目解析

❶ 此題詢問的是《怪獸與牠們的產地》鎖定的觀眾群為何者。選項 (A) 為青少年；選項 (B) 為幼兒；選項 (C) 為兒童；選項 (D) 為成人。錄音檔的前段即明確指出 "Unlike the *Potter* movies … *Fantastic Beasts* is for an adult audience." 故答案選 (D)，此題若沒有把握 "adult" 此單字，也可用 "unlike … young" 來反推。

❷ 此題詢問的是《怪獸與牠們的產地》的電影編劇。選項 (A) 為 J.R.R.托爾金；選項 (B) 為J.K. 羅琳；選項 (C) 為 C‧S 路易斯；選項 (D) 為狄更斯。在錄音檔前段部分即有說明 "*Fantastic Beasts and Where to Find Them*, a screenplay by J. K. Rowling ...", 本題考的是考生是否知道a screenplay by J. K. Rowling是同位語，用來修飾前面的*Fantastic Beasts and Where to Find Them*，故答案選(B)，聆聽時需特別注意。另外，(A)、(B)、(D) 皆是西方著名的文學巨擘。

❸ 此題詢問的是巫師紐特‧斯卡曼德到了哪個城市旅行。選項 (A) 為紐約市；選項 (B) 為奧克拉荷馬市；選項 (C) 為休士頓；選項 (D) 為鳳凰城。錄音檔中段提到 "After getting through customs and immigration, he travels through New York City."故答案選 (A)，此題僅需仔細聆聽注意細節。

❹ 此題詢問的是魔法安全部主任的真實身分。選項 (A) 為普通人；選項 (B) 為警察；選項 (C) 為危險的黑魔王；選項 (D) 為麵包師傅。錄音檔後段有提到 "... the director turns out to be Gellert Grindelwald, a powerful and dangerous Dark Wizard."本題也是考 "a powerful and dangerous Dark Wizard" 做為同位語的用法，用來修飾前面的蓋瑞‧葛林戴華德（Gellert Grindelwald），故答案選 (C)。

❺ 此題詢問紐特‧斯卡曼德承諾蒂娜什麼事。選項 (A) 為他再也不會到美國旅遊；選項 (B) 為他將再回到紐約；選項 (C) 為他將不會再見到她；選項 (D) 為他將想念她。根據錄音檔最後，我們可以得知 "Newt

... promising to return to give Tina a copy of his book on beasts in person." 故答案選(B)。

閱讀題目解析

❶ 此題詢問的是紐特和雅各在不知情的情況下互換了彼此的皮箱，結果發生了什麼事。選項 (A) 為紐特被逮捕了；選項 (B) 為雅各從紐特的皮箱得到很多錢；選項 (C) 為蒂娜覷覷著紐特的皮箱；選項 (D) 為許多紐特藏在皮箱裡的怪獸跑出來了。答案可見內文第二段最後一句，本題考的是考生是否知道result in這個片語的意思是「導致」，故答案選 (D)。

❷ 此題詢問的是我們可以從文章中得知魁登斯的養母是什麼樣的人。選項 (A) 為她有虐待傾向；選項 (B) 為她很慈祥；選項 (C) 為她的心胸開闊；選項 (D) 為她很安靜。答案可見第三段第一句 "Credence, an abused child pressured by his foster mother to be normal ..." 可知養母對他並不包容與關愛，故答案為 (A)。

補充單字

☆ 1. prequal	n.	前傳
☆ 2. aspiring	adj.	有抱負的；有志氣的
☆ 3. unwittingly	adv.	不知情地；無意地
☆ 4. manifest	v.	出現；顯露
☆ 5. massive	v.	大規模的

Level 1
Level 2
Level 3
Level 4
Level 5
Level 6

Level 3

持續精進 × 挑戰自我

Level 3
01 Different Ways to Treat Your Guests

英美待客的差異

聽力測驗 Track 041

在學習英文的過程中，「聽」可能是最直接的第一線接觸，也可能是大家最想要快速習得的能力。現在，就讓我們來熟悉各種英文情境，提升自己的英文臨場感吧！

(   ) 1 .In the article, the English are friendly and _____.
      (A) warm   (B) cruel
      (C) cold   (D) arrogant

(   ) 2. Below are gifts mentioned in the article, except for _____?
      (A) chocolate   (B) wine
      (C) flowers   (D) pet

(   ) 3. Americans like to treat guests _____.
      (A) in the open air
      (B) in the hotel
      (C) in restaurants
      (D) at home

(   ) 4. What does the word "prior" mean in the article?
      (A) in advance   (B) later
      (C) after   (D) never

(   ) 5. What does the word "appreciation" mean in the article?
      (A) dislike   (B) argument
      (C) grateful   (D) anger

剛剛的聽力測驗是否因為答題不順而感到遺憾？或是覺得自己有某些地方掌握地不夠好？現在就讓我們來直接「看」剛剛的聽力測驗，並透過後面的閱讀測驗來補齊聽力上的不足，同時考驗自己的閱讀能力吧！

American and British people have different cultures, for example, life styles, eating habits, hobbies and others. Even the ways people treat their guests are different as well.

The English are friendly and warm. They are honest, kind and have a certain sense of **humor**[1]. The British often invite guests to their home, but unless you are familiar with your friends, it is not polite to visit a family without even a phone call. In other words, a sudden visit isn't appropriate. If a person has accepted an invitation to dine at another's home, it will be seen as a very formal appointment. If you can't make it to the appointment on time, it will be considered impolite. If you really want to cancel the appointment, you must inform the host beforehand. To **avoid**[2] **embarrassment**[3], you must let the host know in advance about the food you don't eat. No matter if you are only staying for a meal or you will be staying longer, it's a custom to bring a gift, such as a bunch of flowers, **chocolates**[4] or a bottle of wine. When you live with a British family, you should be **cautious**[5] at any time. You should be on time for dinners, if there is a need for you to miss a meal, you should give your host a prior notice. You should keep the room clean. Let the owner know if you have to go home late, so that they do not worry about you. Usually when you volunteer to do housework, the host will reject but still be grateful.

What about the Americans? They like to treat guests at home rather than go to a restaurant as the Americans think that this is more cordial and friendly. There are two ways to serve dinner at home. A family style is when the guests and the host sit at a rectangular dining table, and the dishes are served in plates which pass around to one another. The other is that the host and hostess serve the guests with food and you can ask for the dishes you want. After you stay overnight or spend a weekend in the host's place, you should send a short letter to show your appreciation.

As a guest of an American family, you needn't always bring gifts. If you do, you should be careful not to make the other guests embarrassed. You can bring a bouquet of flowers for the hostess or a bottle of wine for the host. At a private banquet, the best gift is a friendship toast, which is a **priceless**[6] gift.

【Question】

( ) 1. Which of the following word is not used to describe British people in the article?
(A) have a certain sense of humor   (B) kind
(C) friendly   (D) ambitious

( ) 2. Which of the following statement is incorrect according to the article?
(A) Going to a restaurant is considered more heart-warming for Americans.
(B) The English may be viewed as having more rules than Americans do.
(C) Offering to help with housework may win you a good impression when you live with a British family.
(D) Getting up to grab the food you need is not normal when it comes to dining with an American family.

【文章中譯】

美國人與英國人擁有不同的文化，例如：生活方式、飲食習慣、嗜好等，就連待客之道也有所不同。

英國人不僅友好，也很熱情。英國人誠實、厚道，也不乏幽默感。英國人經常在家裡待客，但是，除非你與朋友非常熟絡，否則事先不撥打電話，問清楚是否方便作客而突然拜訪是不合適的。如果某人邀請你到家裡作客，那是很正式的約會。如果接受後又不出席將被認為是不禮貌的，如果你非得取消邀請，一定要事先通知主人。如果有些東西自己不吃，一定要事先讓主人知道，以免尷尬。不管是僅僅吃一頓飯還是更久的作客，習慣上都要給主人帶件小禮物，比如鮮花、巧克力或一瓶酒。如果你與一戶英國家庭住在一起，隨時都要謹言慎行。做到準時吃飯，如果需要取消一頓飯，一定事先通知主人。保持房間整潔；讓主人知道你外出要很晚回家，他們才不會為你擔心；如果你主動幫忙做家事，主人通常會拒絕，但仍會表示由衷的感謝。

美國人喜歡在家宴請客人，而不是去餐廳吃飯，因為美國人認為這麼做更加親切與友善。美國人在家請客一般有兩種方式：一種是家庭式，客人與主人圍坐在長方飯桌旁，食物則裝在盤子裡，依序傳給每個人；或是由男女主人依序為每人裝食物，每個人需要什麼就拿什麼。留下來過夜或是到主人家共渡週末後，應隨後寄一封簡短的感謝信。到美國人家裡作客，並不一定帶禮物去，因此送禮時應慎重，才不會讓其他客人感到尷尬。可以為女主人帶一束鮮花，也可以送主人一瓶酒。在家宴中最能使主人高興的禮物是充滿友誼的祝酒詞，這種禮物是無價之寶。

聽力題目解析

❶ 此題詢問的是根據內文，英國人友善又如何。選項 (A) 為溫暖的；選項 (B) 為殘忍的；選項 (C) 為冷淡的；選項 (D) 為傲慢的。在錄音檔的開頭不久之後，我們即可聽見與題目相近的陳述句，答案為 (A)，此選項也較符合內文邏輯。

❷ 此題詢問的是選項中的禮物何者沒有出現在內文中。選項 (A) 為巧克力；選項 (B) 為酒；選項 (C) 為花；選項 (D) 為寵物。答案為 (D)，此題建議先看過題目，以便快速掌握；若疏忽掉細節，也可以推論出寵物為較不合理之選項。

❸ 此題詢問的是美國人喜歡在何處接待客人。選項 (A) 為在露天的場所；選項 (B) 為在旅館中；選項 (C) 為在餐廳裡；選項 (D) 為在家裡。根據錄音檔，我們可以在針對英國人的討論之後，聽見 "What about the Americans? They like to treat guests at home …"，故答案為 (D)。

❹ 此題詢問的是單字 "prior" 之意。選項 (A) 為事先的；選項 (B) 為遲的；選項 (C) 為之後的；選項 (D) 為絕不。根據錄音檔，此單字出現在 "you should give your host a prior notice" 之句子裡，按照上下文，可推答案為 (A)，意及「你應該要事先通知主人」。

❺ 此題詢問的是單字 "appreciation" 之意。選項 (A) 為不喜歡；選項 (B) 為爭論；選項 (C) 為感激的；選項 (D) 為憤怒。根據錄音檔，此單字出現在 "you should send a short letter to show your appreciation"，且此句出現在「留下來過夜或是到主人家共渡週末後」，故答案為 (C)，在接受款待之後表達感謝。

閱讀題目解析

❶ 此題詢問的是選項中哪一個單字沒有被用來形容英國人。選項 (A) 為具有一定程度的幽默感；選項 (B) 為友好的；選項 (C) 為善意的；選項 (D) 為有野心的。答案可詳見內文第二段開頭，選 (D)。

❷ 此題詢問的是選項中根據內文所做之陳述何者是不正確的。選項 (A) 為對美國人來説，去餐廳待客比較溫暖人心；選項 (B) 為與美國人相比，英國人可能會被視為擁有較多規矩；選項 (C) 為當你和英國家庭同住時，主動提議幫忙做家事可能會替你建立好印象；選項 (D) 為與美國家庭用餐時，自己起身拿食物是不正常的。答案為 (A)，可詳見內文最後一段，美國人認為在家宴客才是更加親切與友善的。

補充單字

☆ 1. humor	n.	幽默感
☆ 2. avoid	v.	避免
☆ 3. embarrassment	n.	尷尬
☆ 4. chocolate	n.	巧克力
☆ 5. cautious	adj.	謹慎的
☆ 6. priceless	adj.	無價的

Queen of Pop — Lady Gaga
女神卡卡

聽力測驗 🎧 Track 042

在學習英文的過程中，「聽」可能是最直接的第一線接觸，也可能是大家最想要快速習得的能力。現在，就讓我們來熟悉各種英文情境，提升自己的英文臨場感吧！

(   ) 1. What do people think about Lady Gaga's fashion?
     (A) eccentric   (B) graceful
     (C) practical   (D) inexpensive

(   ) 2. What nickname does Lady Gaga call her fans?
     (A) sweethearts   (B) sugar
     (C) little Monsters   (D) cuties

(   ) 3. Where does Lady Gaga usually communicate with her fans?
     (A) at grocery stores
     (B) on her community website
     (C) in the supermarket
     (D) in city halls

(   ) 4. What is Lady Gaga also known for?
     (A) clothes business   (B) organic cosmetics
     (C) gym business   (D) philanthropic work

(   ) 5. What is Lady Gaga's non-profit organization called?
     (A) Born This Way Foundation
     (B) Band-aide
     (C) Fulbright Foundation
     (D) Born Free

 **閱讀測驗**

剛剛的聽力測驗是否因為答題不順而感到遺憾？或是覺得自己有某些地方掌握地不夠好？現在就讓我們來直接「看」剛剛的聽力測驗，並透過後面的閱讀測驗來補齊聽力上的不足，同時考驗自己的閱讀能力吧！

For her fans, Lady Gaga is a talented singer, songwriter, and actress. For others, she is a controversial singer with her somewhat **eccentric**[1] fashion. She rose from a quirky girl playing in small clubs in New York City to a celebrity appearing on the list of Forbes in 2012, and she has also graced the cover of Time magazine's 100 Most Influential People. Her rise to popularity is simply **phenomenal**[2]. However, is it sheer luck, or is there truly something unique about her?

Although Lady Gaga is not everyone's cup of tea, she certainly is devoted to her fans, the base of which has now reached millions. She **dubs**[3] her fans "Little Monsters," and she shows concerns about them at every concert. To interact with her fans, she even has a website dedicated entirely to them. This allows fans from all over the world to connect and share their passion about her. In addition, she spends a considerable amount of time on her community site, replying messages personally to her fans and **engaging**[4] in genuine conversations with them.

Apart from her music career, Lady Gaga is known for her **philanthropic**[5] work and social activism. She has raised money for areas that have been hit by natural disasters in order to help them rebuild their homeland, and she also fought hard for LGBT right. After the suicide of her fan, Jamey Rodemeyer, an American gay teenager who was severely bullied because of his sexuality, Lady Gaga established a non-profit organization, Born This Way Foundation, to help empower young people and combat bullying in every form.

【Question】

( ) 1. How does Lady Gaga treat her fans?
    (A) with negligence   (B) with much respect
    (C) with ignorance   (D) with gourmet food

( ) 2. Why did Lady Gaga's fan, Jamey Rodemeyer, commit suicide?
    (A) He was too crazy about Lady Gaga.
    (B) He was severely bullied for his gay identity.
    (C) He wanted to get Lady Gaga's attention.
    (D) He wanted to be famous.

【文章中譯】

對於女神卡卡的粉絲來說,她是天賦異稟的歌手、作曲家、女演員。對有些人來說,她則是一位頗具爭議性、時尚品味有點搞怪的歌手。這位古靈精怪的女孩從紐約的小俱樂部駐唱發跡,到出現在 2012 年富比士的名人榜單上,甚至也成為了美國時代雜誌所列之全球 100 位最具影響力的人物之一。她大受歡迎的程度簡直到了驚人的地步。然而,這是她運氣好,還是她真有什麼獨到之處?

雖然不是每個人都喜歡女神卡卡,不過她對粉絲的確好得沒話說,現在她的粉絲群已達到數百萬人了。她暱稱粉絲們為「小怪獸」,並在每場演唱會向他們表達關心。為了與粉絲互動,她還有為歌迷打造的專屬網站,世界各地的粉絲可以在這個平台上互連並分享他們對於這位流行歌星的熱愛。此外,女神卡卡也花了很多時間在這個社群網站,親自回覆訊息給歌迷,並誠摯地與他們對話。

除了她的歌唱事業,女神卡卡也因從事慈善事業和社會運動而廣為人知。她為多個遭到天災襲擊的地區募款重建,並為多元性別族群爭取他們的權益。在她的一位美國粉絲傑米‧羅德梅耶因其同性戀傾向不堪嚴重霸凌最後自殺後,她成立了一個「天生完美基金會」非營利機構,旨在賦予年輕人力量並對抗霸凌。

註：LGBT 是由女同性戀 lesbian、男同戀者 gay、雙性戀者 bisexual 與跨性別者transgender 的英文首字母縮寫而成。

聽力題目解析

❶ 此題詢問的是人們怎麼看待女神卡卡的時尚品味。選項 (A) 為搞怪的；選項 (B) 為優雅的；選項 (C) 為實用的；選項 (D) 為不奢華的。在錄音檔的前段即明確指出 "For some, she is a controversial singer with her somewhat eccentric fashion." 本題考的是考生是否知道eccentric的意思，故答案選 (A)。
（補充：字首ex- 遠離；字根centric中心的：遠離中心的，意即古怪的。）

❷ 此題詢問的是女神卡卡對粉絲的暱稱是什麼。選項 (A) 為甜心；選項 (B) 為糖糖；選項 (C) 為小怪物；選項 (D) 為可人兒。錄音檔中段有說明 "She dubbed her fans 'Little Monsters.' "故答案選 (C)，此答案只出現一次，需注意題型。

❸ 此題詢問的是女神卡卡通常在哪裡跟粉絲對話。選項 (A) 為雜貨店；選項 (B) 為她的社群網站；選項 (C) 為超市；選項 (D) 為市政大廳。在錄音檔中段，我們可以得知 "To interact with her fans, she has a website devoted entirely to them."可知她是透過網站經營與粉絲的關係，故答案選 (B)，若此部分沒有聽見，也可以掌握 "fans from all over the world" 和 "replying messages in person" 來推測。

❹ 此題詢問的是女神卡卡也以什麼聞名。選項 (A) 為服飾業；選項 (B) 為有機化妝品；選項 (C) 為健身事業；選項 (D) 為慈善事業。在錄音檔中後段提到 "Apart from ... is known for her philanthropic work and social activism."可知她除了歌唱事業，也熱心公益和社會運動，故答案選 (D)。而選項(A)、(B)、(C)三種產業，她都沒有從事，也並未出現在內文中。

❺ 此題詢問女神卡卡的非營利組織名稱為何。選項 (A) 為天生完美；選項 (B) 為 OK繃；選項 (C) 為傅爾布萊特基金會；選項 (D) 為生而自由。錄音檔最後即告訴我們答案為 (B)，若有先看過題目便能在內文介紹傑米·羅德梅耶後特別注意。

閱讀題目解析

❶ 此題詢問的是女神卡卡用什麼態度對待她的粉絲。選項 (A) 為疏忽；選項 (B) 為尊重；選項 (C) 為無知；選項 (D) 為美食。答案可見內文第二段最後一句，她 "personally replying messages to her fans and engaging in genuine conversations"，以及第三段提到 "After the suicide of her fan Jamey Rodemeyer ... Lady Gaga established a non-profit organization, Born This Way Foundation ..." 由此可知答案為 (B)。

❷ 此題詢問的是為什麼女神卡卡的粉絲傑米·羅德梅耶自殺。選項 (A) 為他對女神卡卡太瘋狂著迷；選項 (B) 為他因同性戀的身分而慘遭霸凌；選項 (C) 為他想藉此引起女神卡卡對他的注意；選項 (D) 為他想出名。答案可見內文第三段 "... the suicide of her fan, Jamey Rodemeyer, an American gay teenager who was severed bullied because of his sexuality..." 此處以同位語 her fan Jamey Rodemeyer 來說明後面 an American gay teenager who was severed bullied because of his sexuality，故答案為 (B)。

補充單字

☆ 1.	eccentric	**adj.**	古怪的
☆ 2.	phenomenal	**adj.**	非凡的；驚人的
☆ 3.	dub	**v.**	暱稱
☆ 4.	engage	**v.**	參與
☆ 5.	philanthropic	**adj.**	慈善的

The British Media
英國媒體

Level 3
03

聽力測驗 🎧 Track 043

在學習英文的過程中，「聽」可能是最直接的第一線接觸，也可能是大家最想要快速習得的能力。現在，就讓我們來熟悉各種英文情境，提升自己的英文臨場感吧！

(   ) 1. The article is about _____.
- (A) British singer
- (B) British actor
- (C) British Prime Minister
- (D) British media

(   ) 2. The Times was established by John Walter in _____.
- (A) 1785   (B) 1789
- (C) 1875   (D) 1788

(   ) 3. Which of the following is not true?
- (A) Of all the media, newspaper has the longest history.
- (B) The Times published in the United States is the original "Times" newspaper.
- (C) The Times was established by John Walter.
- (D) The Times was the first paper to have war correspondents

(   ) 4. Which of the following isn't the distinguish features of penny press?
- (A) expensive price
- (B) cheaper price
- (C) compact size
- (D) interesting stories

 閱讀測驗

剛剛的聽力測驗是否因為答題不順而感到遺憾？或是覺得自己有某些地方掌握地不夠好？現在就讓我們來直接「看」剛剛的聽力測驗，並透過後面的閱讀測驗來補齊聽力上的不足，同時考驗自己的閱讀能力吧！

Media is important to the public. Newspapers, **broadcasts**[1], and television play an important role in delivering news and advancing communication and culture. Of them all, newspaper has the longest history and remains a large effect to the public.

The word "Times" has been used in quite some newspapers all around the world. For most people, New York Times and The Times of India are the common known papers when mentioning. However, The Times published in the United Kingdom is the original "Times" newspaper. It is one of the oldest and most influential papers in Britain. Among the papers in Britain, The Times is known to be one of the greatest papers along with The Guardian and The Daily Telegraph.

The Times was established by John Walter in 1785. The paper was first named The Daily Universal Register, and renamed in 1788. The title of the paper was mistakenly translated in Chinese due to its similar pronunciation to the River Thames. However, the paper has no relationship with the river at all. To differentiate from the others, it is sometimes referred to The London Times or The Times of London by foreigners. In 1803, John Walter handed his business to his son who has the same name. The paper then started to obtain news from the Continent, especially France. It not only featured politic and financial news but also covered the fields of science, art and **literature**[2]. The wealthy income made The Times the first paper to have war **correspondents**[3] and provide readers with the latest war news.

Objectivity is a significant principle of newspapers, and The Times has always held an independent standpoint. With its **broadsheet**[4] format and neat

typesetting[5,] by merely holding The Times on hand allowed one to feel knowledgeable. Unfortunately, the rise of the penny press had cause great sufferings for The Times. Penny press attracted a wider reader by printed in compact size, selling in cheaper price and human interest stories. In 1981, The Times was **purchased**[6] by Australian Rupert Murdoch who also bought The Sun. With new printing/editing technology, The Times made a great change, regaining a high circulation. In 2004, the broadsheet edition of The Times no longer exists since it decided to print in compact size in demand of the market. With the advance of the Internet, readers all around the world can now read the news through the Internet.

【Question】

(　　) 1. Which of the following newspaper was also purchased by Murdoch?
    (A) The Sun   (B) The New York Times
    (C) The Daily Telegraph   (D) The Times of India

(　　) 2. Which can we infer from the article?
    (A) Broadsheet is useless when it comes to reading newspaper.
    (B) Sticking to objectivity may be the main reason why The Times began to print in compact size.
    (C) The Times covers a wide range of fields.
    (D) War correspondents of the Times were sponsored by the government.

【文章中譯】

媒體對大眾的影響深遠，透過報章雜誌、電台廣播、電視，媒體不僅能傳播訊息，也扮演著推動溝通與文化的重要角色。而新聞報紙可謂眾多傳播媒體中，歷史較為悠久、流傳廣泛的媒介。

提到報章，大多數人的腦海會浮現《紐約時報》、《印度時報》等名稱中帶有「時代」字眼的報章，然而第一張以「時代」命名的報章，卻是出現在英國；而每日發行的英國《泰晤士報》，可說是英國歷史最悠久、最具影響力的報紙之一。在眾多新聞報章中，《泰晤士報》與《衛報》、《每日電訊報》同為英國三大報章。

《泰晤士報》於 1785 年創立，創始人約翰華爾特開始將之命名為《世鑒日報》，並於 1788年改名為《泰晤士報》。關於名稱，有一小插曲，此報與泰晤士河毫無關聯，只因發音相近的緣故而被誤譯為《泰晤士報》，所以後來有些人稱之為《倫敦時報》。1803 年與父親同名的華爾特接手報社後，《泰晤士報》報導內容擴及歐洲地區，尤其是法國。不僅涉獵政治、經濟的報導，《泰晤士報》對於科學、藝術、文學等領域的報導也不遺餘力。優厚的利潤致使《泰晤士報》得以成為第一家擁有駐戰地記者的報社，讓讀者得以即刻掌握戰地狀況。

對報章媒體來說，維持報導的客觀性是一大宗旨，而《泰晤士報》的立場也不受他人影響，始終保持獨立。其大開版與嚴謹的排版，穩健的象徵，讓閱讀者拿在手上似乎多了一份知識氣息。然而，隨著後來崛起的小報充斥著市場，《泰晤士報》的生存與發展嚴重受到打擊。小報的開版小、價格較為廉價，且內容多了偏大眾化的題材，吸引不少讀者。1981 年，來自澳洲的魯本‧梅鐸收購了《泰晤士報》與《太陽報》。在新的印刷／編輯技術的影響下，《泰晤士報》展現了全新風貌，挽回了萎靡許久的銷售量。為了因應市場的需求，《泰晤士報》於 2004 年改成普遍的小開版，傳統的大開版至此走入歷史。隨著網路的發達，現在只要透過網路即可上網閱讀《泰晤士報》。

聽力題目解析

❶ 此題詢問的是文章的討論對象。選項 (A) 為英國歌手；選項 (B) 為英國男演員；選項 (C) 為英國首相；選項 (D) 為英國媒體。錄音檔的一開始即告訴我們答案，答案為 (D)。

❷ 此題詢問的是約翰華爾特創辦《泰晤士報》的年份。答案為 (A) 1785，此種選擇年份的題型僅能注意細節，認真聆聽，建議先看過題目及選項以便掌握。

❸ 此題要求我們選出陳述不正確的選項。選項 (A) 為在所有媒體中，報紙的歷史最為悠久；選項 (B) 為在美國出版的名稱有 "Times" 之報紙是 "Times" 系列的始祖；選項 (C) 為《泰晤士報》是由約翰華爾特所創立；選項 (D) 為《泰晤士報》是第一份擁有戰地記者的報紙。答案

為 (B)，我們可以就音檔的探討內容得知，The Times published in the United Kingdom is the original "Times" newspaper.，而非選項中的 The United States。此題難度較高，為綜合理解題，若能先看過選項會較好拿分。

④ 此題詢問的是選項何者不是小報的特徵。選項 (A) 為昂貴的價格；選項 (B) 為便宜的價格；選項 (C) 為開版小；選項 (D) 為有趣的故事。在錄音檔最後，我們可以聽見 cheaper price此關鍵字，故 (A) 為錯誤之選項。若疏忽細節，我們也可以透過內文推斷，若小報價格昂貴，那麼其應難以在最後完全取代大開版。

閱讀題目解析

① 此題詢問的是選項何者同時也被梅鐸收購。可見內文最後一段，選擇 (A)。

② 此題詢問的是我們可以從文章中推論出哪一個選項。選項 (A) 為大開版就讀報來說沒有用處；選項 (B) 為堅守客觀性可能是《泰晤士報》決定開始印小開版的原因；選項 (C) 為《泰晤士報》的內容涵蓋了多種領域；選項 (D) 為《泰晤士報》的戰地記者是由政府所資助的。答案可見內文第三段，選擇 (C)；此題需注意選項 (B)，雖然堅守客觀性也是《泰晤士報》的特色之一，但是這並不是大開版走入歷史的原因，決定開始印小開版是為因應市場需求。

補充單字

☆ 1. broadcast	n.	廣播
☆ 2. literature	n.	文學
☆ 3. correspondent	n.	記者
☆ 4. broadsheet	n.	大開版的
☆ 5. typesetting	n.	排版
☆ 6. purchase	v.	購買

Different Eating Habits
不同的飲食習慣

🎧**聽力測驗** 🎧Track 044

在學習英文的過程中，「聽」可能是最直接的第一線接觸，也可能是大家最想要快速習得的能力。現在，就讓我們來熟悉各種英文情境，提升自己的英文臨場感吧！

( ) 1. The article talks about _____.
　　(A) hobbies　　　　　　(B) relationship
　　(C) eating habits　　　(D) sports

( ) 2. Which of the following is not Eastern food?
　　(A) rice　　　　　　　(B) porridge
　　(C) pasta　　　　　　(D) tofu

( ) 3 Which of the following belongs to Japanese food?
　　(A) udon　　　　　　(B) pizza
　　(C) sandwiches　　　(D) French fries

( ) 4. Which of the following is not western food?
　　(A) burger　　　　　(B) hot dogs
　　(C) curry　　　　　(D) omelet

( ) 5. Which of the following belongs to French food?
　　(A) dumpling
　　(B) croissant
　　(C) buckwheat noodle
　　(D) baked beans

233

 **閱讀測驗**

剛剛的聽力測驗是否因為答題不順而感到遺憾？或是覺得自己有某些地方掌握地不夠好？現在就讓我們來直接「看」剛剛的聽力測驗，並透過後面的閱讀測驗來補齊聽力上的不足，同時考驗自己的閱讀能力吧！

Eating **habits**[1] are different all around the world. If you have a chance to travel to another country, it's important to know other people's eating habits. When in Rome, do as the Romans do.

Rice is Eastern people's main food. Asians eat rice almost every day, even in the morning. Some elder people prefer having porridge for breakfast because porridge is easy to digest. Soybean milk and steamed buns are traditional Chinese breakfast. For Chinese, rice is **served**[2] with some other dishes, such as vegetables, tofu, poultry, or eggs. Other than rice, Chinese also eat noodles or dumplings. Japanese eat noodles as main food as well. Ramen, udon, and buckwheat noodles are the main types of noodles served in Japan. Due to the hot weather in Southeast Asia, **residents**[3] there prefer to have spicy and sour food. They used a lot of coconut and curry in their dishes. Most of the Asian people like to go to night market, a place where you can enjoy different kind of food at a time.

As for Western people, eating habits differ in each country as well. Americans enjoy having cereal, toast or omelet for breakfast. Hot dogs, burgers, sandwiches are popular American fast food that you can also grab-and-go. These fast foods are usually served with carbonated soft drinks. Besides fast food, steaks, mashed potatoes and seafood can also be found on an American's dining table. As for British people, they have morning tea after getting up from bed. It helps to get rid of their drowsiness. They have eggs, sausages, bacon, and toast for breakfast. Cereal is also popular. A hot meal is preferable for lunch. Employees usually have simple food for **convenience**[4], such as sandwiches. British are very particular about afternoon tea or high tea. Black tea is usually served with light snacks, cakes or cheese. Invite friends for afternoon tea is a social way. As for dinner, people tend to have meat, vegetables, baked beans and potatoes.

France is well-known for its **exquisite**[5] cuisine and wine. French enjoy eating, and they **savor**[6] their food. Generally, they have croissants or pastry with coffee for breakfast, several but small courses for lunch, and something lighter in the evening. Like most of the Westerners, French like to have dessert after their meal, such as cakes, cookies, and pastries.

【Question】

(　　) 1. Which of the following statement is correct according to the article?
(A) Breakfasts are the same in every country.
(B) Croissants usually go with coffee for French people for lunch.
(C) British people will have a cup of tea to wake themselves up.

(　　) 2. Which kind of food does not belong to the Japanese origin?
(A) ramen　　　　　　(B) porridge
(C) udon　　　　　　(D) buckwheat noodles

【文章中譯】

世界各國的飲食習慣大不相同。若要前往其他國家旅遊，最好能入境隨俗，事先瞭解他國的飲食習慣。

米飯是東方人的主食。亞洲人幾乎每天都吃飯，甚至早餐也不例外。年紀稍長的人喜歡早餐時吃粥，因為粥品比較容易消化。豆漿與饅頭也是中國人的傳統早餐。中國人吃飯會搭配蔬菜、豆腐、家禽肉或蛋一同享用。除了米飯，中國人也吃麵食和餃子。日本人也會把麵食當主食，日式拉麵、烏龍麵和蕎麥麵是常見的麵食。東南亞國家氣候炎熱，因此當地居民喜歡吃辛辣和酸的食物。椰漿和咖哩是常見的食材。大多數亞洲人喜歡逛夜市，因為夜市可同時吃到各種不同的食物。

西方國家也有不同的飲食習慣。美國人早餐會吃麥片、土司和煎蛋捲。而午餐通常是熱狗、漢堡或三明治，這類速食也方便外帶，並且搭配碳酸飲料一起享用。除了速食餐點，牛排、馬鈴薯泥和海鮮料理也很普遍。英國人則喜歡起床後先喝一杯茶醒醒腦。他們的早餐多為雞蛋、香腸、培根和土司，有時也會吃麥片。午餐通常為熟食。上班族為了方便，午餐通常以輕食為主，像是三明治。英國人有喝下午茶的習慣，下午茶多為紅茶搭配小點心、蛋糕或起司。邀請朋友一同喝下午茶也是他們的社交活動之一。英國人晚餐會吃肉類、蔬菜、燉豆子和馬鈴薯。

法國以其精緻的料理與美酒聞名。法國人熱衷於飲食，他們會細細品嚐料理。法國人早餐通常是可頌麵包或酥皮點心，再搭配一杯咖啡；午餐是小份量但多道的料理，晚餐偏清淡。法國人也喜歡在餐後吃甜點，像是蛋糕、餅乾、酥皮點心等甜食。

聽力題目解析

❶ 此題詢問的是文章的探討對象。選項 (A) 為嗜好；選項 (B) 為感情；選項 (C) 為飲食習慣；選項 (D) 為運動。錄音檔在一開始即破題給了我們答案，選擇 (C)。

❷ 此題詢問的是選項何者並不是東方食物。選項 (A) 為米飯；選項 (B) 為粥；選項 (C) 為義大利麵食；選項 (D) 為豆腐。根據音檔內容，pasta 在末段介紹義大利食物時才出現，故選擇 (C)。建議在先看過題目及選項以把握關鍵字。

❸ 此題詢問的是選項何者為日本食物。選項 (A) 為烏龍麵；選項 (B) 為披薩；選項 (C) 為三明治；選項 (D) 為薯條。根據音檔內容，烏龍麵是屬於日本主食麵的一種，故選擇 (A)。此題同上，建議在先看過題目及選項以把握關鍵字。

❹ 此題詢問的是選項何者並不是真正的西方食物。選項 (A) 為漢堡；選項 (B) 為熱狗；選項 (C) 為咖哩；選項 (D) 為歐姆蛋。根據錄音檔，curry 是在介紹東南亞國家時才出現，故可快速排除其作為西方食物的可能性，選擇 (C)。此題同上，建議在先看過題目及選項以把握細節，需特

別注意介紹各國食物特性時，出現了什麼說明，以幫助記憶。

❺ 此題詢問的是選項何者為法國食物。選項 (A) 為餃子；選項 (B) 為可頌；選項 (C) 為蕎麥麵；選項 (D) 為烤豆。根據錄音檔，我們可以得知法國人會吃可頌配咖啡，故選 (B)。

● ●

閱讀題目解析

❶ 此題詢問的是哪一個選項為正確的陳述。選項 (A) 為早餐在每個國家都是一樣的；選項 (B) 為法國人午餐時會喝咖啡配可頌；選項 (C) 為英國人會喝茶醒腦。答案可見內文倒數兩段，選 (C)。

❷ 此題詢問的是選項何種並不是日本食物。選項 (A) 為拉麵；選項 (B) 為粥；選項 (C) 為烏龍麵；選項 (D) 為蕎麥麵。答案可見內文第二段，選 (B)。

補充單字

☆ 1. habit	n.	習慣
☆ 2. serve	v.	享用
☆ 3. resident	n.	居民
☆ 4. convenience	n.	方便
☆ 5. exquisite	adj.	精緻的
☆ 6. savor	v.	品嚐

Level 3
05
Tech Giant — Elon Musk

科技巨人——伊隆‧馬斯克

聽力測驗 🎧Track 045

在學習英文的過程中，「聽」可能是最直接的第一線接觸，也可能是大家最想要快速習得的能力。現在，就讓我們來熟悉各種英文情境，提升自己的英文臨場感吧！

(   ) 1. What does Elon Musk currently plan to do?
       (A) invent super food   (B) finish his Ph.D. at Stanford
       (C) colonize Mars   (D) retire

(   ) 2. When Musk was a child, what did his mother discover about him?
       (A) He had a photographic memory.   (B) He learned slowly.
       (C) He was popular at school.   (D) He didn't like learning.

(   ) 3. Why did Musk drop out from Stanford?
       (A) He couldn't understand his professor's lectures.
       (B) He wanted to start his dotcom company.
       (C) He was eager to get married.
       (D) He couldn't afford the tuition.

(   ) 4. What is Musk's childhood dream?
       (A) being an educator   (B) becoming a banker
       (C) space exploration   (D) being a daydreamer

(   ) 5. What is Musk's goal by 2040?
       (A) to retire   (B) to travel around the world
       (C) to build a school   (D) to establish a Mars colony

 閱讀測驗

剛剛的聽力測驗是否因為答題不順而感到遺憾？或是覺得自己有某些地方掌握地不夠好？現在就讓我們來直接「看」剛剛的聽力測驗，並透過後面的閱讀測驗來補齊聽力上的不足，同時考驗自己的閱讀能力吧！

If you haven't heard of Elon Musk, you'd better find out all about this man. He is one of the world's richest tech billionaires. He is the chief engineer and the CEO of SpaceX, a company that develops rockets for space explorations. He is also the CEO of Tesla, which is **revolutionizing**[1] the auto industry with their new electric cars. His current projects include a plan to colonize Mars and the development of Hyperloop that will take you from LA to San Francisco or New York to Washington in just 30 minutes.

Musk was born to a South African father and a Canadian mother. When Musk was a child, his mother was **stunned**[2] by her son's brilliance. He had a photographic memory. He read two **encyclopedias**[3] and remembered everything. But school life was a torture for him. He was bullied a lot at school, and once even had to miss a whole week of school due to the severe beating.

After receiving the bachelor's degrees in physics and economics at the University of Pennsylvania, Musk began a Ph.D. in applied physics and material sciences at Stanford University, but he **dropped out**[4] after only two days because he was eager to jump on the **dotcom**[5] bandwagon. He successfully founded an online bank, which later became PayPal and was bought by eBay for $1.5 billion in 2002. With the huge fortune, he started pursuing his childhood dream—founding SpaceX in order to send humans to Mars. The company has been awarded a contract by NASA to transport cargo to the International Space Station since 2006. His goal is to establish a Mars colony by 2040.

【 Question 】

(　　) 1. What impact does Tesla have on the auto industry?
　　　　(A) Tesla cars will bring more pollution than the traditional ones with petrol engines.
　　　　(B) It only has a temporary impact on the auto industry.
　　　　(C) It doesn't help the development of a more eco-friendly car.
　　　　(D) It is revolutionizing the auto industry with their new electric vehicles.

(　　) 2. How many minutes will it take for people to travel from LA to San Francisco by Hyperloop?
　　　　(A) 30 minutes.　　　　　(B) 50 minutes.
　　　　(C) 1 hour.　　　　　　　(D) 2 hours.

【文章中譯】

如果你還沒聽說過伊隆·馬斯克，你最好惡補有關他的一切消息。他是全球科技業身價最高的億萬富豪之一，也是太空探索技術公司的首席工程師暨執行長，該公司專門研發太空探索的火箭。他同時也身兼特斯拉的執行長，該公司在汽車業掀起了一波電動車的革命。他目前的計畫還包括火星殖民和超迴路列車的研發，這種列車系統能在三十分鐘內讓你從洛杉磯抵達舊金山，或從紐約抵達華盛頓。

馬斯克的父親是南非人，母親是加拿大人。在他小時候，他的母親對於他的聰明才智感到大吃一驚。他有過目不忘的本領，小小年紀就讀完兩套百科全書，並記得裡面所有的內容。但是學校生活對他而言是個折磨，他在校經常被霸凌，有一次甚至被痛毆到整整一個禮拜無法去上學。

他在美國賓州大學取得物理學和經濟學的雙學士學位後，即赴史丹福大學攻讀應用物理學和材料科學博士學位，但只唸了兩天就休學，因為他趕著投入網路公司的創業熱潮，並成功成立了一家網路銀行，其後來改名為PayPal，並被eBay以十五億美元收購。帶著這筆鉅額的財富，他開始追尋兒時的夢想，成立太空探索技術公司，以便把人類送上火星。該公司已於2006年獲得美國太空總署商業軌道運輸服務的合約，而他的目標是於2040年之前要在火星建立殖民地。

聽力題目解析

❶ 第一題詢問的是馬斯克目前計畫做什麼事。選項 (A) 為發明超級食物；選項 (B) 為完成他在史丹福的博士學位；選項 (C) 為火星殖民；選項 (D) 為退休。錄音檔的前段即明確指出 "His current projects also include a plan to colonize Mars and the development of Hyperloop." 指馬斯克目前計畫火星殖民和研發超迴路列車，此題考的是考生 "colonize" 此單字的掌握度，故答案選(C)。

❷ 此題詢問的是在馬斯克孩堤時期，他的媽媽發現他有什麼特質。選項 (A) 為他有過目不忘的本領；選項 (B) 為他學東西很慢；選項 (C) 為他在學校很受歡迎；選項 (D) 為他並不好學。在錄音檔中段部分即有說 "When Musk was a child, ... He had a photographic memory."，本題考的是考生是否知道photographic memory的意思是「如相片般清晰的記憶」，意即「過目不忘」，若不清楚 "photographic" 的意思，也可以先把握 "memory" 來做推測，故答案選 (A)。

❸ 此題詢問的是為什麼馬斯克從史丹福大學輟學。選項 (A) 為他無法理解教授講課內容；選項 (B) 為他想成立自己的網路公司；選項 (C) 為他渴望結婚；選項 (D) 為他負擔不起學費。本題考的是考生是否知道jump on the wagon片語是「趕搭（某）熱潮」的意思，若無法掌握，其他選項皆無提及，可用刪除法選 (B)。

❹ 此題詢問的是馬斯克孩堤時的夢想是什麼。選項 (A) 為當一位教育家；選項 (B) 為成為一位銀行家；選項 (C) 為太空探險；選項 (D) 整天做白日夢。錄音檔後段提到 "... he started pursuing his childhood dream—founding SpaceX in order to send humans to Mars." 故答案選(C)。

❺ 此題詢問馬斯克希望在2040年之前達到的目標為何。選項 (A) 為退休；選項 (B) 為環遊世界；選項 (C) 為興建一所學校；選項 (D) 為把人類送到火星。錄音檔最後一句提到"His goal is to establish a Mars colony by 2040." 這邊考得是學生是否清楚 "colony" 之意，此題也可用 "Mars" 來做推測，故答案選(D)。

閱讀題目解析

❶ 第一題詢問的是特斯拉對汽車業產生了什麼影響。選項 (A) 為特斯拉汽車將比傳統使用汽油引擎的車子更污染環境；選項 (B) 為特斯拉只對汽車業有短暫影響；選項 (C) 為特斯拉對於汽車業研發更環保的車子毫無益處；選項 (D) 為特斯拉正以其研發的新型電動車在汽車業掀起了一波的革命。答案可見內文第一段，可知特斯拉在電動車的研發帶動汽車業大廠紛紛投入將傳統汽車轉型為電動車，故答案選 (D)。

❷ 第二題詢問的是人們若搭超迴路列車從洛杉磯到舊金山需要多久的時間。選項(A) 為30分鐘；選項 (B) 為50分鐘；選項 (C) 為1小時；選項 (D) 為2小時。答案可見內文第一段最後一句，選 (A)。

補充單字

☆ 1. revolutionize	v.	革命
☆ 2. stun	v.	吃驚
☆ 3. encyclopedia	n.	百科全書
☆ 4. drop out	v.	休學
☆ 5. dotcom	n.	網路公司

Differences Between Football and Soccer

英式足球與美式足球的區別

🎧 **聽力測驗** 🎧Track 046

在學習英文的過程中,「聽」可能是最直接的第一線接觸,也可能是大家最想要快速習得的能力。現在,就讓我們來熟悉各種英文情境,提升自己的英文臨場感吧!

( ) 1. Choose the correct statement:
　　(A) American football is originated from the rugby football.
　　(B) American football is originated from the tennis.
　　(C) American football is originated from the baseball.
　　(D) American football is originated form the basketball.

( ) 2. Both of the games are team sport consisting of ＿＿＿＿ teams playing against each other.
　　(A) one
　　(B) two
　　(C) three
　　(D) four

( ) 3. Which statement is not true?
　　(A) In American football, each game holds for four quarters.
　　(B) Only goal keepers are allowed to use their hands and arms to stop or catch the ball.
　　(C) For American football players, they will get a blue penalty card when they break the rules.
　　(D) American football players can use their hand in the game.

剛剛的聽力測驗是否因為答題不順而感到遺憾？或是覺得自己有某些地方掌握地不夠好？現在就讓我們來直接「看」剛剛的聽力測驗，並透過後面的閱讀測驗來補齊聽力上的不足，同時考驗自己的閱讀能力吧！

American football is usually confused with association football played widely in England. American football originated from the rugby football. On the other hand, association football is commonly known as soccer. They share some similarities, but definitely show differences as well.

A rectangular field is required for both games. Both the games are team sport consisting of two teams playing against each other. In a game of football or soccer, each team has eleven players. The football or soccer team which scores the most points wins the game. These two games are mainly about to **offense**[1] and **defense**[2]. Certain rules are imposed in the game which players must obey, or else they will receive penalties.

American football is a collision sport. As a result, protective equipment is needed to protect the players from severe **injuries**[3], such as padded plastic helmet, shoulder pads, hip pads and knee pads. This is also the easiest and fastest way to differentiate American football from association football. Duration of the two games is not alike. In American football, each game holds for four quarters, each quarter lasts 15 minutes. As for soccer, a game lasts for two periods (also called halves), each period has 45 minutes. There is a 15-minute break between halves.

In a soccer game, players can **dribble**[4], pass or shoot the ball by kicking the ball with their feet. They can also use their torso and head to hold up a ball. Only goal keepers are allowed to use their hands and arms to stop or catch a ball. Physical contact is strictly prohibited. Soccer player score points by shooting the ball into their opponent's goal. When a soccer player pushes or trips his opponent, or conducts an unsporting behavior, he will be considered as misconduct. **Referee**[5] can punish the player by a caution (yellow card) or sending-off (red card). In contrast to soccer, American football players can use their hands by carrying the ball. In addition, players can tackle, or knock down opponents in order to stop them from **advancing**[6] the ball. They score points by carrying the ball over the opponent's goal line, kick the ball through the goal posts at the opponent's end zone, and many other ways. For American football players, they will get a yellow penalty flag when they break the rules. For example, they are not allowed to illegally pull or grasp an opponent other than the ball-carrier, or grasp another player's face.

American football and soccer are much alike in some ways, but are completely different in others. Either way you look at it, the two sports are just as aggressive and competitive and can be very enjoyable to watch and play.

【Question】

(　　) 1. Which of the following word has an opposite meaning with "unsporting" based on the article?
　　　(A) cheating　　　　　　　(B) sportsmanship
　　　(C) halves　　　　　　　　(D) prohibited

(　　) 2. Which of the following equipment is not worn in American football games?
　　　(A) padded plastic helmet　(B) shoulder pads
　　　(C) hip pads　　　　　　　(D) ear pads

【文章中譯】

人們常會把美式足球和在英國非常受歡迎的足球搞混。美式足球源自英式橄欖球，而英式足球也就是我們平常指的足球。

兩者有些地方相似，但也有不同點。兩者的比賽都是在一長方形球場進行。美式足球與英式足球都屬團隊性運動，比賽方式是兩個隊伍互相競爭，每隊皆有 11 名球員。比賽中，贏得最多分的隊伍就算獲勝。此兩種比賽不外乎進攻與防守。球員必須按照某些特定的規則比賽，否則得接受處罰。

美式足球涉及身體的衝撞，為了避免球員受重傷，球員必須穿戴塑膠頭盔，保護肩膀、臀部與膝蓋的護具。這點也是分辨美式足球與英式足球最簡單及最快的方式。兩種運動的比賽時間也不一樣。美式足球的比賽進行四節，每一節的比賽為 15 分鐘；英式足球的比賽總共有兩局，每局有45分鐘，中場則會有 15 分鐘的休息時間。

在足球比賽裡，球員用腳運球、傳球並射門，也能用身體和頭擋球。只有守門員能用手和手臂擋球或接球。肢體的碰撞是不被允許的。比賽時，球員把球射入對手的球門即可得分。若推倒、絆倒對手，或是做出違背體育精神的行為，球員將被判犯規，此時裁判可給予黃牌以示警告，或紅牌將球員判離場。與足球不同的是，美式足球球員可用手持球。除此之外，為了阻擋對手進攻，球員可阻截或阻擋對手。得分的方法不只一種，像是持球跑進對手的達陣區，以及把球踢過對手達陣區的橫檔等。美式足球球員若犯規，裁判將給予黃色旗子以示處罰，可能的犯規像是球員不得非法地拉扯或擒抱持球以外的對手，或是拉扯對手的面罩。

足球和美式足球有些相似處，但卻是兩種不一樣的運動。不管怎麼樣，這兩種運動不僅激昂，更具競爭性。觀賞比賽或是親自下場比賽，都是有趣的經驗。

聽力題目解析

❶ 此題詢問的是何者為正確選項。選項 (A) 為美國足球起源於英式橄欖球選項 (B) 為美國足球起源於網球；選項 (C) 為美國足球起源於棒球；選項 (D) 為美國足球起源於籃球。錄音檔的一開始即給我們答案，答案為 (A)。

❷ 此題詢問的是兩種運動皆是幾組隊伍來進行對戰。在錄音檔開始介紹美式足球和英式足球的異同處時，我們便可得知兩種的比賽方式都是由兩個隊伍互相競爭，故選擇 (B)。

❸ 此題詢問的是何者為錯誤之選項。選項 (A) 為在美式足球中,每場比賽共有四節;選項 (B) 為只有守門員可以用手和手臂來擋球或接球;選項 (C) 就美式足球而言,球員若犯規便會得到一張藍卡;選項 (D) 為美式足球員可以在比賽中使用手。根據錄音檔的後段,我們可以得知在美式足球中,球員若犯規是得到一張黃卡,非藍卡,且在內文並沒有出現過藍卡 (blue card) 此單字,故選擇 (C)。此題僅需注意細節,建議先看過選項,以便把握。此種題型也適合在腦中想像加深記憶。

閱讀題目解析

❶ 此題詢問的是選項中哪個單字和內文的 "unsporting" 持相對意思。選項 (A) 為作弊的;選項 (B) 為運動家精神;選項 (C) 為一節;選項 (D) 為被禁止的。根據內文,"an unsporting behavior" 出現在犯規處置的介紹之前,故可以推測其意應與不正當的的犯規行為相關,實意則為「不具運動家精神的」,故選 (B)。

❷ 此題詢問的是選項何者沒有出現在美式足球的裝備內。選項 (A) 為有襯墊的塑膠頭盔;選項 (B) 為護肩;選項 (C) 為臀部襯墊;選項 (D) 為耳墊。答案可見內文第三段開頭,選擇 (D)

補充單字

☆ 1. offense	n.	進攻
☆ 2. defense	n.	防守
☆ 3. injury	n.	傷害
☆ 4. dribble	v.	運球
☆ 5. referee	n.	裁判
☆ 6. advance	v.	前進

Generation Gap Age Disparity VS. Happiness

老少配會幸福嗎？

聽力測驗 🎧 Track 047

在學習英文的過程中，「聽」可能是最直接的第一線接觸，也可能是大家最想要快速習得的能力。現在，就讓我們來熟悉各種英文情境，提升自己的英文臨場感吧！

(   ) 1. According to the article, what does "May-December Romance" mean?
     (A) seasonal greetings   (B) age-gap relationships
     (C) puppy love   (D) emergency calling

(   ) 2. In the movie Phantom Thread, how many years apart in age are there between the dressmaker and the young waitress?
     (A) 26   (B) 28
     (C) 30   (D) 32

(   ) 3. What kind of perspective does the article use to examine May-December Romance?
     (A) historical perspective   (B) engineering perspective
     (C) environmental perspective   (D) socio-cultural perspective

(   ) 4. Can an age-gap relationship succeed?
     (A) It won't succeed.   (B) It always works.
     (C) It depends.   (D) It will end sadly.

(   ) 5. According to the article, what really matters in a relationship?
     (A) How people manage their relationships.
     (B) The older a man is, the better his marriage is.

(C) The younger a woman is, the more likely her marriage will succeed.

(D) Whether the couple have the same job.

 閱讀測驗

剛剛的聽力測驗是否因為答題不順而感到遺憾？或是覺得自己有某些地方掌握地不夠好？現在就讓我們來直接「看」剛剛的聽力測驗，並透過後面的閱讀測驗來補齊聽力上的不足，同時考驗自己的閱讀能力吧！

The movie, Phantom Thread, was nominated for the 2018 Academy Award for Best Picture. The story is about the passionate relationship between a highly successful London **dressmaker**[1] and a young waitress. They are 26 years apart in age. This kind of age gap, however, is not unusual, such as George Clooney and his wife Amal, Michael Douglas and Catherine Zeta-Jones, and French president, Emmanuel Macron, and his wife Brigitte.

It is widely known that men tend to marry women younger than themselves, but if a man is **literally**[2] old enough to be a woman's father, or vice versa, people start to look at the relationship with **skepticism**[3]. To understand the pairing of older men and younger women, we can examine it from the socio-cultural perspective. Younger women seem **physically**[4] more attractive to aging males, while older men with greater power or better financial status are likely to lead his younger partner to want to bond with him.

So can a relationship succeed if one partner is much older? It depends on how similar the two are, for instance, whether they enjoy similar **leisure**[5] activities or reach an agreement on how to spend money. In addition, having supportive friends and family could be particularly useful for age-gap relationships. So, age might just be a number. It all comes down to how people manage their relationship.

Level 1
Level 2
Level 3
Level 4
Level 5
Level 6

【Question】

(　　) 1. What does the word "literally" in the second paragraph mean?
             (A) literary　　　　　(B) liberally
             (C) frankly　　　　　(D) actually

(　　) 2. What is especially important for age-gap relationships?
             (A) the support from friends and family
             (B) people's skepticism
             (C) public criticism
             (D) people's gossip

【文章中譯】

《霓裳魅影》這部電影曾榮獲2018年奧斯卡金像獎提名為最佳影片，故事內容敘述一位在倫敦享譽盛名的裁縫師與一名年輕女服務生熱戀的故事，他們兩人的年齡相差二十六歲。然而，這類年齡懸殊的老少配並非罕見，例如，喬治·克隆尼和妻子艾默、麥可·道格拉斯和妻子凱薩琳·麗塔-瓊斯，以及法國總統馬克宏和妻子布莉姬特。

眾所皆知，男性傾向娶比自己年齡小的妻子，但是如果一個男人的年齡大到足以當妻子的父親，或反之亦然，人們就會開始用猜疑的眼光來看待他們的關係。為了解爺孫戀，我們可以從社會文化的觀點來檢視這類戀情。年輕女性的外貌對年邁的男性十分具有吸引力，而年長的男性若具有較大的權勢或更優渥的經濟條件，也會讓年輕的另一伴比較想與他結為伴侶。

所以老少配能幸福嗎？這取決於這對戀人有多相似，例如他們是否共同享有類似的休閒活動或對於金錢觀是否達成共識。另外，擁有親朋好友的支持對於老少配的戀人而言特別重要。因此，年齡可能只是數字，最終仍取決於是人們如何經營他們的感情。

聽力題目解析

❶ 第一題詢問的是根據本文，"May-December Romance"是什麼意思。選項 (A) 為季節性問候；選項 (B) 為年齡相差懸殊的老少配；選項 (C) 為兩小無猜純純的愛；選項 (D) 為緊急呼救。在錄音檔一開始即以《霓裳魅影》這部電影破題，指出男女主角年齡差距懸殊 "They are 26 years apart in age. This kind of age gap is not unusual." 接著錄音檔中間再開始分析老少配的原因，故答案選 (B)。

❷ 此題詢問的是在《霓裳魅影》這部電影裡，裁縫師與一名年輕女服務生年齡相差幾歲。選項 (A) 為26歲；選項 (B) 為28歲；選項 (C) 為30歲；選項 (D) 為32歲。在錄音檔前段部分即有說"They are 26 years apart in age."，聽力測驗會考文中的數字，請考生聽到數字應特別注意，故答案選 (A)。

❸ 此題詢問的是本文用何種觀點檢視老少配。選項 (A) 為歷史觀點；選項 (B) 為工程觀點；選項 (C) 為環境觀點；選項 (D) 社會文化觀點。錄音檔中段為 "To understand ... from the socio-cultural perspective." 可知本文用的是社會文化觀點，可從組合的兩個單字 "social" 和 "cultural" 來推測，故答案選 (D)。

❹ 此題詢問的是老少配是否能成功。選項 (A) 為絕對不會成功；選項 (B) 為總是成功；選項 (C) 為看情形；選項 (D) 為結局是悲情的。錄音檔後段提到 "It depends on how similar the couple are, for instance..." 考得是 "it depends on ..." 作為「取決於……」的常用片語用法，故答案選 (C)。

❺ 此題詢問在感情中，什麼是重要的。選項 (A) 為人們如何經營他們的感情；選項 (B) 為男人越老，對他的婚姻越有幫助；選項 (C) 為女人越年輕，她的婚姻更有可能成功；選項 (D) 為夫妻是否有相同的工作。錄音檔最後一句提到 "It all comes down to how people manage their relationship." 考得是 "manage" 作為「經營」之意，故答案選(A)。

閱讀題目解析

❶ 第一題詢問的是literally這個單字的意思，選項(A)文學的；(B)自由地；(C)坦白地；(D)實際上地。在本篇的補充單字有收錄這個單字，意思是actually、in fact，故答案選(D)。

❷ 第二題詢問的是對老少戀而言，什麼特別重要，選項(A)親朋好友的支持；(B)人們懷疑的眼光；(C)大眾的批判；(D)人們的八卦。文章第三段指出，"In addition, having supportive friends and family could be particularly useful for age-gap relationships."，故答案為(A)。

補充單字

☆	單字	詞性	中文
☆	1. dressmaker	n.	裁縫師
☆	2. literally	v.	實際上地
☆	3. skepticism	n.	懷疑的態度
☆	4. physically	v.	外貌上地
☆	5. leisure	n.	休閒

New British Royal Member—Meghan Markle

英國皇室新成員——梅根・馬克爾

🦻**聽力測驗** 🎧Track 048

在學習英文的過程中，「聽」可能是最直接的第一線接觸，也可能是大家最想要快速習得的能力。現在，就讓我們來熟悉各種英文情境，提升自己的英文臨場感吧！

( ) 1. Who is Meghan Markle's husband?
    (A) an actor in Suit   (B) the director of Suit
    (C) Prince Harry   (D) Prince Eric

( ) 2. When did Meghan start playing small roles in TV series and films?
    (A) when she was a child
    (B) when she was a high school student
    (C) when she became a new member of the British royal family
    (D) when she was a university student

( ) 3. What did Meghan do before she became a household name?
    (A) She taught calligraphy.
    (B) She taught acting.
    (C) She was a yoga instructor.
    (D) She was a chef.

( ) 4. What else did Meghan do apart from her acting career?
    (A) lighting director   (B) charity work
    (C) psychotherapist   (D) lawyer

(   ) 5. For the United Nations Women, which country did Meghan travel to?
      (A) Botswana   (B) Rwanda
      (C) Zaire   (D) Sierra Leone

 閱讀測驗

剛剛的聽力測驗是否因為答題不順而感到遺憾？或是覺得自己有某些地方掌握地不夠好？現在就讓我們來直接「看」剛剛的聽力測驗，並透過後面的閱讀測驗來補齊聽力上的不足，同時考驗自己的閱讀能力吧！

She is the lady who just stole a royal's heart, but she has led a colorful life before meeting Prince Harry. She was an American actress who played Rachel Zane in a TV series called Suits, but she **ditched**[1] the role to become a British royal bride instead. She is Meghan Markle, a new member of one of the world's most popular royal families.

Meghan's father is white and her mother is African American. When she studied at Northwestern University, she began playing small roles in several American TV series and films. Before her career took off, she was known for teaching **calligraphy**[2] classes. She worked hard, and after years of being **persistent**[3] and developing her talent, she became a **household**[4] name for her role in Suits.

Apart from her acting career, she was an advocate for United Nations Women, and had travelled to Rwanda to raise awareness for the local people. She was also an **ambassador**[5] for the World Vision Clear Water campaign. Her devotion to charity work reminds people of Princess Diana, for she is also an advocate for those who are less fortunate in all parts of the world. Now Prince Harry has found true happiness with Meghan, and together they will continue their commitment to charity and provide care to those who are in need.

Level 1
Level 2
Level 3
Level 4
Level 5
Level 6

【 Question 】

(　　) 1. What does the word "persistent" mean?
  (A) perishing
  (B) continuing to do something, even though it is difficult
  (C) giving up on something because it is difficult
  (D) desisting to do something

(　　) 2. With her devotion to charity work, who does Markle remind people of?
  (A) Princess Anne. (B) King Edward.
  (C) Princess Diana. (D) Prince Philips.

【 文章中譯 】

她是一位偷走了一名皇室成員的心的女子，不過在遇見哈利王子之前，她早已過著多彩多姿的生活。她是一位美國女演員，在電視劇《金裝律師》中扮演瑞秋·詹恩的角色，但隨後為了迎接英國皇室新娘這個身份而辭演。她就是梅根·馬克爾，全球最受歡迎的皇室新成員。

梅根的爸爸是白人，媽媽則是非裔美籍人。她在西北大學就讀時，即開始在數個美國電視劇和電影接演一些跑龍套的小角色。在她的事業飛黃騰達之前，她以教書法而聞名。她努力工作，經過數年的努力不懈和用心發展她的天分之後，梅根終於以《金裝律師》的角色打響知名度，成為家喻戶曉的人物。

除了演藝事業之外，她也擔任過聯合國婦女組織的倡議者，走訪盧安達以喚起世人對於該國人民的關注，同時也擔任世界展望會淨水計畫的全球大使。她對慈善工作的投入令人想起了黛安娜王妃，因為她也在為世界各地不幸的人們發聲。如今哈利王子在梅根身上找到真正的幸福，兩人將繼續積極投入慈善工作，關懷需要幫助的人們。

聽力題目解析

❶ 第一題詢問的是梅根·馬克爾的丈夫是誰。選項 (A) 為《金裝律師》的男演員；選項 (B) 為《金裝律師》的導演；選項 (C) 為哈利王子；選項 (D) 為艾利克王子。在錄音檔一開始即指出 "She is the lady who just stole a royal's heart, but she has led a colorful life before meeting Prince Harry." 這邊考得是考生能不能將 "a royal's heart" 和 "Prince Harry" 連結在一起，答案選 (C)。

❷ 此題詢問的是梅根什麼時候開始接演一些跑龍套的小角色。選項 (A) 為小時候；選項 (B) 為高中生時期；選項 (C) 為成為皇室成員時；選項 (D) 為大學生時期。在錄音檔中段部分即有說 "When she studied at Northwestern University, she began playing small roles in several American TV series and films."，梅根就讀美國名校西北大學時，就開始接演一些小角色，故答案選 (D)，掌握 "studied at" 和 "play roles" 等關鍵字即可。

❸ 此題詢問的是梅根成為家喻戶曉的人物之前曾從事什麼職業。選項 (A) 為她教西洋書法；選項 (B) 為她教演戲；選項 (C) 為她是瑜伽老師；選項 (D) 為她是主廚。在錄音檔中段提到 "Before her career took off, she was known for teaching calligraphy classes." 本題考的是考生是否知道 "take off" 這個片語是「起飛」的意思，事業如同飛機起飛，即飛黃騰達。另外，"calligraphy" 是書法，故答案選 (A)。

❹ 此題詢問的是梅根除了演戲之外還從事什麼工作。選項 (A) 為燈光技術指導；選項 (B) 為慈善工作；選項 (C) 為心理治療師；選項 (D) 為律師。錄音檔中後段我們即可聽見 "... she was an advocate for United Nations Women ... was also an ambassador for the World Vision Clear Water campaign." 這邊可把握 "advocate" 和 "ambassador" 兩個單字，為「倡議者」和「大使」之意，答案選 (B)。

❺ 此題詢問的是梅根為了聯合國婦女組織走訪哪個國家。選項 (A) 為波紮那；選項 (B) 為盧安達；選項 (C) 為薩伊；選項 (D) 為獅子山共和國。

錄音檔後段提到 "... has travelled to Rwanda to raise awareness...",
故答案選 (B)。

閱讀題目解析

❶ 第一題詢問的是 "persistent" 這個單字的意思。選項 (A) 為凋零的；選項 (B)為堅持不懈的，即使遭遇困難；選項 (C) 為放棄某事，因為遭遇困難；選項 (D)為中止不做的。在本篇的補充單字有收錄這個單字，字首per-意思是through，字根sistent（拉丁文sistere而來）意思是to cause to stand，所以這個字是指即使面對困難也堅持下去，故答案選 (B)。

❷ 第二題詢問的是梅根對慈善工作的熱誠令人想起誰。選項 (A) 為安妮公主；選項 (B) 為艾德華國王；選項 (C) 為黛安娜王妃；選項 (D) 為菲利普親王。答案可見內文第三段，答案為 (C)。

補充單字

☆ 1. ditch	**v.**	拋棄；丟棄
☆ 2. calligraphy	**n.**	書法
☆ 3. persistent	**adj.**	堅持不懈的
☆ 4. household	**adj.**	家喻戶曉的
☆ 5. ambassador	**n.**	大使

Level 3 09

A Foreign Company's Requirements for Your English Resume

外商公司對英文履歷的要求

聽力測驗 🎧 Track 049

在學習英文的過程中，「聽」可能是最直接的第一線接觸，也可能是大家最想要快速習得的能力。現在，就讓我們來熟悉各種英文情境，提升自己的英文臨場感吧！

(　　) 1. The article is about _____.
    (A) English resume
    (B) foreign companies
    (C) hobbies
    (D) career planning

(　　) 2. How many types of resume are mentioned in the article?
    (A) four   (B) three
    (C) two   (D) one

(　　) 3. Choose the correct statement.
    (A) Resume is a tool.
    (B) Chronological resume is written according to places.
    (C) Resume should be cliché.
    (D) English is not an important requirement for foreign companies.

(　　) 4. What does the word "duties" mean in the article?
    (A) supervisor
    (B) colleague
    (C) holiday
    (D) responsibility

閱讀測驗

剛剛的聽力測驗是否因為答題不順而感到遺憾？或是覺得自己有某些地方掌握地不夠好？現在就讓我們來直接「看」剛剛的聽力測驗，並透過後面的閱讀測驗來補齊聽力上的不足，同時考驗自己的閱讀能力吧！

English is a widely used language in foreign countries such as the United States, England, Canada, Australia and others. Since more and more foreign companies establish their **branch**[1] offices in Taiwan, English has become a basic requirement for employers. Foreign companies tend to require a brief and concise resume, not to mention they will pay more attention on your English ability. If you plan to apply for a job in a foreign company, take a look at the below notes before you send it out.

Keep in mind that most companies have a busy **schedule**[2], and they need to run through hundreds of resumes a day. Thus, too many cliché will discredit your resume. It's important for a job hunter to provide an **effective**[3] resume. A resume can be written chronologically or functionally. Whichever format you prefer, you should remember to put your name, contacts, address, and objective for the job at the very beginning of your resume. Most companies are not interested in knowing your height, weight, and blood type when they first read your resume. The **excluding**[4] of the above information is recommended.

In a chronological resume, you should mention your working experience and educational experience by time. You should write your latest experience first, following the second latest and so forth. Don't mention only your past job duties and job descriptions. You should emphasize your **accomplishments**[5] and skills from your past work history. Describe each accomplishment and skill in a powerful but simple statement. As for your educational background, it's better not to mention your kindergarten or primary school. University degrees or higher educational experiences are more important and useful.

A functional resume doesn't need to be written in chronological order. It emphasizes on your qualifications, accomplishments, and **relevant**[6] skills. These are important key points you should describe separately and independently in your resume. Make strong and brief descriptions for each point. A brief working history is required as well. Last but not least, you should remember to mention your educational background.

A resume is not merely your personnel document, but a tool instead. It is a marketing tool which you use to introduce yourself to a new company. To convince a company of your qualifications and abilities, you should make your resume as effective as possible. A careful check for spelling and grammar mistakes is indeed very important. You wouldn't want your outstanding resume to be spoiled by a careless mistake.

【Question】

(　　) 1. Which of the following information shouldn't be put into a normal resume?
(A) blood type
(B) past working experience
(C) higher educational background
(D) accomplishments from past work hitory

(　　) 2. Which of the following word is not relevant to the description of a well-written resume?
(A) effective　　　　(B) organized
(C) functional　　　　(D) excluding

【文章中譯】

英文在國外是通用的語言，不管是在美國、英國、加拿大、澳洲和其他國家，都會使用英文。隨著越來越多外商到台灣設立分公司，英文成為員工必須具備的能力。外商公司通常會要求簡潔扼要的英文履歷，更不用說他們會著重你的英文能力。若你正打算應徵外商公司的職務，請花時間閱讀以下幾點建議。

大公司每天要處理的事情很多，而且每天會收到上百封的履歷，過於冗長的履歷反倒會讓對方留下不好印象。因此，履歷應簡潔有力。英文履歷約有兩種格式，一種為依時間順序排列，另一種則是強調功能性。不管你選擇用哪一種方式寫履歷，記得必須在履歷最開頭寫上你的姓名、聯絡電話、地址和目標。一般的公司對於求職者身高、體重和血型等資料不太在意，所以建議省略這類的資料。

若履歷是依時間順序排列，那麼就得依時間順序列出工作經驗和教育程度。先說明最近期的工作經驗，再以此類推。別只是單純地介紹職務和工作內容，而是強調過去工作經驗所取得的成就和累積的工作能力。詳加細數每項成就與能力，但僅記要簡明扼要。提到教育程度時，可省略幼稚園和國中的敘述，因為大學和以上的學歷較為重要。

若你想準備一份功能性履歷，則履歷內容不需依時間順序排列。這類履歷得依照幾個重點分別進行描述，例如：符合相關職務的資格、工作成就和相關技能。針對重點，務必提出有力且概要的證據。在此之後，再簡單地說明過去曾在哪些地方就業，最後也別忘了介紹自己的學歷。

履歷不僅僅是個人資料的介紹，它是一個工具。透過這個行銷工具，你才能向陌生的公司推銷自己。一份有效的履歷，能讓求職者展現其條件與能力，得到應徵公司的肯定。不僅如此，英文單字的拼寫與文法也是必須注意的重點。粗心的失誤會讓一份好的履歷扣分不少。

聽力題目解析

❶ 此題詢問的是內文的主旨。選項 (A) 為英文履歷；選項 (B) 為外國公司；選項 (C) 為嗜好；選項 (D) 為職涯規劃。在錄音檔開始不久後，我們即可得知此篇的重點在 "If you plan to apply for a job in a foreign company, kindly take a look at the below notes and recheck your resume before you send it out." 故答案選 (A)，切記勿被選項 (B) 混淆，若此篇的主旨是外商，那麼接下來不應細談履歷寫法。

❷ 此題詢問的是內文中共提及幾種履歷表格式。選項 (A) 為四種；選項 (B) 為三種；選項 (C) 為兩種；選項 (D) 為一種。根據錄音檔，我們可以得知 "A resume can be written chronologically or functionally."，故答案為 (C)。若此句沒有掌握到，我們也可以透過後續的解說來判斷履歷表有根據時間性和功能性這兩種寫法。

❸ 此題要求我們選出正確的陳述。選項 (A) 為履歷表是種工具；選項 (B)

為按照時序排列的履歷表是根據地點所寫；選項 (C) 為履歷表應該要寫陳腔濫調；選項 (D) 為對外商企業來說，英文不是重要的條件。在錄音檔的後段，我們即可聽見 "A resume is ... a tool instead." 故可直接選擇 (A)。此題同樣為綜合理解的題型，只能緊記細節，或者把握開頭和結尾，因這兩個部分通常為精華主旨所在。

❹ 此題詢問第三段中的 "duties" 為何意。選項 (A) 為監督人；選項 (B) 為同事；選項 (C) 為假期；選項 (D) 為責任。根據錄音檔，我們可以聽見 "job duties" 和 "job descriptions" 被放在一起，故按照推測，此單字應與工作內容有關。選項 (A) 至 (C) 的單字之意皆不符合，故選擇 (D)。

閱讀題目解析

❶ 此題詢問的是選項何者不應被放正常的履歷表中。選項 (A) 為血型；選項 (B) 為過去的工作經驗；選項 (C) 為較高的學歷；選項 (D) 為工作歷史中的成就。答案可詳見內文第二段，一般的公司對於求職者身高、體重和血型等資料不太在意，故選擇 (A)。

❷ 此題詢問的是選項何者和拿來形容一份書寫流暢的履歷表的敘述無關。選項 (A) 為簡潔有力的；選項 (B) 為有組織的；選項 (C) 為功能性的；選項 (D) 為除外的。答案可見內文第二段，我們可以得知 excluding 此單字是出現在「建議省略這類的資料」中的，與可以拿來形容履歷表的單字無關，故答案為 (D)。

補充單字

☆ 1. branch	n.	分公司
☆ 2. schedule	n.	時間表
☆ 3. effective	adj.	有效的
☆ 4. exclude	v.	排除
☆ 5. accomplishment	n.	成就
☆ 6. relevant	adj.	有關的

The Differences Between British and American Cultures

英美文化的差異

聽力測驗 🎧 Track 050

在學習英文的過程中,「聽」可能是最直接的第一線接觸,也可能是大家最想要快速習得的能力。現在,就讓我們來熟悉各種英文情境,提升自己的英文臨場感吧!

( ) 1. Which of the following statement is true?
(A) British literature is similar to American literature.
(B) Captain John Smith is an American.
(C) England is one of America's colonies.
(D) America is one of England's colonies.

( ) 2. Which of the following is not by William Shakespeare?
(A) Twelfth Night
(B) Adventures of Huckleberry Finn
(C) A Midsummer Night's Dream
(D) Macbeth

( ) 3. Which of the following does not belong to William Shakespeare's four tragedies?
(A) Macbeth   (B) Romeo and Juliet
(C) King Lear   (D) Hamlet

( ) 4. What does the word "remarkable" mean in the article?
(A) comment   (B) excellent
(C) horrible   (D) puzzled

 閱讀測驗

剛剛的聽力測驗是否因為答題不順而感到遺憾？或是覺得自己有某些地方掌握地不夠好？現在就讓我們來直接「看」剛剛的聽力測驗，並透過後面的閱讀測驗來補齊聽力上的不足，同時考驗自己的閱讀能力吧！

British and American cultures are popular around the world. Most learners of English are familiar with British and American art, literature, lifestyle, and culture. However, while the two share some similarities, they are different in some ways, and literature plays an important role since literature defines the people and the country.

Obviously, England and America **authors**[1] have different cultural backgrounds. British **literature**[2] has long **existed**[3] in the history, which dated back to the early Middle Ages and the works were written in Old English. Later, a new form of English now known as the Middle English was established during the late medieval period. During the 16th century, sonnet and other Italian literature were introduced into English and enriched the British literature. William Shakespeare is believed to be the most significant author of the age. Other than sonnets, he also produced plays. During his early age, Shakespeare's plays are mostly **comedies**[4]. A Midsummer Night's Dream, Twelfth Night, The Taming of the Shrew, and As You Like It are called the four comedies. Later on, he started to write **tragedy**[5] plays. Hamlet, Othello, King Lear, and Macbeth are his four tragedies. At the end of the 18th century, England entered the time of Romanticism, the era of which people concentrated more on individuality. Novels are widely produced in the 19th century. Famous authors of the time are Jane Austen and Charles Dickens.

As one of the British colonies, early American literature shares a link with the English literature. Colonial literature could be considered as the earliest American literature. Settlers from England and Ireland wrote books about their colonies, including the interaction and conflicts between the Indians. Captain John Smith, an English man who did an **expedition**[6] to New England, was the most famous among them all. The first American novel could be The Power of Sympathy. It was published in 1789. The book was written by William Hill Brown who was born in Boston. Americans established their own literature style during the 19th century. Remarkable authors of the age include Washington Irving and Edgar Allen Poe. Edgar Allen Poe was the first American to produce short stories. Author Mark Twain was also famous for using local dialect and regional accents in his works, such as his masterpiece Adventures of Huckleberry Finn. The 20th century marked a new era for American literature. Stories cover both high and low societies, and sometimes naturalism. War was also a subject matter that concerned some of the American writers.

【Question】

(　　) 1. Which novel is considered as the potential first American novel?
    (A) King Lear
    (B) Edger Allen Poe's short story
    (C) Adventures of Huckleberry Finn
    (D) The Power of Sympathy

(　　) 2. Which of the following statement is incorrect based on the article?
    (A) The 20th century American literature touches on a wider range of topics.
    (B) Jane Austen and John Smith were both from England.
    (C) Ireland had nothing to do with America when the latter one was colonized by England.
    (D) Literature is a way to see the differences between American and British culture.

【文章中譯】

世界各國對於英國與美國文化並不陌生。大多數學習英語的人也瞭解英國或美國的藝術、文學、生活方式和文化。不過，雖然這兩種文化略為相同，英美文化仍存有差異，其中文學扮演著重要的角色，因為文學代表著人民和國家。

很顯然地，兩國的作者擁有的文學背景不同。英國文學發展悠久，可追溯至中世紀時期，當時的作品皆以古英文書寫。中世紀後期，出現了一種新式英文，稱為中古英文。而 16 世紀時，十四行詩和其他義大利文學傳入英國，讓英國文學變得更為豐富。威廉莎士比亞被視為該時期最重要的作家。除了十四行詩，莎士比亞也寫劇本。早期其大多寫喜劇，四大喜劇為《仲夏夜之夢》、《第十二夜》、《馴悍記》和《皆大歡喜》。之後，他開始寫悲劇，而《哈姆雷特》、《奧塞羅》、《李爾王》和《馬克白》為他的四大悲劇。18 世紀末，英國進入浪漫時期，強調人本主義；19 世紀開始則出現越來越多小說，此時期有名的作家如珍奧斯丁和查爾斯狄更斯。

美國是英國殖民地之一，因此早期美國的文學發展與英國有些許的關連。殖民文學被視為最早的美國文學。從英國與愛爾蘭到美國的開拓者會記錄他們在殖民地的生活，述說與印地安人相處與和他們產生分歧的情形，其中較為人知的是到新大陸探險的約翰史密斯上尉。於 1789 年出版的《憐憫的力量》為第一本美國小說，作者為出生於波士頓的威廉希爾布朗。19世紀時，美國發展出獨特的文學風格，此時期傑出的作者有華盛頓歐文和艾倫坡。後者為美國第一位寫短篇故事的作家。馬克吐溫則在作品中使用方言與地方性語調，《頑童流浪記》就是他的作品。美國文學在 20 世紀走向一個新的發展，這個時期的作品敘述著上流與下層社會的生活，有些作品也會探討自然主義。戰爭也成為探討主題之一。

聽力題目解析

❶ 此題詢問的是何者為正確之選項。選項 (A) 為英國文學和美國文學相當類似；選項 (B) 為約翰史密斯船長是美國人；選項 (C) 為英國是美國的殖民地之一；選項 (D) 為美國是英國的殖民地之一。在錄音檔中後段我們可以聽見 "As one of the British colonies, early American literature …" 故答案選則 (D)。選項 (A) 錯誤因為內文有提到美國和英國具有相當不同的歷史。

❷ 此題詢問的是選項何者非莎士比亞所寫。根據錄音檔的末段，我們可以得知《頑童歷險記》為 Mark Twain 所寫，故答案為 (B)。

❸ 此題詢問的是選項何者並不屬於莎士比亞的四大悲劇。在介紹英國文學時，我們可以得知其四大悲劇為《哈姆雷特》、《奧塞羅》、《李爾王》和《馬克白》，且內文並沒有出現《羅密歐與茱麗葉》，故選 (B)。

❹ 此題詢問的是 "remarkable" 之意為何。選項 (A) 為發言；選項 (B) 為傑出的；選項 (C) 為可怕的；選項 (D) 為困惑的。按照文意理解，答案為 (B)，可透過前後文對於美國文學的正面介紹來推測此單字應具有讚賞之意。

• •

閱讀題目解析

❶ 此題詢問的是選項何者可能為美國史上第一本小說。答案可見內文最後一段之中間，選擇 (D)。

❷ 此題詢問的是選項何者為不正確之陳述。選項 (A) 為二十世紀的美國文學觸及了廣泛的題材；選項 (B) 為珍奧斯丁和約翰史密斯都是英國人；選項 (C) 為在美國受英國殖民期間，愛爾蘭和美國毫無關聯；選項 (D) 為文學是辨別美國和英國文化之差異的一種方法。答案可見內文最後一段，答案選擇 (C)。

補充單字

☆			
☆ 1. author	n.	作者
☆ 2. literature	n.	文學
☆ 3. exist	v.	存在
☆ 4. comedy	n.	喜劇
☆ 5. tragedy	n.	悲劇
☆ 6. expedition	n.	探險

Level 3 11 IQ Test
智商測驗

聽力測驗 🎧 Track 051

在學習英文的過程中，「聽」可能是最直接的第一線接觸，也可能是大家最想要快速習得的能力。現在，就讓我們來熟悉各種英文情境，提升自己的英文臨場感吧！

(   ) 1. The story talks about _____.
    (A) politics   (B) environment issue
    (C) robots   (D) IQ test

(   ) 2. What does IQ stands for?
    (A) Intelligence Quotient
    (B) Individual Quota
    (C) Indignity Quotient
    (D) Integral Quotient

(   ) 3. Which of the following is true?
    (A) The original purpose of IQ test is to detect aliens of lower intelligence.
    (B) The original purpose of IQ test is to detect children of lower intelligence.
    (C) The original purpose of IQ test is to detect animals of lower intelligence.
    (D) The original purpose of IQ test is to detect adults of lower intelligence.

(   ) 4. Binet and Simon's test can detect all the following abilities, except for?
    (A) reasoning   (B) practical knowledge
    (C) memory   (D) drawing

閱讀測驗

剛剛的聽力測驗是否因為答題不順而感到遺憾？或是覺得自己有某些地方掌握地不夠好？現在就讓我們來直接「看」剛剛的聽力測驗，並透過後面的閱讀測驗來補齊聽力上的不足，同時考驗自己的閱讀能力吧！

Level 1 Level 2 Level 3 Level 4 Level 5 Level 6

IQ, is the abbreviation of **Intelligence**[1] Quotient. IQ test is a test used to measure intelligence. The original purpose of the IQ test is to **detect**[2] children of lower intelligence in order to put them in special education programs. The IQ test is meant to test a child's intelligence compared to the child's age. If a child obtains high scores, he/she is said to be smarter than other normal children of his/her age. On the other hand, lower scores represented that the child is less intelligent.

Sir Frances Galton, a scientist from England, was the first to study the differences between individual people's **mental**[3] ability. Under the request of the French government, French psychologist Alfred Binet and Theodore Simon first established a test to **predict**[4] academic success. Through the test, they would know if children in the public schools would be able to fit with formal education. The test is of practical knowledge, reasoning, memory, vocabulary and problem solving. It is said that their test was better than Galton's because his test is merely a sensory test. Binet and Simon also invented the idea of mental age. However, their **formula**[5] is not widely used in their homeland. The IQ test invented by Binet and Simon was then brought to the United States by Henry Goddard. He is a director of a school for mentally challenged students. Goddard translated the formula into English and uses it to test students for mental retardation. Following that, an American psychologist Lewis Terman began to use the test on adults. He set up new standards of average ability of people at each age, and his formula was called Stanford-Binet Intelligence Scale. In the test, Terman replaced mental age into a single score, which he called intelligence quotient. Unfortunately, his formula didn't work well on adults.

IQ were used and mentioned in many research, articles and other contexts. Social scientists use IQ test results to predict educational achievements and special needs for students. Companies also apply IQ tests to test for an employee's job performances. However, more and more researchers are in doubt about the **accuracy**[6] and practicality of IQ tests. They believe that intelligence can change over time. Some people said that brain functions can be affected by certain mental activities. Nowadays, our society values more on emotional intelligence. Emotional intelligence involves an individual's personality and his or her capacity or skill to manage his/her emotions. Now, before a company hires an employee, the employee no longer takes an IQ test, instead they need to fill out a personality or EQ test.

【Question】

( ) 1. Who was the first to research on each individual's mental capacity?
(A) Alfrend Binet   (B) Theodore Simon
(C) Henry Goddard   (D) Sir Frances Galton

( ) 2. Whose formula was later introduced into America, and by whom?
(A) Sir Frances Galton; Alfred Binet
(B) Afred Binet and Theodore Simon; Henry Goddard
(C) Henry Goddard and Theodore Simon; Sir Frances Galton
(D) Henry Goddard; Sir Frances Galton

【文章中譯】

IQ 指的就是智力商數，智商測驗就是用以檢測智商的一個測驗指標。智商測驗最初是用來檢測智商較低的孩童，進而安排他們接受特殊教育。智商測驗原意為測驗孩童的智能是否與其年齡應有的智能相符。如果 IQ 取得較高的分數，則代表比其他同年齡的小孩聰明；相對的，若是分數較低，則略為遜色。

英國科學家法蘭西斯・加爾頓爵士為第一位研究個體心智差異的人。在法國政府的要求下，法國心理學家艾佛・貝寧特和希爾多・賽門最先建立一個測驗系統，以預測教育的實施是否成功。透過測驗，他們能判斷公立學校的學生能否接受正規教育。他們所研發的測驗主要針對受測對象的實務知識、判斷力、記憶力、字彙能力和解決問題的能力進行測驗。據說他們的測驗比加爾頓的好，因為加爾頓的測驗僅能針對知覺。與此同時，貝寧特與賽門也提出了心智年齡的理論。可惜，他們研發的測驗沒有在法國廣泛運用。亨利‧戈達將兩人的測驗引進美國，戈達是一家學校的董事，其學校主要接收有智能缺陷的學生。戈達將測驗內容翻譯成英文，再用以檢測學生是否智能不足。在此之後，美國心理學家路易斯‧特曼將此測驗套用於成人身上，他設立了新的標準，劃分出每個年齡層的成人該有的一般能力，他更將測驗命名為史丹福貝寧特智商等級。特曼將測驗中的心智年齡轉換成分數，而此就是所謂的智力商數。然而，針對成人的測驗成效不如預期。

許多研究、文章和其他文本都曾提過智商測驗。藉由智商測驗取得的結果，社會科學家能預測教育制度的成效，也能找出學生的特別需求。企業與公司也會用智商測驗測試員工的工作表現。然而，越來越多學者對智商測驗的準確度和可行性提出質疑，因為他們認為智商是可以隨時間改變的，也有人認為某些心理活動也會影響大腦功能的進行。現今，社會比較注重情緒管理，這包含了個體控制自我情緒的性格分析、能力和技巧。現今企業雇用新人時，新人不再進行智商測驗，取而代之的是人格特質或情緒智商測驗。

聽力題目解析

❶ 此題詢問的是故事主旨。選項 (A) 為政治；選項 (B) 為環境議題；選項 (C) 為機器人；選項 (D) 為智商測驗。錄音檔在一開始即破題，且內文皆在探討 IQ 測驗的演變，故選 (D)。

❷ 此題詢問的是 "IQ" 所個別代表的單字為何。錄音檔在一開始即告訴我們答案，仔細聽即可掌握，選擇 (A)。 "Quotient" 為「商；程度」之意。

❸ 此題詢問的是選項何者正確。選項 (A) 為智商測驗的原始目的是測量低智商的外星人；選項 (B) 為智商測驗的原始目的是測量低智商的孩童；選項 (C) 為智商測驗的原始目的是測量低智商的動物；選項 (D) 為智商測驗的原始目的是測量低智商的成人。在錄音檔開始不久後，我們即可以聽見 "IQ test is to detect children of lower intelligence in order to put them in special education programs."，故答案為 (B)，且內文並沒有提到替外星人和動物測量智商。

❹ 此題詢問的是貝寧特和賽門的測驗系統不能偵測選項何者。選項 (A) 為推理；選項 (B) 為實用知識；選項 (C) 為記憶力；選項 (D) 為畫畫。答案為 (D)，此題建議先看過題目和選項，以便在聆聽時做掌握，將已出現之單字先行刪去。

閱讀題目解析

❶ 此題詢問的是第一個研究個體心智差異的人為何者。選項 (A) 為艾佛‧貝寧特；選項 (B) 為希爾多‧賽門；選項 (C) 為亨利‧戈達；選項 (D) 為法蘭西斯‧加爾頓爵士。答案可見內文第二段第一行，選擇 (D)。

❷ 此題詢問的是何者研發的測驗被引入美國，以及是何人引進的。選項 (A) 為法蘭西斯‧加爾頓爵士／艾佛‧貝寧特；選項 (B) 為艾佛‧貝寧特及希爾多‧賽門／亨利‧戈達；選項 (C) 為亨利‧戈達及希爾多‧賽門／法蘭西斯‧加爾頓爵士；選項 (D) 為亨利‧戈達／法蘭西斯‧加爾頓爵士。答案詳見內文第二段的中間部分，儘管貝寧特與賽門的理論同時提出了心智年齡的理論，他們研發的測驗並沒有在法國被廣泛地運用，後來亨利‧戈達則將兩人的測驗引進美國，故答案選 (B)。

補充單字

☆ 1. intelligence	n.	智能
☆ 2. detect	v.	查出
☆ 3. mental	adj.	精神的、智商的
☆ 4. predict	v.	預測
☆ 5. formula	n.	算式
☆ 6. accuracy	n.	正確性

Level 3
12 On Which Day are Americans the Busiest?

美國人最忙的一天

聽力測驗 🎧 Track 052

在學習英文的過程中，「聽」可能是最直接的第一線接觸，也可能是大家最想要快速習得的能力。現在，就讓我們來熟悉各種英文情境，提升自己的英文臨場感吧！

(　　) 1. Which of the following statement is true?
    (A) Americans need not pay income taxes.
    (B) Americans paid income taxes long before the country established.
    (C) All taxpayers in America should pay local taxes.
    (D) April 15th is America's tax day.

(　　) 2. Below are people who should have a Social Security Number, except for?
    (A) citizens of America
    (B) permanent residents of America
    (C) temporary working residents
    (D) tourist

(　　) 3. Which department is responsible for collecting tax in America?
    (A) Internal Revenue Service   (B) Health Department
    (C) Supreme Court   (D) FBI

(　　) 4. Social Security Number can also be used as a(an) _____?
    (A) birthday card   (B) air ticket
    (C) identifier   (D) phone number

 **閱讀測驗**

剛剛的聽力測驗是否因為答題不順而感到遺憾？或是覺得自己有某些地方掌握地不夠好？現在就讓我們來直接「看」剛剛的聽力測驗，並透過後面的閱讀測驗來補齊聽力上的不足，同時考驗自己的閱讀能力吧！

If you ask Americans which day in a year they are the busiest, you probably will get the answer of April 15th. It is the tax day for Americans, and April 15th is the due date for paying taxes. Like Taiwanese people and other countries, all employed Americans are **obligated**[1] to pay federal **income**[2] taxes.

Running a country is difficult and a country needs a lot of money to cover some of the government expenses, hence the government has to raise money by asking the people to pay taxes. An income tax was first collected during the Civil War, but it didn't last long. In 1894, President Grover Cleveland tried to make yearly income taxes regular, but his suggestion was rejected by the Supreme Court. It was until 1913, Congress could legally collect taxes on income. The Internal Revenue Service (IRS) is a department responsible for collecting federal income taxes in the United States. A person should pay certain taxes according to how much money he/she earned in a year. The Congress allowed some **deductions**[3] of the taxes which taxpayers need not include in their income taxes, such as alimony and charitable **contributions**[4]. Some states in America allow individual cities to levy an additional income tax. On the other hand, in some states, local taxes can be deducted for federal tax purpose.

Americans used to spend a lot of time on filing out tax returns. In the past, people had to wait in a long line and fill in different kinds of forms, and mail their forms through postal services as they ran through all procedures. Luckily, computer and Internet help to improve the operations. Taxpayers can now file their tax returns electronically. No matter how you file your tax returns, there are certain documents one needs to prepare. The Social Security Number is a number issued to U.S. citizens, **permanent**[5] **residents**[6] and temporary working residents. The United States government issued Social Security Number to track citizens for taxation purposes. It can also be an identifier for individuals within America. Besides Social Security Number, documents which prove one's salary and incomes are also required.

If taxpayers failed to file their tax returns before April 15th, they will need to pay late payment penalty and late payment interest. To make filling tax returns much more efficient and to save time, the Postal office suggests taxypayers mail their tax forms earlier. Taxpayers are recommended to submit their income taxes by the Internet since it saves time and saves both the taxpayers and IRS's work.

【Question】

(　　) 1. Which of the following document is not required when filing out tax returns?
(A) Social Security Number　　(B) proof of salary
(C) proof of income　　(D) proof of health

(　　) 2. When did it become legal for the Congress to collect taxes on income?
(A) when Cleveland was in power
(B) in 1894
(C) in 1913
(D) when the Supreme Court denied the proposal again

【文章中譯】

若你問美國人，一年當中他們最忙的一天是哪一天，答案一定是 4 月 15 日。這一天是美國的報稅日，美國人必須在 4 月 15 日以前完成所得稅申報。和台灣人與其他國家的公民一樣，有僱傭關係的美國人也必須繳納所得稅。

治理國家並不容易，必須負擔許多政府開銷，因此政府會向人民徵收稅務以籌措治國經費。美國政府第一次向國民徵收所得稅，是在美國內戰時期，但並沒有持續太久。1894 年，克立夫蘭總統提倡每年徵收所得稅，結果他的建議遭到最高法院駁回。一直到1913年，美國國會才得以合法地徵收所得稅。負責徵收美國聯邦政府稅的是國稅局。國人依據各自一年的年收入，繳納所得稅。美國國會允許國民享有部分扣繳，例如：贍養費和慈善捐獻。美國境內部份的州允許城市加收額外的稅務。另一方面，某些州則會因聯邦稅收的因素將州稅列入扣除額裡。

過去申報稅務會佔用美國人很長的時間，除了必須排隊等候，還得花時間填寫各式不同的表格，然後還得將填妥的表格郵寄出去。所幸電腦與網路省下不少作業時間，因為納稅人現在可用電子報稅的方法繳稅。不管是用何種方式申報所得稅，納稅人必須準備一些相關資料與文件。美國政府給予每個公民、永久居民和臨時居民一個社會安全號碼，目的在於追查納稅人是否逃稅。不僅如此，社會安全號碼也可當作身份證明。另外，申報所得稅時還得備妥薪資與收入證明。

若納稅人無法在截止日期以前完成申報作業，將會被罰款，除了得繳納罰金，還得支付利息。為了使申報作業更有效率、省時，郵政局建議民眾提早寄出稅單。政府也建議納稅人透過網路申報，不僅省時，也省去納稅人和國稅局辦公人員的作業。

聽力題目解析

❶ 此題詢問的是何者為正確選項。選項 (A) 為美國人不需要繳所得稅；選項 (B) 為美國人早在建國前就開始繳所得稅了；選項 (C) 為所有美國納稅人都需要繳交地方稅；選項 (D) 為四月十五日日美國的納稅日。錄音檔的一開始即告訴我們若美國人一年當中最忙的一天是 4 月 15 日，答案為 (D)。

❷ 此題詢問的是選項何者沒有社會安全號碼。選項 (A) 為美國公民；選項 (B) 為美國的永久居民；選項 (C) 為短期工作居民；選項 (D) 為遊客。在錄音檔的末段，我們可以聽見 "Social Security Number is a number issued to US citizens, permanent residents, and temporary working residents." 故選擇 (D)。

❸ 此題訊問的是哪個部門負責稅收。選項 (A) 為國家稅務局；選項 (B) 為健康部門；選項 (C) 為高等法院；選項 (D) 為聯邦調查局。在我們得知徵收所得稅合法之後，我們接著可以聽見 "the Internal Revenue Service is responsible ..."，故選擇 (A)。

❹ 此題詢問的是社會安全號碼可以同時被使用為選項何者。選項 (A) 為生日卡片；選項 (B) 為機票；選項 (C) 為識別證；選項 (D) 為電話號碼。在錄音檔末段，我們可以把握住 "identifier" 此關鍵字，選擇 (C)，且其他選項皆未曾出現。

閱讀題目解析

❶ 此題詢問的是報稅時不需要哪種文件。選項 (A) 為社會安全號碼；選項 (B) 為薪資證明；選項 (C) 為收入證明；選項 (D) 為健康證明。答案可見內文倒數第二段的最後一句，故選擇 (D)。

❷ 此題詢問的是美國國會在什麼時候得以開始合法徵收所得稅。選項 (A) 為當克立夫蘭執政時；選項 (B) 為於1894年時；選項 (C) 為於1913年時；選項 (D) 為當最高法院再度駁回請求時。答案可見內文第二段的中間，選擇 (C)。

補充單字

☆ 1. oblige	**v.**	必須
☆ 2. income	**n.**	收入
☆ 3. deduction	**n.**	扣除
☆ 4. contribution	**n.**	貢獻
☆ 5. permanent	**adj.**	永久的
☆ 6. resident	**n.**	居民

The Fantasy in Paris
巴黎風情

Level 3
13

聽力測驗 🎧Track 053

在學習英文的過程中，「聽」可能是最直接的第一線接觸，也可能是大家最想要快速習得的能力。現在，就讓我們來熟悉各種英文情境，提升自己的英文臨場感吧！

(   ) 1. The article introduces about the fantasy in _____.
     (A) Puerto Rico   (B) Portugal
     (C) Paris   (D) Phuket

(   ) 2. Paris is the capital of _____.
     (A) France   (B) Italy
     (C) Germany   (D) Japan

(   ) 3. According to the article, which of the following is correct?
     (A) Paris has a lot of big emporium.
     (B) Paris has a lot of temples.
     (C) Paris has a lot of museums.
     (D) Paris has a lot of night market.

(   ) 4. Avenue Montaigne is a _____.
     (A) playground for children
     (B) night market
     (C) golf club
     (D) shopping spot

(   ) 5. Which of the following is a traditional French dessert?
     (A) donut   (B) macaroon
     (C) green tea ice cream   (D) bird's nest soup

Level 1
Level 2
Level 3
Level 4
Level 5
Level 6

 閱讀測驗

剛剛的聽力測驗是否因為答題不順而感到遺憾？或是覺得自己有某些地方掌握地不夠好？現在就讓我們來直接「看」剛剛的聽力測驗，並透過後面的閱讀測驗來補齊聽力上的不足，同時考驗自己的閱讀能力吧！

Situated on the river Seine, Paris is the largest city in France. As the capital of France, Paris is one of the most popular tourist **destinations**[1] in the world. **Romantic**[2] and gracious are some of the descriptions you will find in most of the travel **brochures**[3] introducing Paris. Put aside the common failings of big cities, Paris is a city full of art, culture, fashion, cuisine, cafes, and other interesting spots.

If you're an art and culture lover, you will definitely love spending some time in museums, opera houses, theaters and other places. The Louvre Museum is one of the most popular spot for visiting. The museum has about 35,000 works of art, including paintings, **sculptures**[4], and antiquities. Not only its collections are art works, the museum itself is an art piece as well. At the main entrance of the museum sits the Louvre Pyramid constructed mainly with glass segments. The pyramid was designed by I. M. Pei, a Chinese born American architect. The Palais Garnier is also located around Louvre Museum. With 2,200 seats, it is served as the main venues of the Parisian Ballet and Opera. Bastille Opera is another place for watching ballets.

Are Fashion and labels much more eyecatching? Spending a day at Champs-Elysees and Avenue Montaigne will definitely satisfy your thirst for clothes, bags, and shoes. At the Champs-Elysees, there are cafes, cinemas, and luxury shops. On Avenue Montaigne, high fashion stores are everywhere. It is another place for tourists to drown in luxury branded clothes, jewelries, and accessories.

Paris is not only well-known for its art and fashion, but also its delicate cuisine. Some of the restaurants in Paris have been awarded Michelin Stars. Foie gras is one of the French's favorites, a food made of the liver of a duck or goose that has been **intentionally**[5] fattened. Foie gras can be served cold or hot. In most Foie gras dishes, it is flavored with truffles, mushrooms, or **figs**[6] on toasted bread or baguette. Most French people also have a sweet tooth; they love to enjoy desserts after meals. Take a stroll down Paris streets, you will definitely find world famous patisserie with some noted desserts like macaroon, madeleine, and mille-feuille. Other than desserts, breads are common in Paris, too. Among breads in France, the baguette (French bread) is the most popular. There is even a law to define a standard baguette.

【Question】

(　　) 1. Which of the following statement about foie gras is incorrect?
　　　　(A) It may be served in many of the restaurants in France.
　　　　(B) It is made of the liver of a chicken.
　　　　(C) The liver where it is made from has been intentionally fattened.
　　　　(D) Foei gras and truffles can go well together.

(　　) 2. What can be said about the Louvre Museum?
　　　　(A) It was designed by a Vietnam-born American architect.
　　　　(B) It houses 35,000 pieces of artwork.
　　　　(C) Near the entrance lies a Pyramid constructed with procelain.
　　　　(D) The Palaise Garnier is very far away from it.

【文章中譯】

座落於塞納河畔旁的巴黎是法國最大的城市。巴黎是法國的首都，也是全球知名的旅遊景點。大多數介紹巴黎的小冊子裡，都會提到巴黎是一個既浪漫又優雅的地方。撇開大城市的通病，巴黎是個充滿藝術、文化氣息、時尚、美食、咖啡廳和其他有趣景點的地方。

若你熱愛藝文，那麼千萬別錯過巴黎的博物館、歌劇院和劇場。羅浮宮是知名的景點，館裡展示了 35,000 件藝術作品，如畫作、雕像和古董。羅浮宮不僅館藏豐富，它本身也可被視為是一項藝術作品。博物館主要入口處有一座玻璃金字塔。羅浮宮金字塔是由華裔美籍建築師貝聿銘所設計。距離羅浮宮不遠處，是巴黎加尼葉歌劇院，裡面可容納2,200 名觀眾，它主要是芭蕾與歌劇的表演場所。想欣賞芭蕾舞演出，還可到巴斯底歌劇院。

覺得時尚和名牌更有吸引力嗎？那麼就要到香榭里舍大道和蒙田大道血拼一番，滿足你對衣服、皮包和鞋子的慾望。巴黎的香榭里舍大道上有咖啡廳、電影院和高級商店。而蒙田大道上則是新潮名店匯集的地方，遊客在這裡可買到高級品牌的衣服、珠寶和配件。

除了藝文與時尚，巴黎的高級料理也是世界知名的。這裡有不少餐廳榮獲米其林星等的評價。以鵝和鴨的肝製成的鵝肝、鴨肝是法國人最愛的料理之一。鵝肝與鴨肝的製作方法是對鵝和鴨灌食，讓牠們的肝變得肥美。鵝肝、鴨肝可熟食也可生食。大多數的料理會將它們與松露、菌類與無花果一起搭配烤過的麵包或棍子麵包。法國人大多也愛吃甜食，他們也喜歡在餐後享用甜點。在巴黎街上晃一晃，不難發現許多知名的甜點屋，裡面擺著著名的法式甜點，如杏仁小圓餅、瑪德蓮和千層派。除了甜點，麵包也是法國常見的食物，各式麵包中，要屬棍子麵包（即法國麵包）最常見，法國甚至有規定正統的棍子麵包應有的標準。

聽力題目解析

❶ 此題訊問的文章介紹了何地的風情。選項 (A) 為波多黎各；選項 (B) 為葡萄牙；選項 (C) 為巴黎；選項 (D) 為普吉島。錄音檔一開始即破題，選擇 (C)。

❷ 此題詢問的是巴黎為何地的首都。選項 (A) 為法國；選項 (B) 為義大利；選項 (C) 為德國；選項 (D) 為日本。答案為 (A)，同上，我們在一開始即可聽見。

❸ 此題詢問的是選項何者的陳述正確。選項 (A) 為巴黎有很多大型商場；選項 (B) 為巴黎有很多寺廟；選項 (C) 為巴黎有很多博物館；選項 (D) 為巴黎有很多夜市。在一開始，我們可以聽見巴黎是一件充滿藝術及文化的城市，接下來，我們也接收到了關於羅浮宮等藝術場所之地的資訊，故答案應選擇 (C)。

❹ 此題詢問的是蒙田大道是何地。選項 (A) 為孩子的遊樂園；選項 (B) 為夜市；選項 (C) 為高爾夫俱樂部；選項 (D) 為購物地點。我們在聽見時尚和名牌購物地的介紹時，便可聽見 "Spend a day at Champs-Elysees and Avenue Montaigne...",故答案為 (D),且選項 (A) 至 (C) 皆沒有出現過。

⑤ 此題詢問的是選項何者為傳統法式點心。選項 (A) 為甜甜圈;選項 (B) 為馬卡龍;選項 (C) 為綠茶冰淇淋;選項 (D) 為燕窩。在錄音檔最後,我們可以得知 "macaroon, madeleine, and mille-feuille" 為法國的常見甜點,故選擇 (B),此種題型建議先看過題目和選項,以便掌握。

• •

閱讀題目解析

❶ 此題詢問的是何者關於肥肝的敘述是不正確的。選項 (A) 為它可能會出現在法國許多的餐廳之中;選項 (B) 為它是由雞肝做成的;選項 (C) 為製成肥肝的肝已被蓄意地填充使其變飽滿;選項 (D) 為肥肝和松露是適合搭配在一起的料理。答案可見內文最後一段第三句,其應是由鵝或鴨的肝製成,故選 (B)。

❷ 此題詢問的是關於羅浮宮,我們可以做出何種陳述。選項 (A) 為它是由越南裔的美國建築師所設計;選項 (B) 為館裡展示了 35,000 件藝術作品;選項 (C) 為博物館主要入口處有一座瓷製金字塔;選項 (D) 為巴黎加尼葉歌劇院離它很遠。答案可見內文第二段全部,唯一正確的選項為 (B)。

補充單字

☆ 1. destination	n.	目的地
☆ 2. romantic	adj.	浪漫的
☆ 3. brochure	n.	小冊子
☆ 4. sculpture	n.	雕像
☆ 5. intentionally	adv.	故意地
☆ 6. fig	n.	無花果

The Common Points between American Psychiatrists and Dentists

美國精神科醫生與牙醫的共同點

聽力測驗 🎧 Track 054

在學習英文的過程中,「聽」可能是最直接的第一線接觸,也可能是大家最想要快速習得的能力。現在,就讓我們來熟悉各種英文情境,提升自己的英文臨場感吧!

( ) 1. In the article, dentists share common points with _____.
    (A) police   (B) nurse
    (C) psychiatrists   (D) artist

( ) 2. Which of the following is not what a dentist does?
    (A) cleaning   (B) filling cavities
    (C) root canals   (D) painting walls

( ) 3. Which of the following is not a subspecialized of psychiatry?
    (A) dental public health   (B) forensic psychiatry
    (C) adult psychiatry   (D) learning disability

( ) 4. If you want to become a dentist, which of the following knowledge should you acquire?
    (A) interpret X-rays of teeth
    (B) how to fix a faucet
    (C) learn about botanic
    (D) mental illness

( ) 5. What does the word "adolescent" mean in the article?
    (A) old people   (B) baby
    (C) teenager

剛剛的聽力測驗是否因為答題不順而感到遺憾？或是覺得自己有某些地方掌握地不夠好？現在就讓我們來直接「看」剛剛的聽力測驗，並透過後面的閱讀測驗來補齊聽力上的不足，同時考驗自己的閱讀能力吧！

Most American people visit a dentist twice a year. The **frequency**[1] is suggested by professional dentists. Americans not only visit the dentist regularly, their **appointments**[2] with psychiatrists are also on their schedule as well. Unlike Asian people, visiting psychiatrists is common and not unusual for Americans. In the United States, seeing a psychiatrist is as usual as seeing a dentist. These two careers seem different, but somehow they share some common points.

Dentists specialize in oral problems. A professional dentist needs to provide care, prevention, **diagnosis**[3], and treatment of diseases of teeth and oral health to his/her patients. Their services cover different areas, such as cleanings, filling cavities, root canals, treatment for gum diseases, and other things. Just like dentist, a psychiatrist specializes in the diagnosis, treatment, and prevention of mental illness. Psychiatrists' job is to deal with all kinds of problems concerning mental health. Different from other mental health practitioners, psychiatrists are one of a few professionals who are fully licensed medical doctors.

Dentists are accredited to be medical professionals. In America, students who wish to become dentists should study and train for several years. One should attend a dental school to acquire basic knowledge; they also need to learn how to fill cavities, straighten teeth, replace damaged and missing teeth with dentures, and **interpret**[4] X-rays of the teeth. Other than general dentistry, there are some dental specialties in the United States, such as dental public health, pediatric dentistry, and others. One should also learn how to **counsel**[5] a patient, run a clinic, and keep up with the latest and cutting edge dentistry technology. To become a psychiatrist, one should be trained in psychotherapy, and complete a Bachelor's degree by finishing study in college. After that, students **enroll**[6] in pre-medical program and choose to study for specific courses. Further psychiatry fields include psychoanalysis, adolescent psychiatry, adult psychiatry, forensic psychiatry, learning disability and others.

Students should then apply for a four-year medical school to complete their medical education. After graduating from medical school, they should complete a four-year residency training in the field of psychiatry.

In the United States, certain associations and organizations of dentist and psychiatry were established. These associations and organizations hold conferences, meetings, and annual sessions, where dentists and psychiatrists can share their knowledge and ideas with each other. They could also get in touch with the latest news and technology concerning their specialties. These organizations can thus provide help to the public by providing suggestions.

【Question】

(　　) 1. What can we infer from the article?
　　(A) Going to a psychiatrist may be considered strange in Asia.
　　(B) It is very expensive to see a dentist in the United States.
　　(C) Licenses are highly accessible for anyone who wants to be a dentist in the U.S.
　　(D) Text books are more important than new trends.

(　　) 2. Which of the following is not included in the field of psychiatry?
　　(A) psychotherapy　　(B) pre-medical program
　　(C) adult psychiatry　　(D) animal psychiatry

【文章中譯】

大多數美國人一年會看兩次牙醫，這是專業牙醫的建議。美國人不只定期看牙醫，也常預約精神科醫生。與亞洲人不同的是，美國人認為看精神科是很普通的事情，一點也不奇怪。牙醫和精神科醫生看似不同，但卻有一些共同點。

牙醫專門醫治與口腔有關的問題。專業牙醫必須照料病人的牙齒與口腔，也得針對牙齒疾病進行預防、診斷和治療的協助。他們提供的服務非常廣泛，例如：洗牙、修補蛀牙、根管與牙齦疾病的治療。和牙醫一樣，精神科醫師必須診斷、治療並預防心理方面的疾病，精神科醫師需處理一切跟心理疾病有關的事情。有別於其他心理健康工作者，精神科醫師和一些專業醫師一樣，擁有醫師執照。

牙醫是合格的專業醫師。在美國，要成為牙醫師必須修讀好幾年。學生需要唸牙醫學院習得基本的知識，還得學會如何補蛀牙、矯正牙齒、將壞掉的牙齒換成假牙，以及看懂牙齒的 X 光片。除了牙科醫學，美國還有許多特殊的牙科專門科，像是牙科公共衛生學、小兒牙科學等。要成為牙醫還得學會給病人諮詢和經營診所，也得隨時跟上最新的尖端牙醫科技。要成為精神科醫師就必須選修精神療法，完成大學的課業並取得學士文憑。之後則進入醫學預科，選讀特殊科目，這類的特殊科目包括精神分析、青少年精神病學、成人精神病學、刑事精神病學，和學習障礙等。在此之後，學生還得在醫學院完成四年的課業，從醫學院畢業後，他們還得花四年的時間，住院實習有關精神醫學方面的技能。

美國成立了不少與牙醫和精神科醫師有關的協會和機構。透過舉辦研討會、會議和年度大會，牙醫與精神科醫師得以互相交流，還能接觸與其相關領域的消息和最新技術。這類的協會和機構也能向民眾提供服務，給予專業建議。

聽力題目解析

❶ 此題詢問的是根據內文，牙醫與選項何者句有共通點。選項 (A) 為警察；選項 (B) 為護士；選項 (C) 為精神科醫生；選項 (D) 為藝術家。根據錄音檔的一開始，我們即可得知 "... somehow they share some common points"，故選 (C)。

❷ 此題詢問的是選項何者並非牙醫之職務。選項 (A) 為清潔；選項 (B) 為補牙；選項 (C) 為根管治療；選項 (D) 為畫牆。答案為 (D)，此題建議先看過題目及選項，便可在介紹牙醫之職務時，把握關鍵字。若疏忽細節，此題也用常理推測。

❸ 此題詢問的是何者不是精神病學的子項。選項 (A) 為牙科公共衛生；選項 (B) 為刑事精神病學；選項 (C) 為成人精神病學；選項 (D) 為學習障礙。答案為 (A)。此題同上，建議先看過題目及選項。若大意錯失關鍵字，也可用常理推判。

❹ 此題詢問的是一名牙醫需要具備何種選項的知識。選項 (A) 為解讀牙齒的X 光照；選項 (B) 為修水龍頭；選項 (C) 為植物學；選項 (D) 為心理疾病。錄音檔指出 "... also need to learn ... (to) interpret X-rays of the teeth"，故選擇 (A)。

❺ 此題詢問的是美國人一年去看幾次牙醫。選項 (A) 為一次；選項 (B) 為兩次；選項 (C) 為四次；選項 (D) 為六次。錄音檔的第一句即告訴我們答案，選擇 (B)。

閱讀題目解析

❶ 此題詢問的是我們可以從內文中推論出何者。選項 (A) 為在亞洲看精神科醫師可能會被人覺得奇怪；選項 (B) 為在美國看牙醫很昂貴；選項 (C) 為在美國任何想要當牙醫的人都可以很輕易地取得證照；選項 (D) 為對精神科醫生來說，教科書比新趨勢重要的多。答案可見內文第一段，選擇 (A)。這題特別要注意到的是，選項 (B) 和 (C) 並沒有在內文被提及，故不論對錯皆無法推測。選項 (D) 為錯誤之選項，可見內文倒數二段。

❷ 此題詢問的是選項何者並不被涵蓋在精神科的領域之內。選項 (A) 為精神療法；選項 (B) 為醫學預科；選項 (C) 為成人精神病學；選項 (D) 為動物精神病學。答案可見內文倒數第二段中間部分，答案為 (D)。

補充單字

☆ 1. frequency	n.	頻率、次數
☆ 2. appointment	n.	（正式的）約會
☆ 3. diagnosis	n.	診斷
☆ 4. interpret	v.	解釋、理解
☆ 5. counsel	v.	勸告
☆ 6. enroll	v.	入學、註冊

American Country Music
美國鄉村音樂

聽力測驗 🎧 Track 055

在學習英文的過程中，「聽」可能是最直接的第一線接觸，也可能是大家最想要快速習得的能力。現在，就讓我們來熟悉各種英文情境，提升自己的英文臨場感吧！

( ) 1. The article talks about _____.
  (A) American Jazz music
  (B) American R&B music
  (C) American Rap music
  (D) American country music

( ) 2. American country music was originated from _____.
  (A) folk music   (B) Indian songs
  (C) symphony   (D) rock and roll

( ) 3. Which of the following is true?
  (A) British settlers brought their music into America.
  (B) Americans don't like country music.
  (C) LeAnn Rimes is an opera singer.
  (D) Grand Ole Opry is a TV broadcasting show.

( ) 4. Which of the following is not a country music singer?
  (A) Billy Ray Cyrus   (B) Mariah Carey
  (C) Carrie Underwood   (D) Tim McGraw

( ) 5. Who was known to be an important country musician in the early age?
  (A) Carrie Underwood   (B) Jimmie Rodgers
  (C) Taylor Swift   (D) Billy Ray Cyrus

 閱讀測驗

剛剛的聽力測驗是否因為答題不順而感到遺憾？或是覺得自己有某些地方掌握地不夠好？現在就讓我們來直接「看」剛剛的聽力測驗，並透過後面的閱讀測驗來補齊聽力上的不足，同時考驗自己的閱讀能力吧！

Country music is an important **genre**[1] in the America music industry. Most the Americans are fond of country music. Not only country music singers are popular, but country music awards are held every year.

When British settlers came to America, they brought along their culture and music. British people learned to **record**[2] history by storytelling, and this tradition was brought into America as well. People who lived in an uneasy life express their feelings by music. Country music originated from traditional folk music and **ballad**[3] of these **miserable**[4] people, such as people living in mountain areas. Americans changed the foreign music into their own songs, and their songs became more personal. Usually, the Americanized songs ended with moral statements. The main instrument used in country music is the fiddle because it is easy to carry around. Later on, other instruments were added in, such as the banjo, electronic guitars, the mandolin, etc.

Jimmie Rodgers and the Carter Family were known to be important country musicians in the early age. In his music, Jimmie Rodgers combined country music with jazz, gospel and folk songs. During that time, more and more musicians **released**[5] records, and some were sold with great results. Due to the Great Depression in 1929, numbers of record were cut down. People at the time could no longer afford to buy records. As a result, they prefer listening to radio and broadcast shows, such as "barn dance shows" which featured country music. The show was popular all over the southern United States, Chicago, and California. One of the most famous and popular broadcasting show was the Grand Ole Opry from Nashville, Tennessee. During the 1930s and 1940s, when Hollywood produced films about Western cowboys, western music was recorded. In the late 1960s, country rock, a new genre, surprised the music industry.

Country music singers are popular in the United States. Well-known singers are Garth Brooks, Faith Hill, Trisha Yearwood, Tim McGraw, Billy Ray Cyrus, and others. In recent years, young singers have become new bloods for country music, and made it more energetic than ever. LeAnn Rimes had her debut album released when she was only 13 years old. Carrie Underwood is a winner of American Idol, a reality show in America. Her debut album was certified seven times **platinum**[6]. Taylor Swift is also now another famouse country-pop singer-songwriter.

【Question】

(　　) 1. Which genre took the music industry by surprise in the late 1960s?
 (A) punk 　　　　　(B) techno
 (C) country music 　(D) rap

(　　) 2. What can we infer from the article?
 (A) Country music at its early age tended to tell personal or moral stories.
 (B) The instruments used in country music are pretty dull.
 (C) People stopped buying records because records became hard to come by.
 (D) Radio shows were all banned because people skipped work for them.

【文章中譯】

鄉村音樂在美國音樂界裡佔有一席重要地位，因為大多數的美國人都喜歡聽鄉村音樂。不僅鄉村音樂歌手大受歡迎，美國每年更舉辦鄉村音樂頒獎典禮。

英國人到美國定居時，他們也引進其文化與音樂。英國人以說故事的方式記錄歷史，這個方法後來也流入美國。生活困苦的人透過音樂抒發心情，鄉村音樂就是源自這些人所作的傳統歌謠，例如：居住在山區的人。美國人將外來的音樂轉變成本土的歌曲，他們的音樂更涉及私人情感。這些經過改良的美式歌曲，通常會以敘述道德作為結尾。鄉村音樂主要使用的樂器為小提琴，因為它方便攜帶。在此之後，鄉村音樂開始加入其他的樂器，像是五弦琴、電子吉他、曼陀林等。

傑米‧羅傑斯和卡特家族被視為是早期重要的鄉村音樂歌手。傑米‧羅傑斯將鄉村音樂、爵士、福音和民歌結合。當時越來越多鄉村歌手推出唱片，有些更取得極佳的銷售成績。然而約於 1929 年發生的經濟大蕭條，唱片發行開始萎靡，經濟拮据的人們無法購買唱片，他們開始收聽電台的廣播節目，像是伴隨著鄉村音樂的穀倉舞節目。這類的節目在美國南部、芝加哥與加州大受歡迎。當時最廣為人知的節目，是田納西州那什維爾的地方節目，名為「大奧普里」。1930 年到1940 年時期，好萊塢開始拍攝西部牛仔影片，此時西部也發行了西部牛仔音樂。在 1960年後期，鄉村搖滾的誕生則成為了音樂界的驚奇。

在美國，鄉村歌手極受歡迎，知名鄉村歌手有葛斯‧布魯克、費絲‧希爾、崔夏‧宜爾伍、提姆‧麥克羅和比利‧瑞塞洛斯等。近幾年來，美國鄉村音樂樂壇也出現了幾名新血，讓鄉村音樂更朝氣蓬勃。黎安‧萊姆絲在 13 歲時就推出首張個人專輯。凱莉‧安德伍是美國實境節目《美國偶像》的冠軍。她的首張專輯獲得七白金的成績。泰勒‧史薇芙特也是另一位有名的鄉村流行樂創作歌手。

聽力題目解析

❶ 此題詢問的是文章主旨。選項 (A) 為美國爵士樂；選項 (B) 為美國節奏藍調；選項 (C) 為美國饒舌樂；選項 (D) 為美國鄉村樂。音檔一開始即給答案，選 (D)。

❷ 此題詢問的是美國鄉村音樂的起源為何者。選項 (A) 為民俗音樂；選項 (B) 為印地安歌謠；選項 (C) 為交響樂；選項 (D) 為搖滾樂。在中段部分，我們可聽見 "Country music originated from traditional folk music and ...",這部分是要考 "originate" 此單字，為「發源於」之意，故選 (A)。

❸ 此題詢問的是選項何者為正確之陳述。選項 (A) 為英國殖民者將他們的音樂帶入美國；選項 (B) 為美國人不喜歡鄉村樂；選項 (C) 為黎安萊姆絲是一名哥劇歌手；選項 (D) 為《大奧普里》是一個電視廣播秀。在介紹鄉村音樂時，我們聽見 "... British settlers came to America, they brought along their culture and music." 後來我們才會聽見美國鄉村音

樂是如何發展成現在的樣子，選 (A)。

④ 此題詢問的是選項何者不是鄉村歌手。選項 (A) 為比利·瑞塞洛斯；選項 (B) 為瑪麗亞凱莉；選項 (C) 為凱莉·安德伍；選項 (D) 為提姆·麥克羅。答案為 (B)，此題型僅需細心聆聽，建議先看過題目及選項，以便掌握。

⑤ 此題詢問的是何者被認為是美國早期鄉村樂的重要人物。選項 (A) 為凱莉·安德伍；選項 (B) 為傑米·羅傑斯；選項 (C) 為泰勒·史薇芙特；選項 (D) 為比利·瑞塞洛斯。同上，答案為 (B)。

閱讀題目解析

① 此題詢問的是哪種樂風在 1960 年代讓音樂界感到驚奇。選項 (A) 為龐克；選項 (B) 為電子音樂；選項 (C) 為鄉村搖滾；選項 (D) 為饒舌。答案可見內文倒數第二段最後二行，選擇 (C)。

② 此題詢問的是我們可以從文章中推論何者。選項 (A) 為鄉村音樂在初期傾向於訴說個人和道德故事；選項 (B) 為鄉村音樂所使用的樂器相當單一乏味；選項 (C) 為人們停止購買唱片因為唱片變得很難取得；選項 (D) 為廣播電台秀被全面禁止因為人們為了聽廣播而翹班。答案見內文第二段，選 (A)。選項 (C) 的錯誤在於當時是因為大蕭條人們才無法買唱片；選項 (D) 並未在文章中提及。

補充單字

☆ 1. genre	n.	類型
☆ 2. record	n.	唱片
☆ 3. ballad	n.	民謠
☆ 4. miserable	adj.	痛苦的、不幸的
☆ 5. release	v.	發行
☆ 6. platinum	n.	白金

Level 4

隨心所欲
×
運用自如

Level 4
01
Crusades
十字軍東征

在學習英文的過程中,「聽」可能是最直接的第一線接觸,也可能是大家最想要快速習得的能力。現在,就讓我們來熟悉各種英文情境,提升自己的英文臨場感吧!

( ) 1. The Crusades were a series of _____ movements approved by the Pope.
(A) peaceful (B) military (C) selling (D) buying

( ) 2. When did the first Crusade happen?
(A) 1095 (B) 1509 (C) 1452 (D) 1059

( ) 3. What did they fight against at first?
(A) the Russia (B) Muslims (C) Jews (D) Mongol

( ) 4. Who won the first war?
(A) Crusaders (B) Muslins (C) Turkey (D) We don't know.

( ) 5. The First Crusade was a big _____.
(A) joke (B) failure (C) mistake (D) success

閱讀測驗

剛剛的聽力測驗是否因為答題不順而感到遺憾?或是覺得自己有某些地方掌握地不夠好?現在就讓我們來直接「看」剛剛的聽力測驗,並透過後面的閱讀測驗來補齊聽力上的不足,同時考驗自己的閱讀能力吧!

The Crusades were a series of **military**[1] movements approved by the Pope that took place during the 11th through 13th centuries. They started off to capture the Holy Land, Jerusalem, from the Muslims but developed into territorial wars.

The First Crusade took place when the Normans had **settled**[2] in France and conquered England. At that time, France and England, and also the Holy Roman Empire, were all stronger than ever. The rulers, therefore, began to think of conquering the Mediterranean and recreating the Roman Empire. Most importantly, they wanted to take Jerusalem, the city of Jesus Christ, away from the Muslims.

In 1095, the Pope **urged**[3] the people to take up weapons and fight for Jerusalem. People were so enthusiastic that even kids and old people wanted to go. They believed that their God would just **destroy**[4] the walls of Jerusalem as soon as they got there, so a lot of them didn't even take weapons with them. But the traveling and fighting were very hard, and most of the people died.

So instead of getting to Jerusalem to fight the Muslims, some Crusaders decided to stop in Germany to fight the Jews. Because Jews were not Christians, these Crusaders **robbed**[5] them and killed thousands of them.

In the fall of 1096, the main Crusade left for Jerusalem and took over it. The Crusaders made a lot of errors in their fighting. But the enemies didn't defend Jerusalem very well, so the Crusaders still took over Jerusalem and some other important cities. They settled down in Jerusalem, their new country. The First Crusade was a big success.

After a period of peace between Christians and Muslims, who coexisted in the Holy Land, Jerusalem, a new crusade formed and marched to Asia Minor. This is known as the Second Crusade. But this time they failed to accomplish any major successes. In 1149, they **returned**[6] to their countries without any result.

The timetable :
1 First Crusade 1095-1099
3 Third Crusade 1187–1192
5 Fifth Crusade 1217–1221
7 Seventh Crusade 1248–1254
9 Ninth Crusade 1271–1272

2 Second Crusade 1147–1149
4 Fourth Crusade 1202–1204
6 Sixth Crusade 1228–1229
8 Eighth Crusade 1270
10 Northern Crusades (Baltic and Germany)

【 Question 】

(   ) 1. What was the reason why some Crusaders fought the Jews in Germany?
(A) The Jews provoked them.
(B) The Pope ordered them to do so, and whoever won could be rewarded.
(C) The traveling and fighting were too hard, and the Jews were not Christians.
(D) They couldn't make it to Jerusalm.

(   ) 2. When did the Sixth Crusade take place?
(A) 1095-1099   (B) 1228-1239
(C) 1271-1272   (D) 1228-1229

【 文章中譯 】

十字軍東征是十一世紀至十三世紀一連串經由教宗認可的軍事行動。他們起始於想從回教徒手中奪取聖地耶路撒冷，但最後發展成領土的戰爭。

第一次十字軍東征發生在諾曼第人在法國定居下來，又征服了英國之時期。那時候的法國、英國和神聖羅馬帝國都比過去強盛。因此，統治者們開始想征服地中海地區，重建羅馬帝國。最重要的是，他們想從回教徒手中奪取耶路撒冷──耶穌基督的城市。

1095年，教宗催促人們拿起武器，為耶路撒冷而戰。人們實在太狂熱了，連小孩老人都想去打仗。他們相信他們的神會在他們抵達耶路撒冷時粉碎耶路撒冷的城牆，因此很多人連武器都沒帶。但是遠征和打仗非常辛苦，大多數的人都死掉了。

所以有些遠征軍放棄前往耶路撒冷跟回教徒打仗，而選擇停留在德國跟猶太人打仗。因為猶太人不是基督徒，所以這些遠征軍掠奪他們並殺了成千的猶太人。

在1096年的秋天，正式的十字軍出發前往耶路撒冷並一舉拿下聖城。十字軍在戰略上犯了很多錯誤，但由於敵人沒有好好保衛耶路撒冷，所以仍讓十字軍拿下了耶路撒冷，連帶收服一些其他重要的城市。他們定居在耶路撒冷，也就是他們的新國家。第一次十字軍東征是個大成功。

一起共居在聖城耶路撒冷的基督徒和回教徒在經過一段平和期後，一支新的十字軍又形成了，並遠征小亞細亞，以第二次十字軍東征為人所知。但是這次他們沒有取得任何重大勝利。在1149年，他們返回他們的國家，沒有任何收穫。

時間表：

1 第一次十字軍東征－1095至1099年　　2 第二次十字軍東征－1147至1149年
3 第三次十字軍東征－1187至1192年　　4 第四次十字軍東征－1202至1204年
5 第五次十字軍東征－1217至1221年　　6 第六次十字軍東征－1228至1229年
7 第七次十字軍東征－1248至1254年　　8 第八次十字軍東征－1270 年
9 第九次十字軍東征－1271至1272年　　10 北方十字軍（波羅的海和德國）

聽力題目解析

❶ 此題詢問的是十字軍東征為一系列由教宗所批准的何種行動。選項 (A) 為和平的；選項 (B) 為軍事的；選項 (C) 為銷售的；選項 (D)為購買的。錄音檔在一開始即給了我們答案，選 (B)。

❷ 此題詢問的是第一場十字軍東征是在何年發生。選項 (A) 為 1095 年；選項 (B) 為 1509 年；選項 (C) 為1452 年；選項 (D)為 1059 年。在錄音檔的最後，我們可以聽見十次十字軍東征的時間表，仔細聆聽即可，答案為 (A)。

❸ 此題詢問的是他們在一開始是與何者對戰。選項 (A) 為俄羅斯；選項 (B) 為穆斯林；選項 (C) 為猶太人；選項 (D)為蒙古人。根據錄音的一開始，我們可以聽見 "They started off to capture the Holy Land, Jerusalem, from the Muslims but developed into territorial wars."，因此只要把握住 "capter ... from"、"Muslims"，以及 "war" 這幾個關鍵字即可得知答案為 (B)。

❹ 此題詢問的是誰贏了第一次的戰爭。選項 (A) 為十字軍；選項 (B) 為穆斯林；選項 (C) 為土耳其；選項 (D)為我們無法從內文得知。我們在聆聽時需注意，此題詢問的是第一次的戰爭，所以我們必須找出關鍵字，

在此處即為 "the frist crusade" 以及在介紹戰爭起源過後出現的 "the main Crusade"，故接下來出現的即為答案 "the main Crusade left for Jerusalem and took it."，答案選擇 (A)。

❺ 此題詢問的是第一次十字軍東征可以用何種單字來形容。選項 (A) 為笑話；選項 (B) 為失敗；選項 (C) 為錯誤；選項 (D)為成功。同上，我們可以聽見內文最後的結論是 "The First Crusade was a big success."，故選擇 (D)。

• •

閱讀題目解析

❶ 此題詢問的是有些十字軍留在德國與猶太人對戰的原因為何。選項 (A) 為猶太人激怒了他們；選項 (B) 為教宗指使，且勝利的人可獲得獎賞；選項 (C) 為旅途太過辛勞，且猶太人不是基督徒；選項 (D)為他們到達不了耶路撒冷。答案可見 "But the traveling and fighting were very hard ... some Crusaders decided to stop in Germany to fight the Jews. Because Jews were not Christians ..."，故選 (C)。

❷ 此題詢問的是第六次十字軍東征為何時。選項 (A) 為 1095-1099 年；選項 (B) 為 1228-1239 年；選項 (C) 為 1271-1272 年；選項 (D)為 1228-1229 年。答案可見內文最後的時間表，選擇 (D)，注意勿被選項 (B) 混淆。

補充單字

☆ 1. military	**adj.**	軍事的
☆ 2. settle	**v.**	定居
☆ 3. urge	**v.**	催促
☆ 4. destroy	**v.**	破壞
☆ 5. rob	**v.**	搶劫
☆ 6. return	**v.**	返回

Level 4 02

Line — One of Asia's Favorite Mobile Messenger Apps

亞洲最受歡迎的手機通訊軟體之一：Line

聽力測驗 🎧Track 057

在學習英文的過程中，「聽」可能是最直接的第一線接觸，也可能是大家最想要快速習得的能力。現在，就讓我們來熟悉各種英文情境，提升自己的英文臨場感吧！

( ) 1. Why was Line developed?
    (A) in response to the telecommunications problem caused by the 2011 Tōhoku earthquake
    (B) to compete against other messengers
    (C) to discourage people from contacting their friends
    (D) to get people's attention

( ) 2. How popular is Line in Japan?
    (A) Few people in Japan are using it.
    (B) It's unpopular in Japan.
    (C) Almost half of the Japanese population are using it.
    (D) All people in Japan are using it.

( ) 3. What does Line mean to its users?
    (A) a place to sing karaoke
    (B) a direct messaging platform
    (C) a place to write blogs
    (D) an online matchmaking site

(   ) 4. Line is popular in many countries except which one?

        (A) Taiwan   (B) Indonesia

        (C) Thailand   (D) Switzerland

(   ) 5. What is one of Line's popular features?

        (A) emojis   (B) word size

        (C) photos   (D) music

 **閱讀測驗**

剛剛的聽力測驗是否因為答題不順而感到遺憾？或是覺得自己有某些地方掌握地不夠好？現在就讓我們來直接「看」剛剛的聽力測驗，並透過後面的閱讀測驗來補齊聽力上的不足，同時考驗自己的閱讀能力吧！

As Internet connections are getting cheaper and faster with 4G technology, more and more people are interested in using their smart phones for video chats. One of users' most popular **messaging**[1] applications is Line. Similar to the way a superhero is born from a tragic life-changing incident, Line was developed by a Korean tech firm's Japanese office in response to the **telecommunications**[2] problem caused by the 2011 Tohoku earthquake.

Never had anyone expected it to end up taking Japan by storm, with almost half of the Japanese population using it. Line is also popular in Asian countries such as Taiwan, Thailand, Indonesia, and Turkmenistan. Although many people think of it as a social networking service, like Facebook and Twitter, what Line really means to its users is its direct messaging **platform**[3]. In Line, messaging comes first, and your social media life comes second.

One of Line's most popular features is **emojis**[4]. You can spice up your chats from stick figures to super cute and popular characters. You can also chat with over 200 friends simultaneously on a group chat. **In a nutshell**[5], Line is about staying in touch with people that matter to you. So, what's your line?

【Question】

(　　) 1. Which country's company developed Line?
　　　(A) Japan
　　　(B) Thailand
　　　(C) Turkmenistan
　　　(D) Korea

(　　) 2. For Line, what comes first?
　　　(A) messaging
　　　(B) vlogs
　　　(C) social media life
　　　(D) films

【文章中譯】

隨著網路第四代科技資訊傳輸越趨便宜及快速，有越來越多的人願意使用智慧型手機進行視訊，而最受用戶歡迎的通訊軟體之一莫過於 Line。就像超級英雄是從悲劇事件中誕生出來的一樣，Line 是由一家韓國科技公司的日本分支開發出來的，當時的契機是為了解決 2011年日本東北大地震造成電訊業癱瘓的問題。

從來沒有人想過 Line 居然會在日本大受歡迎，現在幾乎有半數日本人都在使用它，它在亞洲國家也很受歡迎，比如台灣、泰國、印尼、土庫曼。雖然許多人認為它就像臉書和推特是社交網路服務的一種，但它對用戶而言實際上是直接通訊的平台。因此 Line 首重通訊，其次才是用戶的社交媒體生活。

Line最受歡迎的特色是表情貼圖，用戶可以在聊天時點選超可愛及熱門角色化身的表情貼圖來增加聊天的樂趣。用戶也可以在群組與超過 200 位朋友同步聊天。簡而言之，Line 就是要你和真正重要的人保持聯繫。那麼，可以跟你要 Line 嗎？

聽力題目解析

❶ 此題詢問的是Line是什麼原因而開發的。選項 (A) 為因應2011年日本東北大地震造成電訊業癱瘓的問題；選項 (B) 是為了與其它通訊軟體競爭；選項 (C) 為使人們不想與朋友聯絡；選項 (D) 是為了引起人們的注意。這邊考得是 "in response to" 作為「因應、回應」的用法，故答案選 (A)。

❷ 此題詢問的是Line在日本有多受歡迎。選項 (A) 為在日本很少人使用它；選項 (B) 為它在日本並不受歡迎；選項 (C) 為幾乎有半數日本人在使用它；選項 (D) 為在日本所有人都使用它。錄音檔中指出 "Never had anyone expected it would end up taking Japan by storm, with almost half the Japanese population using it."，本題考的是考生是否聽得懂這句倒裝句，和片語 "take...by storm"（風靡、大受歡迎），故答案選 (C)。

❸ 此題詢問的是對用戶而言 Line的意義是什麼。選項 (A) 為唱卡啦OK的地方；選項 (B) 為直接通訊的平台；選項 (C) 為寫部落格的地方；選項 (D) 為相親網站。錄音檔中後段提到 "what Line really means to its users is its direct messaging platform" 故答案選 (B)。

❹ 此題詢問的是Line在多國受到歡迎，除了哪國以外。選項 (A) 為台灣；選項 (B) 為印尼；選項 (C) 為泰國；選項 (D) 為瑞士。錄音檔提到 Taiwan, Thailand, Indonesia, and Turkmenistan，可知Line在亞洲國家較受歡迎，（註：西方國家以Snapchat、Whatsapp、Wechat等較受歡迎）故答案選 (D)。

❺ 此題詢問的是何者是Line受歡迎的特色。選項 (A) 為表情貼圖；選項 (B) 為字體大小；選項 (C) 為相片；選項 (D) 為音樂。錄音檔後段提到 "One of Line's most popular features is emojis." 這邊需注意 "feature"（特色）此單字，選 (A)。

閱讀題目解析

❶ 第一題詢問的是Line為哪國公司所開發的。選項 (A) 為日本；選項 (B) 為泰國；選項 (C) 為土庫曼；選項 (D) 為韓國。答案可見內文第一段，選 (D)。

❷ 第二題詢問的是Line首重什麼功能。選項 (A) 為通訊；選項 (B) 為影像部落格（video weblog或video blog，簡稱vlog）；選項 (C) 為社交媒體生活；選項 (D)為影片。答案可見內文第二段，選 (A)。

補充單字

☆	1. messaging	n.	通訊
☆	2. telecommunications	n.	電訊業
☆	3. platform	n.	平台
☆	4. emoji	n.	表情貼
☆	5. in a nutshell	ph.	簡而言之

Fashion Legend — Hubert de Givenchy

紀梵希的品牌創始人 —— 紀梵希先生

聽力測驗 🎧Track 058

在學習英文的過程中,「聽」可能是最直接的第一線接觸,也可能是大家最想要快速習得的能力。現在,就讓我們來熟悉各種英文情境,提升自己的英文臨場感吧!

( ) 1. Who was Givenchy's most devoted client and muse?
    (A) Rihanna   (B) Audrey Hepburn
    (C) Julianne Moore   (D) Shirley Temple

( ) 2. What did Givenchy's family wanted him to be?
    (A) a lawyer   (B) a doctor
    (C) a banker   (D) a politician

( ) 3. When did Givenchy found his own fashion house?
    (A) 1990   (B) 1980
    (C) 1952   (D) 1920

( ) 4. What was the characteristic of Givenchy's clothes?
    (A) complicated design
    (B) eccentricity
    (C) exaggeration
    (D) extreme elegance

( ) 5. What did Givenchy believe when it came to fashion design?
   (A) Less is more.
   (B) The cuter, the better.
   (C) The weirder, the more beautiful.
   (D) The more ostentatious, the better.

 閱讀測驗

剛剛的聽力測驗是否因為答題不順而感到遺憾？或是覺得自己有某些地方掌握地不夠好？現在就讓我們來直接「看」剛剛的聽力測驗，並透過後面的閱讀測驗來補齊聽力上的不足，同時考驗自己的閱讀能力吧！

When legendary fashion designer Hubert de Givenchy passed away at the age of 91 in March 2018, the photos that accompanied his **obituaries**[1] featured Audrey Hepburn, his most devoted client and **muse**[2], who trusted him to design her ensembles on and off the screen.

When Givenchy was young, he was fascinated by his grandfather's collection of clothes from around the world. Despite the fact that his family wanted him to become a lawyer, Givenchy persuaded them to allow him to pursue his dream as a fashion designer. After working for several famous designers, he founded his own fashion house in 1952 and soon met actress Audrey Hepburn, who became his lifelong friend. They became the most influential team of star and designer in the fashion history.

Throughout his career, the French designer went on to make clothes for celebrities such as Princess Grace of Monaco and Greta Garbo. His work was marked by Parisian extreme elegance and **sophistication**[3]. Givenchy believed less was more when it came to fashion design, preferring the simple but perfectly-stylish cut to the **ostentatious**[4] one. Today, people still see his impact on the silver screen, the red carpet, and the **choicest**[5] of women.

【Question】

(　　) 1. What does the word ensemble mean in the first paragraph?
        (A) a set of clothes which have been chosen to look nice together
        (B) a single piece of clothes
        (C) a shirt
        (D) a trouser

(　　) 2. What was Givenchy's nationality?
        (A) USA   (B) Canada
        (C) UK   (D) France

【文章中譯】

于貝爾‧德‧紀梵希是一位傳奇的時尚設計師，甫於2018年3月以91歲的高齡辭世。在他的訃文我們可以看見奧黛麗‧赫本的相片，她是紀梵希最忠誠的客戶，也是他的設計靈感源泉。奧黛麗對他十分信任，不論在銀光幕上下都穿著他設計的整套服飾。

當紀梵希還小時，他對祖父從世界各地收集來的衣服感到很著迷。儘管家人希望他成為律師，他仍說服他們讓他追尋成為時尚設計師的夢想。他曾在幾位知名設計師麾下工作，隨後於 1952 年成立個人時尚工作室，並很快地遇見了奧黛麗‧赫本。他們兩人不但成為終生的朋友，更是時尚史上最具影響力的明星與設計師組合。

這位法國設計師為許多名人設計服裝，包括摩納哥的葛麗絲王妃和好萊塢女星葛麗泰‧嘉寶。他的作品散發巴黎極簡風格及細膩氣質，他相信簡單勝過繁複，並偏好簡單、完美的時尚剪裁，而非浮誇的裝飾。如今，人們仍能在大銀幕上、紅毯、和最挑剔的女人身上看到他的影響力。

❶ 此題詢問的是紀梵希最忠誠的客戶和靈感的源泉是誰。選項 (A) 為蕾哈娜；選項 (B) 為奧黛麗‧赫本；選項 (C) 為茱莉安‧摩爾；選項 (D) 為秀蘭‧鄧波爾。錄音檔前段指出 "Audrey Hepburn, his most devoted client and muse, who trusted him to design her ensembles on and off the screen" 本題考的是考生是否了解同位語 "his most devoted client and muse" 用來修飾逗號前面的人，選 (B)。

❷ 此題詢問的是紀梵希的家人原希望他從事什麼行業。選項 (A) 為律師；選項 (B) 為醫生；選項 (C) 為銀行家；選項 (D) 為政治家。在錄音檔中段部分即有說 "his family wanted him to become a lawyer" 故答案選 (A)。

❸ 此題詢問的是紀梵希何時成立個人時尚工作室。考題經常會考數字，請考生特別注意，答案選 (C)。

❹ 此題詢問的是紀梵希設計的衣服特色是什麼。選項 (A) 為複雜的設計；選項 (B) 為搞怪；選項 (C) 為誇張；選項 (D) 為極為優雅。錄音檔中後段提到 "His work was marked by Parisian extreme elegance and sophistication." 這邊可把握 "marked by"（以……著稱）此關鍵字，故答案選 (D)。

❺ 此題詢問的是何者為紀梵希對於時尚設計的理念是什麼。選項 (A) 為簡單勝過繁複；選項 (B) 為越可愛越好；選項 (C) 為越怪異越美；選項 (D) 為越浮誇越好。錄音檔後段提到 "Givenchy believed less was more ..." 故答案選 (A)。

閱讀題目解析

❶ 此題詢問的是第一段中 "ensemble" 這個單字意思為何。選項 (A) 為搭配好的一整套衣服；選項 (B) 為單件衣服；選項 (C) 為一件襯衫；選項 (D) 為一件褲子。雖然這個字未被列入補充單字，但值得補充給讀者學習，答案選 (A)。

❷ 此題詢問的是紀梵希的國籍。選項 (A) 為美國；選項 (B) 為加拿大；選項 (C)為英國；選項 (D) 為法國。答案可件內文第三段第一句，答案為 (D)。

補充單字

☆ 1. obituary	n.	訃文
☆ 2. muse	n.	靈感源泉；繆思
☆ 3. sophistication	n.	細膩氣質
☆ 4. ostentatious	adj.	浮誇的
☆ 5. choice	adj.	挑剔的

The Great Discovery: The Terracotta Warriors and Horses of the Qin Dynasty in China

世紀大發現──中國秦兵馬俑

聽力測驗 🎧 Track 059

在學習英文的過程中，「聽」可能是最直接的第一線接觸，也可能是大家最想要快速習得的能力。現在，就讓我們來熟悉各種英文情境，提升自己的英文臨場感吧！

( ) 1. Where were the terracotta warriors and horses discovered?
  (A) China   (B) Shanxi province
  (C) Shanxi, China   (D) all of the above

( ) 2. Who discovered it?
  (A) specialist   (B) some farmers
  (C) some villagers   (D) some artists

( ) 3.How long did it take to build it?
  (A) 20 years   (B) 28 years
  (C) 38 years

( ) 4 . Who built it?
  (A) the emperor's father (B) the emperor's son
  (C) the emperor himself (D) close to a million of workers

( ) 5. It was included in the World Heritage List by _____.
  (A) UNESCO   (B) Guinness
  (C) The United Nations (D) China

 **閱讀測驗**

剛剛的聽力測驗是否因為答題不順而感到遺憾？或是覺得自己有某些地方掌握地不夠好？現在就讓我們來直接「看」剛剛的聽力測驗，並透過後面的閱讀測驗來補齊聽力上的不足，同時考驗自己的閱讀能力吧！

But for the **discovery**[1] of the terracotta warriors and horses at Xiyang Village in Lintong County of Shanxi Province, China would have never drawn the world's attention as it does today. This great discovery took place in the spring of 1974. Some villagers were digging a well. When they reached about four meters deep, they found a clay man in the pit. Its head, body, arms, and legs had been broken. These villagers were excited and **reported**[2] to the authorities at once.

Archaeologists reacted to the big discovery immediately. They didn't expect that they would take part in such a major archaeological discovery in China in the twentieth century. Those who discovered the terracotta warriors and horses really made a great discovery!

Today when people go into the Museum of Terracotta Warriors and Horses Guarding the Mausoleum of the First Emperor of Qin, they are shocked by the grand **view**[3]. But what they see is only a small part of the outer area of the mausoleum. More than 2,000 years ago, Sima Qian, the most prominent historian in ancient China, wrote about the grandeur of the Mausoleum of the First Emperor of Qin in his great work, Records of the Historian,which is still of great value to the history study.

It was a legendary and boundless underground world. In the burial chamber, magnificent palace buildings were built up, the universe, the starry sky and the geographical features were duplicated, and a large quantity of mercury was filled in to **represent**[4] ponds, rivers, and oceans. In 221 B.C., the First Emperor of Qin unified China. Construction of his mausoleum started in the same year. More than 700,000 laborers worked on the site year in and year out. The 38-year vast project was completed after the death of the emperor.

The underground military array was almost a reproduction of the grand army of the Empire of Qin. It achieved the unification of China for the

First Emperor of Qin. Then it undertook the new mission to defend the unified empire and its founder. But the **powerful**[5] empire fell apart three years after the death of the First Emperor of Qin. The rebel troops attacked Xianyang, the capital of the empire. The magnificent and splendid palaces and halls built during the rule of the First Emperor of Qin were burnt down in a big fire. His mausoleum was not spared. In 1987, the Terracotta Warriors and Horses of Qin were included in the World Heritage List by UNESCO. It **attracts**[6] millions of visitors from all over the world every year.

【Question】

(　　) 1. How did the magnificent places and halls of the rule of the First Emperor of Qin end up?
　　　　(A) It was drown in a flood.
　　　　(B) It was burned down in a big fire.
　　　　(C) It was reused by the rebel troops.
　　　　(D) It was torn down.

(　　) 2. Which of the following statement about the Mausoleum is correct?
　　　　(A) It went unnoticed only after the modern discovery.
　　　　(B) It was built within a short period of time.
　　　　(C) It was copied mostly from the real-life military array of the Empire of Qin.
　　　　(D) It was not valuable to historical studies.

【文章中譯】

如果沒有兵馬俑的發現，中國陝西省臨潼縣昔陽村將永遠不會像現在一樣吸引全世界的目光。這個世紀大發現發生在1974年春天。當時一些村民正在挖掘一口井，當他們挖到大約四米深的時候，發現了一個泥人在坑裡。這個泥人的頭部、身體、胳膊和腿已斷掉。村民們很興奮，並立刻向有關單位報告。

考古學家立即對村民的發現做出反應。他們從來沒有料到他們將在中國開始一項二十世紀的重大的考古發現。那些找到兵馬俑這個偉大發現的村民們真的做了一個偉大的貢獻！

今天，當人們進入守衛秦始皇陵園兵馬俑的博物館，他們會被宏偉的景觀震懾住。但是，他們所看到的只是陵墓地區外的一小部分。兩千多年前，中國古代最著名的歷史學家司馬遷，在他的出色作品史記中曾介紹了皇帝秦始皇宏偉的陵墓。這本書至今對於歷史的研究仍極具價值。

那真是一個神話般無邊無界的地下世界。在墓室裡，宏偉的宮殿建築物被修建起來，模仿了宇宙、星空和地域特徵，以及填補大量的汞來代表池塘，河流和海洋。西元前221年，秦始皇統一中國。同一年他的陵墓開始施工。70多萬勞動者在工地年復一年地工作。歷時38年的工程最後在皇帝死後竣工。

這個地下世界裡的軍陣幾乎是複製秦帝國的大規模軍隊。它讓秦始皇統一了中國，然後進行了新的變革，維護著統一的帝國和它的創始人。但是，秦始皇死亡後三年，強大的帝國崩潰。叛亂士兵攻擊帝國的首都咸陽。秦始皇時期修建的宏偉的宮殿和室館被大火燒毀。他的陵墓也不能倖免。最後於1987年，聯合國教科文組織將兵馬俑秦為收錄於世界遺產。現在每年都吸引了數以百萬來自世界各地的遊客參觀兵馬俑。

聽力題目解析

❶ 此題詢問的是秦兵馬俑是在何處發現的。選項 (A) 為中國；選項 (B) 為陝西省；選項 (C) 為中國陝西；選項 (D)為以上皆是。錄音檔的一開始即告訴我們答案 "the discovery ... at Xiyang Village in Lintong County of Shanxi Province, China ..."故答案選 (D)。

❷ 此題詢問的是何人發現了秦兵馬俑。選項 (A) 為專家；選項 (B) 為幾位農夫；選項 (C) 為幾位村民；選項 (D)為幾位藝術家。我們在聽見 "This great discovery took place in the spring of 1974." 時，便可推測接下來會出現「人物」，因此只要把握住關鍵字即可，答案為 (C) 幾位村民。

❸ 此題詢問的是秦兵馬俑費時幾年。答案為 (C) 38 年，此種題型若能先看過題目及選項會較好把握。

❹ 此題詢問的是秦兵馬俑是誰建造的。選項 (A) 為皇帝的父親；選項 (B)

為皇帝的兒子；選項 (C) 為皇帝本人；選項 (D)為近百萬名工人。根據錄音檔，在開始介紹秦始皇的陵墓之後，我們便能聽見 "More than 700,000 laborers worked on the site ..." 故答案為 (D)。

❺ 此題詢問的是秦兵馬俑被何組織列為世界遺產。選項 (A) 為聯合國教科文組織；選項 (B) 為金氏世界記錄；選項 (C) 為聯合國；選項 (D) 為中國。錄音檔的最後即給了我們答案 "...were included in the World Heritage List by UNESCO."，故答案為 (A)。

閱讀題目解析

❶ 此題詢問的是秦始皇時期修建的宏偉宮殿和室館最後的下場為何。選項 (A) 為被水災淹沒；選項 (B) 為在大火中燃燒殆盡；選項 (C) 為被叛軍重新使用；選項 (D)為被拆毀。答案可見內文最後一段，選擇 (B)。

❷ 此題詢問的是何者關於陵墓的陳述是正確的。選項 (A) 為它一直到現代的發現之前都不為人所知；選項 (B) 為它在短時間內即建造完成；選項 (C) 為它大多是複製於秦帝國的大規模軍隊；選項 (D)為它對歷史研究來說不具價值。答案可見內文倒數最後一段 "was almost a reproduction of the grand army of the Empire of Qin"，故選擇 (C)。選項 (A) 不對，因中國古代歷史學家司馬遷曾介紹過秦始皇的陵墓。

補充單字

☆ 1. discovery	n.	發現
☆ 2. report	v.	報告
☆ 3. view	n.	景觀
☆ 4. represent	v.	代表
☆ 5. powerful	a.	強大的
☆ 6. attract	v.	吸引

What Are Content Farms?
什麼是內容農場？

聽力測驗 Track 060

在學習英文的過程中，「聽」可能是最直接的第一線接觸，也可能是大家最想要快速習得的能力。現在，就讓我們來熟悉各種英文情境，提升自己的英文臨場感吧！

( ) 1. Is content farm a reliable source?
    (A) Yes, it is.   (B) No, it isn't.
    (C) always   (D) It is highly reliable.

( ) 2. Who is the target of content farms?
    (A) search engines   (B) people
    (C) book lovers   (D) elementary school students

( ) 3. What is the purpose of content farms?
    (A) to provide highly reliable information
    (B) to help college students write their papers
    (C) to produce authoritative content
    (D) to charge for advertisements

( ) 4. What matters to content farms?
    (A) search engine rankings   (B) accuracy of information
    (C) utility of information   (D) user experience

( ) 5. Which of the following characteristic is NOT included in a content farm?
    (A) very brief articles
    (B) lots of ads
    (C) accurate information
    (D) information that has been copied and pasted from other websites

 **閱讀測驗**

剛剛的聽力測驗是否因為答題不順而感到遺憾？或是覺得自己有某些地方掌握地不夠好？現在就讓我們來直接「看」剛剛的聽力測驗，並透過後面的閱讀測驗來補齊聽力上的不足，同時考驗自己的閱讀能力吧！

Maybe you haven't heard of the term "**content farm**"[1], but you surely have visited one. It is a website that produces hundreds of low-quality article and stories each day. For example, when you click a search result looking for something useful, and you find seductive headlines, or click baits, but the article on the website is **invariably**[2] disappointing.

To content farms, quality and **utility**[3] are not important. All that matters is search engine rankings in order to charge for advertisements. Pieces of the articles are often very short, image-based, and lack of **accuracy**[4]. So, in fact, content farm material is written for search engines, not for people. It's designed to be popular. When more people click on their website, they embrace the overwhelming amount of advertisements that can be further included on their weside page.

The question will now be: how do we know if we just **stumble upon**[5] content farms? Well, they have a quite consistent pattern as follows: very brief articles; lots of ads; links to other sites; information that has been copied and pasted from other websites. So if you land on a content farm's website, be careful about the quality, accuracy, and reliability of its content.

【Question】

(   ) 1. What does the word "seductive" mean in the first paragraph?
    (A) reducing   (B) attractive
    (C) boring   (D) agonizing

(   ) 2. How many characteristics does the article provide for readers to distinguish useful information from a content farm?
    (A) two   (B) three
    (C) four   (D) five

也許你從沒聽過內容農場這個專有名詞,但你肯定看過它。它是一個每天專門製造上百篇低品質文章和故事的網站。就像是,當你在搜尋引擎點選搜尋結果並希望找到有用的資訊,而你也發現很誘人的標題或是釣魚標題時,點入內容農場的文章進行閱覽,卻總是令你感到非常失望。

對內容農場而言,品質和實用性並不重要,重要的是搜尋引擎的排名,以藉此賺取更多廣告費。這類文章內容通常很短,以圖像式為主,並欠缺正確性。因此實際上,內容農場的題材是為了搜尋引擎而非人們而寫的。它是為了受歡迎程度而寫出來的內容,當越多人點閱這類文章,代表它們可以在頁面上夾帶更多的廣告。

現在的問題在於,我們要如何知道我們是否點進了內容農場。它們有非常一貫的模式,如下:文章篇幅短、很多廣告、很多對外連結、資訊是從其它網站複製貼上的。若你湊巧點入內容農場的網站,請小心它的品質、正確度和可靠性。

聽力題目解析

❶ 此題詢問的是內容農場是否為可靠的消息來源。選項 (A) 為是的;選項 (B) 為不是;選項 (C) 為總是;選項 (D) 為高度可靠。錄音檔前段即指出 "It is a website that produces hundreds of low-quality articles and stories each day." 故選 (B)。

❷ 此題詢問的是內容農場是為誰所寫的。選項 (A) 為搜尋引擎;選項 (B) 為人們;選項 (C) 為愛書人;選項 (D) 為小學生。錄音檔中段指出 "... content farm material is written for search engines, not for people." 掌握 "written for"(為……而寫)即可,故答案選 (A)。

❸ 此題詢問的是內容農場的目的為何。選項 (A) 為提供高度可靠的資訊;選項 (B) 為幫助大學生寫論文;選項 (C) 為產出有權威的文章內容;選項 (D) 為收取廣告費用。本題在錄音檔中段提到 "All that matters is search engine rankings in order to charge for advertisements." 把握 "charge"（收費）此字即可，答案選 (D)。

❹ 此題詢問的是內容農場在乎的是什麼。選項 (A) 為搜尋引擎的排名；選項 (B)為資訊精確度；選項 (C) 為資訊實用性；選項 (D) 為使用者經驗。同上，選(A)。

❺ 此題詢問的是以下何者並非內容農場的特色。選項 (A) 為文章簡短；選項 (B)為廣告很多；選項 (C) 為精確的資訊；選項 (D) 為從其它網站複製貼上的資訊。這邊可以在內文將要列舉細項時特別注意，選 (C)。

• •

閱讀題目解析

❶ 第一題詢問的是第一段中seductive這個單字意思為何。選項 (A) 為減少的；選項 (B) 為吸引人的；選項 (C) 為無聊的；選項 (D) 為痛苦的。雖然這個字未被列入補充單字，但值得補充給讀者學習，意為「吸引人的；引誘人的」，也可以從前後文來推測，說明標題吸引人點進去文章，答案選 (B)。

❷ 第二題詢問的是本篇文章提供幾個內容農場的特色讓讀者能區別它。選項 (A)為兩項；選項 (B) 為三項；選項 (C) 為四項；選項 (D) 為五項。答案可見內文第三段，選 (C)。

補充單字

☆ 1. content farm	n.	內容農場
☆ 2. invariably	adv.	一定地；總是
☆ 3. utility	n.	實用性
☆ 4. accuracy	n.	正確度
☆ 5. stumble upon	v.	巧遇

Level 4
06

Augmented Reality
擴增實境

在學習英文的過程中,「聽」可能是最直接的第一線接觸,也可能是大家最想要快速習得的能力。現在,就讓我們來熟悉各種英文情境,提升自己的英文臨場感吧!

( ) 1. With new developments in augmented reality, what happened to our world?
(A) The technology industry isn't interested in developing augmented reality.
(B) Engineers are reluctant to develop augmented reality.
(C) The line between real and virtual life has become increasingly blurry.
(D) The development of augmented reality doesn't have a future.

( ) 2. Which of the following is a famous example of augmented reality?
(A) Doraemon   (B) Little Mermaid
(C) Snoopy   (D) Pokemon Go

( ) 3. What device do people use to play the Pokemon Go?
(A) smart phone   (B) laptop computer
(C) digital camera   (D) thumb drive

( ) 4. Who are the fans of the Pokemon Go?
(A) mostly children
(B) children and adults
(C) mostly adults
(D) only children

(   ) 5. Which of the following is NOT true?

    (A) Augmented reality can be applied in medicine.

    (B) Augmented reality can only be applied in games.

    (C) Augmented reality can be applied in business.

    (D) Pokemon Go is one of the most famous examples that apply augmented reality technology.

剛剛的聽力測驗是否因為答題不順而感到遺憾？或是覺得自己有某些地方掌握地不夠好？現在就讓我們來直接「看」剛剛的聽力測驗，並透過後面的閱讀測驗來補齊聽力上的不足，同時考驗自己的閱讀能力吧！

With new developments in the digital revolution, The Matrix becomes more like reality. That's because hardware and software engineers continue to enhance their **augmented**[1] reality technologies, making the line between real and virtual life increasingly **blurry**[2].

Augmented reality is the blending of interactive digital elements, like visual **overlays**[3] and other sensory projections, into our real-world environments. The Pokemon Go is a famous example. This mobile game allows users to see the world around them through their smart phone cameras which project game items, such as onscreen icons and Pokemon creatures, as overlays that make them seem as if they are right in our real-life environment. The design of the game was so successful that it sent millions of children and adults walking through their real-world backyards in search of **virtual**[4] prizes.

Augmented reality is more than just a smart phone game. It's also a technology that can be applied in business and medicine. The possibilities of AR tech are limitless. The only uncertainty is how smoothly and quickly developers will **integrate**[5] these capabilities into devices that we use on a daily basis.

【Question】

(　　) 1. Why does the movie The Matrix become more like reality?
　　(A) Because hardware and software engineers continue to enhance augmented reality technologies.
　　(B) Because the world is affected by climate change.
　　(C) Because virtual reality is replacing augmented reality.
　　(D) Because mobile devices are evolving themselves.

(　　) 2. What are developers of augmented reality (AR) technology trying to do?
　　(A) They will abandon the AR technology.
　　(B) They are trying to integrate the AR technology into devices that we use on a daily basis.
　　(C) They don't think it's practical.
　　(D) They will try to phase out AR technology.

【文章中譯】

隨著數位革命的發展，電影《駭客任務》劇情變得更加真實了，因為硬體和軟體工程師不斷地在研發擴增實境的科技，讓真實和虛擬生活的界線變得更加模糊了。

擴增實境是運用視覺重疊、感官投射的數位互動元素來混入我們真實世界的環境中，而寶可夢是最有名的例子。這個手機遊戲讓使用者能透過智慧型手機的相機看到周遭的世界，配合投射的遊戲物件如螢幕圖示和寶可夢的神奇寶貝，讓使用者視覺看到虛擬和真實物件在真實環境中同時呈現。這款遊戲的設計相當成功，讓數百萬的大人和小孩都在現實世界的後院尋找虛擬的獎勵。

擴增實境不僅限於手機遊戲的技術，它也能應用在商業和醫療等重要的領域。擴增實境技術的可能性是無限的，唯一不確定的是開發商何時能流暢地把它整合在我們每天使用的裝置中。

聽力題目解析

❶ 此題詢問的是隨著擴增實境的新發展，我們的世界發生什麼改變。選項 (A) 為科技業對發展擴增實境不感興趣；選項 (B) 為工程師很遲疑是否要發展擴增實境；選項 (C) 為真實與虛擬生活的界線變得越來越模糊；選項 (D) 為擴增實境的發展沒有前景。在錄音檔前段即指出 "... making the line between real and virtual life increasingly blurry." 把握 "blurry"（模糊的）此關鍵字，選 (C)。

❷ 此題詢問的是擴增實境的著名例子。選項 (A) 為多拉A夢；選項 (B) 為小美人魚；選項 (C) 為史努比；選項 (D) 為寶可夢。錄音檔中前段部分有提到擴增實境的例子："The Pokemon Go is a famous example." 故答案選 (D)。

❸ 此題詢問的是人們用何種裝置玩寶可夢。選項 (A) 為智慧型手機；選項 (B) 為筆電；選項 (C) 為數位相機；選項 (D) 為隨身碟（thumb drive）。本題在錄音檔中段提到"This mobile game allows users to ... through their smart phone cameras which project game items ...",強調寶可夢是手機遊戲，故答案選 (A)。

❹ 此題詢問的是誰是寶可夢的粉絲。選項 (A) 為主要是小孩；選項 (B) 為小孩和成人；選項 (C) 為主要是成人；選項 (D) 為只有小孩。錄音檔中後段提到 "... it sent millions of children and adults walking through their real-world backyards in search of virtual4 prizes." 故答案選(B)。

❺ 此題詢問的是何者為非。選項 (A) 為擴增實境可被應用在醫療；選項 (B) 為擴增實境僅限被應用在遊戲；選項 (C) 為擴增實境可被應用在商業；選項 (D) 為寶可夢遊戲是應用擴增實境的知名例子。錄音檔後段提到 "Augmented reality is ... also a technology that can be applied in business and medicine.",這邊考的是 "be applied to"（應用至……），故選項 (B) 為非。

閱讀題目解析

❶ 此題詢問的是為什麼電影《駭客任務》劇情變得更加真實了。選項 (A) 為因為硬體和軟體工程師不斷地在研發擴增實境的科技；選項 (B) 為因為世界受到氣候變遷所影響；選項 (C) 為因為虛擬實境在替代擴增實境；選項 (D) 為因為手機能自行進化。答案可見內文第一段，選 (A)。

❷ 此題詢問的是擴增實境的研發商正試圖怎麼做。選項 (A) 為他們將放棄擴增實境技術；選項 (B) 為他們將把擴增實境技術整合在我們每天使用的裝置中；選項 (C) 為他們不認為擴增實境是可行的；選項 (D) 為他們將淘汰（phase out）擴增實境。答案可見內文第三段，文章第三段指出，選 (B)。

補充單字

☆ 1. augmented	**adj.**	擴增的
☆ 2. blurry	**adj.**	模糊的
☆ 3. overlay	**n.**	覆蓋
☆ 4. virtual	**adj.**	虛擬的
☆ 5. integrate	**v.**	整合

Level 4
07

Amazing Auroras
神奇的極光

聽力測驗 🎧 Track 062

在學習英文的過程中，「聽」可能是最直接的第一線接觸，也可能是大家最想要快速習得的能力。現在，就讓我們來熟悉各種英文情境，提升自己的英文臨場感吧！

(　　) 1. Auroras are also called _____.
    (A) lighter   (B) spotlight
    (C) neon lights   (D) polar lights

(　　) 2. Auroras are a phenomenon which occurs in _____ latitudes of both hemispheres.
    (A) low
    (B) east
    (C) high

(　　) 3. The term "aurora" was coined by _____ in 1621.
    (A) an Asian scholar
    (B) an American professor
    (C) a local farmer
    (D) a French astronomer

(　　) 4. Auroras are most often seen in an impressive _____ color.
    (A) black   (B) purple
    (C) red   (D) green

(　　) 5. Auroras are formed when _____ approaches the globe.
    (A) atmosphere
    (B) lunar wind
    (C) starry wind
    (D) solar wind

 **閱讀測驗**

剛剛的聽力測驗是否因為答題不順而感到遺憾？或是覺得自己有某些地方掌握地不夠好？現在就讓我們來直接「看」剛剛的聽力測驗，並透過後面的閱讀測驗來補齊聽力上的不足，同時考驗自己的閱讀能力吧！

Auroras, also called polar lights, found 100- 400km above the earth **surface**[1] (the bottom edge is at around 100km altitude), are the extraordinary **phenomenon**[2] which occurs in high latitudes of both hemispheres. The term "aurora" was coined by a French astronomer in 1621. The aurora borealis (the northern polar lights) and the aurora australis (the southern polar lights) have always enthralld humans. People even travel all the way to the poles just to see the magic light shows in the planet Earth's atmosphere. Auroras, both **surrounding**[3] the magnetic poles happen when storms on the sun form solar winds and highly charged electrons from the solar wind interact with elements in the earth's atmosphere.

Auroras are a luminous natural phenomenon of the upper atmosphere in the form of magnificent, colorful, and irregular lights. They appear as many different shapes and colors, and also change in time. Thus, no two auroras are the same. Auroras are a glow of greenish light **stretching**[4] across the sky on a clear dark night. They are most often seen in an impressive green color, but it also shows off its **numerous**[5] colors ranging from red to purple, dark to light. The colors of auroras can cover the entire spectrum. Auroras are formed when solar wind **approaches**[6] the globe. They are caused by energetic particles that enter the atmosphere from above. The composition and density of the atmosphere and the altitude of the aurora decides the possible colors of auroras.

While auroras have long fascinated people in high altitudes regions of the Arctic and Antarctic, aurora australis is not seen as often as the aurora borealis. After all, aurora australis takes place in a very thinly populated part of the Earth. Auroras occurs most often in regions known as the "auroral ovals". Now, scientific facts reveal that the aurora also occurs on other planets such as Jupiter.

【 Question 】

(   ) 1. What is the name of the area where auroras occur most often?
      (A) aurora borealis   (B) auroral ovals
      (C) auroral ovens   (D) auroral winds

(   ) 2. Which of the following statement is correct based on the article?
      (A) Aurora australis is seen as often as aurora borealis.
      (B) Auroras happen in all places with high altitudes.
      (C) Without the sun, we might not have a chance to witness auroras.
      (D) Auroras appear mostly in red.

【 文章中譯 】

極光，出現在離地球表面100-400公里地方（最底點是大約海拔100公里），是出現在南北半球高緯度的神奇現象。「極光」這個詞是在 1621 年由一名法國天文學家所造。北極光和南極光始終令人類心醉神迷。人們甚至長途跋涉到極地，只為了看在地球大氣的神奇極光。圍繞著磁極的極光是經由太陽磁爆產生的太陽風和太陽風產生的帶負電荷之電子與大氣中的元素相互影響而生成的。

極光是在大氣中發光的自然現象，具有壯麗、多彩、不規則的光線。它們有各種形狀與顏色，並會隨著時間改變。因此，每種極光都是獨一無二的。極光是清朗的夜空中，一道劃過天空的綠色光影。儘管大部分的極光呈現令人印象深刻的綠色，但其實他涵蓋了整個光譜的顏色，從藍到紫，由淺到深。當太陽風接近地球時，高能粒子進入大氣時，極光就會形成。大氣的組成和密度以及極光的高度決定極光可能出現的顏色。

出現在高緯度的南極和北極的極光長久以來令人著迷。不過南極光不如北極光那樣常見，畢竟南極是個幾乎沒有人煙的地方。極光多出現在「極光橢圓區」。現在，科學上的資料顯示極光也曾在其他星球發生，例如在木星。

❶ 此題詢問的是極光的別稱為何。選項 (A) 為打火機；選項 (B) 為聚光燈；選項 (C) 為霓虹燈；選項 (D) 為北極光。錄音檔在一開始即給我們答案，為 (D)。

❷ 此題詢問的是極光是一種出現在兩極何種緯度的現象。選項 (A) 為低的；選項 (B) 為東邊的；選項 (C) 為高的。同上，答案為 (C)，這邊可以注意 "... are the extraordinary phenomenon which occurs in high latitudes of both hemispheres." 之中的 "which" 之子句用法，用來補充形容前面的北極光，便能掌握答案。

❸ 此題詢問的是「aurora」一詞是被何人於 1621 年創立。選項 (A) 為一名亞洲學者；選項 (B) 為一名美國教授；選項 (C) 為一名本地農夫；選項 (D)為一名法國天文學家。同上，答案為 (D)，此題建議先看過題目及選項。

❹ 此題詢問的是極光大多都以令人驚奇的何種顏色出現。選項 (A) 為黑色；選項 (B) 為紫色；選項 (C) 為紅色；選項 (D) 為綠色。答案為 (D)，此題型無特殊技巧，僅能仔細注意細節，或是先看過題目及選項以便把握關鍵字。

❺ 此題詢問的是極光是當何物接近地球時所形成的。選項 (A) 為大氣；選項 (B) 為月球風；選項 (C) 為繁星風；選項 (D) 為太陽風。在錄音檔開始不久，我們便能聽見關於極光的介紹，此題考的是我們認不認識 "solar" 這個單字，答案為 (D)，或者我們也可以用 "stroms on the sun" 來推測 "solar" 應與太陽有關。

閱讀題目解析

❶ 此題詢問的是極光最常出現的區域又叫做什麼。選項 (A) 為北極光；選項 (B) 為北極橢圓區；選項 (C) 為北極烤箱；選項 (D) 為北極風。答案可見內文最後一段，選擇 (B)。

❷ 此題詢問的是何者根據內文所做的推測正確。選項 (A) 為南極光和北極光一樣常見；選項 (B) 為極光在所有高緯度的地方都會出現；選項 (C) 為沒有太陽，我們可能就會看不到極光；選項 (D) 為極光大多以紅色出現。答案為 (C)，根據內文第一段最後，我們可以得知極光的產生與太陽風等等多項作用有關，故可以就此推測。

補充單字

☆	1. surface	**n.**	表面
☆	2. phenomenon	**n.**	現象
☆	3. surround	**v.**	包圍
☆	4. stretch	**v.**	伸展
☆	5. numerous	**adj.**	許多的
☆	6. approach	**v.**	接近

Robot Doctors on Duty
機器人醫生問世

聽力測驗 🎧 Track 063

在學習英文的過程中，「聽」可能是最直接的第一線接觸，也可能是大家最想要快速習得的能力。現在，就讓我們來熟悉各種英文情境，提升自己的英文臨場感吧！

(　　) 1. Doctors can maneuver the robot by using a _____ to check on their patients via the Internet.
(A) joystick　　　(B) joyride　　　(C) chopstick

(　　) 2. The purpose of the robo-doc is to make it more _____ for physicians to check on their patients.
(A) convenient　　(B) difficult　　(C) complicated

(　　) 3. Robot doctors' assistance will play a _____ role in the future of health care.
(A) simple　　　(B) momentous　　(C) weak

(　　) 4. This new technology can also provide care to patients in _____ areas.
(A) outer space　　(B) earth's core　　(C) rural and remote

(　　) 5. This latest technology is not intended to replace _____.
(A) a human doctor　(B) a robot doctor　(C) an animal doctor

閱讀測驗

剛剛的聽力測驗是否因為答題不順而感到遺憾？或是覺得自己有某些地方掌握地不夠好？現在就讓我們來直接「看」剛剛的聽力測驗，並透過後面的閱讀測驗來補齊聽力上的不足，同時考驗自己的閱讀能力吧！

Most doctors wish they could be in two or three places at once. Now some of them can because robot doctors are currently being tested at the **hospitals**[2] in several countries such as the United States, Canada, and Britain. They are experimenting with the robots that let doctors examine their **patients**[3] remotely, saving hours of travel time, which means that patients can be accessed more quickly.

With a flat video screen, a microphone, a video camera, and databases, it permits doctors and patients to **interact**[4] with each other almost as they were talking face to face. The doctor can converse with a patient's family, nurses or other **physicians**[5] through the robot. This new technology can also provide medical care to patients in rural and remote areas.

Doctors can maneuver this new type of robot by using a joystick to check on their patients from another place, even another country, via the Internet. The doctor's face will show on the robot's screen and they can communicate with the patient through the microphones and speakers. The purpose of the robo-doc is to make it more convenient for physicians to check on their patients, and for patients to get direct and immediate access to their doctors who are not at the hospital.

According to the survey, eighty percent of the patients who took part in the study believed the robo-doc would increase accessibility to their doctors, and seventy-five percent thought robo-doc would allow their doctors to provide more medical information. Most patients participating in the survey were very satisfied with this new kind of technology. Many patients say that they prefer virtual visits to real visits from the doctor, though this latest technology is not intended to replace a human doctor.

Through a live, two-way audio and video connection, doctors can operate the robot and move the robot's head to see important signs on charts and monitors. Physicians say that robot doctors' **assistance**[6] will play a momentous role in the future of medical care. They will allow doctors to reach patients in outlying areas. The robot doctor is a precious tool.

Due to the fact that more specialties may be added to the robots later, it is believed that they will be able to perform a variety of services themselves. Also, the emergency department might be able to provide treatment for stroke patients through the robot in the near future.

【Question】

(　　) 1. What may the word "outlying" possibly mean in the fifth paragraph?
(A) urban　　　　(B) city　　　　(C) remote　　　　(D) seaside

(　　) 2. What medical symptom may be taken care of by the robot in the near future?
(A) arthritis　　　(B) cellulitis　　　(C) stroke　　　(D) rash

【文章中譯】

大多數的醫生都希望自己有分身術，能快速移動至各個地方。現在有些醫生可以擁有這項特技了，因為目前機器人醫生正在美國、加拿大及英國這幾個國家的醫院進行測試。醫生可以透過測試中的機器人遠距為病人看診，節省了數小時往返的時間，這表示醫生可以更快速地接觸病人。

機器人不會自己提供診療，而是配有螢幕、麥克風、攝影機和資料庫，讓醫生和病人可以彼此互動，就好像面對面說話一樣。醫生可以透過機器人和病人家屬、護士或其他醫生交談。這項新科技也可以為住在偏遠郊區的病人提供醫療服務。

透過網路，醫生可以在別的地方、甚至別的國家，利用搖桿操作這種新型態機器人，來達到巡房的目的。醫生的臉會顯示在機器人的螢幕上，並且可以透過麥克風和喇叭和病人溝通。機器人醫生的目的是讓醫生能更方便照顧病患，也讓病患能和本人不在醫院裡的醫生直接立即的接觸。

根據調查報告顯示，八成參加研究的病人相信機器人醫生能使他們更快速地接觸到醫生，七成的病人認為機器人醫生能讓他們的醫生提供更多的醫療資訊。大部分參加調查的病人都非常滿意這項新科技。很多病人說他們喜歡醫生的虛擬診巡房勝過醫生親自巡房，儘管這項最新科技並不是要用來取代真人醫生的。

透過現場、雙向影音的聯繫，醫生可以操作機器人，移動機器人的頭部來察看監測器及圖表上重要的徵兆。醫生說機器人醫生的協助將會在未來的醫療照護上扮演重大的角色。它們可以讓醫生接觸到邊遠地區的病人。機器人醫生是個珍貴的工具。

由於往後機器人會加入更多的功能，相信它們本身將能夠提供更多元化的服務，而或許急診部門在不久的將來也能夠透過機器人為中風患者提供治療。

聽力題目解析

❶ 此題詢問的是醫生可以使用何物操控機器人來透過網路檢查病人。選項 (A) 為搖桿；選項 (B) 為兜風；選項 (C) 為筷子。答案為 (A)，在錄音檔中間，我們可以聽見 "Doctors can maneuver this new type of robot by using a joystick ..."此題考的是我們對 "maneuver"（v. 操控）這個字是否熟悉，若無法把握，也可試著從 "by using ..."（透過使用……）來推測。

❷ 此題詢問的是機器人醫生的目的是使醫生監測病人的方式變得更加如何。選項 (A) 為便利的；選項 (B) 為困難的；選項 (C) 為複雜的。在介紹完醫生會如何操作機器人後，我們可以得知 "The purpose of robodoc is to make it more convenient ..." 故答案為 (A)，此題也可以透過全文的寫作方向來刪去其它選項。

❸ 此題詢問的是機器人醫生的協助將會在醫療保護的未來扮演什麼樣的角色。選項 (A) 為簡單的；選項 (B) 為強而有力的；選項 (C) 為虛弱的。答案為 (B)，此題考的是我們熟不熟悉 "momentus" 此單字。或者我們可以透過前後文推測，後面我們聽見一個相對簡單的句子 "The robot doctor is a precious tool." 便可知答案應為一正向之單字，此時便能將中性的 (A) 和負面的 (C) 排除。

❹ 此題詢問的是這項新科技可以提供住在何種地區的病人照護。選項 (A) 為外太空；選項 (B) 為地核；選項 (C) 為農業的和偏遠的。在中後段，

我們可以聽見幾乎與題目相同之句子，答案為 (C)，此題也可用常理將其它選項刪去。

❺ 此題詢問的是此種最新科技並不是用來取代何者。選項 (A) 為人類醫生；選項 (B) 為機器人醫生；選項 (C) 為動物醫生。在調查報告後，我們可以聽見 "... although this latest technology is not intended to replace a human doctor." 故選擇 (B)，此題可以用前面的 "prefer" 和接續的 "although" 來進行推測。

* * *

閱讀題目解析

❶ 此題詢問的是內文第五段中出現的 outlying 意思可能為何。選項 (A) 為都市的；選項 (B) 為城市；選項 (C) 為偏遠的；選項 (D) 為海邊的。答案可從前後文推測，都市醫療本較便利，故常理判斷答案為 (C)，且此句也曾以 "rural" 及 "remote" 兩個相近字來表達過。

❷ 此題詢問的是何種醫學症狀在未來也可能會有機器人醫生來照顧。選項 (A) 為關節炎；選項 (B) 為蜂窩性組織炎；選項 (C) 為中風；選項 (D) 為疹子。答案可見內文最後一段最後一句，選 (C)。

補充單字

☆ 1. robot	n.	機器人
☆ 2. hospital	n.	醫院
☆ 3. patient	n.	病人
☆ 4. physician	n.	醫生
☆ 5. interact	v.	互動
☆ 6. assistance	n.	協助

A Concise History of English Language

英語的發展歷史

聽力測驗 🎧 Track 064

在學習英文的過程中，「聽」可能是最直接的第一線接觸，也可能是大家最想要快速習得的能力。現在，就讓我們來熟悉各種英文情境，提升自己的英文臨場感吧！

( ) 1. Half of the most commonly used words in Modern English have Old English _____.
(A) roots   (B) roof   (C) rust

( ) 2. The Duke of Normandy is also known as _____.
(A) Shakespeare
(B) William the Conqueror
(C) Oxford
(D) Alexander the Great

( ) 3. The first English dictionary was published in_____.
(A) 1804   (B) 1504   (C) 1604

( ) 4. According to the text, American English is more like the English of _____.
(A) Shakespeare   (B) Cambridge   (C) Victoria

( ) 5. _____English has many words adopted foreign vocabulary from countries around the world.
(A) Modern   (B) Middle   (C) Old

 **閱讀測驗**

剛剛的聽力測驗是否因為答題不順而感到遺憾？或是覺得自己有某些地方掌握地不夠好？現在就讓我們來直接「看」剛剛的聽力測驗，並透過後面的閱讀測驗來補齊聽力上的不足，同時考驗自己的閱讀能力吧！

The history of the English language began with the invasion of Britain by three Germanic tribes, the Anglos, the Saxons and the Jutes during the 5th century A.D.. At that time, the inhabitants of Britain spoke a Celtic language. The Anglos came from England and their language was called English, which the words "England" and "English" were **derived**[1] from.

The **invading**[2] three tribes spoke similar languages, and the languages **evolved**[3] into so-called Old English. Old English did not sound or look like English today. Native English speakers today would have difficulty understanding Old English. However, about half of the most commonly used words in **Modern**[4] English have Old English roots.

The Duke of Normandy, also known as William the Conqueror, conquered England in 1066. The new conquerors spoke a sort of French. At that time, the lower classes spoke English while the upper classes spoke French. Later in the 14th century, English became dominant in Britain again, but with many French words added, it was called Middle English and would still be difficult for native English speakers today to understand.

At the end of Middle English, a change in pronunciation started, with vowels being pronounced shorter. The British people got in contact with many peoples from around the world, which meant that many new words and phrases were added to the language. At that time, books became cheaper and more people started to read. Printing also brought standardization to English. **Spelling**[5] and grammar were fixed as well. The first English dictionary was published in 1604.

Modern English has many words adopted from foreign **vocabularies**[6] from countries around the world. And there are many British words which are different from American words. Some of the spellings are not the same, either. Here are some very common examples as follows.

British spellings	American spellings
cheque	check
colour	color
cosy	cozy
dialogue	dialog
favourite	favorite
humour	humor
jewellery	jewelry
kilometre	kilometer
realise	realize
theatre	theater
traveller	traveler
tyre	tire

American English is more like the English of Shakespeare. Spanish had a great influence on American English. French words also greatly influenced American English. Besides American English and British English, there are many other varieties of English around the world such as Canadian English, Australian English, New Zealand English, Indian English, South African English and so on.

【Question】

(　　) 1. Which of the following tribe did not take part in the invasion of Britain based on the article?
(A) the Anglos (B) the Jutes
(C) the Saxons (D) the French

(　　) 2. Which of the statement is incorrect according to the article?
(A) The spellings between British and American English are slightly different.
(B) There was a change of how the words are pronounced at the end of Middle English.

(C) American English is only a branch among many other varieties of English.

(D) The first English Dictionary was published in the last few decades.

【文章中譯】

英語的歷史由三個日耳曼部族，即，盎格魯族、撒克遜族、朱特族，於西元五世紀侵略英國展開。當時英國人說的是凱爾特語。盎格魯族來自英格蘭，他們的語言稱為「English」，英文的「England」和「English」都是由這個字衍生出來的。

這三個侵略英國的部族說的是相似的語言，這三種語言逐漸發展成所謂的古英文。古英文聽起來、看起來皆與現代英語不同。現今的英美本國人也很難理解古英文。然而，現在英文中大約有一半的最常使用字彙有古英文字根。

法國諾曼第公爵，又稱威廉大帝，在1066年征服英國。這個新的征服者說的是某種法語。當時，下層階級說的是英文，而上層階級說的是法文。之後到了十四世紀，英文又變成英國主要的語言，但是已加入許多的法語。這個時期的英文稱做中古英文，現今的英美本國人也很難理解中古英文。到了中古英文末期，開始了發音的轉變，母音發得越來越短。英國人和世界各國的民族有往來，這意味著許多新字詞加入了這個語言。當時，書籍變得越來越便宜，許多人開始閱讀。印刷術也為英文帶來準則，拼字和文法也固定了。第一本英文字典於1604年出版。

現代英文有很多世界各國的外來的字彙。英式英文有很多字和美式英文不同，有些拼法也不一樣。以下列舉一些常見的例子：

英式拼法	美式拼法
cheque	check （支票）
colour	color （顏色）
cosy	cozy （舒適的）
dialogue	dialog （對話）
favourite	favorite（最愛的）

humour	humor （幽默）	
jewellery	jewelry （珠寶）	
kilometre	kilometer （公里）	
realise	realize （明瞭）	
theatre	theater （戲院）	
traveller	traveler （旅客）	
tyre	tire （輪胎）	

美式英文比較像莎士比亞時期的英文。西班牙文深深影響了美式英文，法文也大大地影響了美式英文。除了美式英文與英式英文，全世界還有各式各樣的英文，例如加拿大英文、澳洲英文、紐西蘭英文、印度英文、南非英文等等。

聽力題目解析

❶ 此題詢問的是現代英語多數的用字都具有古英語的什麼。選項 (A) 為根源；選項 (B) 為屋頂；選項 (C) 為生鏽。在錄音檔中段，我們可以聽見一樣的 "... Modern English have Old English roots." 故選 (A)，也可從內文的討論來推測。

❷ 此題詢問的是諾曼第公爵的別稱為何。選項 (A) 為莎士比亞；選項 (B) 為威廉大帝；選項 (C) 為牛津；選項 (D) 為亞歷山大大帝。這邊考的是 "also known as" 作為「又稱作 ......」的用法，選擇 (B)。

❸ 此題詢問的是第一本英文字典於幾年發行。選 (C)，此類年份題需特別注意。

❹ 此題詢問的是根據內文，美式英語更像是屬於何人或何地使用的英式英語。選項 (A) 為莎士比亞；選項 (B) 為康橋；選項 (C) 為維多利亞。在錄音檔後段，我們可以聽見一樣的 "American English is more like the English of Shakespeare." 掌握細節即可，選擇 (A)。

❺ 此題詢問的是哪一時期的英語具有許多採用世界各地外文單字的特質。選項 (A) 為現代的；選項 (B) 為中世紀的；選項 (C) 為古代的。在介紹英式英語和美式英語的拼法之前，我們可以得知 "Modern English has many words adopted from foreign vocabularies ..." 故選 (A)，這邊考的是 "adopt"（採用）和 "foreign"（外國的；外來的）這兩個關鍵字，也可從後面舉例的各國英文來推判。

● ● ● ● ● ● ● ● ● ● ● ● ● ● ● ● ● ● ●

閱讀題目解析

❶ 此題詢問的是根據內文，選項何者沒有參與入侵英國。選項 (A) 為盎格魯族；選項 (B) 為朱特族；選項 (C) 為撒克遜族；選項 (D) 為法國人。答案可見內文第一段，選擇 (D)。

❷ 此題詢問的是何者選項為非。選項 (A) 為英式英語和美式英語的拼音有些微差別；選項 (B) 為在中世紀，單字的發音有產生改變；選項 (C) 為美式英語只是英語眾多的分支之一；選項 (D) 為第一本英語字典在近幾十年發行了。答案為 (D)，第一本英語字典是在第四段最後一句出現的「1604年」出版。其餘的選項皆可在內文中得知。

補充單字

☆ 1. derive	v.	衍生出
☆ 2. invade	v.	入侵
☆ 3. evolve	v.	發展、進化
☆ 4. modern	adj.	現代的
☆ 5. spelling	n.	拼字
☆ 6. vocabulary	n.	字彙

聽力測驗 🎧 Track 065

在學習英文的過程中，「聽」可能是最直接的第一線接觸，也可能是大家最想要快速習得的能力。現在，就讓我們來熟悉各種英文情境，提升自己的英文臨場感吧！

(　) 1. According to the article, we should stay away from people who is always influencing us _____.
　　(A) in a good way　(B) greatly　(C) positively　(D) negatively

(　) 2. To be happy, we can go see a movie. It'll _____ our imagination.
　　(A) enrich　　(B) narrow　(C) reduce　　(D) decrease

(　) 3. We should _____ express how we feel and what we want to feel happier.
　　(A) politely　　(B) rudely　(C) impolitely　(D) loudly

(　) 4. As one of the rules to seek happiness, _____ is the best policy.
　　(A) exercise　　(B) honesty　(C) reading

(　) 5. According to the text, we should count our _____ every day.
　　(A) blessings　　(B) money　(C) books　　(D) families

閱讀測驗

剛剛的聽力測驗是否因為答題不順而感到遺憾？或是覺得自己有某些地方掌握地不夠好？現在就讓我們來直接「看」剛剛的聽力測驗，並透過後面的閱讀測驗來補齊聽力上的不足，同時考驗自己的閱讀能力吧！

think the most important goal in life is the **pursuit**[1] of happiness. I believe happiness is a state of mind. It is not something that can be defined concretely. We can change our state of mind in many ways. Here are some simple tips on how to live a happy life. Life is really very simple, unless you **complicate**[2] it on purpose. Go ahead and be happier.

1. Nothing is more precious than your health, so be healthy physically and mentally.
2. Keep in touch with your close friends. You'll need their love and support at some point.
3. Stay away from people who are always influencing you negatively.
4. Have a pet and stroke them often.
5. Honesty surely is the best policy.
6. Always say what you mean and mean what you say.
7. Politely express how you feel and what you want because people around you can't be mind readers.
8. Always wear a smile.
9. Laugh out loud every day.
10. Spend less than you earn.
11. Give contributions to charities regularly.
12. Do not use your credit card and borrow money unless you really have to.
13. Do not lend people money unless you truly don't mind if it's not repaid.
14. Do not gamble because in the long run, you can't win.
15. Give lots of **compliments**[3]. Giving is more blessed than receiving. This will give you pleasure and make others feel good.
16. Read newspapers and books on a daily basis.
17. Try to enjoy classical music. It will soothe your mind and soul.
18. Watch reruns of classic sitcoms that never fail to make you laugh.
19. Watch "A Christmas Carol" on Christmas every year. It'll reaffirm your belief in love.
20. Go see a good movie sometimes. It'll enrich your imagination.
21. Stay close to nature often.
22. Exercise three times a week. It'll lift your spirit and make you feel good.
23. **Travel**[4] to different countries if you can afford it, and savor different

cultures.

24. Write good memories in your diary or journal so you can revisit good times.

25. Write solutions to bad events that happened to you in your diary or journal so you can avoid them next time and have positive thinking.

26. Make a list of things you're grateful for and count your blessings every day.

27. Try to write a poem or **create**[5] a song. You'll be surprised to find your inner artist.

28. When you are gloomy, imagine the feeling of the sun on your skin and the sound of the waves against the shore. It'll cheer you up.

29. **Seize**[6] the day. Rather than waiting to do something tomorrow, why not do it today?

30. Live a simple and meaningful life.

【Question】

(　　) 1. Which of the following is not mentioned in the article as a way to be happy?
    (A) traveling
    (B) keep a journal
    (C) imagine the feeling of the sun
    (D) go to the library everyday

(　　) 2. Which of the following is not mentioned in the article as something to avoid?
    (A) do not gamble
    (B) do not borrow money
    (C) do not spend more than you earn
    (D) do not say what you mean

【文章中譯】

我認為人生中最重要的目標是追求快樂。我相信快樂是一種心境，它並不是一種可以具體定義的東西。我們可以在很多方面改變自己的心境。以下是一些如何過一個快樂人生的簡單小秘訣。人生其實非常簡單,除非你刻意使它複雜化。讓自己更快樂吧。

1. 沒有什麼比你的健康更珍貴,所以請保持身心健康。
2. 與你的好友們保持聯繫。你會需要他們的愛和支持。
3. 遠離總是負面影響你的人。
4. 養隻寵物,常常輕撫牠們。
5. 誠實為上策。
6. 永遠心口合一,不要言不由衷。
7. 有禮地説出你的感覺和你想要的,因為你周遭的人可不會讀心術。
8. 臉上永遠掛著微笑。
9. 每天都放聲大笑。
10. 量入為出。
11. 定期做慈善捐獻。
12. 除非不得已,不要使用信用卡、不要借錢。
13. 除非你真心不介意錢收不回來,否則不要借錢給別人。
14. 不要賭博,因為你終究會輸的。
15. 多多讚美別人。施比受有福,你會從中得到喜樂,別人也會因此感到愉快。
16. 每天閱讀書報。
17. 試著享受古典音樂,它會舒緩你的身心。
18. 看會讓你一笑再笑的重播的情境喜劇。
19. 每年聖誕節看電視播出的「聖誕頌歌」,這會讓你更堅定愛的信仰。
20. 常常看部好電影,這會豐富你的想像力。
21. 常常接觸大自然。
22. 每週運動三次,這會提振你的精神, 讓你感覺很棒。
23. 如果負擔得起,可以到不同國家旅行,品嚐各國不同的文化。
24. 將好的回憶寫在日記或手扎裡,這樣你就可以重溫好時光。
25. 為發生在你身上的壞事提出解決之道,並寫在日記或手扎裡,這樣你下次就可以避免,而且會有正面的思維。
26. 列出一張感謝清單,每日細數恩典。
27. 試著寫首詩或創作一首歌。你會驚訝地發覺你的藝術天分。
28. 當你鬱鬱寡歡時,想像陽光親吻肌膚的感覺和海浪打在岸上的聲音。這樣會讓你開心起來。

29. 把握今日。與其等待明天,何不現在就去做?
30. 過一個簡單、有意義的人生。

聽力題目解析

❶ 此題詢問的是我們應該遠離總是會如何影響我們的人。選項 (A) 為以好的方式;選項 (B) 為大大地;選項 (C) 為正向地;選項 (D) 為負面地。在錄音檔開始介紹小祕訣後,我們可以聽到 "Stay away from people who are always influencing you negatively." 故選 (D),這邊考的是 "negatively"(負面地)此單字。

❷ 此題詢問的是為了快樂,我們可以去看場電影,它可以使我們的想像力如何。選項 (A) 為充實;選項 (B) 為變狹窄;選項 (C) 為減少;選項 (D) 為降低。同上,選 (A),除此之外,我們可以發現其餘選項皆是「變窄」或「減少」之意,故在沒有特殊脈絡之下,可以一併排除。此處考的變是 "enrich"(充實)之意。

❸ 此題詢問的是我們可以如何表達我們的意見和我們的渴望來感到更快樂。選項 (A) 為禮貌地;選項 (B) 為粗魯地;選項 (C) 為不禮貌地;選項 (D) 為大聲地。同上,選擇 (A),這邊我們也可以透過 (A) 作為唯一具正向意涵之單字來做簡單的刪去。

❹ 此題詢問的是作為一種尋找快樂的方法,何者為上策。選項 (A) 為運動;選項 (B) 為誠實;選項 (C) 為閱讀。同上,選 (B),此題僅需注意聆聽內文。

❺ 此題詢問的是根據內文,我們應該要每天細數何者。選項 (A) 為恩典;選項 (B) 為金錢;選項 (C) 為書籍;選項 (D) 為家人。同上,選擇 (A),此類型的題目除了在聆聽時把握內文之外,還可透過與主題相呼應這個路線,依照「尋找快樂」來做簡單的常理推判。

Level 1
Level 2
Level 3
Level 4
Level 5
Level 6

閱讀題目解析

❶ 此題詢問的是何者並非內文所提及之快樂的方法。選項 (A) 為旅遊；選項 (B) 為寫日記；選項 (C) 為想像太陽的觸感；選項 (D) 為每天去圖書館。答案可見內文第 23、24、第28點，選擇 (D)。

❷ 此題詢問的是何者並非內文所提及之需避免的事。選項 (A) 為不要賭博；選項 (B) 為不要借錢；選項 (C) 為不要花超過自己賺的錢；選項 (D) 為不要心口合一。答案可見內文第10、12、13點，選擇 (D)。這邊需注意選項 (C) 的寫法稍為複雜，且 (D) 為陷阱題。

補充單字

☆ 1. pursuit	n.	追求
☆ 2. complicate	v.	使複雜
☆ 3. compliment	n.	恭維
☆ 4. travel	v.	旅行
☆ 5. create	v.	創造
☆ 6. seize	v.	把握

The Differences Between Asian and Western Cultures

東西文化的差異

🎧 聽力測驗 🎧 Track 066

在學習英文的過程中,「聽」可能是最直接的第一線接觸,也可能是大家最想要快速習得的能力。現在,就讓我們來熟悉各種英文情境,提升自己的英文臨場感吧!

(　　) 1. According to the text, the biggest difference between Asian and Western cultures is _____.
(A) school　　　　　　(B) family
(C) work　　　　　　　(D) freinds

(　　) 2. Few old people in Asia end up in a _____.
(A) nursing home　　　(B) daycare center
(C) hospital　　　　　(D) clinic

(　　) 3. _____ families are more popular in Asian culture.
(A) Patriarchal　　　　(B) Matrilineal
(C) Homosexual　　　　(D) Polygamous

(　　) 4. Western culture lays great stress on _____.
(A) family　　　　　　(B) individualism
(C) conformity　　　　(D) parents

(　　) 5. Asia culture put emphasis on _____.
(A) school　　　　　　(B) individualism
(C) conformity　　　　(D) work

剛剛的聽力測驗是否因為答題不順而感到遺憾？或是覺得自己有某些地方掌握地不夠好？現在就讓我們來直接「看」剛剛的聽力測驗，並透過後面的閱讀測驗來補齊聽力上的不足，同時考驗自己的閱讀能力吧！

There are many differences between **Western**[1] and **Asian**[2] cultures. But the biggest difference between them could be defined in one word—family. The concept of family members living under the same roof is generally more emphasized in the Asian world than in the West since most people in Asia believe good family education is strongly related to a child's quality and behavior, and also related to the future of their **country**[3].

In Asian culture, family is the most important thing. Asian parents tend to have more children than their Western counterparts. Parents and children, even their relatives, tend to live together or live close together, which Westerners would consider old-fashioned. Few old people in Asia end up in a nursing home because their families will look after them.

But you will find things quite different in the West. Western people usually move away from home to attend college, make their own living in a new city, and then have their own family far away from their hometown. As the pressure of raising their own children and fulfilling their lives grows bigger, they visit their parents less and less each year. And old people, in western culture, will be brought to the nursing home under the care of the care givers since they have no time to take good care of their old people in their own homes.

In Asian culture, the young show **respect**[4] to the elder by calling them uncle or aunt. But in Western culture, young people just call the elder ones by their names. Sons- and daughters-inlaw also call their parents-in-law directly by their names. In the Asian culture, sons- and daughtersin- law call their parents-in-law Mom and Dad.

Patriarchal families are more popular in Asian culture. It is believed that the man is in charge of the house in most countries in Asia. Nowadays, however, the Western ideas have influenced many Asian nations. Western influence, economic pressure and changing ways of living are all making a great impact on the **traditional**[5] Confucianist-led lifestyle in

Asian countries.

Western culture lays great stress on individualism, whereas Asian culture put emphasis on conformity. Asian students are expected to memorize the right answers for exams, while in the West, students are encouraged to have more in-class discussion and problem-solving exercises. What this results in is that Asia produces more doctors and scientists, and the West produces more artists and musicians.

Of course, there are always exceptions to both Asian and Western patterns of behavior. With **different**[6] family educations, both Eastern or Western family concepts have their own merits. We ought to fully understand the differences between them, make up for the deficiencies by learning from the advantages, and make the world a more compatible place to live.

【Question】

( ) 1. According to the article, what do sons- and daughters-in-law call their parents-in-law in the West?
    (A) mom and dad   (B) uncle and aunt
    (C) by their names   (D) They usually don't call them anything.

( ) 2. According to the article, what may be the main reason why the West produces more artists and musicians?
    (A) Students in the West love arts more than those in the East.
    (B) Parents in the West force their children to practice music.
    (C) Students in the East all want to become doctors or scientists.
    (D) Students in the East are asked to memorize the right answers.

【文章中譯】

亞洲和西方文化間有許多差異。但最大的差異可以用一個詞來定義，即家庭。一家人同住在屋簷下的觀念通常在亞洲社會被加以強調，因大部分的亞洲人相信良好的家庭教育跟孩童的素質和行為有很大的關連，跟國家的未來也大有關係。

在亞洲文化中，家庭是最重要的。亞洲父母傾向生育許多小孩，西方父母則不然。父母、小孩，甚至親戚住在一起或住得很近，在西方人看來是很過時的觀念。而亞洲的老人很少會在療養院度過晚年，因為家人們會照護他們。

在西方社會則大不同。西方人通常會離家上大學，在新的城市裡賺錢生活，然後在遠離家鄉的地方成家立業。隨著撫養小孩及實現生活理想的壓力變大，他們回家看父母的次數也會逐年遞減。在西方文化中，老年人會被帶至療養院交給看護照顧，因為他們沒有時間在自己家裡照顧老年人。

在亞洲文化中，年輕人會尊敬地稱呼長輩某某叔叔、某某阿姨。但在西方文化中，年輕人會直呼長輩的名字。女婿和媳婦也會直呼公婆及丈人和丈母娘的名字。在亞洲文化中，女婿和媳婦則都稱呼公婆及丈人和丈母娘為爸爸、媽媽。

父系社會在亞洲文化中最普遍，因為大部分的亞洲國家相信男人是一家之主。然而，現今的西方思維已影響了許多亞洲國家。西方的影響、經濟的壓力，以及生活方式的轉變都大大衝擊了亞洲國家其由傳統儒家主導的生活形態。

西方文化非常重視個人主義，反之，亞洲文化強調則順從。亞洲教育希望學生背誦正確答案以求考試高分，然而西方教育鼓勵學生多多在課堂上討論，並練習解決問題，最後造就了亞洲出醫生及科學家，西方出藝術家及音樂家的現象。

當然，關於亞洲及西方的行為模式一定有例外。由於不同的家庭教育，東西雙方的家庭概念都有其優點。我們應該完全理解兩者間的差異，截長補短，使這個世界更能和平共存。

聽力題目解析

❶ 此題詢問的是根據內文，東西文化最大的差異為何。選項 (A) 為學校；選項 (B) 為家庭；選項 (C) 為工作；選項 (D) 為朋友。錄音檔開始即給我們答案，選 (B)。

❷ 此題詢問的是很少有亞洲年長的人最後會被安置於何處。選項 (A) 為安養院；選項 (B) 為日間照護中心；選項 (C) 為醫院；選項 (D) 為診所。這邊考得是 "end up" 作為「最後處於、最後成為」之意，故選 (A)。

❸ 此題詢問的是何種家庭在亞洲較常見。選項 (A) 為父系的；選項 (B) 為母系的；選項 (C) 為同性的；選項 (D) 為一夫多妻的。在錄音檔中後段，我們可以聽見 "Patriarchal families are more popular ..."，這邊若無法把握此單字，可先記得發音來進行刪去法。選擇 (A)。

❹ 此題詢問的是西方文化較著重於何者。選項 (A) 為家庭；選項 (B) 為個人主義；選項 (C) 為順從；選項 (D) 為父母親。答案為 (B)，此題僅需注意聆聽，或者可以透過後續的教育文化不同來推測。

❺ 此題詢問的是亞洲文化強調何者。選項 (A) 為學校；選項 (B) 為個人主義；選項 (C) 為順從；選項 (D) 為工作。答案為 (C)，同上。

閱讀題目解析

❶ 此題詢問的是根據內文，西方人的女婿和媳婦會稱自己的公婆、丈人和丈母娘為什麼。選項 (A) 為爸爸和媽媽；選項 (B) 為叔叔和阿姨；選項 (C) 為直呼名字；選項 (D) 為他們不會稱呼他們。答案可見內文第四段末，選 (C)。

❷ 此題詢問的是根據內文，何者為西方造就較多藝術家和音樂家的主要原因。選項 (A) 為西方的學生比起東方的學生更愛藝術；選項 (B) 為西方的家長強迫孩子練習音樂；選項 (C) 為東方的學生全都想要成為醫生或科學家；選項 (D) 為東方的學生被要求背誦正確答案。答案可見內文倒數第二段，選 (D)。

補充單字

☆ 1. Western	a.	西方的
☆ 2. Asian	a.	亞洲的
☆ 3. country	n.	國家
☆ 4. respect	n.	尊敬
☆ 5. traditional	adj.	傳統的
☆ 6. different	adj.	不同的

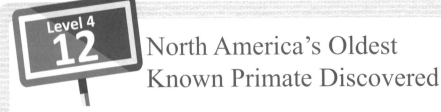

North America's Oldest Known Primate Discovered

北美發現最古老靈長類化石

聽力測驗 🎧 Track 067

在學習英文的過程中,「聽」可能是最直接的第一線接觸,也可能是大家最想要快速習得的能力。現在,就讓我們來熟悉各種英文情境,提升自己的英文臨場感吧!

( ) 1. What is the species found in North America called?
   (A) Teilhardina magnoliana
   (B) Hibiscus syriacus
   (C) Oncorhynchus masou formosanus

( ) 2. It is said that this newly found species were very small and weighed no more than _____.
   (A) one inch   (B) one ounce   (C) one meter

( ) 3. The scientists estimate that newly found species dates to about _____ million years ago.
   (A) 78   (B) 48
   (C) 55.8   (D) 85.5

( ) 4. _____ was the route of many migrations over the eons, including dinosaurs.
   (A) The Bering land bridge
   (B) The London bridge
   (C) The Brooklyn bridge
   (D) The Golden Gate bridge

(　　) 5. The newly found species is as small as _____?
    (A) a cat   (B) a dog
    (C) a mouse

 閱讀測驗

剛剛的聽力測驗是否因為答題不順而感到遺憾？或是覺得自己有某些地方掌握地不夠好？現在就讓我們來直接「看」剛剛的聽力測驗，並透過後面的閱讀測驗來補齊聽力上的不足，同時考驗自己的閱讀能力吧！

A **paleontologist**[1] recently discovered North America's oldest known **primate**[2] **fossil**[3]. The newly-found animal appears to have been as small as the palm of a hand. This tiny **species**[4], called Teilhardina magnoliana, is very, very old. Scientists have known that it was a relative of some similarly-aged fossils from Europe, China, and Wyoming's Bighorn Basin.

The Teilhardina fossils found in Mississippi are older than the ones that have been found in Europe. It is said that this newly-discovered species was as small as mice and weighed no more than one ounce. Its fossils proved that it had migrated from Asia to North America across the Bering land bridge long before humans, and then continued its migration to Europe. The Bering land bridge was the route of many migrations over the eons, including dinosaurs. Many scientists believe the first modern human beings went into North America sometime between 30,000 to 12,000 years ago over the same route.

The scientists estimate that Teilhardina magnoliana, the leaping, **furry**[5] mini-monkey, dates back to about 55.8 million years ago. The layer of rock in which the fossils were found also proved the fact that the fossil of Teilhardina magnoliana might indeed be North America's oldest primate fossil.

Teilhardina magnoliana once **inhabited**[6] North America for many thousands of years, but none of its distant relatives, such as monkeys, currently lives there because most primates only inhabit humid tropical or subtropical regions. So, when Earth began to cool down about 35 million years ago, Teilhardina magnoliana disappeared from North America and Europe. Today, modern human beings have already grown accustomed to living in different climates.

【Question】

( ) 1. Why did Teilhardina magnoliana begin to disappear from North America and Europe?
   (A) They were hunted down.
   (B) The weather cooled down.
   (C) They were killed by monkeys.
   (D) There was an asteroid that crashed onto the Earth.

( ) 2. Which of the following statement is incorrect about Teilhardina magnoliana?
   (A) They were distant relatives of some similar aged fossils found in Europe.
   (B) It was estimated that Teilhardina magnoliana dates back to about 20 millions ago.
   (C) Teilhardina magnoliana was resided in North America.
   (D) The fossils of Teilhardina magnoliana found in Mississippi were older than those in Europe.

【文章中譯】

一名考古學家最近在北美發現了目前所知最古老的靈長類化石。這個新發現的動物似乎和人的手掌一樣小。這個小型物種叫做「Teilhardina magnoliana（德氏猴）」，是非常、非常古老的動物。科學家已經知道牠與在歐洲、中國和美國懷俄明州的大角羊盆地所發現的差不多年代的化石有親戚關係。

這個在密西西比發現的德氏猴化石比在歐洲發現的還要古老。據説這個新發現的物種和老鼠一樣小隻，體重不超過一盎司。化石也證明了這個物種是經由白令陸橋從亞洲遷移到北美，遠比人類還要早，並繼續遷移至歐洲。白令陸橋是許多物種亙古遷移的路徑，包括恐龍在內。許多科學家相信現代人類大約在 30,000 到 12,000 年前經由同樣的路徑進入北美。

科學家估計「Teilhardina magnoliana」這種跳躍的、毛茸茸的迷你猴子，源自5580萬年前。發現化石的岩層也證明了在北美發現的「Teilhardina magnoliana」可能真的是最古老的靈長類化石。

「Teilhardina magnoliana」曾經棲息在北美數千年之久，但牠的其他遠親，例如猴子，目前都不住在那裡，因為大部分的靈長類只生活在潮濕的熱帶或副熱帶地區，因此當地球在 3500 萬年前開始冷卻時，「Teilhardina magnoliana」便從北美及歐洲消失。不過今日，現代人類已經適應了在各種不同的氣候下生存。

聽力題目解析

❶ 此題詢問的是在北美被發現的物種叫做什麼。選項 (A) 為德氏猴；選項 (B) 為木槿花；選項 (C) 為櫻花鉤吻鮭。這邊考得是同位語的用法，"This tiny species, called Teilhardina magnoliana, is very, very old." 只需要把握逗號間 "called" 作為前面 "species" 的補充即可，選 (A)。

❷ 此題詢問的是據說此新發現的物種體積極小，不會超過幾公斤。選項 (A) 為一公吋；選項 (B) 為一盎司；選項 (C) 為一公尺。答案為 (B)，這邊考的是考生能否把握單位的英文寫法進而選出答案，為 (B)。

❸ 此題詢問的是科學家預測此新發現的物種可以追溯到多少年前。答案為 (C)，除了考 "date to" 作為「追溯到」之意，還測驗學生是否能記住數字型的資訊。

❹ 此題詢問的是何者為包括恐龍等萬古以來眾多遷徙會行經之處。選項 (A) 為白令陸橋；選項 (B) 為倫敦大橋；選項 (C) 為布魯克林橋；選項 (D) 為金門大橋。在錄音檔中我們即可聽見同樣的句子，故仔細聆聽把握細節即可，選 (A)。

❺ 此題詢問的是此新發現的物種和何者一樣體積狹小。選項 (A) 為貓；選項 (B) 為狗；選項 (C) 為老鼠。這邊考得是 "as ... as ..." 作為「和……一樣……」的用法，故選擇 (C)。

閱讀題目解析

❶ 此題詢問的是為什麼德氏猴消失在北美和歐洲。選項 (A) 為他們被獵殺；選項 (B) 為氣候冷卻：選項 (C) 為他們被猴子殺光；選項 (D) 為有行星撞擊地球。答案可見內文最後一段，選擇 (B)。

❷ 此題詢問的是何者關於德氏猴的陳述不正確。選項 (A) 為牠們是猴子的遠親；選項 (B) 為據傳德氏猴可以被追溯到二十萬年前：選項 (C) 為德氏猴曾住在北美；選項 (D) 為在密西西比找到的德氏猴化石比在歐洲找到的還要古老。答案為 (B)，可見內文倒數第二段，其餘選項可見內文第二段及倒數最後一段。

補充單字

☆ 1. paleontologist	n.	古生物學家
☆ 2. primate	n.	靈長類的
☆ 3. fossil	n.	化石
☆ 4. species	n.	物種
☆ 5. furry	adj.	毛茸茸的
☆ 6. inhabit	v.	居住於

Introduction for TOEFL Test Takers

托福簡介

聽力測驗 🎧 Track 068

在學習英文的過程中，「聽」可能是最直接的第一線接觸，也可能是大家最想要快速習得的能力。現在，就讓我們來熟悉各種英文情境，提升自己的英文臨場感吧！

(　　) 1. What kind of English proficiency test does this article introduce?
(A) Test of English as a Foreign Language
(B) International English Language Testing System
(C) General English Proficiency Test
(D) Test of English for International Communication

(　　) 2. Who are the test takers of TOEFL?
(A) English native speakers
(B) American high school students
(C) non-English speaking people
(D) kindergarten students

(　　) 3. What is the total score of TOEFL?
(A) 80　　　　(B) 100　　　　(C) 120　　　　(D) 140

(　　) 4. What is the range of TOEFL score that most universities require?
(A) 30-50　　　(B) 50-70　　　(C) 70-80　　　(D) 80-100

(　　) 5. What is important when practicing TOEFL?
(A) to select 4 universities that you want to apply
(B) to go over your mistakes and practice the areas that you consider difficult

(C) to lay back and watch movies

(D) to apply for a job at a foreign institution

 閱讀測驗

剛剛的聽力測驗是否因為答題不順而感到遺憾？或是覺得自己有某些地方掌握地不夠好？現在就讓我們來直接「看」剛剛的聽力測驗，並透過後面的閱讀測驗來補齊聽力上的不足，同時考驗自己的閱讀能力吧！

Have you received any formal training in English? I bet you did, but this isn't enough to prove that you have a good command of English. The Test of English as a Foreign Language (TOEFL) is the world's most widely accepted and renowned test you must take to prove that your **grasp**[1] of English is **adequate**[2] enough to study at a US-based university or apply for a job at a foreign institution. In fact, many universities in Europe also accept TOEFL.

Designed to measure the English levels of non-English speaking people, the test **consists of**[3] four sections — reading, listening, speaking, and writing. Each section of TOEFL has a maximum score of 30, and the total score is 120. The validity of TOEFL score is two years from the date of test. Most universities require TOEFL score ranging from 80 to 100. Score will be posted online within two weeks from the test date. In addition, students can select four Universities on their test date to send their scores for free.

Preparing for a TOEFL may sound **daunting**[4]. So why not pick your favorite film, watch it, and then read the script? To enhance reading **comprehension**[5], you can choose a book with short, interesting, but not too easy stories, for example, detective stories. To practice speaking, you can correspond online in English. Last not but least, you should practice taking the test and assess your progress. It's important to go over your mistakes and practice the areas that you consider difficult. With persistence and hard work, you will no doubt pass your TOEFL!

【Question】

(　　) 1. How long will it take for the TOEFL test takers to know their scores?
    (A) within two days of the test day
    (B) within one week of the test day
    (C) within two weeks of the test date
    (D) after one month of the test day

(　　) 2. How many sections are there in a TOEFL?
    (A) one　　　　　　(B) two
    (C) three　　　　　(D) four

【文章中譯】

你曾接受正式的英語訓練嗎？我相信你有，但是這並不足以證明你的英文能力很好。若要證明你對英文的掌握能力足以應付美國大學學業或應徵外商工作，你一定要考托福，因為它是全球最廣為接受並享有盛名的英語能力測驗。事實上，很多歐洲國家的大學也接受托福成績。

托福是為測驗非英語人士的英文程度而設計的，它包含四個部分：閱讀、聽力、口說、寫作。每部分滿分是30分，總分是120分。托福成績的有效期限是從測驗當日起後的兩年內，大部分大學所要求的托福成績落在80分到100分之間。成績會在測驗日後的兩星期內公布，學生可選擇將托福成績傳送至四所大學，此項服務是不收費的。

準備托福聽起來可能很令人退卻，所以何不挑選你最喜歡的電影來看，然後細讀劇本？為增強閱讀理解能力，你可以選擇短篇、有趣但又不會過於簡單的故事來讀，例如偵探故事。為練習口說能力，你可以在網路上與別人用英語通訊。最後，你應練習托福考題並評估進步程度。複習寫錯的試題並強化練習你覺得困難的部分是很重要的，只要持續不懈和用功，你一定可以通過托福測驗的！

聽力題目解析

❶ 此題詢問的是本文介紹的是哪一種英文能力測驗。選項 (A) 為托福測驗；選項 (B) 為雅思測驗；選項 (C) 為全民英檢；選項 (D) 為多益測驗。在錄音檔前段即指出 "The Test of English as a Foreign Language (TOEFL) is ...",本題考的是考生是否可把握TOEFL的全名,選 (A)。

❷ 此題詢問的是托福的考生是誰。選項 (A) 為英語為母語的人士；選項 (B) 為美國高中生；選項 (C) 為非英文為母語的人士；選項 (D) 為幼稚園學生。在錄音檔中前段部分提到 "Designed to measure the English levels of non-English speaking people..." 把握 "design"（設計）和 "measure"（測量）即可,選 (C)。

❸ 此題詢問的是托福的總分是幾分。在錄音檔中段提到 "Each section of TOEFL has a maximum score of 30, and the total score is 120." 注意數字即可,選 (C)。

❹ 此題詢問的是大部分美國學校要求托福成績範圍是幾分。錄音檔中後段提到"Most universities require TOEFL score ranging from 80 to 100.",數字是考試常見的考題,請考生注意,答案選 (D)。（註：申請美國大學的托福成績範圍是一般常識,若要申請美國常春藤名校至少要達105分）

❺ 此題詢問的是練習托福時很重要的是什麼。選項 (A) 為選擇四所想申請的大學；選項 (B) 為複習寫錯的試題並強化練習你覺得困難的部分；選項 (C) 為悠閒地看電影；選項 (D) 為向外商應徵工作。錄音檔後段提到 "It's important to go over your mistakes and practice the areas that you feel difficult." 也考 "go over"作為「複習」之片語用法,答案選 (B)。

閱讀題目解析

❶ 此題詢問的是托福的考生要等多久才能知道考試成績。選項 (A) 為測驗當天後的兩日內;選項 (B) 為測驗當天後的一個星期;選項 (C) 為測驗當天後的兩個星期;選項 (D) 為測驗當天後的一個月後。答案可見內文第二段,選 (C)。

❷ 第二題詢問的是托福有幾部分的測驗。選項 (A) 為一部分;選項 (B) 為兩部分;選項 (C) 為三部分;選項 (D) 為四部分。答案可見內文第二段,選 (D)。

補充單字

☆	1. grasp	n.	理解;掌握
☆	2. adequate	adj.	適當的
☆	3. consist of	v.	構成
☆	4. daunting	adj.	令人生畏的
☆	5. comprehension	n.	理解力

Level 1
Level 2
Level 3
Level 4
Level 5
Level 6

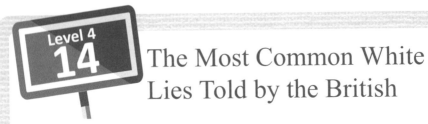

🔊 **聽力測驗** 🎧Track 069

在學習英文的過程中，「聽」可能是最直接的第一線接觸，也可能是大家最想要快速習得的能力。現在，就讓我們來熟悉各種英文情境，提升自己的英文臨場感吧！

( ) 1. According to a new survey, how many times does a British male lie a day?
　　(A) never 　　　　　　　(B) two times
　　(C) four times 　　　　　(D) five times.

( ) 2. What is the number one white lie told by the british?
　　(A) Nothing's wrong; I'm fine.
　　(B) Nice to meet you.
　　(C) I am on the way.
　　(D) My car is broken.

( ) 3. British scientists find out _____ are better liars.
　　(A) men 　　　(B) males 　　　(C) women

( ) 4. British scientists also discovered that men generated more _____ than women while speaking.
　　(A) smiles 　　　(B) pauses 　　　(C) words

( ) 5. Twenty-five percent of respondents have lied about _____ they are in.
　　(A) the place of work 　　(B) the amount of debt
　　(C) the amount of time

剛剛的聽力測驗是否因為答題不順而感到遺憾？或是覺得自己有某些地方掌握地不夠好？現在就讓我們來直接「看」剛剛的聽力測驗，並透過後面的閱讀測驗來補齊聽力上的不足，同時考驗自己的閱讀能力吧！

Do you **mind**[1] telling white lies? British people probably don't mind telling a **fib**[2] because, according to the latest **survey**[3], an average British male lies five times a day, while an average British female lies at least three times a day. Most of these white lies occur when people are too polite to tell the truth. People always respond "I'm fine" when, as a matter of fact, they're having a hard day.

According to the survey, the ten most **common**[4] white lies are as follows: 1) Nothing's wrong; I'm fine. 2) Nice to see you. 3) Sorry, I missed your call. 4) I'm afraid I haven't got any cash on me. 5) I'll give you a ring. 6) I don't have any spare change. 7) No, I'm afraid I haven't got a spare five minutes. 8) I'll give up tomorrow. 9) It's just what I've always wanted. 10) We'll have to meet up soon.

The survey says most common white lies also include "No, your bum doesn't look big in that"; "I'm stuck in traffic"; "What text message?"; "I had no signal"; "Of course I love you"; "My alarm didn't go off" ;"The check is in the post"; "My battery died"; "The train was delayed"; "I'll phone you back in a minute"; "This tastes delicious" and "I'm going to the gym tonight".

Another investigation says that about thirty percent of the respondents have lied about being sick; twenty-five percent about the amount of debt they are in. Eighteen percent of the respondents have denied having an affair and ten percent have lied on their resume. Six percent have told a white lie after bumping into another car. But an incredible sixty percent of the respondents said they don't feel guilty about lying.

Although men tell more lies than women, British scientists find that women are better liars. The research reveals that women are more persuasive in telling lies than men since women are more talkative than men. So it is easier for women to tell fibs.

British scientists also discovered that men participating in the investigation generated more pauses than women while speaking. The pauses arise spontaneously because men need to take more time to make their words sound better. When men have to tell lies, these pauses become more **frequent**[5]. Men need more time to make up a logically and syntactically correct sentence, connected with the previous and following sentences at the same time, whereas women first grow used to a **character**[6] they invent, and only after that they start talking.

【Question】

(　　) 1. According to the article, why are women better at lying?
　　　(A) Women are well-trained.
　　　(B) Men are asked to tell worse lies.
　　　(C) Women get themselves accustomed to the character they create first.
　　　(D) Women have more secrets to hide.

(　　) 2. What percentage of people does not feel guilty about lying?
　　　(A) 40　　　　　(B) 50　　　　(C) 60　　　　(D) 20

【文章中譯】

你介意説善意謊言嗎？英國人可能不會介意撒撒小謊，因為根據一份最新報告，一個普通英國男性一天會撒五次謊，而普通的英國女性一天會撒至少三次謊。大部分的善意謊言都是起因於人們不好意思説真話。人們總是會回答「我很好」，其實卻過了倒楣透頂的一天。

根據調查顯示，以下是十個最普遍的善意謊言：1）沒事，我很好。2）很高興見到你。3）抱歉，我沒接到你的電話。4）我沒帶現金在身上耶。5）我會打電話給你。6）我沒有多餘的零錢。7）不行，我連五分鐘的空閒都沒有。8）我明天就會放棄。9）這是我一直想要的。10）我們一定要快點聚一聚。

這份報告還指出其他最普遍的善意謊言包括：「不會，妳穿那件屁股看起來不會很大。」「我在塞車。」「有嗎？什麼簡訊？」「我手機收不到訊號。」「我當然愛你。」「我的鬧鐘沒有響。」「支票已經寄出了。」「我的電池沒電了。」「火車誤點了。」「我等一下回電話給你。」「這真好吃。」以及「我今晚要去健身房。」

另一項調查顯示，大約百分之三十的受訪者曾謊稱生病；百分之二十五沒有說出實際的債務數字；百分之十八的受訪者曾否認有婚外情；百分之十曾寄出不實的履歷表；而百分之六曾在撞到別人的車時撒了善意謊言。但有相當驚人的百分之六十的受訪者說他們撒謊時不會覺得有罪惡感。

儘管男性說的謊比女性多，但英國科學家發現女性說謊的技巧比較高明。研究顯示女性說出的謊言比男性更有說服力。原因在於女性比男性多話，所以比較容易撒撒小謊。

英國科學家也發現了，受訪的男性在說話時會產生許多停頓，這樣的情形比女性多。男性會不由自主地停頓，因為他們需要花更多的時間讓話語聽起來合理。當男人非得要說謊時，停頓的次數就會變得頻繁起來，因為男性需要更多時間來造出語意與結構上和邏輯正確的句子，同時要與前後的句子相關連。反之女性會先讓自己熟悉自己所發明的角色，然後才會開始說話。

聽力題目解析

❶ 此題詢問的是，根據內文提及的調查，英國男性平均一天共說了多少謊。錄音檔以問句起頭之後，便直接進入英國人的說謊習慣，因此在這邊便需特別注意。答案出現在 "an average British male lies five times a day"，故答案為 (D)。

❷ 此題詢問的是英國人最常說的善意謊言第一名為何。我們可以聽見文章第二段的開頭便告訴我們接下來會是調查的順序，因此只要仔細聽即可。答案為 (A) Nothing's wrong; I'm fine。

❸ 此題詢問的是英國科學家發現何種性別較會說謊。在我們聽完一大段關於多少百分比的人說了何種謊言之後，錄音檔接著說明：Although men tell more lies than women, British scientists find that women are better liars. 在這個部分，我們便能知道答案為 (C)。即便沒有注意到這

個明顯的開頭，後續的討論也都是環繞在為什麼女性比較會說謊。

❹ 接續第三題，此題詢問在說謊的過程中，男性較女性多了何種特徵。此題應可很快地選擇 (B) 停頓，因錄音檔節尾多次出現 "pauses" 此單字，且後續皆是在解釋為什麼男性需要比女性更多的 "pauses"，像是男性需要更多時間來造出語意與結構上邏輯正確的句子等等。

❺ 此題詢問的是百分之二十五的人會在何種方面說謊。此題較為困難，因內文將所有統計數字放置在一起，易造成混淆或難以記憶。最好的情況便是在聽音檔時，注意統計數字出現之時，並加以留心，便能較快抓住答案。此題答案為 (B) 債務方面。

閱讀題目解析

❶ 此題詢問的是，女性的說謊技巧為何比較高明。根據內文的最後兩段，我們得知男性需要較多時間來組織架構，因此男性會有較多的停頓（pauses），而女性則是會讓自己先熟悉該角色，然後才會開始說話。故答案選 (C)。選項 (A) 是女性受過好的訓練；選項 (B) 是男性被要求說較糟的謊言；選項 (D) 是女性擁有較多需要隱藏的秘密。

❷ 此題詢問的是共有多少百分比的人不會因說謊而有罪惡感。此題若仔細閱讀文章，便可發現答案在內文第四段。答案為 (C)。

補充單字

☆ 1. mind	**v.**	介意
☆ 2. fib	**n.**	小謊
☆ 3. survey	**n.**	調查
☆ 4. common	**adj.**	普遍的
☆ 5. frequent	**adj.**	頻繁的
☆ 6. character	**n.**	角色

The Importance of Sleep
睡眠的重要性

聽力測驗 🎧 Track 070

在學習英文的過程中，「聽」可能是最直接的第一線接觸，也可能是大家最想要快速習得的能力。現在，就讓我們來熟悉各種英文情境，提升自己的英文臨場感吧！

(   ) 1. According to the text, a good night's sleep will do you much more good than _____ before a big exam.
(A) exercising a lot   (B) pulling an all-nighter
(C) dancing all night   (D) having a light meal

(   ) 2. _____ makes the timing for sleep regular.
(A) An alarm clock   (B) A biological clock
(C) A biological control   (D) A pocket watch

(   ) 3. Adults need approximately _____ hours of sleep every night.
(A) 8   (B) 10   (C) 5   (D) 12

(   ) 4. Traveling also disorders sleep because _____ can disturb your biological clock.
(A) jet lag   (B) jet plane   (C) jazz dance   (D) jogging

閱讀測驗

剛剛的聽力測驗是否因為答題不順而感到遺憾？或是覺得自己有某些地方掌握地不夠好？現在就讓我們來直接「看」剛剛的聽力測驗，並透過後面的閱讀測驗來補齊聽力上的不足，同時考驗自己的閱讀能力吧！

A good night's sleep will do you much more good than pulling an all-nighter before a big exam even though why sleep is good for the **memory**[1] remains a mystery. One theory says that sleep is when long-term memories form. The other says the memories are actually formed during the day, but then "refined" at night to get rid of what is unnecessary.

Sleep is a **basic**[2] human need. It is an essential part of a person's life. However, few people know about how important it is, and some people even try to get by with very little sleep. Sleep, like eating and exercise, is important for our minds and bodies to work normally. In fact, sleep is essential for survival.

A **biological**[3] clock makes the timing for sleep regular. It trains a person to automatically feel sleepy during the nighttime and to be active during the daytime. Light is the signal that synchronizes the biological clock to the 24-hour cycle of day and night.

Sleepiness due to constant lack of sufficient sleep is a serious problem and affects a lot of children as well as adults. Children and teenagers need at least 9 hours of sleep every night to perform well. Adults need approximately 8 hours of sleep every night. Sleeping less than you need each night can lead to problem sleepiness that happens when you should be wide awake and lead to a decrease in your ability to function, which interferes with your daily routine and activities and causes you to fall asleep at improper or even dangerous times.

Sleep is essential for a person's health. However, millions of people do not get enough sleep and many suffer from insomnia. Most of those with sleep problems go undiagnosed and untreated. **Stress**[4] is the number one cause of short-term sleep problems. Usually the sleep problem vanishes when stress goes away. However, if short-term sleep problems, such as **insomnia**[5], aren't managed properly from the beginning, they can last long after the original stress has passed. Traveling also disorders sleep because jet lag can disturb your biological clock.

Inadequate sleep can cause increases in lapses of memory, accidents, injuries, behavior and mood problems. And some signs of sleep disorders include snoring, breathing pauses during sleep, insomnia, having trouble staying awake during the daytime, and a decrease in daytime performance for unknown reasons. According to sleep experts, here are some tips on how to **overcome**[6] common sleep problems: Keep a regular sleep schedule; do not consume caffeine six hours before sleep and reduce daytime use; avoid alcohol and heavy meals before bed; minimize light and noise where you sleep; try to go to bed earlier every night so it can ensure that you get enough sleep; exercise regularly.

【Question】

(   ) 1. Which of the following is not caused by an inadequate sleep?
    (A) mood problems   (B) snoring
    (C) insomnia   (D) cramps

(   ) 2. Which of the following should not be considered as a tip for a good sleep?
    (A) avoid alcohol
    (B) stay away from caffeine six hours prior to sleep
    (C) reduce chances of having heavy meal before bed
    (D) exercise a lot to get tired before sleep

【文章中譯】

在大考前，一夜好眠遠比整晚不睡開夜車來得有幫助，儘管目前為何睡眠對記憶力有益仍舊是個謎。有一派理論提出長期記憶是在睡眠時形成的；另一派的說法則是記憶的形成是在白天，但晚上是讓記憶「去蕪存菁」的時候。

睡眠是人類基本的需求，是一個人生命的一個重要部分。然而，很少人知道睡眠有多重要，有些人甚至一天到晚都不睡覺。睡眠，就像吃飯和運動一樣，是讓我們的心智和體魄正常運作的重要環節。事實上，人要生存下來，睡眠是不可或缺的。

生理時鐘使我們的睡眠時間變得規律，使人養成在夜間想睡覺、在日間想活動的習慣。光線是讓生理時鐘順著日夜二十四小時規律運轉的訊號。長期缺乏充足睡眠所導致的睡意是個嚴重的問題，影響了許多成年人與孩童。孩童和青少年每晚需要至少九個小時的睡眠才能有好的日常表現。而成年人每晚需要大約八個小時的睡眠。睡眠時間不夠會使你在應該完全清醒的時候產生睡意，導致日常表現能力降低，干擾你的日常工作及活動，也會使你在不適當的時候產生睡意而導致危險。

睡眠是一個人健康的基本需求。然而，數以百萬計的人們得不到足夠的睡眠，而且很多人為失眠所苦。而大多數有睡眠問題的人都沒有尋求醫生的診斷與治療。壓力是短期睡眠問題的首要因素。通常當壓力解除時，睡眠問題就會消失。然而，如果短期的睡眠問題，例如失眠症，一開始沒有適當地處理，可能會演變成長期問題，這樣一來，即使原始的壓力消失了，睡眠問題也無法解決。長途旅行也會擾亂睡眠，因為時差會干擾你的生理時鐘。

睡眠不足會導致記憶力降低、意外、受傷、行為及情緒問題。睡眠失調的徵兆包括：打呼、睡覺時呼吸暫停、失眠、白天很難保持清醒、以及日間表現能力因不明原因而降低。根據睡眠專家的建議，以下是克服睡眠問題的一些小秘訣：維持規律的睡眠時間、睡前六小時不要攝取咖啡因，白天也要減少用量、睡前避免酒精及難以消化的食物、將睡眠場所的光線及噪音降至最低、試著每晚提早上床睡覺，這樣才能確保你得到充足的睡眠，還有規律性地運動。

聽力題目解析

❶ 此題詢問的是根據內文，一夜好眠會比在考試前做何事還能帶來更多好處。選項 (A) 為大量運動；選項 (B) 為熬夜；選項 (C) 為通宵跳舞；選項 (D) 為少量進食。錄音檔在一開始即給我們答案，這邊可以把握 "pull an all-nighter" 作為「熬夜」的用法，選擇 (B)。

❷ 此題詢問的是何者可以讓睡眠時間變得規律。選項 (A) 為一個鬧鐘；選項 (B) 為一個生理時鐘；選項 (C) 為一個生理上的掌控；選項 (D) 為

一個口袋錶。在錄音檔中間，我們可以得知 "a biological clock makes the timing ..." 故選 (B)，這邊要注意選項 (C) 的陷阱，"control" 為「控制」之意。

❸ 此題詢問的是成人每晚大約需要幾小時的睡眠。選 (A)，請注意數字型考題。

❹ 此題詢問的是旅行也會擾亂睡眠因為何者會干擾生理時鐘。選項 (A) 為時差；選項 (B) 為噴氣式飛機；選項 (C) 為爵士舞；選項 (D) 為慢跑。這邊我們可以聽見同樣的句子，需注意其它選項的混淆，選 (A)。

閱讀題目解析

❶ 此題詢問的是何者不是由睡眠不足所造成的。選項 (A) 為情緒問題；選項 (B) 為打呼；選項 (C) 為失眠；選項 (D) 為抽筋。答案可見內文最後，選 (D)。

❷ 此題詢問的是何者不應被視為一夜好眠的小秘訣。選項 (A) 為避免酒精；選項 (B) 為睡前六小時不攝取咖啡因；選項 (C) 為睡前減少大量進食；選項 (D)為睡前大量運動使身體勞累。答案可見內文倒數最後一段，選 (D)。

補充單字

☆ 1. memory	n.	記憶
☆ 2. basic	adj.	基本的
☆ 3. biological	adj.	生物的
☆ 4. stress	n.	壓力
☆ 5. insomnia	n.	失眠症
☆ 6. overcome	v.	克服

Level 5

驚艷老外
×
嘖嘖稱奇

Secrets to Career Success
職場成功小秘訣

聽力測驗 🎧 Track 071

在學習英文的過程中,「聽」可能是最直接的第一線接觸,也可能是大家最想要快速習得的能力。現在,就讓我們來熟悉各種英文情境,提升自己的英文臨場感吧!

( ) 1. What is the first secret to career success in the article?
   (A) Be honest with all people.　　(B) Love your job.
   (C) Have a supportive spouse.　　(D) Have a good mentor.

( ) 2. Which is wrong about being honest with all people?
   (A) It sounds simple, but it requires courage.
   (B) It is accessible to anyone.
   (C) It's the first success factor.
   (D) It is useful to play tricks.

( ) 3. Which of the following statements is true according to the passage?
   (A) You need only principles in your work.
   (B) If you have a supportive spouse, you can have a rest and let him or her do all the work.
   (C) You can take any financial risk without doing market research.
   (D) If your mind and body won't function well, your job performance will be affected.

( ) 4. If you want to succeed, you should _____.
   (A) always ask your spouse and friends for everything
   (B) change your work if you meet with difficulties
   (C) have strong leadership qualities
   (D) waste your time

閱讀測驗

剛剛的聽力測驗是否因為答題不順而感到遺憾？或是覺得自己有某些地方掌握地不夠好？現在就讓我們來直接「看」剛剛的聽力測驗，並透過後面的閱讀測驗來補齊聽力上的不足，同時考驗自己的閱讀能力吧！

I've been **joining**[1] a book club after work with my friend Judy for the last two months. Judy and I went to high school together and now we both work in the digital publishing field. The topic we've been discussing at the book club for over the last two months is about how to be successful at work. From the group discussion I learned not only about what it takes to become successful in the workplace, but also about how to think differently and live a better life.

First of all, one of the success secrets, according to the conclusion from our group discussion, is being honest with all people. This may sound too simple to all of you, yet in my opinion, it takes a lot of courage to just be honest. The great thing about being honest is that it makes you approachable because instead of finding fault, you think of people positively to make things easier. So, start doing it right now. You will find yourself getting along with people well. There is no such business or career that has no involvement with people, right?

Secondly, you must love and appreciate your job. Combine your **passion**[2] with your discipline. This will make your work more than just daily routines. Of course, it could be hard at times. Sometimes you might be too **upset**[3] to love your job. But you don't have to be so. You can change your attitude. The trick is that if you act like you are having fun with your work, you may start feeling great and passionate again. Try this trick. You'll be surprised and won't be sorry!

Thirdly, a **supportive**[4] spouse can greatly help with your career. We all know that being attracted to someone is really important, but it's probably not the sole criterion you should use to find your significant other. In my own view, I would say that having a kind, responsible, and supportive spouse who shares similar goals and plans with you is much more important. If you choose to be single, that is all right as well. All you need

Level 1
Level 2
Level 3
Level 4
Level 5
Level 6

is good mentors. You can learn amazing qualities from highly successful people. It is easier than learning the ropes on your own. As long as your mentality is in the right place and your actions are performed, success will follow.

Fourthly, you need to be physically fit and exercise at least three times a week. If you do not take good care of your health, your mind and body won't **function**[5] well and this will affect your job performance. One of the success factors is having strong leadership qualities. Once your mind doesn't work optimally, you are unable to concentrate on more important issues and may fail to apply your leadership skills. So, being mentally and physically healthy is critical.

Fifthly, you need to recognize business opportunities when you see them. The truth is that if you are in an already over-saturated market, you will have too much competition to make any differences. Of course you might stand out and rise to the top, but the chance might be as slim as being struck by lightening. Thus, try to find an unoccupied market, and instead of putting your money in the stock market, invest it in your own business if you have one. There's no way that you can't have more control over the stock market than your own business.

Sixthly, find yourself an excellent investment adviser. You don't want to risk losing your money, and an investment expert will know the best place to put your money. You may have very high incomes, but you also need to learn how to make money grow. You must pave your way for the future, not just enjoy the moment and waste your time. In this way, you might reach a point where you could live off the interest of your investments.

Lastly, unless you live below your means, you will never save a good amount of money, even if you have a big income. Try to control your spending and saving by creating a budget or a cash plan. Always think about what you buy and track your expenses. Spend less than you earn.

Finally, I believe all of us can live a better quality of life by **implementing**[6] these secrets to career success. Good luck!

【Question】

(　　) 1. How did the author come up with these success factors?
  (A) from a financial book　　　(B) from a mentor's advice
  (C) from a book club discussion　(D) from a frend's suggestions

(　　) 2. Why does the word "over-saturated" mean in the article?
  (A) to lack something　　(B) to have too much of something
  (C) to outdo something　　(D) to be oustanding

【文章中譯】

過去這兩個月，我和朋友茱蒂一起參加了一個讀書會。茱蒂和我是高中同學，而我們倆現在都在電子出版業工作。過去這兩個月我們讀書會討論的主題是如何在工作上有所成就。從小組討論中，我不只學到了事業成功的要素，也學會了如何換個方式思考，以及如何過更好的生活。

首先，根據討論結果，其中一個成功秘訣是對所有的人都要誠實。這點聽起來簡單，但對別人誠實需要花上許多勇氣。誠實的好處是很容易和別人親近。而且你會看到別人的好處與優點，而不會只想找碴。所以現在就開始執行吧。你會發現自己能和別人融洽相處。天底下沒有一種行業是不需要接近人的，不是嗎？

第二，你要熱愛和感謝你的工作。把熱情與紀律結合起來，如此一來，工作就不僅僅只是工作而已。當然有時要做到這點很難，有時候你會因為太沮喪而無法熱愛你的工作。但是你其實可以不必沮喪的。你可以改變你的態度。秘訣就在於你要表現出你很享受這份工作，這樣一來，你就會開始覺得很愉快，熱情也會再度湧現。試試看這個秘訣。你會感到驚奇而且不會後悔的。

第三，擁有一個支持你的伴侶可以幫助你的事業。我們都知道對方是否吸引你是很重要且必須的，但這可能不是選擇伴侶的唯一標準。就我認為，擁有一個善良、有責任感、支持你、和你有著相似人生目標與計畫的配偶更重要。如果你選擇單身，那也沒關係。你所需要的是良師益友。你可以從一些很成功的人身上學到許多優秀的特質，這要比你自己摸索容易得多。當你的想法正確了，行動也付諸實行了，成功就會跟著來了。

第四，你需要身心都健康，而且每週運動三次。如果你不留意你的健康，那麼你的精神與身體是無法好好運轉的，而且這會影響你的工作表現。成功要素之一包含領導特質。一旦你的精神不在最佳狀態，你會無法專心在重要的議題上，也就無法表現出你的領導素質。所以保持身心健康是很重要的。

第五，你需要識別商機。事實上，在一個過度飽和的市場中，你會遇到許多競爭，出頭會很難。當然你也可能出人頭地，但那種可能性就像是被雷打到一樣低，所以你可以試著發掘大家還沒有發現的新市場。再來，與其把錢放在股票市場，不如投資在你自己的事業上。你對自己事業的掌控度一定會大於對股票市場的掌控度。

第六，幫你自己找一個優秀的投資理財顧問。你一定不想冒著損失金錢的風險，而一個投資專家知道如何最完善地配置你的金錢。你可以賺很多錢，但你也同樣需要讓錢滾錢。你必須為你的未來鋪路，而不是只享受當下、浪費時光。如此一來你就可以達到只靠你投資所產生的利息生活的狀態。

最後，除非你量入為出，否則你永遠存不到錢，即使你有很好的收入。試著利用預算或現金流計畫控制你的花費及儲蓄。永遠都要思考一下你買了甚麼並追蹤花費。切記要量入為出。

最終我相信我們都可以藉由履行這些成功秘訣，過更有品質的生活。祝你好運！

聽力題目解析

❶ 此題詢問的是內文提出的第一個成功要素為何。選項 (A) 為對所有人誠實；選項 (B) 為熱愛工作；選項 (C) 為擁有一個支持你的另一半；選項 (D) 為擁有一位良師益友。答案為 (A)，這邊若有先看過題目及選項便可輕鬆把握。

❷ 此題詢問的是針對對所有人誠實這件事，何者為非。選項 (A) 為聽起來簡單，實際上則需要勇氣；選項 (B) 為它讓你變得容易親近；選項 (C) 為這是第一個成功要素；選項 (D) 為它很適合拿來當作秘技。錄音檔中，"trick" 這單字是出現在 "Secondly, ..." 這個部分的介紹，需注意此篇的分段重點，選 (D)。

❸ 此題要求我們選出正確陳述。選項 (A) 為在職場上你只需要原則；選項 (B) 為如果你有一位支持你的伴侶，你可以休息並叫對方做所有事；選項 (C) 為你可以在沒有做任何市場調查的情況下承擔金融風險；選項 (D) 為如果你的身心無法正常運作，你的工作表現會受到影響。我們在聽見規律運動的段落時，即可得聽見選項 (D) 此答案。選項 (A) 為非，因此篇文章已列舉多種原則以外的因素。

❹ 此題詢問的是如果你想要成功，你必須做何事。選項 (A) 為總是要求你的伴侶和朋友做所有事；選項 (B) 為遇到困難時就換工作；選項 (C) 為擁有強大的領導特質；選項 (D) 為浪費時間。在強調身心健康的重要性後，接著 "leadership qualities" 便出現用以重申精神與身體正常運作的重要性，故選擇 (C)。

閱讀題目解析

❶ 此題詢問的是作者如何得到這些成功要素。選項 (A) 為從一本金融書；選項 (B) 為從一位良師益友的建言；選項 (C) 為從一個讀書會的討論；選項 (D) 為從一位朋友的建議。答案可見內文第一段開頭，選 (C)。

❷ 此題詢問的是文內 "over-saturated" 的意思為何。選項 (A) 為缺少某物；選項 (B) 為擁有過多某物；選項 (C) 為勝過某物；選項 (D) 為變得出眾。答案為 (B)，"saturate" 本身之意為「滲透」，故加上字首 over- 即表「過度飽和」之意。這邊也可以透過內文推敲，此單字出現後內文接著指出 "... you will have too much competition to may any differences" 意思為競爭過多，難以出頭。

補充單字

☆ 1. join	v.	參加
☆ 2. passion	n.	熱情
☆ 3. upset	adj.	生氣的、沮喪的
☆ 4. supportive	adj.	支持的
☆ 5. function	v.	運轉
☆ 6. implement	v.	履行、實行

Level 5
02 Executive Compensation in U.S. Companies

美國高階主管的薪資

聽力測驗 🎧 Track 072

在學習英文的過程中，「聽」可能是最直接的第一線接觸，也可能是大家最想要快速習得的能力。現在，就讓我們來熟悉各種英文情境，提升自己的英文臨場感吧！

( ) 1. "Ten years" means _____.
(A) a century (B) a decade
(C) a fortnight (D) a quarter

( ) 2. After a public-comment period, a final vote will be conducted in _____.
(A) winter (B) summer
(C) spring (D) fall

( ) 3. Revelation reforms in 1992 also resulted from similar public outrage over _____.
(A) proper executive pay (B) poor executive pay
(C) adequate executive pay (D) excessive executive pay

( ) 4. Chief executive officers who are _____ are possibly in higher demand than ever before.
(A) quite tall (B) very wealthy (C) highly skilled

( ) 5. Executive salaries normally consist of _____ ,annual bonus and stock options.
(A) baseball payment (B) basic allowance
(C) base pay (D) basement

Level 1
Level 2
Level 3
Level 4
Level 5
Level 6

剛剛的聽力測驗是否因為答題不順而感到遺憾？或是覺得自己有某些地方掌握地不夠好？現在就讓我們來直接「看」剛剛的聽力測驗，並透過後面的閱讀測驗來補齊聽力上的不足，同時考驗自己的閱讀能力吧！

Salaries for Chief Executive Officers in the United States have skyrocketed over the past ten years, and critics accuse the self-serving insiders of having damaged stockholders' interests. In **reply**[1] to this controversial issue, the Securities and Exchange Commission took the initiative to let stockholders understand better on how much the company pays their top executives.

Pushed by the Commission's new chairman, the changes would for the first time demand companies and corporations to clearly state the total pay figure for each of the top executives. Revelation would include the **values**[2] of stock options, severance plans, pension, and perks worth over ten thousand U.S. dollars. After a public-comment period, a final vote will be conducted in spring. Most observers predict that the Commission will **adopt**[3] the rules, but executive compensation will still probably not be diminished by all this.

Some scholars argued that executive compensation is not necessarily as excessive and unreasonable as some extreme cases suggest. Yet, all of them agreed a more complete and clear revelation would be better for the system. Some even teased that when a person is forced to get undressed in public, they pay close attention to their figure. People have been criticizing that executive pay is too high for several years, and they will always be critical of it. Revelation reforms in 1992 also resulted from similar public outrage over excessive executive pay. Executive salaries normally consist of base pay, annual bonus based on work performance, grants of stock, stock options, retirement contributions, and perks, which can include almost everything from contributions to charities to personal use of company limo and jet.

Now, it is very difficult to find out the total value of top executive's pay from company filings because they don't reveal the value of the stock options or show much about pension plans and perks. But it is quite

obvious[4] that salaries have been driven upward by greater use of stock options because it gives the top executives the right to buy corporate stock at a set price anytime over a number of years. Value of options can skyrocket if the price of **stock**[5] increases above the set price.

It can't be emphasized enough that the use of stock options has exploded. Options only accounted for about twenty percent of the typical chief executive officer's compensation in the early 1990s. But that had grown to fifty percent by the year two thousand. However, some scholars don't think the typical chief executive officer's compensation is higher than expected since most of those top executives work twelve hours a day for probably over 350 days a year.

The world has become more complex, global trade is inevitable, and technology is moving faster than ever, all of which have resulted in the soar of executive compensation in the past 15 years. And chief executive officers who are highly skilled are possibly in higher demand than ever before. Besides, they face higher risks from litigation and a stricker regulatory environment. And lastly they are required to keep a large portion of their personal wealth tied up in corporate stock and options, usually as much as fifty percent to seventy-five percent of their net worth. For these reasons, a top executive faces serious risk of loss if the stock price drops. Thus, today's top executives will demand more pay to neutralize the risk.

The Securities and Exchange Commission should, ideally, demand corporations to reveal this link, but that is currently not among the commission's executive-compensation **proposals**[6]. Yet, the executive-compensation proposals should still give stockholders better insight into executive pay.

【 Question 】

(   ) 1. Why is it difficult to find out the total value of top executive's pay?
   (A) because stock options do not affect much on the executive salaries

(B) because they don't reveal the value of stock options
(C) because the executive officers want to hide the information
(D) because it is illegal to make such information go public

(　　) 2. According to the article, the executive-compensation proposal may give whom better insights into executive pay?
(A) chief executive offers　　(B) scholars
(C) the public　　(D) stockholders

【文章中譯】

美國首席執行長的薪資在過去十年間暴增，批評家們指控這些自私自利的業界人士故意損害股東的利益。美國證券交易委員會為了回應此一爭議，迅速邁出了第一步，希望透過制定規定，能讓股東好好地瞭解他們高階主管的薪資。

在委員會新任主席的敦促下，新的規定首次要求公司必須清楚說明每位高階主管的薪資。公開的內容包括股票期權的價值、離職計畫、退休金和超過一萬美元的額外收入。在公眾評論期之後，委員會將在春天舉行最後的投票，大多數觀察家預測委員會會通過這些規定，雖然影響應該不大。

有些學者認為高階主管的薪資並不一定都如同那些極端案例一樣過高或不合理。然而，全部的人都認同，一個完善全面的公開將會改進這一體制。有些人甚至挪揄說，當人們被迫在大庭廣眾之下脫光衣服時，他們就會好好注意自己的身材。人們批評高階主管的薪資過高已經好幾年了，而且還會繼續批評下去。管理階層薪水暴增所引起的眾怒也曾導致了1992 年的公開機制改革。高階主管的薪資通常包括基本薪資、依工作表現頒發的紅利、股票、股票期權、退休金提撥和額外收入。額外收入包含慈善機構的捐款和公司豪華轎車和飛機的使用等。

目前很難從公司的檔案中發現高階主管的薪資總價值，因為公司並未公開股票期權的價值，也沒有顯示退休金和額外收入的金額。但很明顯的是，股票期權的大量使用增進了薪資的成長，因為高階主管有權在幾年之內以預定價格購買公司的股票。如果股票價格超過預定價格，期權的價值就會暴增。

期權早已開始被大範圍使用,這點是需要再三強調的。在九〇年代早期,期權僅占一般首席執行長薪資的百分之二十左右。但到了二千年,期權已增長為薪資的一半。但是,有些學者認為一般首席執行長的薪資金額並不會太誇張,因為大多數首席執行長一年工作可能超過三百五十天。

世界已經變得越來越複雜,全球貿易無可避免,科技的發展速度比以前要快,所有這些因素都導致了高階主管的薪資在過去十五年大幅上漲。對於有高超技能的首席執行長的需求可能比過去都來得高。此外,他們更面臨了更高風險的訴訟和更為嚴峻的監督環境。最後,他們還被要求將個人的大部分財產與其公司的股票和期權綁在一起,一般是他們資產淨值的一半到七成五。根據以上所述,高階主管承擔了一旦公司股票價值下跌,就會面臨巨大損失的風險,因此,現在的高階主管都會要求更高的薪資來平衡風險。

證交會理應要求公司公開此關聯,不過目前委員會的高階主管薪資提案中並沒有如此要求。話雖如此,高階主管薪資提案應仍要能讓股東清楚瞭解高階人員的薪資狀況。

聽力題目解析

❶ 此題詢問的是 "ten years" 之意。選項 (A) 為一世紀;選項 (B) 為十年;選項 (C) 為兩星期;選項 (D) 為四分之一。答案為 (B),這邊考的是 "decade"(十年)此單字,選 (B)。

❷ 此題詢問的是在公眾評論期之後,委員會將於何時舉行最後的投票。選項 (A) 為冬天;選項 (B) 為夏天;選項 (C) 為春天;選項 (D) 為秋天。答案為 (C),建議先看過題目以便掌握,答案在內文只出現過一次。

❸ 此題詢問的是 1992 年的公開機制改革同時導致大眾對於何事的憤怒。選項 (A) 為適當的管理階層薪水;選項 (B) 為過低的管理階層薪水;選項 (C) 為適宜的管理階層薪水;選項 (D) 為過高的管理階層薪水。在內文提及公開機制改革前,我們即可得知 "People have been criticizing that executive pay is too high for several years ...",故就算沒有掌握 "excessive"(過高的;過量的)也可推測選 (D)。

❹ 此題詢問的是具有何種特質的執行長可能已達到了前所未有的需求量。選項 (A) 為相當高的；選項 (B) 為非常有錢的；選項 (C) 為極具技能的。內文提到 "The world has become more complex ..." 藉此推測「技能性」的重要，故選 (C)。

❺ 管理階層薪水通常由年度紅利、股票，及何者組成。選項 (A) 為棒球費用；選項 (B) 為基本免稅額；選項 (C) 為底薪；選項 (D) 為地下室。答案為 (C)，這邊考的是易混淆字，注意拼字即可。

閱讀題目解析

❶ 此題詢問的是為何目前很難得知高階主管的薪資總價值。選項 (A) 為因為股票對管理階層薪水的影響不大；選項 (B) 為因為他們並未公開股票期權的價值；選項 (C) 為因為管理階層想要隱藏此資訊；選項 (D) 為因為公開這類資訊是違法的。答案可見 "Now it is very difficult … because they don't reveal the value of the stock options or show much about pension plans and perks." 故選 (B)。

❷ 此題詢問的是根據內文，高階主管薪資提案中應能讓何者瞭解高階人員的薪資狀況。選項 (A) 為執行長；選項 (B) 為學者；選項 (C) 為大眾；選項 (D) 為股東。答案可見內文最後一段，選 (D)。

補充單字

☆	1. reply	n.	回應
☆	2. value	n.	價值
☆	3. adopt	v.	正式通過、接受、採用
☆	4. obvious	adj.	顯然的
☆	5. stock	n.	股票
☆	6. proposal	n.	提案、提議

A Healthy Diet for Better Health

健康飲食有益健康

在學習英文的過程中,「聽」可能是最直接的第一線接觸,也可能是大家最想要快速習得的能力。現在,就讓我們來熟悉各種英文情境,提升自己的英文臨場感吧!

(   ) 1. According to the article, what is Meghan Markle's favorite snack?
      (A) apple slices with almond butter and sea salt
      (B) fried chicken and beer
      (C) popcorn
      (D) caviar

(   ) 2. What kind of nutrient helps reduce DNA damage and lead to a reduction in cancer risk?
      (A) saturated fats   (B) trans fats
      (C) antioxidants   (D) cholesterol

(   ) 3. What does research consistently show?
      (A) People who eat mainly red meat have the lowest risk of many diseases.
      (B) People who eat vegetables and fruit on a daily basis have the lowest risk of many diseases.
      (C) People who eat a lot of snacks are healthier.
      (D) People who have a healthy diet are less healthy.

(   ) 4. How many servings of vegetables and fruit per day do researchers recommend?
      (A) 7   (B) 8   (C) 9   (D) 10

(   ) 5. What is the conclusion of the article?
      (A) People should enjoy vegetables and fruit to reap as many health benefits as possible.
      (B) Eating vegetables and fruit is a hassle.
      (C) We should take vitamin pills.
      (D) The best way to get antioxidants is from frozen food.

 閱讀測驗

剛剛的聽力測驗是否因為答題不順而感到遺憾？或是覺得自己有某些地方掌握地不夠好？現在就讓我們來直接「看」剛剛的聽力測驗，並透過後面的閱讀測驗來補齊聽力上的不足，同時考驗自己的閱讀能力吧！

Meghan Markle, the former American actress and the new **Duchess**[1] of Sussex after she married Prince Harry, has healthy eating habits long before she met her husband. She is a foodie and enjoys plant-based diet. According to a piece of news article, one of her favorite snacks is apple slices with almond butter and sea salt. Her healthy diet is her secret to looking slim and glowing.

Why is eating vegetables and fruit every day so beneficial to our health? It is because they provide essential vitamins, minerals, and other nutrients, such as fiber and **antioxidants**[2]. Research consistently shows that people who eat vegetables and fruit on a daily basis have the lowest risk of contracting diseases, including cancer and **chronic**[3] diseases, for antioxidants can reduce DNA damage and lead to the reduction in cancer risk.

So, how much vegetables and fruit should we have in our daily diet? Researchers found that the benefits come from eating 10 **servings**[4] of fruit and vegetables a day. That may seem like a lot, but it won't be a **hassle**[5] if we have three to four servings in both lunch and dinner, and one to two servings of fruit or vegetables in breakfast and as snacks. Now, let's enjoy the tastes of vegetables and fruit daily and to reap as many health benefits as possible!

【 Question 】

(　　) 1. What does the word "foodie" mean in the first paragraph?
      (A) a person who likes frozen food
      (B) a person who enjoys different types of good food
      (C) a person who likes processed food
      (D) a food factory

(　　) 2. Which of the following nutrients do vegetables and fruit not contain?
      (A) vitamins   (B) minerals
      (C) trans fats   (D) antioxidants

【 文章中譯 】

梅根‧馬克爾是美國前女演員，嫁給哈利王子後成為薩塞克斯公爵夫人，不過她在婚前就有健康的飲食習慣。她是美食主義者，喜歡以蔬果為基礎的飲食。根據一篇新聞報導，她最愛的零嘴之一是蘋果切片沾上杏仁醬並灑一點海鹽，且她的健康飲食就是她保持苗條和容光煥發的秘訣。

為什麼每日攝取蔬果對我們的健康如此有益？因為它們提供人體必須的維他命、礦物質和其他營養，如纖維和抗氧化劑。研究一致顯示每天攝取蔬果的人罹患像是癌症和慢性疾病的風險較低，因為抗氧化劑能降低人體DNA的受損，進而降低罹癌的機率。

所以我們每天應該攝取多少蔬果呢？研究人員發現每天吃十份的蔬果效益最大，這看起來似乎很多，但若把它變成習慣就不會是件麻煩事，可以在中餐和晚餐各攝取三到四份蔬果，早餐和點心則攝取一到二份蔬果。現在，就讓我們一起享受各式蔬果帶給我們的好處吧！

聽力題目解析

❶ 第一題詢問的是根據本文敘述，何者是梅根‧馬克爾最愛的零嘴，選項 (A) 為蘋果切片沾上杏仁醬並灑一點海鹽；選項 (B) 為炸雞和啤酒；選項 (C) 為爆米花；選項 (D) 為魚子醬。錄音檔前段即給了我們答案，把握 "one of her favorite snacks" 此關鍵字即可，選 (A)。

❷ 此題詢問的是何種營養有助降低人體DNA的受損，進而減少罹癌風險，選項 (A) 為飽和脂肪；選項 (B) 為反式脂肪；選項 (C) 為抗氧化劑；選項 (D) 為膽固醇。在錄音檔中後段部分提到 "That's because antioxidants can reduce DNA damage and lead to a reduction in cancer risk."，故答案選 (C)。

❸ 此題詢問的是研究一致發現什麼，選項 (A) 為吃大量紅肉的人罹患多種疾病的風險最低；選項 (B) 為常攝取蔬果的人罹患多種疾病的風險最低；選項 (C) 為吃大量零嘴的人較健康；選項 (D) 為飲食健康的人比較不健康。本題在錄音檔中段提到 "... people who eat vegetables and fruit on a daily basis have the lowest risk of many diseases ..."，故答案選 (B)。

❹ 此題詢問的是研究人員建議每天吃幾份蔬果為佳。答案選 (D)，數字是考試常見的考題，請考生多加注意。

❺ 此題詢問的是本篇文章的結論為何。選項 (A) 人們應享受蔬果以獲取最大量其對健康的好處；選項 (B) 為吃蔬果很麻煩；選項 (C) 為我們應該吃維他命錠；選項 (D) 為攝取抗氧化劑最好的方式是透過冷凍食品。本文均探討蔬果帶來的健康益處，故答案選(A)。

閱讀題目解析

❶ 此題詢問的是第一段「foodie」的意思為何。選項 (A) 為喜食冷凍食品的人；選項 (B) 為享受各式美食的人；選項 (C) 為喜食加工食品的人；選項 (D) 為食品工廠。本文雖未收錄這個單字，但它是常用簡易的生活單字，選 (B)。

❷ 此題詢問的是何者是蔬果不包含的營養。選項 (A) 為維他命；選項 (B) 為礦物質；選項 (C) 為反式脂肪；選項 (D) 為抗氧化劑。答案見第二段，選 (C)。

補充單字

☆ 1. duchess	n.	公爵夫人
☆ 2. antioxidant	n.	抗氧化劑
☆ 3. chronic	adj.	慢性的
☆ 4. serving	n.	份數；一份
☆ 5. hassle	n.	麻煩

Level 5 04 Will Syrian Civil War Ever End?

敘利亞內戰，和平遙遙無期？

🎧 聽力測驗 Track 074

在學習英文的過程中，「聽」可能是最直接的第一線接觸，也可能是大家最想要快速習得的能力。現在，就讓我們來熟悉各種英文情境，提升自己的英文臨場感吧！

( ) 1. Where does the deadliest civil war of the 21st century take place?
(A) Lebanon　　　　　(B) Syria
(C) Iraq　　　　　　　(D) Turkey

( ) 2. How many people are displaced due to Syrian Civil War?
(A) 100,000 people　　(B) 500,000 people
(C) 1 million people　　(D) 6 million people

( ) 3. What was the period called when Syrians staged protests against the government and high unemployment rate?
(A) Arab Spring　　　　(B) Arab Dream
(C) Middle East Protest　(D) Middle East Reform

( ) 4. How many entities was Syria divided into?
(A) 1　　　(B) 2　　　(C) 3　　　(D) 4

( ) 5. What do many countries supply to fighters in Syria?
(A) internet and smart phones　(B) weapons and money
(C) korans　　　　　　　　　　(D) literary classics

 **閱讀測驗**

剛剛的聽力測驗是否因為答題不順而感到遺憾？或是覺得自己有某些地方掌握地不夠好？現在就讓我們來直接「看」剛剛的聽力測驗，並透過後面的閱讀測驗來補齊聽力上的不足，同時考驗自己的閱讀能力吧！

The deadliest civil war of the 21st century is taking place in Syria, a nation in the Middle East. According to the UN **Envoy**[1] for Syria, an estimated 400,000 Syrians were killed. As of November 2018, more than 5.6 million Syrians have fled the country, and over 6 million people are **displaced**[2] in the country.

Syria has been ruled by the al-Assad family since 1970. When Bashar al-Assad succeeded his father Hafez as president in 2000, he allowed citizens to have access to the Internet so they could see what life was like in other countries. However, corruption **seeps**[3] into the government during Assad's reign. In 2011, many young citizens began to protest the injustice of the government and the country's high unemployment rate. This period was called the Arab Spring.

However, it did not bring positive changes in Syria. Instead, the government clamped down on protesters, even killing dissidents. Such acts **inflamed**[4] public anger, dividing Syria into three groups — the Assad government, people who wanted Assad to step down, and **extremists**[5]. Meanwhile, many countries supply weapons and money to fighters on three sides. Today, there is still no telling whether the Syrian Civil War will come to an end in the near future.

【**Question**】

(　　) 1. Who is the current president of Syria?
    (A) Asma al-Assad　　　(B) Mohammed al-Assad
    (C) Hafez al-Assad　　　(D) Bashar al-Assad

(　　) 2. What does the word "dissidents" mean in the third paragraph?
    (A) people who publicly criticize their government

(B) people who support their government
(C) people who play devil's advocates
(D) people who are rebels

【文章中譯】

二十一世紀死傷最慘重的內戰發生於位在中東的國家敘利亞。根據聯合國特使表示，約有40萬名敘利亞人喪生，而截至2018年11月，超過560萬名敘利亞人逃離該國，另有逾6百萬人民因內戰而流離失所。

敘利亞自1970年起即由阿薩德家族統治。2000年巴沙爾·阿薩德繼承父親哈菲茲統治該國，並允許人民使用網路一窺外面的世界，然而阿薩德執政期間，貪腐也滲入了政府。2011年有許多年輕人開始抗議政府不公和高失業率的問題，這段時期被稱為「阿拉伯之春」。

然而這並未帶給敘利亞正面效應，政府反而鎮壓了抗議者，甚至血洗異議人士，這引發了大眾的不滿，將該國分裂成三方勢力：阿薩德政府、希望阿薩德下台的人士、和極端份子。於此同時，多國分別提供三方勢力武器和金錢以對抗彼此，至今人們仍不知道敘利亞內戰在短期的未來會不會有結束的一天。

聽力題目解析

❶ 此題詢問的是二十一世死傷最慘重的內戰發生在哪裡。選項 (A) 為黎巴嫩；選項 (B) 為敘利亞；選項 (C) 為伊拉克；選項 (D) 為土耳其。錄音檔開頭即指出 "The deadliest civil war of the 21st century is taking place in Syria..." 故選 (B)。

❷ 此題詢問的是由於敘利亞內戰，有多少人民因此流離失所。本題答案選 (D)，數字是考試常見的考題，請考生注意。

❸ 此題詢問的是敘利亞年輕人抗議政府和高失業率的那段時期，被外界稱做什麼。選項 (A) 為阿拉伯之春；選項 (B) 為阿拉伯夢想；選項 (C) 為中東抗議事件；選項 (D) 為中東改革。此題把握 "protest the injustice of the government" 及 "high unemployment rate" 後即可一併記住答案 "This period was called the Arab Spring."故答案選 (A)。

④ 此題詢問的是敘利亞被分成了幾派勢力。錄音檔後段提到 "... dividing Syria into three entities—the Assad government, those who wanted Assad to step down, and extremists." 掌握 "divide"（分割；區分）此單字即可。答案選 (C)。（註：原本還有第四派勢力是恐怖份子，在全球反恐的情勢下，第四派勢力已漸失勢。）

⑤ 此題詢問的是多國提供什麼給敘利亞的三方勢力人士。選項 (A) 為網路和智慧型手機；選項 (B) 為武器和金錢；選項 (C) 為可蘭經；選項 (D) 為文學經典書籍。此題掌握 "supply"（提供）此關鍵字即應能一同掌握後面的 "weapons and money" 故答案選 (B)。

閱讀題目解析

① 此題詢問的是敘利亞現任總統是誰。答案可見內文第二段 "When Bashar al-Assad succeeded his father Hafez as president in 2000..."。這邊需注意 "succeed" 是「繼承」的意思。答案選 (D)。

② 第二題詢問的是「dissidents」這個單字的意思。選項 (A) 為公開批評政府的人士；選項 (B) 為支持政府的人士；選項 (C) 為刻意唱反調的人士；選項 (D) 為反抗軍。dissident（單數可數名詞）是一般所稱的「政治異議人士」，為英文新聞裡常見的單字，答案選 (A)。

補充單字

☆ 1. envoy	n.	特使
☆ 2. displace	v.	迫使（某人）離開原居住的地方
☆ 3. seep	v.	滲透
☆ 4. inflame	v.	激怒
☆ 5. extremist	n.	極端主義者

Level 5
05 Key of Success to Cloned Sheep
複製羊的成敗關鍵

聽力測驗 🎧 Track 075

在學習英文的過程中,「聽」可能是最直接的第一線接觸,也可能是大家最想要快速習得的能力。現在,就讓我們來熟悉各種英文情境,提升自己的英文臨場感吧!

( ) 1. This passage is talking about _____.
(A) cloning of plants
(B) cloning of animals
(C) cloning of documents
(D) cloning of human beings

( ) 2. An obscure _____ scientist succeeded in cloning a sheep.
(A) Russian (B) Chinese
(C) German (D) Scottish

( ) 3. The difficulty in using transgenic animals to improve medicine is getting enough _____.
(A) animals (B) plants
(C) food (D) metal

( ) 4. For _____ nuclear transplant experiments were attempted without success.
(A) 25 months (B) 25 years
(C) 25 weeks (D) 25 centuries

( ) 5. The idea of cloning animals was first suggested _____ by the German embryologist.
(A) in 1938 (B) in 1914
(C) in 1925 (D) in 1952

閱讀測驗

剛剛的聽力測驗是否因為答題不順而感到遺憾？或是覺得自己有某些地方掌握地不夠好？現在就讓我們來直接「看」剛剛的聽力測驗，並透過後面的閱讀測驗來補齊聽力上的不足，同時考驗自己的閱讀能力吧！

The globe was **fascinated**[1] by the announcement of the success in cloning a sheep by an obscure Scottish scientist. He took cells from an adult sheep and used them to make another sheep. Although much of the press **coverage**[2] concentrated on the future possibility of cloning humans, the immediate impact is in genetic engineering. By microinjecting DNA into fertilized eggs, biologists have been able to engineer preferable traits into goats, sheep, cows, and other animals for a few years.

On the other hand, it's difficult to get enough animals to make more transgenic animals to improve agriculture and medicine. Breeding produces offspring slowly. It is ideal then, one would think, to duplicate genes. The notion of cloning animals was first offered by the German embryologist, Hans Spemann, in 1938. He proposed what he called a "fantastical experiment": remove the nucleus from an egg cell, and put in a nucleus from another cell. It was more than fifteen years before technology moved far enough for people to take up this challenge.

In 1952, two U.S. scientists used hollow glass tubes which were very fine pipettes to suck the nucleus out of a frog egg, and **replace**[3] it with a nucleus sucked from a body cell of an adult frog. They did not succeed. Partial success, however, was achieved approximately twenty years later by the British developmental biologist John Gurdon. He did the experiment again, but inserted nuclei from advanced toad embryos. The toad eggs developed into tadpoles, but died before they grew up.

For the past twenty-five years, nuclear transplant experiments were done with failure. With the advance of technology, finally, in 1984, Steen Willesden, who was a Danish embryologist and work in Texas, succeeded in cloning a sheep using a nucleus from a cell of an early embryo. The key to his success was in choosing a cell very early in development. Others soon replicated this exciting result in a host of other organisms such as pigs, monkeys, and cattle.

It seemed that only early embryo could work. But after numerous **attempts**[4] to transfer older nuclei, researchers believed that after the first few cell divisions of the developing embryo, animal cells would become irreversibly committed. The key advance for figuring out this enigma was made by Scottish geneticist Keith Campbell, who studied the cell cycle of agricultural animals and so forth. Knowledge of how the cell grows and division cycle works had now led to an understanding that cells don't divide until conditions are **appropriate**[5]. The cell only starts cell division when everything needed is at hand, just as a washer only begins the spin cycle when water has been completely discharged. This result proved to be a key breakthrough.

Therefore, in1995, by first **starving**[6] the cells so that they stopped at the beginning of the cell cycle, the scientists succeeded in cloning animals from advanced embryos. Two starved cells are thus synchronized in the cell cycle. Other scientists then wanted to achieved another major breakthrough. They started out by transfering the nucleus from an adult distinguished cell into an enucleated egg, which would allow the embryo to develop in a surrogate mother, and a healthy animal was produced.

【Question】

(   ) 1. What was the key advance brought out by Keith Campbell?
       (A) Only early embryo works.
       (B) Cell divisions are reversible.
       (C) Cells don't divide until an appropriate condition is provided.
       (D) The nucleus of a toad has lesser chance to be transplanted than animals.

(   ) 2. How did the scientists stop the beginning of the cell cycle according to the article?
       (A) starve the cells   (B) water the cells
       (C) feed the cells   (D) suck out the cells

【文章中譯】

一個名不見經傳的蘇格蘭科學家已經成功地複製了綿羊。他以成年綿羊的細胞來製造另一隻羊。雖然大多數新聞報導的重點都放在使用這種方法來複製人類的可能性，但科學的直接影響是在基因工程。近年來，透過將DNA顯微注射入受精卵，生物學家已經可以將較好的特質移植入山羊、綿羊、牛，以及其他動物。

另一方面，利用基因轉殖動物改善農業和醫藥的困難點在於必須獲得足夠的動物。育種產生後代是緩慢的。有人的認為理想的方法是要複製。複製動物的想法最早是在 1938 年由德國胚胎學家漢斯施佩曼提出的。他稱呼它為「荒誕實驗」，即為：將細胞核由該卵細胞中移除，並放入另一個卵細胞的細胞核。然而過了 15 年之後，人們才有足夠的技術延續施佩曼提出的挑戰。

1952 年，兩名美國科學家使用非常細的中空玻璃鋼管當作移液器，從一個青蛙卵中吸出細胞核，並改放入成年青蛙細胞的細胞核。這項實驗並沒有成功，但這種方式，卻在大約二十年後由英國發育生物學家約翰歌登取得部分成功。他重複了實驗，放入的是蟾蜍胚胎。蟾蜍卵雖長成了蝌蚪，但還沒長大前就死了。

過去 25 年來，細胞核移殖實驗一直未獲成功。隨著技術持續發展，最後一直到 1984 年，由在德州工作的丹麥胚胎學者斯蒂恩維拉德森，成功地從一個早期胚胎裡取出細胞核複製了綿羊。他成功的關鍵是挑選發育早期的細胞。這一令人興奮的結果很快推廣到其他一系列的生物體，包括豬、猴子和牛。

看來似乎只有發育早期的胚胎才有作用。但經過多次試圖轉移較老的細胞核後，研究人員相信發育中胚胎在起頭幾個細胞分裂之後，動物細胞即是不可逆的。做農業動物細胞等研究的蘇格蘭遺傳學家基斯坎貝爾最後解開了這個謎。由細胞如何生長和分裂的知識所得到的理解是，細胞一直要到條件適當才會分裂，就像洗衣機自動偵測水已完全排出後才會開始脫水一樣，細胞也會偵測所需的一切都到位後才開始細胞分裂。這樣的結果證明了其深刻的洞察力。

因此，在 1995 年，藉由在細胞週期初讓細胞挨餓，科學家成功從晚期胚胎複製了動物，兩個饑餓的細胞因此在細胞週期同步化。其他科學家也嘗試突破，著手進行將成年可區分細胞中取出的細胞核放到另一個已摘除細胞核的卵，想讓由此產生的胚胎在代理母親的孕育下成長，並希望生產出一個健康的動物。

聽力題目解析

❶ 此題詢問的是文章主旨。選項 (A) 為複製植物；選項 (B) 為複製動物；選項 (C) 為複製文件；選項 (D) 為複製人。這邊考的是 "clone"（複製）此單字，且在一開始我們可以聽見 "cloning a sheep"，故可知答案為 (B) 複製動物。

❷ 此題詢問的是一名來自何處的名不經傳科學家成功地複製一隻羊。選項 (A) 為俄羅斯；選項 (B) 為中國；選項 (C) 為德國；選項 (D) 為蘇格蘭。答案為 (D)，可知 "... by an obscure Scottish scientist" 因此只要把握職業前的形容詞即可。

❸ 此題詢問的是利用基因轉殖動物來改善醫藥的困難點在於必須獲得足夠的何物。選項 (A) 為動物；選項 (B) 為植物；選項 (C) 為食物；選項 (D) 為金屬。在錄音檔開始介紹基因轉殖後，我們可聽見此技術之難處在於 "It's difficult to get enough animals ..." 或者可以透過前後文的談論對象來推測答案為 (A)。

❹ 此題詢問的是多久以來細胞核移植一直無法成功。選 (B)，掌握數字即可。

❺ 此題詢問的是複製動物此想法是在何年第一次由一位德國胚胎學家所提出。選 (A)，此類年份題僅需仔細聆聽，並注意年份經常被放在事件之後，掌握即可。

閱讀題目解析

❶ 此題詢問的是基斯坎貝爾提出了什麼成功關鍵。選項 (A) 為只有早期的胚胎才有效；選項 (B) 為細胞分裂是可逆的；選項 (C) 為細胞只有在合適的情況下才會分裂；選項 (D) 為青蛙的細胞核比起動物移植成功的機會較低。答案可見內文倒數第二段，選 (C)，注意選項 (D) 並沒有被提及。

❷ 此題詢問的是根據內文，科學家是如何停止細胞週期。選項 (A) 為讓細胞挨餓；選項 (B) 為讓細胞喝水；選項 (C) 為餵食細胞；選項 (D) 為將細胞吸出。答案可見內文最後一段第一句，選 (A)。

補充單字

☆ 1. fascinate	**v.**	使著迷
☆ 2. coverage	**n.**	報導
☆ 3. replace	**v.**	取代
☆ 4. attempt	**n.**	企圖、嘗試
☆ 5. appropriate	**adj.**	適當的
☆ 6. starve	**v.**	餓死

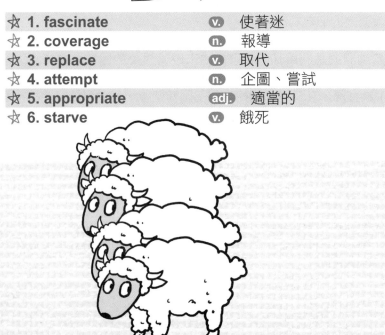

Brexit Consequences for UK
英國脫歐

聽力測驗 🎧 Track 076

在學習英文的過程中，「聽」可能是最直接的第一線接觸，也可能是大家最想要快速習得的能力。現在，就讓我們來熟悉各種英文情境，提升自己的英文臨場感吧！

(   ) 1. What has Britain been debating about for decades?
      (A) pros and cons of the EU membership
      (B) possibilities of space exploration
      (C) how much it will cost for Britain's exit from the EU
      (D) Brexit's consequences for the United States

(   ) 2. Who called for a referendum on the Brexit deal?
      (A) Tony Blair   (B) Gordon Brown
      (C) David Cameron   (D) Theresa May

(   ) 3. Who were pro-Brexit voters?
      (A) younger people in the UK
      (B) voters in London
      (C) Britons living overseas
      (D) older, working-class voters in England's countryside

(   ) 4. What did pro-Brexit voters worry about?
      (A) the UK's medical care
      (B) free movement of immigrants and refugees
      (C) the UK's education
      (D) free movement of capital and trade

(   ) 5. How much will the UK pay for its exit from the EU?
      (A) €50.7 billion   (B) zero
      (C) US$ 50.7 billion   (D) We don't know.

 **閱讀測驗**

剛剛的聽力測驗是否因為答題不順而感到遺憾？或是覺得自己有某些地方掌握地不夠好？現在就讓我們來直接「看」剛剛的聽力測驗，並透過後面的閱讀測驗來補齊聽力上的不足，同時考驗自己的閱讀能力吧！

Britain has been debating the pros and cons of membership in the European Union (EU) for decades. To silence pro-**Brexit**[1] opponents within his Conservative party, then Prime Minister David Cameron called for a **referendum**[2] in June 2016. He thought the referendum would resolve the issue in his favor. But it turned out that the anti-immigration and anti-EU arguments won. Britons voted for Brexit by nearly 52% to 48%.

Most of the pro-Brexit voters were older, **working-class**[3] people in England's countryside. They were worried about the free movement of immigrants and refugees. They felt that EU was changing their national identity, and they didn't like the budgetary system and regulations the EU **imposed**[4]. What they didn't see was how the free movement of capital and trade with the EU benefited them.

Younger voters and those in London, Scotland, and Northern Ireland preferred to stay in the EU, but they were **outnumbered**[5] by older voters who were in favor of Brexit. As a result, the UK will pay a €50.7 billion "divorce bill" for its exit from the EU. Brexit's biggest disadvantage is that it might slow down the UK's economic growth. Most of this has been due to the uncertainty surrounding the UK's future and its investment environment.

【 Question 】

(   ) 1. In addition to immigrants and refugee issues, what did pro-Brexits voters worry about?

      (A) northern Ireland issue

      (B) global warming

      (C) The EU was changing the UK's national identity.

      (D) relations between the UK and the US

(   ) 2. What is Brexit's biggest disadvantage?

      (A) The UK won't be able to return to the EU.

      (B) It might slow down the UK's economic growth.

      (C) Capital and trade can move freely in the UK.

      (D) The referendum held in 2016 did not decide whether Britain will exit or remain in the EU.

【 文章中譯 】

英國數十年來都在辯論成為歐盟會員國的利與弊。為了平息保守黨內支持脫歐的聲浪，當時的英國首相大衛‧卡麥隆在2016年6月提出了公投案，他以為公投結果脫歐不會過關，這麼一來就解決了這個爭議；沒想到有人炒作反移民和反歐盟的議題，使得脫歐過關了，英國公投結果以 52% 比 48% 同意脫歐。

大多數支持英國脫歐的選民是英格蘭鄉間較年長、藍領階級人士，他們很憂心移民和難民能在英國自由出入，並覺得歐盟在改變他們的國家認同感。他們也不喜歡歐盟對會員國施加的預算制度和法規，但是他們沒注意到英國因是歐盟會員國而享受到資金和貿易得以自由流通的經濟益處。

傾向留在歐盟的選民為年輕人和居住在倫敦、蘇格蘭和北愛爾蘭地區的人民，不過他們的人數不敵選擇脫歐的年長選民。結果是英國為了脫歐，要付出高達507億歐元的「分手費」。英國脫歐最大的弊病在於它可能會使英國經濟成長趨緩，因為脫歐導致英國的未來和其投資環境存在了許多不確定的因素。

 聽力題目解析

❶ 此題詢問的是英國辯論數十年的議題是什麼。選項 (A) 為成為歐盟會員國的利弊；選項 (B) 為太空探索的可能性；選項 (C) 為英國脫歐要付多少錢；選項 (D) 為英國脫歐對美國的影響。錄音檔開頭即指出 "Britain has been debating the pros and cons of membership in the European Union (EU) for decades."，本題考的是考生是否能掌握 "debate"（辯論）此關鍵字，答案選 (A)。

❷ 此題詢問的是誰提出英國脫歐公投案。錄音檔前段部分提到 "To silence pro-Brexit opponents within his Conservative party, then Prime Minister David Cameron called for a referendum in June 2016." 故答案選 (C)。（註：答案 (A)、(B)為英國前首相，(D)為英國現任首相。）

❸ 此題詢問的是支持脫歐的選民是誰。選項 (A) 為英國年輕人；選項 (B) 為倫敦選民；選項 (C) 為僑居海外的英國人；選項 (D) 為英格蘭鄉間年長、藍領階級的選民。本題掌握任何 "pro-Brexit voters" 出現的句子即可，選 (D)。

❹ 此題詢問的是支持英國脫歐的選民是擔憂什麼事。選項 (A) 為英國的醫療照護；選項 (B) 為移民和難民能在英國自由出入；選項 (C) 為英國的教育；選項 (D) 為資金和貿易能在英國自由出入。錄音檔中段直接給了答案 "They were worried about the free movement of immigrants and refugees." 答案選 (B)。（註：原本還有第四派勢力是恐怖份子，在全球反恐的情勢下，第四派勢力已漸失勢。）

❺ 此題詢問的是英國脫歐要付出多少錢。錄音檔最後提到 "As a result, the UK will pay a €50.7 billion 'divorce bill' for its exit from the EU." 答案選 (A)。

閱讀題目解析

❶ 此題詢問的是除了移民和難民議題，支持英國脫歐的選民還憂心何事。選項 (A) 為北愛爾蘭問題；選項 (B) 為全球暖化；選項 (C) 為歐盟在改變英國的國家認同感；選項 (D) 為英美兩國關係。答案可見內文第二段，答案選 (C)。

❷ 第二題詢問的是何者為脫歐最大的弊病。選項 (A) 為英國無法重返歐盟；選項 (B) 為它可能會使英國經濟成長趨緩；選項 (C) 為資金和貿易能在英國自由流通；選項 (D) 為2016年的公投案並未決定英國在歐盟的去留。答案可見內文第三段末段，選 (B)。

補充單字

☆ 1. Brexit	**n.**	英國脫歐
		（由 Britain + exit 所形成的新字）
☆ 2. referendum	**n.**	公投
☆ 3. working-class	**adj.**	藍領階級的
☆ 4. impose	**v.**	徵（稅）
☆ 5. outnumber	**v.**	在數量上超過

Level 5 07 The Opening Ceremony of 2016 Rio Olympics

2016里約奧運開幕式

聽力測驗 🎧Track 077

在學習英文的過程中，「聽」可能是最直接的第一線接觸，也可能是大家最想要快速習得的能力。現在，就讓我們來熟悉各種英文情境，提升自己的英文臨場感吧！

(   ) 1. Which of the following was the host country of the 2016 Rio Olympics?

    (A) Puerto Rico   (B) Brazil

    (C) Ecuador   (D) Chile

(   ) 2. What was the video about in the opening of the 2016 Rio Olympics?

    (A) global warming and climate change

    (B) Brazil's famous supermodel Gisele Bundchen

    (C) Maracana Stadium

    (D) Zika virus

(   ) 3. What happened to Brazil's Amazon rainforests?

    (A) They have been well-preserved.

    (B) They are all gone.

    (C) They remain intact.

    (D) Chunks of them have been lost due to deforestation.

(   ) 4. What kind of weather is expected in Brazil in the coming years?

    (A) colder weather   (B) ideally comfortable weather

    (C) cool weather   (D) drier and hotter weather

(　　) 5. What kind of mosquito-borne disease will cause serious birth defects in infants?
    (A) dengue fever   (B) Zika
    (C) flu   (D) jaundice

 閱讀測驗

剛剛的聽力測驗是否因為答題不順而感到遺憾？或是覺得自己有某些地方掌握地不夠好？現在就讓我們來直接「看」剛剛的聽力測驗，並透過後面的閱讀測驗來補齊聽力上的不足，同時考驗自己的閱讀能力吧！

The 2016 Rio Olympics officially kicked off on the evening of August 5th with the opening ceremony held in the Maracana Stadium in the seaside city of Brazil. It marked the first time a South American city hosted the summer games, and showcased one of Brazil's famous supermodel exports, Gisele Bundchen, as she **sashayed**[1] down "the world's longest runway."

However, the glamorous supermodels were not the only dashing moments of the opening ceremony of the Olympics. Brazil also showed a video that intended to raise awareness about global warming and climate change. Narrated by the Academy Award-winning actress, Judi Dench, the video included maps and **graphics**[2] showing how rapidly the earth's temperature has increased over time, and how steadily sea levels are rising around the world.

Home to about one-third of the world's rainforests, **chunks**[3] of Brazil's Amazon rainforests have disappeared due to deforestation. Drier and hotter weather is thus expected to become more severe in the coming years. The changing environmental conditions could **accelerate**[4] outbreaks of **mosquito-borne**[5] diseases such as Zika, which have led to serious birth defects in infants. The climate change interlude of the opening ceremony won the praise from environmentalists, who hoped the world would pay more attention to the challenges facing our planet.

【 Question 】

(　　) 1. What made the 2016 Rio Olympics so special?
　　　　(A) The Maracana Stadium was the hugest site for the Olympics in its history.
　　　　(B) The weather was the best in the Olympic history.
　　　　(C) Many athletes were infected with Zika.
　　　　(D) It was the first time a South American country hosted the Olympics.

(　　) 2. Why does Brazil play a key role in global temperature regulation?
　　　　(A) It is home to about one-third of the world's rainforests.
　　　　(B) It has developed and used solar energy nationwide.
　　　　(C) It has invented a new technology to address global warming.
　　　　(D) It is a leader of clean energy transition.

【 文章中譯 】

里約奧運在2016年8月5日晚間正式開幕，地點是馬拉卡納體育場。這屆奧運是首次由南美洲國家舉辦的夏季運動盛會，並由巴西超級名模吉賽爾·邦臣出場亮相，在「全球最長的伸展台」走秀。

然而，開幕儀式的精彩亮點不只有光彩亮麗的超模，巴西藉此機會播放一段影片，期盼世人關注全球暖化和氣候變遷的議題。影片旁白由奧斯卡得主的女演員茱蒂·丹契擔綱口述，影片呈現各國地圖及地球快速升溫的圖表，還有海平面持續上升的景況。

全球有近三分之一的熱帶雨林位在巴西境內，但是由於森林砍伐，該國大片亞馬遜熱帶雨林已經消失了，因此預計未來幾年氣候將越來越乾熱。環境的改變也將加速以蚊蟲為媒介的疾病在各地肆虐，例如造成嬰兒出生時即帶有嚴重缺陷的茲卡病毒。氣候變遷成為開幕式的穿插節目贏得環境保護人士的一致讚賞，並企盼全球能多加關注地球此刻面臨的重大挑戰。

聽力題目解析

❶ 第一題詢問的是2016里約奧運的主辦國是何者，選項 (A) 為波多黎各；選項 (B) 為巴西；選項 (C) 為厄瓜多；選項 (D) 為智利。本題考的是考生是否知道host country是「主辦國」的意思。另外，里約熱內盧（Rio de Janeiro）是巴西的舊首都，故答案選 (B)。

❷ 此題詢問的是2016里約奧運開幕儀式播放的影片是關於什麼，選項 (A) 為全球暖化和氣候變遷；選項 (B) 為巴西知名超模吉賽爾·邦臣；選項 (C) 為馬拉卡納體育場；選項 (D) 為茲卡病毒。在錄音檔中段部分提到 "... a video that intended to raise awareness about global warming and climate change."，故答案選 (A)。

❸ 此題詢問的是巴西的亞馬遜熱帶雨林發生什麼事。選項 (A) 為它們被保護得很好；選項 (B) 為它們全不見了；選項 (C) 為它們維持地完整無缺；選項 (D) 為由於森林砍伐，大片亞馬遜熱帶雨林已經消失。本題在錄音檔中後段提到 "... disappeared due to deforestation." 若未能掌握 "deforestation" 也可藉由 "disappeared" 來推測，故答案選 (D)。

❹ 此題詢問的是巴西未來幾年的天氣預計會是如何。選項 (A) 為更冷的天氣；選項 (B) 為理想宜人的天氣；選項 (C) 為涼爽的天氣；選項 (D) 為更乾熱的天氣。錄音檔中後段提到 "Drier and hotter weather is expected to become more severe in the coming years."，故答案選 (D)。

❺ 此題詢問的是何種以蚊蟲作為媒介的疾病將造成嬰兒出生即帶有嚴重的缺陷。選項 (A) 為登革熱；選項 (B) 為茲卡病毒；選項 (C) 為流感；選項 (D) 為黃疸。錄音檔提到 "... mosquito-borne diseases such as Zika, which have led to serious birth defects in infants." 這邊把握 "which" 作為 "Zika" 的補充即可，選 (B)。

閱讀題目解析

❶ 第一題詢問的是2016里約奧運有什麼特別之處。選項 (A) 為馬拉卡納體育場是奧運史上最大的舉辦場地;選項 (B) 為氣候是奧運史上最佳的;選項 (C) 為許多運動員感染了茲卡病毒;選項 (D) 為是南美洲國家首度舉辦的夏季運動盛會。答案可見本文第一段,答案選 (D)。

❷ 第二題詢問的是為何巴西在全球氣候調節中扮演重要的角色。選項 (A) 為全球有近三分之一的熱帶雨林位在巴西境內;選項 (B) 為該國已發展太陽能,並全國使用;選項 (C) 為該國已發明對付全球暖化的新科技;選項 (D) 為該國是轉型為潔淨能源的先驅。答案可見內文第三段,選 (A)。

補充單字

☆ 1. sashay	**v.**	搖曳生姿地走路
☆ 2. graphics	**n.**	圖像
☆ 3. chunk	**n.**	大部分
☆ 4. accelerate	**v.**	加速
☆ 5. mosquito-borne	**adj.**	由蚊子傳播的

Level 1
Level 2
Level 3
Level 4
Level 5
Level 6

Level 5
08 Clean Energy for a Sustainable Future

潔淨能源帶來永續未來

聽力測驗 🎧 Track 078

在學習英文的過程中，「聽」可能是最直接的第一線接觸，也可能是大家最想要快速習得的能力。現在，就讓我們來熟悉各種英文情境，提升自己的英文臨場感吧！

(　　) 1. What is the world's urgent problem?
　　　　(A) falling sea levels
　　　　(B) extinction of penguins
　　　　(C) climate change
　　　　(D) Wikileaks

(　　) 2. What should we do to reduce carbon emissions?
　　　　(A) to burn coals
　　　　(B) to switch from fossil fuel-based power to clean energy
　　　　(C) to cut down more trees
　　　　(D) to plant flowers

(　　) 3. What encouraging trends do we see in 2018?
　　　　(A) In Europe, major renewable energy projects have started to take root without direct subsidies.
　　　　(B) Every country in the world has cut carbon emissions on a massive scale.
　　　　(C) Clean energy has completely replaced fossil fuel-based energy.
　　　　(D) Sea level is not rising.

( ) 4. What kind of energy will Ikea and Apple use to power their operations?

(A) coal-fired energy   (B) fossil fuel-based energy

(C) renewable energy   (D) nuclear energy

( ) 5. Who should join the efforts to build a sustainable future?

(A) both private and public sectors

(B) public sector only

(C) every country except the US

(D) private sector only

 閱讀測驗

剛剛的聽力測驗是否因為答題不順而感到遺憾？或是覺得自己有某些地方掌握地不夠好？現在就讓我們來直接「看」剛剛的聽力測驗，並透過後面的閱讀測驗來補齊聽力上的不足，同時考驗自己的閱讀能力吧！

Climate change is unquestionably an urgent problem in the world today, and the **transition**[1] away from fossil fuels is the biggest challenge humanity has ever faced. To reduce carbon emissions, the world needs to switch from fossil fuel-based power to clean energy, such as solar, wind, hydro, and **biomass**[2].

Here are some encouraging trends we can see in 2018. In Europe, major **renewable**[3] energy projects have started to take root without direct **subsidies**[4]. In the US, renewables are rapidly closing up the gap with natural gas power plants. Furthermore, a number of huge enterprises signed record-breaking purchasing deals for renewables. For instance, at least 158 companies, including Allianz, Ikea, and Apple, have set targets for 100% renewable energy to power their operations. Google has also bought enough renewable energy to match its annual energy demand.

These trends show that people have a better sense of what it takes to meet climate goals. The challenge now is to build the global will from both private and public sectors to launch ourselves further and faster than ever before toward a **sustainable**[5] future without carbon emissions.

【Question】

(   ) 1. Which of the following is NOT clean energy?
      (A) hydro energy
      (B) biomass
      (C) fossil fuels
      (D) wind energy

(   ) 2. What development has the US made in terms of energy transition?
      (A) More nuclear power plants have been built.
      (B) Clean coal technology has been widely deployed.
      (C) Geothermal energy has long been successfully deployed in all states.
      (D) Renewables are rapidly closing up the gap with natural gas power plants.

【文章中譯】

氣候變遷無疑是當今全球迫切的問題，這也使汰除石化燃料成為人類至今面臨最大的挑戰。為了減少碳排放，全球極需將以石化燃料為主的能源轉換為以潔淨燃料為主的能源，例如太陽能、風能、水力發電、生質能源等。

在2018年，我們可以看到一些令人振奮的趨勢。在歐洲，重大再生能源計畫在沒有獲得官方直接的補助下已生根發展。在美國，再生能源的蓬勃發展也迅速消弭其與天然氣發電廠之間的差距。此外，許多大企業均以天價簽購再生能源；例如，包括安聯集團、宜家家居、蘋果等至少158家公司都設定使用100%再生能源來營運公司的目標，而谷歌也已購買足以供應其用電一整年的再生能源。

這些趨勢顯示人們對於如何達成氣候目標更有概念了，現在的挑戰是結合全球政府與民間的意願，齊心比往年更進一步地加速邁向無碳排放的永續未來。

聽力題目解析

❶ 此題詢問的是世界面臨的急迫問題是什麼。選項 (A) 為降低的海平面；選項 (B) 為企鵝的絕種；選項 (C) 為氣候變遷；選項 (D) 為維基解密。錄音檔開頭即指出 "Climate change is unquestionably an urgent problem ..."，故答案選 (C)。

❷ 此題詢問的是我們應該採取什麼行動來減少碳排放。選項 (A) 為燒煤炭；選項 (B) 為將石化燃料為主的能源轉換為使用潔淨能源；選項 (C) 為砍更多的樹；選項 (D) 為種植花朵。錄音檔前段部分提到 "To reduce carbon emissions, the world needs to switch from fossil fuel-based power to clean energy ..." 本題考的是「switch from A to B」的片語，意思是「從A物轉換成B物」，故答案選 (B)。

❸ 此題詢問的是我們在2018年看到了什麼振奮人心的趨勢。選項 (A) 為在歐洲，重大再生能源計畫在沒有獲得官方直接的補助下已生根發展；選項 (B) 為世界每國都已大幅度減少碳排放了；選項 (C) 為潔淨能源已完全取代石化燃料為主的能源；選項 (D) 為海水不再上升。錄音檔中段提到 "Here are some encouraging trends in 2018. In Europe, major renewable energy projects have ..." 故選 (A)。

❹ 此題詢問的是宜家家居和蘋果將用何種能源維持企業的營運。選項 (A) 為燃煤能源；選項 (B) 為石化燃料為主的能源；選項 (C) 為再生能源；選項 (D) 為核能。此即考的是考生能否把握 "including" 作為中間補充的用法，故選 (C)。

❺ 此題詢問的是誰應為了共創永續未來而一起努力。選項 (A) 為公、私部門都要；選項 (B) 為公部門即可；選項 (C) 為每個國家，除了美國以外；選項 (D) 為私部門即可。錄音檔後段提到 "The challenge now is building the global will from both private and public sectors ..." 本題重點是private sector（私部門，指民間企業）和public sector（公部門，指公家機關、政府）都要齊力為無碳排放的永續未來而努力，故答案選 (A)。

閱讀題目解析

❶ 此題詢問的是以下何者不是潔淨能源。選項 (A) 為水力發電能源;選項 (B)為生質能源;選項 (C) 為石化燃料;選項 (D) 為風能。答案可見內文第一段,答案選 (C)。

❷ 此詢問的是美國在能源轉型方面有什麼發展。選項 (A) 為更多核能發電廠已開始興建;選項 (B) 為淨煤技術已被廣泛佈局於全美各地;選項 (C) 為地熱發電已在全美各州成功地設置;選項 (D) 為再生能源的蓬勃發展正迅速消弭其與天然氣工廠之間的差距。答案可見內文第二段,答案選 (D)。

補充單字

☆ 1. transition	**v.**	轉換
☆ 2. biomass	**n.**	生質能源
☆ 3. renewable	**adj.**	再生的
☆ 4. subsidy	**n.**	補助
☆ 5. sustainable	**adj.**	永續的

The History of Paper and Printing

紙與印刷的歷史

聽力測驗 Track 079

在學習英文的過程中，「聽」可能是最直接的第一線接觸，也可能是大家最想要快速習得的能力。現在，就讓我們來熟悉各種英文情境，提升自己的英文臨場感吧！

(   ) 1. Most of our important records are written on _____.
    (A) trees   (B) paper
    (C) clothes   (D) walls

(   ) 2. Paper is a _____ material which can be used in many different ways.
    (A) boring   (B) heavy
    (C) versatile   (D) ridiculous

(   ) 3. Before the invention of _____, all writing was done by hand.
    (A) ink   (B) color
    (C) painting   (D) printing

(   ) 4. In 1453, a man named _____ created the first printed Bible.
    (A) Babylon   (B) Gordon   (C) Gutenberg

(   ) 5. E-books, short for _____, are books published in electronic form
    (A) electric books
    (B) electronic books
    (C) equipment books

剛剛的聽力測驗是否因為答題不順而感到遺憾？或是覺得自己有某些地方掌握地不夠好？現在就讓我們來直接「看」剛剛的聽力測驗，並透過後面的閱讀測驗來補齊聽力上的不足，同時考驗自己的閱讀能力吧！

Written communication has been the spotlight of civilization and **culture**[1] for centuries. Most of our important records are on written paper. Although writing has been invented and around for a long time, paper hasn't.

People had tried to **produce**[2] something easier and cheaper to write on, but it took almost three thousand years to create paper. Paper is believed to be first created in 100 B.C. and is credited to a Chinese man named Tsai Lun. Tsai Lun's paper was a huge achievement, and started to be used all over China. People in India started to make paper by 400 A.D.. But it took another thousand years before people were using paper all over Europe and Asia. By 1411, people in Germany began to produce their own paper. After they had learned to make paper, they were also interested in learning about Chinese printing. And in 1453, a man named Gutenberg created the first printed Bible.

Now paper is a type of thin flat material. It's a versatile material which can be used in many ways, such as printing. Printing is the process of producing copies of documents, publications, or images, and is a highly important part of **publishing**[3] and **transaction**[4] printing. Before the invention of printing, all writing was done by hand. So this made books very pricey, and only the richest people could have them. A faster and more convenient method was later invented in the Tang Dynasty of China around 650 A.D. There was a man who had the idea of carving wooden blocks with a page of text. He inked the block and pressed paper on to it to print a page. This method of making printed books was quite innovative, but later, in about 1000 A.D., a Chinese alchemist called Pi Sheng invented a more elastic system of Chinese moveable type. He carved each Chinese character separately on small fired clay blocks and arranged them to make phrases and sentences. Approximately five hundred years later, people all over Europe and Asia started to use moveable metal type. In 1453, Johannes Gutenberg then used moveable metal type to print a Christian Bible.

The invention of the printing press made books less expensive and helped ideas spread quickly. It also made things less difficult for the reform of the Church and the development of modern science. Early in the 18th century, John Harris was printing **tasteful**[5], quality little books for kids. The method for adding color by hand had turned into a small home-based business. He employed young people to paint the books at his home. During the 1860s, chromolithography was used to print cheaper books with **vivid**[6] colors. Chromolithography was a faster and cheaper way to produce books with color compared to the hand-colored illustrations.

E-books, short for electronic books, are books published in electronic form. E-books show mankind's need to use technology. And just imagine all the trees e-books would save! However, printed books are believed to prevail by some people. Many consider it exceptionally important to keep the printed books around.

【Question】

(   ) 1. How many years did it take for paper to be created?
      (A) 1000 years   (B) 3000 years
      (C) 300 years   (D) 1300 years

(   ) 2. Which of the following statement about printing is incorrect?
      (A) It is a process of producing copies.
      (B) It plays an important part in publishing.
      (C) Books are pricey before the invention of printing.
      (D) Printing methods did not evolve much until today.

【文章中譯】

幾個世紀以來，書寫溝通一直是文明和文化中的亮點。我們大部分的記錄都源自於紙上。儘管人們發明書寫很長一段時間了，可是紙並沒有很早就出現。

人們一直想製造出一種更容易也更便宜的書寫材料。可是，經歷了幾乎三千年之久的時間，人們才發明出紙來。人們普遍認為紙的發明應該歸功於中國人，蔡倫。是他在西元前110年，首次創造出了紙。蔡倫發明的紙是一項非常重大的成就，之後普及全中國。到了西元400年的時候，印度人也開始製作紙。但是，在所有的歐洲和亞洲廣泛使用紙之前，期間又經過了一千年的時間。到1411年，德國人也開始製造他們自己的紙。他們學會造紙之後，同時也開始熱衷於學習中國的印刷術。在1453年，一個名叫古騰堡的人創造了第一本印刷版的聖經。

現在的紙又平又薄，它是一種多用途的材料，人們能透過多種方式來對其加以利用，像是印刷。印刷指的是對文件、出版物或是圖像進行複印的一個過程。印刷是出版和交易印刷中非常重要的一部分。在印刷術被發明之前，所有的書寫都是手寫完成的。這使得書的價格昂貴，只有有錢人才能買得起。後來，在西元650 年，中國唐朝的時候，人們發明出一種更為快捷方便的方法。那時，有個人想到可以手工雕刻木板來記錄一頁文章的內容，他先是在木板上塗上墨水，然後把紙按壓在上面，就印出了一頁文章的內容。這種印書的方法相當新穎，之後大約到了西元1000 年，中國的一位煉金術士，畢升，發明了一套更為靈活的方法。他把漢字單獨刻在被燒好的小泥塊上，然後進行排版，使泥塊上的漢字能編排成很多的短語和句子。大約五百年之後，歐洲和亞洲人就都開始使用金屬活版印刷術了。在 1453 年的歐

洲，古騰堡用活字版印出了一本基督教聖經。

印刷機的發明使得書籍不再那麼昂貴，也促進了思想的快速傳播。同時，還為宗教改革的進行和現代科學發展減少了阻礙。在 18 世紀早期，約翰·哈里斯出版了給兒童看的雅緻高檔小書。這種手繪的方式發展成了一種家庭工業。他雇用年輕人到家中給書手繪著色。在 19 世紀六十年代期間，彩色石印術被用來給更便宜的書籍印上鮮豔的色彩。彩色石印術比起手工繪色插圖的技術來，在出版彩色書籍方面顯得更快捷，也更便宜。

電子書是電子書籍的簡稱，它指的是以電子檔形式出版的書籍。電子書體現了人們對應用技術的需求。只要想像一下電子書可以為我們節省多少的樹木就可以知道了！不過，許多人不認為紙本書會絕跡，且肯定紙本書在身邊的重要性。

聽力題目解析

❶ 此題詢問的是我們許多重要紀錄都是寫在何物上。選項 (A) 為樹木；選項 (B) 為紙張；選項 (C) 為衣服；選項 (D) 為牆壁。錄音檔一開始即給了答案，為 (B)。

❷ 此題詢問的是紙張是何種可以被多重利用的材質。選項 (A) 為無趣的；選項 (B) 為沉重的；選項 (C) 為多樣性的；選項 (D) 為可笑的。答案為 (C)，這邊考的即是 "versatile"（多樣性的）此單字，延伸字為 "variety"（多樣性）。

❸ 此題詢問的是在何物的發明以前，所有的紀錄都是透過手寫來進行。選項 (A) 為墨水；選項 (B) 為顏色；選項 (C) 為顏料；選項 (D) 為印刷。這邊考的是 "printing" 作為「印刷」之意，且其它選項可因做為手寫用料而一併排除，選 (D)。

❹ 此題詢問的是在1453年，一位名叫什麼的男子創造了第一本印刷聖經。選項 (A) 為巴比倫；選項 (B) 為高登；選項 (C) 為古騰堡。答案為 (C)，在介紹完紙在歐亞的大致發行順序後，我們即可聽見人名，注意 "a man named" 這裡，文章後段也有再次提及。

❺ 此題詢問的是 E-books，也就是以電子形式發行的書，其原名為何。選項 (A) 為電力書籍；選項 (B) 為電子書籍；選項 (C) 為設備書籍。錄音檔最後我們可聽見 "... short for electronic books ..."，選 (B)，注意勿被其它選項的單字混淆。

● ●

閱讀題目解析

❶ 此題詢問的是歷經了多少年後，人們才發明紙張。答案可見內文第二段第一句，選擇 (B)，這邊注意勿被選項的數字混淆。

❷ 此處詢問的是何者關於印刷的陳述不正確。選項 (A) 為印刷是一個複印的過程；選項 (B) 為印刷對出版來說非常重要；選項 (C) 為在印刷被發明前，書的價格相當昂貴；選項 (D) 為印刷術直到現今才有比較多變革。根據內文，我們可以得知印刷歷經了雕刻木板到活版印刷，最後演變至電子書，故選 (D)。

補充單字

☆ 1. culture	n.	文化
☆ 2. produce	v.	生產
☆ 3. publish	v.	出版
☆ 4. transaction	n.	交易
☆ 5. tasteful	adj.	雅緻的
☆ 6. vivid	adj.	鮮明的

聽力測驗 🎧Track 080

在學習英文的過程中，「聽」可能是最直接的第一線接觸，也可能是大家最想要快速習得的能力。現在，就讓我們來熟悉各種英文情境，提升自己的英文臨場感吧！

(   ) 1. What happened to the 70-year-old man?
        (A) He was conscious when he was sent to the hospital.
        (B) He could chat with his daughter in the hospital.
        (C) He told the doctor he was hungry.
        (D) He had a heart attack and was admitted to the intensive care unit.

(   ) 2. What had the 70-year-old patient written?
        (A) a Do-Not-Resuscitate form and a living will
        (B) an organ donation card
        (C) a body donation consent form
        (D) a blood donation card

(   ) 3. What is palliative care?
        (A) a treatment that can cure all illnesses
        (B) a medical care for only small children
        (C) a treatment that relieves but does not cure an illness
        (D) a medical care for only old people

(   ) 4. What does palliative care focus on?
        (A) physical, psychological, and spiritual well-being of a dying person, and those close to him or her
        (B) avian flu viruses
        (C) mental diseases
        (D) Zika virus

(　　) 5. What can help a very sick patient and his family members cope better?

(A) avoid talking anything about death

(B) plan ahead for palliative care

(C) stay in a surgical ward

(D) ho mountain climbing

 閱讀測驗

剛剛的聽力測驗是否因為答題不順而感到遺憾？或是覺得自己有某些地方掌握地不夠好？現在就讓我們來直接「看」剛剛的聽力測驗，並透過後面的閱讀測驗來補齊聽力上的不足，同時考驗自己的閱讀能力吧！

A 70-year-old man had a heart attack and was admitted to the intensive care unit (ICU). He had no spontaneous breathing and had gone without oxygen for approximately 15 minutes. When his daughter arrived, she found her father **intubated**[1] and unresponsive to pain. The patient had a written a **Do Not Resuscitate**[2] (DNR) form, and a living will, in which he made it clear to his physician, family, and friends that living without his full cerebral function in a nursing home was to be avoided at all costs.

End-of-life care is a complicated topic, especially in a society where talks of death are customarily avoided. But death is inevitable; planning death with the loved ones is a part of having a good death. **Palliative**[3] care is a treatment that relieves but does not cure an illness. It focuses on the physical, psychological, and spiritual well-being of the dying person and those close to him or her. It can be the difference between a calm serene death or one **fraught with**[4] dread, agony, and suffering.

Open conversations and planning ahead for palliative care can help patients and their family members cope better with situations of **imminent**[5] death. They may feel a sense of peace knowing that they help their loved ones leave the world with their wishes fulfilled.

【Question】

( ) 1. What did the 70-year-old man emphasize in his living will?
　　(A) He wanted to live in a nursing home for the rest of his life.
　　(B) Living without his full cerebral function in a nursing home was to be avoided at all costs.
　　(C) He didn't want to see a doctor.
　　(D) He wanted his daughter to take care of him.

( ) 2. Why would family members feel a sense of peace if palliative care is planned in advance?
　　(A) They do not need to make any decision.
　　(B) They do not need to handle anything.
　　(C) They would know that they help their loved ones leave the world with their wishes fulfilled.
　　(D) Palliative care can cure illnesses.

【文章中譯】

一位70歲的先生因心臟病發被送進加護病房，他無法自主呼吸，且已缺氧約15分鐘。當他的女兒趕到醫院時，她見到父親插管並對疼痛沒有反應。他的父親曾簽過放棄急救同意書並寫過生前遺囑，其中對醫師、家人和朋友聲明要盡可能協助他避免在喪失腦部功能的情況下於安養院度過餘生。

臨終照護是個複雜的話題，尤其是在傳統忌憚談論死亡的社會。但是死亡是無可避免的，與心愛的人安排臨終方式是使生命善終的一部分。安寧照護是一種舒緩病人痛苦但無法治癒疾病的療養方式，著重在臨終病人和其親友在身、心、靈上的照護。它能幫助使病人離世的過程是安祥的，而非充滿恐懼、痛苦和折磨。

公開討論並預先安排安寧照護可以幫助病人和家人調適面對即將來臨的死亡，因為他們能了解這麼做是依照病人的意願離世，而能平靜地接受這一切。

聽力題目解析

❶ 此題詢問的是本文中的70歲老翁發生什麼事。選項 (A) 為他被送進醫院時仍意識清楚；選項 (B) 為他在醫院仍能跟女兒閒聊；選項 (C) 為他告訴醫師他肚子餓；選項 (D) 為他心臟病發被送到加護病房。這裡的關鍵字為 "heart attack" 及 "intensive care unit (ICU)"，故答案選 (D)。

❷ 此題詢問的是這位70歲先生曾寫過什麼。選項 (A) 為放棄急救同意書及生前遺囑；選項 (B) 為器捐卡；選項 (C) 為大體捐贈書；選項 (D) 為捐血卡。這裡考的是 "Do Not Resuscitate (DNR) form" 及 "a living will"，也可從前後文推斷，故答案選 (A)。

❸ 此題詢問的是何謂安寧照護。選項 (A) 為可治癒所有疾病的療法；選項 (B) 為僅供孩童的醫療照護；選項 (C) 為舒緩痛苦但無法治癒疾病的療養方式；選項 (D) 為僅供老年人的醫療照護。錄音檔中段即給出與選項相同之陳述，選 (C)。

❹ 此題詢問的是安寧照護的重點是什麼。選項 (A) 為臨終病人和其親友在身、心、靈上的照護；選項 (B) 為禽流感病毒；選項 (C) 為心理疾病；選項 (D) 為茲卡病毒。同上，把握即可，答案選 (A)。

❺ 此題詢問的是何者能幫助病況嚴重的病人和其家屬調適得更好。選項 (A) 為避談死亡；選項 (B) 為預先安排安寧照護；選項 (C) 為留在手術室；選項 (D) 為出外爬山。同上，可先快速看過題目及選項，以便掌握關鍵字，答案選 (B)。

閱讀題目解析

❶ 此題詢問的是本文中70歲的先生在生前遺囑裡強調什麼。選項 (A) 為他想在安養院度過餘生；選項 (B) 為他們要盡可能避免讓他在喪失腦部功能的情況下於安養院度過餘生；選項 (C) 為他不想看醫師；選項 (D) 為他希望女兒照顧他。答案可見內文第一段，選 (B)。

❷ 此題詢問的是為何預先安排安寧照護，家屬心情會感到比較平靜。選項 (A) 為他們不需做任何決定；選項 (B) 為他們不需處理任何事情；選項 (C) 為他們能了解這麼做是依照病人的意願離世；選項 (D) 為安寧照護可以治癒疾病，答案見內文第三段，選 (C)。

補充單字

☆ 1. intubate	**v.**	插管
☆ 2. Do Not Resuscitate	**ph.**	放棄急救
☆ 3. palliative	**adj.**	緩和的
☆ 4. fraught with	**adj.**	充滿（問題）……的
☆ 5. imminent	**adj.**	即將發生的

Level 6

頂尖高手
×
滿分到手

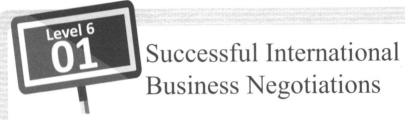

Level 6
01 Successful International Business Negotiations

成功的國際商務談判

在學習英文的過程中，「聽」可能是最直接的第一線接觸，也可能是大家最想要快速習得的能力。現在，就讓我們來熟悉各種英文情境，提升自己的英文臨場感吧！

(   ) 1. The success of international business relationships relies on effective business _____.
    (A) meetings
    (B) dinners
    (C) phone calls
    (D) negotiations

(   ) 2. _____ differences can make simple communication complicated.
    (A) Weight   (B) Height
    (C) Document   (D) Cultural

(   ) 3. The _____ barrier is the biggest hurdle.
    (A) language
    (B) vocal
    (C) spelling
    (D) dramatic

(   ) 4. Negotiations should involve creating _____ for all parties.
    (A) checks   (B) change
    (C) debt   (D) value

 **閱讀測驗**

剛剛的聽力測驗是否因為答題不順而感到遺憾？或是覺得自己有某些地方掌握地不夠好？現在就讓我們來直接「看」剛剛的聽力測驗，並透過後面的閱讀測驗來補齊聽力上的不足，同時考驗自己的閱讀能力吧！

The success of international business relationships **relies**[1] on effective business negotiations. Some company leaders assume that they can simply extend their **successful**[2] domestic experience to the international setting. But that's incorrect. In order to make successful deals, business executives should be better educated about international negotiations. International business negotiations are basically different from domestic negotiations, and need different knowledge and skills.

Cultural differences can make simple communication **complicated**[3]. The correct way of doing things differs from culture to culture in business environments. Remember to confirm who you are negotiating with early in your communications. And good cross-cultural communication skills are all about trust and clearness of expression.

International alliances have produced a substantial increase in the number of multinational business agreements. But in international negotiations, there is a great potential for misunderstanding and misinterpreted messages. The language barrier is the biggest **hurdle**[4]. When two persons communicate, they may be hardly talking about exactly the same subject, since meaning is based on a different cultural conditioning. So the failure of international negotiations is often **related**[5] to misunderstanding. Cultural differences are a major factor in international negotiations.

Negotiators must be well-**prepared**[6]. Here are some tips that will save a lot of time and trouble for everyone involved: Whenever you are involved in global negotiations or international meetings, keep in mind that you might be working with the same person for the next few decades. Negotiations should involve creating value for all parties. Negotiations should be straightforward and open. Hidden agendas will in the end be revealed and make the next meeting very hard. Trust being established is a highly important moment in meetings. Be honest and state your intentions clearly, and listen and evaluate what your business partner is requesting. At the end, turn the negotiations into win-win outcomes for all parties.

Lastly, unexpected changes in governmental currency policies can have major effects on international business deals. Different nations may have very distinct ideas about profit, private investment and individual rights. Since the relative value of different currencies differs over time, the actual value of the prices or payments may differ and cause losses or gains. Successful negotiators will be aware of differences in all aspects. International ventures are vulnerable to sudden and major changes in uncontrollable conditions. Events such as war, currency devaluation, or changes in government can have a strong effect on international businesses.

【Question】

(   ) 1. What may be the top factor to be considered when in business meetings?
(A) love
(B) trust
(C) hatred
(D) secrecy

(   ) 2. Which of the following may have major effects on international business according to the article?
(A) personal affairs
(B) cost of living
(C) gas prices
(D) governmental currency policies

【文章中譯】

成功的國際商務關係依賴於有效的商務談判。有一些企業領導人認為,他們可以很容易地把國內成功的經驗拓展到國際環境當中。但是,這個觀點是不正確的。為了使交易成功,企業主管更要好好地瞭解國際談判。國際商務談判與國內談判有本質上的不同。前者需要的知識和技能是有別於後者的。

文化差異使得原本簡單的交流變複雜了。在商務環境下,每個文化對於正確做事方式的認知是不一樣的。記得在交談剛開始的時候就確認一下你談判的對象是誰,且所謂的良好的跨文化溝通技巧指的就是信任和清楚的表述。

國際聯盟促成了大量的跨國商務協定。但是,國際談判卻可能潛藏著很多的誤解和誤導資訊。語言障礙是最大的一道阻礙。當兩個人在溝通的時候,他們可能會幾乎沒有談到同一個主題,因為語義是基於不同的文化條件而存在的。這一策略的失敗通常與誤解有關。文化差異是影響國際談判的一個主要因素。

談判必須做好充分準備。下面有些小提示可以幫大家節約不少時間和省去諸多麻煩。不管你何時參加國際談判或是國際會議,你都要記住,你以後可能會跟同一個人合作好幾十年。談判涉及到給參與各方創造價值。談判要開誠佈公。檯面下的動機最終都會被揭穿的,而且,還會讓下一次的會議很難進行。會議上信任的確立是很重要的時刻。你要誠實,並要清楚地說明自己的請求,還要傾聽和評估對方的請求,最後使談判達到一個雙贏的結果。

最後,政府貨幣政策出現的不可意料的變動對國際商貿也會產生很大的影響。不同的國家很可能會對利潤、私人投資和個人權利方面有很不同的想法。因為不同貨幣的相對價值因時而異,價格或是付款的實際價值很可能會有所變動,從而造成損失或是產生收益。成功的談判要會覺察到各個方面的差異。國際企業在不可控制的條件下,面對突如其來的重大變動會變得不堪一擊。諸如戰爭、貨幣貶值或是政府變動這些事件都會對國際商貿產生很大的影響。

聽力題目解析

❶ 此題詢問的是國際企業關係的成功是仰賴有效的商業 _____。選項 (A) 為會議;選項 (B) 為晚餐;選項 (C) 為通話;選項 (D) 為協商。錄音檔的一開始即給了我們答案,為 (D)。

❷ 此題詢問的是何種差異會使簡單的溝通變得複雜。選項 (A) 為重量;選項 (B) 為高度;選項 (C) 為文件;選項 (D) 為文化。在介紹國內外商務之不同後,內文接著談起國際商務的不同之處,因此在聆聽之外也可透過脈絡推測,選 (D)。

❸ 此題詢問的是何種障礙會是最大的阻撓。選項 (A) 為語言;選項 (B) 為歌唱的;選項 (C) 為拼音;選項 (D) 為戲劇性的。在錄音檔中段,我們可以聽見與題目一樣的句子,選 (A),或者可以透過「溝通」此主旨來推測。

❹ 此題詢問的是協商應涉及創造雙方的何物。選項 (A) 為支票;選項 (B) 為改變;選項 (C) 為債務;選項 (D) 為價值。答案為 (D),此句出現在探討協商的段落內,若不確定答案,可透過後續出現的 "win-win outcomes"(雙贏結果)來推測。

• •

閱讀題目解析

❶ 此題詢問的是在商業會議中,何者可能是最優先被考慮的要素。選項 (A) 為愛;選項 (B) 為信任;選項 (C) 為仇恨;選項 (D) 為秘密。答案可見內文倒數第二段,選 (B)。

❷ 此題詢問的是根據內文，選項何者可能會對國際商貿產生很大的影響。選項 (A) 為私人事務；選項 (B) 為物價；選項 (C) 為油價；選項 (D) 為政府貨幣政策。答案可見內文最後一段第一句，選 (D)。

補充單字

☆ 1. rely	v.	仰賴、依靠
☆ 2. successful	adj.	成功的
☆ 3. complicated	adj.	複雜的
☆ 4. hurdle	n.	障礙、困難
☆ 5. relate	v.	使有關
☆ 6. prepare	v.	準備

Level 1
Level 2
Level 3
Level 4
Level 5
Level 6

White-Collar Employees Nowadays

白領階級現況

🔊 聽力測驗 🎧 Track 082

在學習英文的過程中，「聽」可能是最直接的第一線接觸，也可能是大家最想要快速習得的能力。現在，就讓我們來熟悉各種英文情境，提升自己的英文臨場感吧！

(   ) 1. The passage is mainly about the white collar's _____.
      (A) love life   (B) hobbies
      (C) pay and tax   (D) work and health

(   ) 2. According to the text, a lot of white-collar workers _____ in their daily jobs.
      (A) play hard
      (B) work against the clock
      (C) play by ear
      (D) have lunch on time

(   ) 3. A great number of white-collar employees _____ decide their own work situation.
      (A) can   (B) refuse to
      (C) choose to   (D) cannot

(   ) 4. According to the text, what do they need after an exhausting work day?
      (A) to work overtime
      (B) to take medicine
      (C) to find time to relax
      (D) to earn more money

 **閱讀測驗**

剛剛的聽力測驗是否因為答題不順而感到遺憾？或是覺得自己有某些地方掌握地不夠好？現在就讓我們來直接「看」剛剛的聽力測驗，並透過後面的閱讀測驗來補齊聽力上的不足，同時考驗自己的閱讀能力吧！

The word "white-collar" refers to jobs that are usually salaried and do not involve manual labor. And the term "white-collar employee" means a salaried professional or an educated worker in the office. The name derives from the **traditional**[1] white, button down shirts worn by employees of such professions. Because white shirts get dirty easily, these workers do not do manual labor work. Usually, the pay is higher among white-collar employees, although many of the "white-collar" employees nowadays are not necessarily in the upper class as the term once implied.

White-collar employees who have university degrees but not necessarily have high salaries are overworked and stressed. They put in more than ten to twelve hours a day on average and have no holidays. They are under growing pressure at work and out of **condition**[2]. Most feel that their health is declining, and most of them suffer from pain in the neck, shoulders, and back. It is believed that these pains are related to the work environment. A lot of white-collar workers work against the clock in their daily jobs. They **skip**[3] their lunch break and other breaks because of the lack of time. The speed of work is extremely high and they are asked to be always quick, **flexible**[4], and available.

The conditions for doing work have changed. Fast technical developments and competition have resulted in major changes for white-collar employees, and they hardly have possibility to decide when to work. They cannot choose where they work or how many hours they work. The speed of life and work are very **intense**[5]. A lot of times the stress from increased work relates to shortages of labor as well. A great number of white-collar employees cannot decide their own work situation. Almost half of them have seen their tasks change over the past few years. However, this does not mean that their jobs are disappointing. Many employees say they have a challenging job, and they generally get along with their colleagues. It's just that when they go home, they are extremely **exhausted**[6]. All they need is to find time to relax.

Another term that arises from the class of white-collar employees is white-collar crimes. White-collar crimes are those crimes performed by professional employees. These crimes include certain forms of fraud, embezzlement, insider trading, forgery and computer crime. It is estimated that a great deal of white collar crime is undiscovered. The term is derived from the typical white-collar, bottom down shirts worn by professionals committing such crimes.

【 Question 】

(　　) 1. Where does the name "white-collar" derive from?
    (A) the designed shirts worn by office workers
    (B) the clothes that have a white collar and other patterns worn by office workers
    (C) the costume worn by employees in the office
    (D) the tradition shirts worn by employees in the office

(　　) 2. Which of the following is not included as a kind of white-collar crimes?
    (A) embezzlement
    (B) forgery
    (C) insider trading
    (D) theft

Level 1
Level 2
Level 3
Level 4
Level 5
Level 6

【文章中譯】

「白領」一詞，是指領取薪水的非勞力相關工作。而「白領階級」則指在辦公室工作的受過良好教育、具備專業知識的工作人員。白領一詞源於傳統上穿著白襯衫從事此類工作的人。因為白色衣服很容易弄髒，所以這些人不會做勞力工作。通常白領階級的薪水比較高，但是現今的白領階級已不像以往那樣一定屬於上層階級了。

具有大學文憑但不一定擁有高薪，白領階級總是超負荷地工作，還要承受很大的壓力。他們平均每天要工作十到十二小時，甚至更多，而且沒有假日。他們的工作壓力越來越大，健康狀況也不好。他們大多覺得自己的身體愈來愈差，且他們大多數人會感到肩頸痛、後背痛。據信，這些疼痛與工作環境密切相關。很多白領每天的工作都很忙碌。因為沒有足夠時間工作，他們會犧牲午餐休息以及其他休息時間。他們的工作速度很快，且他們也被要求要一直保持快速、彈性，且有空處理工作。

工作環境已經改變了，快速發展的科技以及競爭已經給白領階級帶來巨大的變化。他們幾乎不能決定什麼時候去工作，他們不能選擇工作地點及工作時數。生活和工作的節奏都非常快，且勞動力的短缺也和工作的壓力有關。很多的白領不能決定他們自己的工作情形，他們當中幾乎有將近一半的人在過去的幾年中，見證了工作任務的改變。但是，這並不意味著他們的工作是讓人失望的。不少員工說他們的工作相當有挑戰性，且他們普遍和同事相處融洽。只是說當他們下班回到家中後，會感到極度疲勞。他們需要的只是找時間放鬆。

另一個從白領階級而起的詞為白領犯罪。白領犯罪即指由專業人員犯罪。這些罪行包括特定形式的詐騙、貪汙、內幕交易、偽造和電腦犯罪。估計還有很多的白領犯罪沒有被揭露出來。白領犯罪這個名詞源自於由穿著帶釦子的白襯衫之專業人士犯下的罪行。

聽力題目解析

❶ 此題詢問的是文章主旨為白領階級的何種層面。選項 (A) 為感情生活；選項 (B) 為嗜好；選項 (C) 為花費與稅務；選項 (D) 為工作與健康。這邊我們可以掌握 "overwork"、"work-related problems"、"health"、"pain" 等字，選 (D)。

❷ 此題詢問的是根據內文，許多白領階級會在日常工作中進行何事。選項 (A) 為瘋狂玩樂；選項 (B) 為不停工作與時間賽跑；選項 (C) 為隨機應變；選項 (D) 為準時吃午餐。這邊考的是 "work against the clock"（工作忙碌）之意，選 (B)。

❸ 此題詢問的是許多白領階級 _____ 決定他們的工作情況。選項 (A) 為可以；選項 (B) 為拒絕；選項 (C) 為選擇；選項 (D) 為無法。在內文提及科技發展導致工作環境產生劇變之後，我們得知此變化使白領階級幾乎無法 (hardly) 決定他們的工作情況，也因此錄音檔才又提及身體之相關病痛，故選 (D)。

❹ 此題詢問的是白領階級在疲倦的一天後需要的是什麼。選項 (A) 為加班；選項 (B) 為吃藥；選項 (C) 為找時間放鬆；選項 (D) 為賺更多錢。錄音檔在介紹完白領工作的轉變之後，便給了我們與選項相同之答案，故仔細聽即可，選 (C)。

閱讀題目解析

❶ 此題詢問的是 "white-collar" 此字的起源。選項 (A) 為辦公族穿的設計襯衫；選項 (B) 為辦公族穿的白領圖樣服飾；選項 (C) 為辦公族穿的戲服；選項 (D) 為辦公族傳統在工作時穿的衣服。答案可見內文第一段，選 (D)。

❷ 此題詢問的是何者不算是白領犯罪的一種。選項 (A) 為貪汙；選項 (B) 為偽造；選項 (C) 為內線交易；選項 (D) 為偷竊。答案可見最後一段，選 (D)。

補充單字

☆			
☆ 1. traditional	**adj.**	傳統的
☆ 2. condition	**n.**	狀態、情況
☆ 3. skip	**v.**	略過、跳過
☆ 4. flexible	**adj.**	有彈性的
☆ 5. intense	**adj.**	密集的；高強度的
☆ 6. exhausted	**adj.**	疲憊不堪的

Level 1
Level 2
Level 3
Level 4
Level 5
Level 6

不可或缺的團隊合作

聽力測驗 🎧Track 083

在學習英文的過程中，「聽」可能是最直接的第一線接觸，也可能是大家最想要快速習得的能力。現在，就讓我們來熟悉各種英文情境，提升自己的英文臨場感吧！

(   ) 1. A group or team is more than two people working together to achieve a _____.
     (A) common day
     (B) common law
     (C) common cold
     (D) common goal

(   ) 2. Effective team leader plays a essential role in establishing a _____ performance team.
     (A) cheating
     (B) aggressive
     (C) high
     (D) low

(   ) 3. It is essential that team members are _____ in their positions.
     (A) silly and hysterical
     (B) selfish and angry
     (C) headless and talkative
     (D) knowledgeable and skillful

(　　) 4. _____ is an essential part of teamwork.
    (A) Lecture
    (B) Speech
    (C) Leadership
    (D) Meeting

 閱讀測驗

剛剛的聽力測驗是否因為答題不順而感到遺憾？或是覺得自己有某些地方掌握地不夠好？現在就讓我們來直接「看」剛剛的聽力測驗，並透過後面的閱讀測驗來補齊聽力上的不足，同時考驗自己的閱讀能力吧！

A group or team is more than two people working **together**[1] to achieve a common goal. A successful team is one that **achieves**[2] high levels of task performance and member satisfaction. Teamwork is able to achieve the goal quicker because there are many people involved. Successful teamwork is not accomplished as easily as getting a group of individuals together. First of all, individuals need to group around a common goal or task that they are trying to achieve before teamwork is formed. This is how individuality is used to create teamwork. If developed and managed correctly, teams or groups can **evolve**[3] into high performing and extremely useful tools in any organization. Nowadays, more businesses and corporations require their employees to work more in a team than individually. Individuality is a characteristic that sets you apart from everyone else. Individuality shows the personality of a character. But if individuality is properly incorporated in a team, as described above, the outcome might be exploding and brilliant.

It is essential that team members are knowledgeable and skillful in their positions. Team members working **harmoniously**[4] and cooperatively together is also important, and this will form into a high performance team. Leadership is thus also an **essential**[5] part of teamwork. One of the most effective factors to team success is leadership. Organizations depend on teams to achieve specific assignments. Leading a team to realize their strengths can then make a group become a high performance team.

Teamwork is a group of people working towards a common goal. It can be a source where complexity is simplified. If team members can share their strengths with other team members, those who possess good skills and wide knowledge will be a valuable resource to the team. The most important ingredient in the formula of success is knowing how to get along with people. In a team environment, members have different strengths, so they can work problems out faster. Today, small firms and worldwide organizations have realized and **integrated**[6] teamwork methods into their planning. And with the management of a strong leader, a team can go very far. Therefore, teamwork plays an essential role in modern corporations.

【Question】

(　　) 1. Which of the following is not the benefit of teamwork according to the article?
(A) Complexity is simplified.
(B) Problems are solved faster.
(C) It highlights the importance of getting along with people.
(D) It brings in more profits than individual works.

(　　) 2. What does the word "individuality" in comparison with "teamwork" mean?
(A) a feature of a group
(B) a characteristic that sets a person apart from others
(C) a mark of a high-performance team
(D) a quality of an excellent teamwork

【文章中譯】

一個團隊是指兩個以上的人為了實現同一目標而一起工作。一個成功的團隊就是一個能達到任務執行和成員滿足感的最高水準團隊。因為團隊中有很多的成員，因此，團隊合作能夠更快地實現該目標。要想團隊合作成功並不僅僅是把個人組成為一個群體那麼簡單。首先，所有人需要聚集在一個共同的目標或是任務之下，而該目標或任務是他們在團隊組成之前就在努力實現著的事情。這就是如何利用個人性來開展團隊合作。如果發展和管理得當的話，團隊或是團體就能在任何一個組織中演變成一個高績效和極其有用的工具。現在，越來越多的企業和公司要求他們的員工以團隊的形式來進行工作，而不是單獨行動。個人性即是把你和別的人區別開來的一個特點。個性展示出了一個人的性格。但如果個人性能如上述般合適地整合在一個團隊裡，那結果可能會非常具爆炸性和出色。

團隊成員必須具備各自崗位上所需要的知識和技能。團隊成員能共同和諧工作也是很重要的，這將有助於在以後形成一個高績效的團隊。領導者同時也是團隊合作的一個必要組成部分。影響團隊成功最有效的因素之一就是領導能力。企業依靠團隊來實現特定的任務。所以領導每個團員去展示出自己的優勢便可以讓一個團隊擁有高績效。

團隊合作是一群人一起為了同一個目標而工作。它可以化繁為簡。如果團隊成員可以和別的團隊成員共用自己的優勢，那麼，那些擁有良好技能和淵博知識的人就將會是這個隊伍的一種珍貴資源。成功秘方最重要的成分就是知道如何與人相處。在一個團隊中，成員具有不同的優勢，因此，他們就能很快的解決問題。今天，從全球組織到小企業的管理，無不意識到了團隊合作的方法，把它整合到自己的計劃中去。因此，團隊合作在現代合作中發揮著必不可少的作用。

Level 1
Level 2
Level 3
Level 4
Level 5
Level 6

❶ 此題詢問的是一個團隊是由超過兩人以上的人來達成何者。選項 (A) 為共同的一天；選項 (B) 為共同的法律；選項 (C) 為共同的冷漠；選項 (D) 為共同的目標。錄音檔一開始即給我們答案，選 (D)。

❷ 此題詢問的是有效率的團隊領導人在建立何種團隊中扮演著不可或缺的角色。選項 (A) 為作弊的；選項 (B) 為具攻擊性的；選項 (C) 為高的；選項 (D) 為低的。這邊考的是考生能不能理解 "high performance"（高效能）之意，選 (C)。

❸ 此題詢問的是隊員在其職位保有何種特質是相當重要的。選項 (A) 為愚蠢且歇斯底里的；選項 (B) 為自私且憤怒的；選項 (C) 為無腦且多話的；選項 (D) 為知識性且有技能的。在介紹團隊合作的重要性之後，錄音檔即給了我們答案 (D)，此題我們也可以使用刪去法，其它選項皆為負面之意，故不構成團隊要素。

❹ 此題詢問的是何者為團隊工作中重要的一部分。選項 (A) 為講課；選項 (B) 為演講；選項 (C) 為領導能力；選項 (D) 為會議。答案為 (C)，"leadership"（領導能力）可從 "leader"（領導人）來推測其意，進而排除其它選項。

- -

閱讀題目解析

❶ 此題詢問的是根據內文，何者不是團隊合作的好處。選項 (A) 為複雜得以被簡化；選項 (B) 為問題得以被更快解決；選項 (C) 為它強調了與人相處的重要性；選項 (D) 為它比個人型態的工作更能帶收益。答案為

(D)，收益這部分並未在內文中被提及。

❷ 此題詢問的是與 "teamwork" 相較之下的 "individuality" 為何意。選項 (A) 為一個團隊的特質；選項 (B) 為將一個人與其他人區別開來的特點；選項 (C) 為一個高效能團隊的標誌；選項 (D) 為一個傑出團隊合作的特色。這邊我們需要考慮前後文：越來越多公司要求團隊合作，以及多元文化等問題可能會 "raised face to face with individuals"，故 "individual" 及 "individuality" 皆與「個人性（的）」有關，故選 (B)，或可透過其他選項皆直指團隊合作特質而使用刪去法剩下 (B)。

補充單字

☆ 1. together	adv.	一起
☆ 2. achieve	v.	達成
☆ 3. evolve	v.	進化
☆ 4. harmoniously	adv.	和諧地
☆ 5. essential	adj.	必要的
☆ 6. integrate	v.	合併；整合

Level 6
04 The Future of Service Industries

服務業的前景展望

聽力測驗

在學習英文的過程中,「聽」可能是最直接的第一線接觸,也可能是大家最想要快速習得的能力。現在,就讓我們來熟悉各種英文情境,提升自己的英文臨場感吧!

( ) 1. Service industries continue to play an _____ role in the local economy.
    (A) essential   (B) unimportant
    (C) trivia   (D) tedious

( ) 2. Service industries keep growing at a _____ pace.
    (A) slow   (B) fast
    (C) mediate   (D) unbearable

( ) 3. Economists divide all economic activities into two large categories: _____.
    (A) goods and services   (B) food and drink
    (C) health and care   (D) big and small

( ) 4. If you are in the service industry, you know what you are selling is _____.
    (A) magazines
    (B) advertisement
    (C) customer satisfaction
    (D) lunchbox

 閱讀測驗

剛剛的聽力測驗是否因為答題不順而感到遺憾？或是覺得自己有某些地方掌握地不夠好？現在就讓我們來直接「看」剛剛的聽力測驗，並透過後面的閱讀測驗來補齊聽力上的不足，同時考驗自己的閱讀能力吧！

What are **Service**[1] Industries? They are those providing products that cannot be stored and are consumed at the place and time of purchase, representing industries that produce services rather than tangible goods. The importance of service industries in the economic system has been rising steadily, and has become one of main drivers for most countries' economic **development**[2].

Service industries continue to play an essential role in the global economy. Economists divide all economic activities into two large categories: goods and services. From mowing lawns to providing health care to delivering parcels, service industries play an important part in everyday activities of millions of people and businesses. Its emphasis is placed on service performance and the delivery of the service. Generally, these services involve only the performance of actions and have no tangible substance. If you are in the service industry, you know what you are selling is customer satisfaction.

Nowadays, service industries occupy more than three-fifths of the global GDP and employ more than one-third of the labor force internationally. Also, according to the statistics, service industries keep **growing**[3] at a fast pace. One of the booming **categories**[4] is the educational service industry. It consists mainly of school-based education offered by both public and private institutions. These institutions offer corporate training in computer technology, foreign languages, etc. Service industries also include **transportation**[5], information services, health care and social assistance services, arts, entertainment, and recreation services, individual and **miscellaneous**[6] services, and so on.

Over the last ten years, service industries have become the most important business in the world, and the web-based services industry will become the major means of providing a new service experience to the customers. Surely, the rapid development of the Internet will continute to stimulate the service industry even more.

【Question】

(   ) 1. Which direction is service industry developing at based on the passage?
     (A) printing advertisement
     (B) web-based services
     (C) street services
     (D) free samples

(   ) 2. Which of the following is considered as a part of educational service industry?
     (A) non-profit fund-raising activities
     (B) medical practice
     (C) software development program
     (D) school-based education offered by public and private institutions

【文章中譯】

什麼是服務業？服務業提供的是那些不能儲存以及在購買時就即時被消費的產品。它們是生產服務而不是生產有形產品的工業。在經濟體制中，服務業的重要性正穩步提升，成為大多數國家經濟發展的主要推動力之一。

服務業持續在全球經濟發展中扮演著十分重要的角色。經濟學家把所有的經濟活動分為兩大類：貨物和服務。從除草到提供衛生保健到發送貨物，服務業在數以百萬計的人們日常生活和商業活動中發揮著重要的作用。它著重強調服務性能和服務傳遞。總體來講，這些服務僅涉及行為的履行而不是有形的實體。如果你在服務業工作，你就會知道你銷售的是顧客滿意。

如今，服務業已佔據了全球 GDP 的五分之三，甚至更多，且全球從事服務業的勞動力超過三分之一。且根據資料顯示，服務業持續快速增長。其中興起有教育服務業，其主要由公立和私立機構提供的學校基礎教育組成。這些機構提供電腦技術、外語及其他培訓。服務業還包括交通運輸、資訊服務、衛生保健服務、社會援助服務、藝術服務、休閒娛樂服務、以及個人和各種社會服務等。

在過去的十年中，服務業已經成為世界上最重要的商業，且網路服務將會成為向客戶提供新型服務體驗的主要服務方式。無疑地，網際網路的快速發展將會持續使服務業更加繁榮。

聽力題目解析

❶ 此題詢問的是服務業持續在地方經濟中扮演何種角色。選項 (A) 為必要的；選項 (B) 為不重要的；選項 (C) 為瑣碎的；選項 (D) 為冗長的。這邊考 "essential" 作為「必要的」之意，且此字也符合整篇強調服務業發展的重點，選(A)。

❷ 此題詢問的是服務業持續以何種速度增長。選項 (A) 為緩慢的；選項 (B) 為快速的；選項 (C) 為排解；選項 (D) 為無可容忍的。答案為 (B)，我們可以從後面提及的服務業之壯大和重要性攀升來做推測，末段也有出現 "rapid" 同義詞。

❸ 此題詢問的是經濟學家將所有經濟活動區分為哪兩種。選項 (A) 為商品和服務；選項 (B) 為食物和飲料；選項 (C) 為健康與照護；選項 (D) 為大與小。此題無特殊技巧，僅需聆聽把握細節，選 (A)。

❹ 此題詢問的是如果你在服務產業，你應知道你在販賣的為何物。選項 (A) 為雜誌；選項 (B) 為廣告；選項 (C) 為客戶滿意；選項 (D) 為午餐盒。答案為 (C)，這邊我們可以注意到前後文涉及 "intangible"（無形的）之銷售過程。

閱讀題目解析

❶ 此題詢問的是根據內文，服務業正以哪個方向發展。選項 (A) 為印刷廣告；選項 (B) 為網路服務；選項 (C) 為街頭服務；選項 (D) 為免費贈品。答案可見內文最後一段，選擇 (B)。

❷ 此題詢問的是何者被視為是教育服務產業的一部分。選項 (A) 為非營利組織的募款活動；選項 (B) 為醫療實踐；選項 (C) 為軟體開發計畫；選項 (D) 為由公立和私立機構提供的學校基礎教育。答案可見內文倒數第二段，選 (D)。

補充單字

☆	1. service	**n.**	服務
☆	2. development	**n.**	發展
☆	3. grow	**v.**	成長
☆	4. category	**n.**	種類；分類
☆	5. transportation	**n.**	運輸
☆	6. miscellaneous	**adj.**	各種各樣的

The Pros and Cons of Outsourcing

企業外包的好與壞

Level 1
Level 2
Level 3
Level 4
Level 5
Level 6

聽力測驗 🎧 Track 085

在學習英文的過程中,「聽」可能是最直接的第一線接觸,也可能是大家最想要快速習得的能力。現在,就讓我們來熟悉各種英文情境,提升自己的英文臨場感吧!

( ) 1. Many large or small companies _____ certain sorts of jobs to workers in foreign countries.
    (A) output   (B) outcome
    (C) outsource   (D) outrage

( ) 2. Outsourcing lowers _____ costs.
    (A) in person   (B) personal
    (C) person   (D) personnel

( ) 3. Lack of communication between the company and its outsourcing employee can result in huge _____.
    (A) success   (B) losses
    (C) money   (D) cash

( ) 4. Money is burned _____ if there are misunderstandings at the start of a project.
    (A) effectively
    (B) slowly
    (C) peacefully
    (D) rapidly

剛剛的聽力測驗是否因為答題不順而感到遺憾？或是覺得自己有某些地方掌握地不夠好？現在就讓我們來直接「看」剛剛的聽力測驗，並透過後面的閱讀測驗來補齊聽力上的不足，同時考驗自己的閱讀能力吧！

Businesses nowadays often choose to employ outsource workers from outside the company. Many large or small companies outsource **certain**[1] sorts of jobs to workers in foreign countries. Some common examples are technical support, payroll and **accountancy**[2] services, catering, and even writing. The employees can be hired temporarily, or they can be outsourced on a regular basis depending on the project. In this case, the companies do not have to **spend**[3] any extra time and money on advancing technology or training current staff. There are many pros and cons to outsourcing work. So try to consider them all and make a **careful**[4] decision.

Pros: 1. Outsourcing reduces cash outflow; money can be spent in other areas, such as research and development./ 2. Outsourcing works both ways./ 3. Outsourcing **boosts**[5] economy by stimulating trade and creating more jobs./ 4. More workers can be hired for the same, or less, amount of money./ 5. Outsourcing lowers personnel costs./ 6. Outsourcing can increase employee productivity./ 7. It saves management time.

Cons: 1. Services outsourced to offshore countries can cause large-scale job losses in developed nations./ 2. A lot of overseas call centers cannot produce desired results for customers due to the accents of overseas employees./ 3. Lack of communication between the company and its outsourcing employees can result in huge losses./ 4. Money is burned rapidly if there are misunderstandings at the start of a project./ 5. Outsourcing can cause quality problems./ 6. Sometimes outsourcing can cause slow resolution time and sluggish response time./ 7. Lower-than-expected profits and results may occur.

Nowadays, businesses often choose to lease or rent workers from a leasing company. These employees can be noted as temps. The leasing company hires highly trained and experienced workers who are brought in only when needed and then are gone at the end. In most cases, leased employees have a certain **expertise**[6], which excludes the company's need to train current workers. Outsourcing can be a useful tool for making any business more productive and profitable if used properly. The major merit of outsourcing is that it makes the corporation able to invest its resources into more profitable areas.

【Question】

(   ) 1. Which of the following is not a pro of outsourcing based on the passage?
    (A) It saves management time.
    (B) It creates chances for business trips.
    (C) It helps to improve workplace productivity.
    (D) It boosts economy.

(   ) 2. What are the employees working under a leasing company called?
    (A) temps   (B) outsourcing man
    (C) worker   (D) officer

【文章中譯】

現在的企業常常會選擇雇用企業以外的外包人員。很多的大小型企業會把某些特定的工作外包給外國工作者來完成，諸如：技術支援、工資和賬務服務、餐飲、甚至是寫作。這些員工可以是臨時雇用的，或者是根據該專案情況而決定。在這種情形之下，企業就無需再花費額外的時間和金錢來發展技術或者是培訓現有員工。工作外包有利也有弊。我們必須將全部納入考量，審慎地做出決定。

優點：1. 外包減少了資金外流，而這些資金可以用於他處，例如研發。／2.不管是發包還是接件，外包起雙向作用。／3. 外包透過刺激貿易和創造更多的工作機會來促進經濟發展。／4. 可以以同樣或是較低的價錢雇用到更多的工作者。／5. 外包降低了人事成本。／6. 外包可以提高員工的工作效率。╱7. 外包節省了管理時間。

缺點：1. 外包到海外的服務會導致已開發國家的人大規模失業。╱2. 由於海外員工的口音，導致很多海外電話客服中心的服務效果不盡如人意。╱3. 企業和外包員工之間若缺乏交流導致巨大的損失。╱4. 專案一開始就出錯會迅速耗費掉資金。╱5. 外包會引起品質的問題。╱6. 有時候，外包會減慢決策時間和反應時間。╱7. 收益和效果可能會低於預期。

現在，人們在業務上常常會選擇從租賃或人力派遣公司找尋員工。這些員工可以被稱為臨時員工。租賃公司會雇傭經驗豐富、訓練有素的工作者，這些工作者在需要的時候被引進，然後在工作結束時離開。在大部分的情況下，被租用的員工具有某種專業知識或技能，這樣就無需再去培訓現有員工了。外包這個工具要是利用得當的話，有助於增加業務成效和收益。而外包的最大優勢則在於它可以使企業把資源投入到利潤更高的領域。

聽力題目解析

❶ 此題詢問的是許多大大小小的公司會將某些業務 ＿＿＿＿ 到國外。選項 (A) 為產出；選項 (B) 為結果；選項 (C) 為外包；選項 (D) 為憤怒。這邊考的是 "outsource" 作為「外包」之意，我們也可以透過詞性的要求刪除其他名詞選項。

❷ 此題詢問的是外包減少了何種費用。選項 (A) 為親自地；選項 (B) 為個人的；選項 (C) 為人；選項 (D) 為人事。這邊測驗的除了 "personnel" 表「人事」之意外，還考易混淆字 "personal"（個人的；私人的），選 (D)。

❸ 此題詢問的是企業和外包人員之間若缺少溝通會導致龐大的 ＿＿＿＿。選項 (A) 為成功；選項 (B) 為損失；選項 (C) 為金錢；選項 (D) 為現金。選擇 (B)，注意此句是出現在外包的缺點之部分，故需選擇一負面單字。

❹ 此題詢問的是如果在企劃開始前出現誤解，金錢將以何種速度燃燒殆盡。選項 (A) 為有效率地；選項 (B) 為緩慢地；選項 (C) 為和平地；選項 (D) 為快速地。選 (D)，同上，"effectively" 此字具正面涵義，故不選。

閱讀題目解析

❶ 此題詢問的是根據內文，何者不是外包的優點之一。選項 (A) 為它減少了管理時間；選項 (B) 為它創造了出差的機會；選項 (C) 為它幫助提升職場效率；選項 (D) 為它促進經濟。答案可細讀內文，選項 (B)沒有被提及。

❷ 此題詢問的是在租賃或人力派遣公司下工作的人被稱為什麼。答案可見內文最後一段，注意 "be noted as" 為「被當作……；被稱作……」之意，選擇 (A)。 "temps" 同時也為 "temporary"（暫時性的）之延伸。

補充單字

☆ 1. certain	adj.	特定的
☆ 2. accountancy	n.	會計
☆ 3. spend	v.	花費
☆ 4. careful	adj.	小心的
☆ 5. boost	v.	提振
☆ 6. expertise	n.	專業技能；專業知識

Level 6
06 Livestreaming Economy
直播經濟

在學習英文的過程中，「聽」可能是最直接的第一線接觸，也可能是大家最想要快速習得的能力。現在，就讓我們來熟悉各種英文情境，提升自己的英文臨場感吧！

( ) 1. What can live-streamers get from their viewers?
(A) water and electricity
(B) toothpaste and soap
(C) money and digital gifts
(D) toothbrush

( ) 2. Where does most live-streaming take place?
(A) in a movie theater
(B) on a virtual stage
(C) in the bathroom
(D) in the waiting room

( ) 3. What kind of live-streaming platform do people in China use to get public attention?
(A) YY
(B) Line
(C) YouTube
(D) WeChat

( ) 4. What do live-streamers perform for their viewers?
(A) gargle and spit
(B) daydream
(C) cut newspapers
(D) sing, dance, or present a talk show program

(　　) 5. How much can top live-streamers earn per month?
　　　　(A) US$100,000
　　　　(B) US$1,000
　　　　(C) US$100
　　　　(D) US$10

 **閱讀測驗**

剛剛的聽力測驗是否因為答題不順而感到遺憾？或是覺得自己有某些地方掌握地不夠好？現在就讓我們來直接「看」剛剛的聽力測驗，並透過後面的閱讀測驗來補齊聽力上的不足，同時考驗自己的閱讀能力吧！

A young Chinese woman sits in front of a video camera on her laptop. After introducing herself and greeting her viewers, she begins to **live-stream**[1] on how to apply makeup step by step. In the meantime, digital gifts start pouring in. Some viewers donate money via the streaming platform, while others give compliments. After finishing her makeup, she has earned several thousand US dollars from admirers, suprisingly in just 15 minutes. It all takes place all on a virtual stage.

Starting as a social media fad, live-streaming has quickly become a **lucrative**[2] **microeconomy**[3] in China that anyone can be a part of, regardless of social status, gender, or income. Live-streamers do not have to be exceptionally gifted or talented. All they need are loyal fans who will eventually become their **munificent**[4] patrons. In real life, this could not happen; but online, it becomes easily possible.

In the US, Canada, or the UK, **would-be**[5] Internet stars use YouTube or Instagram as a platform to get people's attention. In China, people use a live-streaming platform called YY, where they sing, dance, or present a talk show program to entertain viewers to get digital gifts. Top streamers can earn at least US$100,000 per month, so lots of people are trying to jump on the bandwagon of live-streaming economy now.

【Question】

(　　) 1. In this article, what did the young Chinese woman live-stream for her viewers?
- (A) how to apply makeup
- (B) how to make tea
- (C) how to write calligraphy
- (D) how to decorate a room

(　　) 2. Essentially, what do live-streamers need?
- (A) chocolate
- (B) munificent patrons
- (C) young viewers
- (D) a new computer

【文章中譯】

一位年輕的中國女子坐在筆電攝影機前面，在簡單自我介紹並和觀眾問候之後，便開始網路直播上妝的步驟。同時，數位禮物開始湧入，有些觀眾透過直播平台贈送金錢，有些則表示讚美。從開始直播到妝容完成，她就從眾多仰慕者那裡賺到數千美元，令人驚奇的是這只發生在十五分鐘之內，且這一切都發生在虛擬的舞台上。

直播剛開始只是社群媒體一時的流行，但很快地便在中國成為利潤頗豐的微型經濟，而且不管社會地位、性別或收入，任何人都能參與其中。直播主不需要特別具有天賦或才華，他們只需要擁有忠實的粉絲，而這群觀眾最後能變成慷慨的主顧即可。這在現實中不太可能發生，但在網路上，這即容易成為可能。

在美國、加拿大、英國，想成為網紅的人會使用YouTube或Instagram做為吸引眾人目光的平台。在中國，人們則利用名為YY的直播平台表演唱歌、舞蹈、脫口秀節目給觀眾看，以獲取數位禮物。頂尖的直播主每個月至少能賺十萬美元，這也就是為什麼目前仍有許多人試圖搭乘直播經濟的順風車。

聽力題目解析

❶ 此題詢問的是直播主能從觀眾方獲取什麼。選項 (A) 為水和電；選項 (B) 為牙膏和肥皂；選項 (C) 為錢和數位禮物；選項 (D) 為牙刷。錄音檔開頭即指出 "...digital gifts start pouring in. Some viewers donate money via the streaming platform..." 這邊掌握 "pour in"（湧入）和 "donate"（捐贈）即可，選(C)。

❷ 此題詢問的是直播大多在哪裡進行。選項 (A) 為在戲院；選項 (B) 為在虛擬舞台；選項 (C) 為在廁所；選項 (D) 為在候診室。這邊考的是 "take place" 作為「發生於」之意，答案選 (B)。

❸ 此題詢問的是中國民眾用哪種直播平台吸引大眾目光。選項 (A) 為歪歪語音（YY）；選項 (B) 為 Line；選項 (C) 為 YouTube；選項 (D) 為 WeChat。錄音檔後段提到 "In China, people use a livestreaming platform called YY ..." 這邊掌握 "called" 作為 "platform" 之補充即可，答案選 (A)。

❹ 此題詢問的是直播主會為觀眾表演什麼節目。選項 (A) 為漱口和吐水；選項 (B) 為做白日夢；選項 (C) 為剪報紙；選項 (D) 為唱歌、舞蹈、脫口秀節目。錄音檔有給我們與選項相同之陳述，故仔細聽即可，答案選 (D)。

❺ 此題詢問的是頂尖直播主每個月能賺多少錢。選項 (A) 為十萬美元；選項 (B) 為一千美元；選項 (C) 為一百美元；選項 (D) 為十美元。同上，答案選 (A)。

閱讀題目解析

❶ 此題詢問的是本文中的年輕中國女子向觀眾直播什麼節目。選項 (A) 為如何上妝；選項 (B) 為如何泡茶；選項 (C) 為如何寫書法；選項 (D) 為如何佈置房間。答案可見內文第一段，選 (A)。

❷ 此題詢問的是直播主實際上需要的是什麼。選項 (A) 為巧克力；選項 (B) 為慷慨的主顧；選項 (C) 為年輕的觀眾；選項 (D) 為一台新電腦。答案詳見內文第二段，答案選 (B)。

補充單字

	單字	詞性	中文
☆	1. live-stream	v.	直播
☆	2. lucrative	adj.	利潤豐厚的
☆	3. microeconomy	n.	微型經濟
☆	4. munificent	adj.	慷慨的
☆	5. would-be	adj.	想要成為的

Level 1
Level 2
Level 3
Level 4
Level 5
Level 6

Level 6
07 AI Virtual Nursing Assistants

人工智慧虛擬護理助理

聽力測驗 🎧 Track 087

在學習英文的過程中，「聽」可能是最直接的第一線接觸，也可能是大家最想要快速習得的能力。現在，就讓我們來熟悉各種英文情境，提升自己的英文臨場感吧！

( ) 1. According to the article, what is revolutionizing healthcare and enhancing the quality of clinical care?
(A) artificial intelligence
(B) virtual reality
(C) Pokemon Go
(D) live streaming

( ) 2. Which of the following service is AI virtual nursing assistants unable to offer patients?
(A) 24/7 data support and monitoring service
(B) quick answers to questions about patients' health condition and medications
(C) reduction of unnecessary hospital visits
(D) food cooking

( ) 3. In what way do AI virtual nursing assistants help medical professionals?
(A) They can take more days off.
(B) They can go on a vacation more often.
(C) They can focus on their jobs more efficiently.
(D) They can relax more at home.

(   ) 4. How many percent of patients reported comfort in the replacement of human nurses with AI virtual nurse assistants?

(A) 30%   (B) 64%

(C) 50%   (D) 100%

(   ) 5. According to the article, do most patients think that AI can replace physicians?

(A) Yes.

(B) No.

(C) Absolutely.

(D) Definitely.

閱讀測驗

剛剛的聽力測驗是否因為答題不順而感到遺憾？或是覺得自己有某些地方掌握地不夠好？現在就讓我們來直接「看」剛剛的聽力測驗，並透過後面的閱讀測驗來補齊聽力上的不足，同時考驗自己的閱讀能力吧！

Artificial[1] intelligence (AI) is revolutionizing healthcare in various ways. With the combination of AI, the application of big data, machine learning, **deep learning**[2], and natural language processing has led to inventions of medical tools that can significantly enhance the quality of clinical care and the overall medical efficiency.

One of those is AI virtual **nursing**[3] assistants, which can offer patients 24/7 data support and **monitoring**[4] service, as well as quick answers to questions about their health condition and medications. This helps reduce the number of unnecessary hospital visits while medical professionals can focus on their jobs more efficiently.

Some AI virtual nursing assistants have been working with patients across the world. According to a survey, while many patients do not think AI can replace physicians, 64% of patients hold a positive attitude toward the **replacement**[5] of human nurses with AI virtual nursing assistants.

【 Question 】

(　　) 1. Which of the following technology is NOT used to develop AI virtual nursing assistants?
　　　(A) machine learning
　　　(B) bibliographic framework
　　　(C) deep learning
　　　(D) natural language processing

(　　) 2. Which of the following is a synonym to enhance?
　　　(A) lessen
　　　(B) exaggerate
　　　(C) debase
　　　(D) improve

【 文章中譯 】

人工智慧在健康照護的領域產生多樣的革命，與人工智慧結合在一起之後，大數據、機器學習、深度學習、及自然語言處理的應用，已促使了能大幅提升臨床照護品質及全面性照護效率的醫學儀器之發明。

其中一項發明是人工智慧虛擬護理助理，它能提供全年無休、每日24小時的數據支援與監測服務，並協助病人迅速獲得有關其健康狀況及醫藥問題的答覆。這有助於減少病人去醫院的次數，也讓醫療專業人士能更有效率地專注在他們的工作上。

有些人工智慧虛擬護理助理已在為世界各地的病人服務。根據一項調查，儘管許多病人不認為人工智慧能取代醫師，但有百分之六十四的病人對於人工智慧虛擬護理助理取代護理人員抱持樂觀態度。

❶ 此題詢問的是根據本文，何者正在照護領域做出革命性的貢獻，並提升臨床照護品質。選項 (A) 為人工智慧；選項 (B) 為虛擬實境；選項 (C) 為寶可夢；選項 (D) 為直播。錄音檔開頭即給出答案，選 (A)。

❷ 此題詢問的是以下何者並非人工智慧虛擬護理助理能對病人提供的協助。選項 (A) 為全年無休、每日二十四小時的數據支援與監測服務；選項 (B) 為迅速獲得有關健康情形或醫藥問題的答覆；選項 (C) 為減少病人去醫院的次數；選項 (D) 為烹調食物。答案選 (D)，此題型僅能特別注意主題的介紹。

❸ 此題詢問的是人工智慧虛擬護理助理能如何協助醫學專家。選項 (A) 為他們能請更多天假；選項 (B) 為他們能更常去渡假；選項 (C) 為他們能更有效率地專注在工作上；選項 (D) 為他們能在家更放鬆。錄音檔中後段提到 "This helps ... while medical professionals can do their jobs more efficiently." 故選 (C)。

❹ 此題詢問的是有多少百分比的病人表示能接受人工智慧虛擬護理助理取代護理人員。錄音檔在聽到 "survey"、"research"，或是 "investigation" 時，都需特別注意接下來可能會出現的數字，因數字為常見考題，此題答案選 (B)。

❺ 此題詢問的是根據調查，大部分病人認為人工智慧是否能取代醫師。選項 (A) 為能；選項 (B) 為不能；選項 (C) 為絕對可以；選項 (D) 為完全可以。答案選 (A)，這邊需要特別注意 "hold a positive attitude"（持正向態度）和過半數的 "64%"。

閱讀題目解析

❶ 第一題詢問的是以下何種科技並未用來發展人工智慧虛擬護理助理。選項 (A) 為機器學習；選項 (B) 為書目框架；選項 (C) 為深度學習；選項 (D) 為自然語言處理。答案可見內文第一段，選 (B)。（註：(B) 選項所提書目框架是專門運於在圖書館。）

❷ 第二題詢問的是以下何者是「enhance」的同義字。選項 (A) 為減少；選項 (B) 為誇大；選項 (C) 為貶低；選項 (D) 為改善。本題考的是考生是否知道題目中synonym是「同義字」的意思（補充：反義字是antonym），答案選 (D)。

補充單字

☆ 1. artificial	adj.	人工的
☆ 2. deep learning	n.	深度學習
☆ 3. nursing	n.	護理
☆ 4. monitor	v.	監測
☆ 5. replacement	n.	取代

The Main Differences between American English and British English

美式英語與英式英語的主要差異

聽力測驗 🎧Track 088

在學習英文的過程中，「聽」可能是最直接的第一線接觸，也可能是大家最想要快速習得的能力。現在，就讓我們來熟悉各種英文情境，提升自己的英文臨場感吧！

( ) 1. This passage is about _____.
　　(A) the English history
　　(B) the English weather
　　(C) the English language
　　(D) the English people

( ) 2. In the article, how many main differences between American English and British English are mentioned?
　　(A) one
　　(B) two
　　(C) three

( ) 3. Which of the following sentences is mostly used in British English?
　　(A) I suggest that the draft should be revised.
　　(B) I just received a call.
　　(C) I have to do something.

(   ) 4. Which is an American expression?

    (A) I've already seen it.

    (B) She's lost her car keys. Can you help her find them?

    (C) I already saw it.

 閱讀測驗

剛剛的聽力測驗是否因為答題不順而感到遺憾？或是覺得自己有某些地方掌握地不夠好？現在就讓我們來直接「看」剛剛的聽力測驗，並透過後面的閱讀測驗來補齊聽力上的不足，同時考驗自己的閱讀能力吧！

English is spoken in many countries. The two commonly used **versions**[1] of English are British and American English. In fact, British and American English are quite **similar**[2]. New media and **globalization**[3] have made more and more people capable of understanding the disparities.

There are three main differences between British and American English. The first is the **spelling**[4] disparities. For example, the "s" in the word "analyse" is replaced by an "z" in America, and the "re" is often reversed in British English, such as "theatre." The second main difference lies in the use of vocabulary. There are a large number of words between British and American English that have the same meaning but look totally different. For example, "fall" becomes "autumn" in British English, or "lift" becomes "elevator" in American English.

The third dissimilarity is the use of the present perfect vs. past tense. In British English, the present perfect is used to express an action that has occurred in the recent past and has an effect on the present moment. For example: "She's lost her car keys. Can you help her find them?" But in American English, the following is also **possible**[5]: "She lost her wallet. Can you help her look for it?" In British English, the above past-tense sentence would be considered incorrect. However, both forms are generally accepted in American English. Here are some other examples of expressions: In

British English (present perfect), we may hear "I've just received a ring."/ "I've already seen it."/ "Have you completed your work yet?"/ "I suggest that the draft should be revised."/ "I have got to do something." In American English (both present perfect and past tense are acceptable), we may hear "I've just received a call." or "I just received a call."/ "I've already seen it." or "I already saw it."/ "Have you done your job?" or "Did you do your job yet?"/ "I suggest that the draft be revised."/ "I have to do something."

To sum up, there are indeed quite a few differences between American English and British English. So if you can get familiar with these main differences, you can better **handle**[6] English in listening, writing, reading, speaking and so on.

【Question】

(   ) 1. What is the British way of spelling "theater" according to the article?
(A) thaeter
(B) theatre
(C) thaetre
(D) theatr

(   ) 2. What is the American way of saying "lift" according to the article?
(A) left
(B) sidewalk
(C) litter
(D) elevator

【文章中譯】

很多國家都講英語，而常用的兩種英語就是英式英語和美式英語。事實上，英式和美式英語大同小異。新媒介的出現和全球化使得越來越多的人能夠更加瞭解這兩種形式的英語。

英式英語和美式英語主要有大三不同，第一個是拼音。舉例來說，在「analyse」中的「s」在美國就會被「z」取代，以及「re」常常在英式英語中被顛倒過來，像是「theater」變成「theatre」。第二個差異在於字彙的使用。在英式英語和美式英語中存在著大量意思相同可是長相完全不同的單字。例如，美式英語中的「fall」在英式英語裡為「autumn」；而在英式英語裡的「lift」則於美式英語中變成「elevator」。

第三個主要的不同在於現在完成式與過去式的使用。在英式英語中，現在完成式表達的是一個發生在不久前的過去的動作對現在所產生的影響。例如：「她已弄丟了她的車鑰匙，你可以幫忙她找嗎？」但是在美式英語中，他們也會這樣說：「她丟了錢包，你可以幫忙她找嗎？」在英式英語中，這個使用過去式的句子就是錯的。不過在美式英語裡，兩者都是可以被接受的。其它的例句如下：在英式英語中（現在完成式），我們會聽見「我剛才收到了一枚戒指。」／「我已經看到它了。」／「你完成你的工作了嗎？」／「我建議草圖應該修改。」／「有些事情我不得不做。」在美式英語中（現在完成式和過去式都可以），我們會聽見「我剛才已接了一通電話。」或者「我剛接了通電話。」／「我已經看到它了。」或者「我看到它了。」／「你已經完成工作了嗎？」或者「你完成你的工作了嗎？」／「我建議草圖進行修改。」／「有些事情我必須做。」

總而言之，美式英語和英式英語之間的確存在著很多差異。因此，如果你掌握好這些主要差異，你就可以在聽說讀寫方面對英語運用自如了。

聽力題目解析

❶ 此題詢問的是文章主旨。選項 (A) 為英語歷史；選項 (B) 為英國天氣；選項 (C) 為英語 為；選項 (D) 為英國人。內文區分了美式英語與英式英語，故選 (C)。

❷ 此題詢問的是根據內文，美式英語與英式英語有幾種不同。錄音檔有提及 "There are three main differences ..." 答案為 (C)，也可透過後面的

介紹來得知。

❸ 此題詢問的是選項何者句型較常出現在英式英語。答案為 (A)，此題型需先記得內文如何區分英式與美式英語的差別，才可以使用刪除法得到答案。

❹ 此題詢問的是選項何者為美式英語的用法。答案為 (C)，同上。

● ●

閱讀題目解析

❶ 此題詢問的是「theater」此字的英式拼法為何。答案見內文第二段，選 (B)。

❷ 此題詢問的是「lift」此字的美式用法為何。答案可見內文第三段，選 (D)。

補充單字

☆ 1. version	n.	版本
☆ 2. similar	adj.	相似的
☆ 3. globalization	n.	全球化
☆ 4. spelling	n.	拼法
☆ 5. possible	adj.	可能的
☆ 6. handle	v.	處理

The So-Called Postmodernism

所謂的後現代主義

聽力測驗 Track 089

在學習英文的過程中，「聽」可能是最直接的第一線接觸，也可能是大家最想要快速習得的能力。現在，就讓我們來熟悉各種英文情境，提升自己的英文臨場感吧！

(　　) 1. This passage is mainly about _____.
   (A) architecture
   (B) drama
   (C) postmodernism
   (D) modernism

(　　) 2. Postmodernism is a literary, political, and social _____.
   (A) philosophy　　　(B) science
   (C) reform　　　(D) problem

(　　) 3. Post modernity focuses on social and political innovations globally, especially since the _____ in the West.
   (A) 1960s　　　(B) 1970s
   (C) 1970s　　　(D) 1980s

(　　) 4. Postmodernism was originally a reaction to _____.
   (A) postmodernism
   (B) naturalism
   (C) supernaturalism
   (D) modernism

閱讀測驗

剛剛的聽力測驗是否因為答題不順而感到遺憾？或是覺得自己有某些地方掌握地不夠好？現在就讓我們來直接「看」剛剛的聽力測驗，並透過後面的閱讀測驗來補齊聽力上的不足，同時考驗自己的閱讀能力吧！

Postmodernism[1] mixes old themes with new and contemporary issues to create beautiful artworks that guide and fascinate all spectators to participate in the discovery of their meanings. Postmodernism is an intricate term, or a set of concepts, that has only come into view as a field of academic study which focuses on social and political innovations globally, especially since the mid-1980s in the West. Postmodernism is an intellectual activity that results from the **intensification**[2], **radicalization**[3], or transformation of the course of modernity. Postmodernism is not easy to define, because it is an idea that emerges in a wide variety of disciplines or fields of study, including art, architecture, film, literature etc.

Postmodernism literally means "after-the-modernist activity." Along with an interior meaning and beauty, postmodernism is used as a form of communication toward social, political, and cultural issues around the world. Also associated with postmodernism is the recent evolution in philosophy and critical theories which have entirely dismantled the idea of a coherent subject, leaving open the very location of signification and even its existence. Anthropologists are thus compelled to **contend**[4] with the changes created by postmodernism in various ways.

It's difficult to locate it temporally or historically because it's not clear exactly when postmodernism commenced. Maybe the most effortless way to think of postmodernism is to start from modernism, the activity from which postmodernism develops. Society was rebelling against modern concepts and had lost belief in the modern ideals. As the reactionary activity against modern activity, postmodernism can be examined from the changes in architecture. The postmodern epoch freed its artists from old traditional barriers that confined them. It employed all methods, materials, forms, and colors available. Postmodernism basically represented the reactions against the nearly **totalitarian**[5] features of Modernist thoughts, which favor personal preferences and conclusive truths or principles.

In sum, traditional thinking has comprehended the world as including both chaos and harmony. While "modern" itself refers to something related to the present, the activity of modernism and the reaction of postmodernism are basically defined by multiple viewpoints, and it is precisely this atmosphere of judgment and **skepticism**[6] that help explain postmodern philosophy.

【Question】

(　　) 1. Which field of knowledge is used as an example to view postmodernism?
(A) literature
(B) music
(C) movie
(D) architecture

(　　) 2. Which of the following is wrong regarding postmodernism?
(A) It challenges authorities.
(B) It frees traditions.
(C) It is an intellectual activity.
(D) It is about sticking to principles.

【文章中譯】

後現代主義融合了新舊時代主題，進而創造出優美的藝術作品，這些作品支配並迷惑所有人去參與到其內涵的發現之旅。後現代主義是一個很複雜的術語，或者也可以說是一種自 1980 年代中期以來出現在學術領域的思潮。後現代主義是一種由現代化過程的加劇、激化和轉化所引發的智力運動。後現代主義很難去界定，因為它是出現在各種學科和研究領域中的概念，包括藝術、建築、電影、文學等。

後現代主義字面上意為「現代主義之後的運動」。伴隨其內在含義及美感，後現代主義已經被當做一種直接針對世界上社會、政治和文化問題的溝通形式來使用。另外與後現代主義相關的是在哲學和批判理論上的發展，其將一連貫主體的觀念拆解，留下了意義位址和存在性的開放問題。人類學家因此被迫應付由後現代主義所引發的各種變化。

後現代主義很難用時間或歷史去劃定，因為目前無法明定後現代主義的起始點。或許思考後現代主義最簡單的方式就是思考現代主義，也就是後現代主義的發源。社會反抗現代觀念，並對現代理想失去信心。而作為一種對現代運動的反動，後現代主義運動可從建築領域中的改變來觀看。後現代主義將藝術家從阻礙他們的牢籠中解放出來。它借鑒所有方法、材料、形式和顏色來表現作品。後現代主義基本上代表著對於現代極權思想、個人偏好，及最終真理和原則的回應。

總結來說，傳統的思想認為世界整體上都包含混亂和和諧。所以儘管「現代」一詞本身牽涉到當下，現代主義運動及後續的後現代主義反應根本上都是由一系列不同的觀點界定的，而也正是這種批判和質疑的氛圍才幫助我們理解後現代主義哲學。

聽力題目解析

❶ 此題詢問的是內文主旨。選項 (A) 為建築；選項 (B) 為戲劇；選項 (C) 為後現代主義；選項 (D) 為現代主義。錄音檔一開始即給我們答案，選 (C)。

❷ 此題詢問後現代是一種文學、政治及社會的 ＿＿＿＿＿。選項 (A) 為哲學；選項 (B) 為科學；選項 (C) 為改革；選項 (D) 為問題。錄音檔最後即給答案，選 (A)。

❸ 此題詢問的是後現代著重於社會和政治的全球性革命，尤其是始於西

方的什麼年代。在一開始介紹後現代主義時，我們可以把握 "has only come into view"（始出現於……）來做為年份的提示，選 (D)。

❹ 此題詢問的是後現代主義起初是對於何種主義的反動。選項 (A) 為後現代主義；選項 (B) 為自然主義；選項 (C) 為超自然主義；選項 (D) 為現代主義。

• •

閱讀題目解析

❶ 此題詢問的是內文使用哪一個領域來做為觀看後現代主義的例子。選項 (A) 為文學；選項 (B) 為音樂；選項 (C) 為電影；選項 (D) 為建築。答案可見內文第三段，選 (D)。

❷ 此題詢問的是選項關於後現代主義的描述何者是錯的。選項 (A) 為它挑戰權威；選項 (B) 為它解放傳統；選項 (C) 為它是一種智識活動；選項 (D) 為它涉及原則的堅守。這邊可以從第三段來推論，後現代主義應是擺脫框框的，選 (D)。

補充單字

☆ 1. postmodernism	n.	後現代主義
☆ 2. intensification	n.	加劇、加強
☆ 3. radicalization	n.	激烈化
☆ 4. contend	v.	抗衡、競爭
☆ 5. totalitarianism	n.	極權主義
☆ 6. skeptism	n.	懷疑、質疑

Level 6
10 E-Commerce and Modern Logistics

大數據與電子商務

🎧 **聽力測驗** 🎧 Track 090

在學習英文的過程中，「聽」可能是最直接的第一線接觸，也可能是大家最想要快速習得的能力。現在，就讓我們來熟悉各種英文情境，提升自己的英文臨場感吧！

(   ) 1. The passage mainly talks about _____.
    (A) machine learning
    (B) live-streaming
    (C) financial industry
    (D) E-commerce

(   ) 2. According to the article, how long are online shops open for business?
    (A) 7 hours
    (B) 10 hours
    (C) 12 hours
    (D) 24 hours

(   ) 3. Many customers prefer to buy goods from e-commerce because it is convenient and _____.
    (A) time-coding
    (B) time-consuming
    (C) time-recording
    (D) time-saving

(　　) 4. According to the article, how do the public feel about e-commerce?
      (A) They prefer to use it for shopping.
      (B) They prefer to go to brick-and-mortar stores for shopping.
      (C) They feel nothing about e-commerce.
      (D) They hold a hostile attitute towrd e-commerce.

 閱讀測驗

剛剛的聽力測驗是否因為答題不順而感到遺憾？或是覺得自己有某些地方掌握地不夠好？現在就讓我們來直接「看」剛剛的聽力測驗，並透過後面的閱讀測驗來補齊聽力上的不足，同時考驗自己的閱讀能力吧！

E-commerce means that companies run their business online, and they are open 24 hours a day and 7 days a week. Such new model of transaction has accordingly changed the relationship between buyers and sellers. Almost anything can be purchased, traded, or sold via the Internet. You select your items, and your e-commerce retailer will get it **delivered**[1] to your door the next day; the price is also slightly cheaper.

Customers can view products, read product descriptions, and sometimes even try samples as long as they have the access to the Internet. In **essence**[2], e-commerce is a broad term describing the electronic exchange of business data between two or more organizations' computers. E-commerce is thus an important factor that makes people's lives more convenient and **efficient**[3]. That also explains why many customers prefer to buy goods from e-commerce. It is more convenient and **time-saving**[4]. The service is fast and the delivery is fast as well. Therefore, **unsuprisingly**[5], e-commerce has developed exponentially in the last few years. Electronic money also makes it easier for smaller businesses to achieve success.

All in all, the Internet has grown from simply sending messages to creating plaforms where different operating systems sell and buy products as if in the tangible world. Customers can click the products they want to buy, and after filling out the customer information, the product will be shipped and received in a few days.

【Question】

(　　) 1. What can we infer from the article about the evolution of the Internet?
　　　(A) It has been continuously simplified.
　　　(B) It became out-dated.
　　　(C) It can handle more complicated tasks.
　　　(D) It remains the same.

(　　) 2. Which of the following is not mentioned in the article as someone would do if connected to the Internet for online shopping?
　　　(A) view products
　　　(B) read e-books
　　　(C) try samples
　　　(D) read product descriptions

【文章中譯】

電子商務意味著商業公司在網路上進行作業,且網路商店一周七天,每天二十四小時營業。這樣的新型態交易方式則相應地改變了買賣雙方的關係。幾乎任何東西都能夠在網際網路上買進、交易或出售。你選擇你要的商品,電子商務零售商第二天就會把它送上門,而且它的價格也會比商場中的便宜一些。

只要連上網路,顧客就可以流覽商品、閱讀產品說明,甚至有時候可以試用樣品。就本質上來說,電子商務就是廣義上描述兩個或更多企業之間電子資料交換的術語。電子商務因此是使人們的生活更便捷、更高效的重要因素。這同時也是為什麼許多顧客喜歡在網上買東西,因為它方便而且節省時間。它的服務快捷,送貨也很快。因此,不意外地,電子商務在過去的幾年裡開始興起。電子貨幣也更容易使小商家獲得成功。

總而言之，網路的發展已從單純傳訊，到創造出能讓不同運作系統彷彿在有形世界中一樣進行買賣的平台。顧客可以透過點選他們想要購買的商品，並在填寫完客戶資訊之後，在幾天內就收到出貨的商品。

聽力題目解析

❶ 此題詢問的是文章主旨。選項 (A) 為機器學習；選項 (B) 為直播；選項 (C) 為金融業；選項 (D) 為電子商務。錄音檔在一開始即給我們答案，選 (D)。

❷ 此題詢問的是根據內文，線上商店的營業時間為多久。這邊考考生是否能把握 "24 hours a day"（一整天）的用法，以及 "open" 作為「營業」之意，選 (D)。

❸ 此題詢問的是許多顧客喜歡透過電商購買物品的原因是便利及選項何者。選項 (A) 為時間編碼的；選項 (B) 為浪費時間的；選項 (C) 為紀錄時間的；選項 (D) 為節省時間的。除了細聽錄音檔之外，我們也可以透過 "time- " 後面銜接的單字來判斷：save 為「節省；拯救；免除」之意，那麼透過內文，與時間搭配在一起便表「節省時間的」之意，故透過前後文可推斷答案為 (D)。（註：選項 (B) 的 consume 為「消耗；消費」之意）

❹ 此題詢問的是根據內文，大眾對於電子商務的感受為何。選項 (A) 為他們現在偏好透過電商購物；選項 (B) 為他們偏好去實體店面購物；選項 (C) 為他們對電商沒有感覺；選項 (D) 為他們對電商抱持敵對態度。在介紹完電商的便利性後，我們聽見 "That also explains why…" 來解釋大眾現在對電商的偏好，選 (A)。

閱讀題目解析

❶ 此題詢問的是我們可以針對網路的演進這個主題從內文推斷出何者。選項 (A) 為它不斷地被簡化；選項 (B) 為它變得過時；選項 (C) 為它可以處理更複雜的任務；選項 (D) 為它維持不變。答案可從內文最後一段的第一句推測，選 (C)。

❷ 此題詢問的是當某人連結到網路來進行網路購物時，他會做的事情根據內文不包括選項何者。選項 (A) 為瀏覽商品；選項 (B) 為讀電子書；選項 (C) 為使用試用品；選項 (D) 為讀產品敘述。答案可見內文第二段，選 (B)。

補充單字

☆ 1. deliver	**v.**	運輸
☆ 2. essence	**n.**	本質；要素
☆ 3. efficient	**adj.**	有效率的
☆ 4. time-saving	**adj.**	節省時間的
☆ 5. unsurprisingly	**adv.**	不令人驚訝地

Level 1
Level 2
Level 3
Level 4
Level 5
Level 6

NOTE

原來如此 系列 E232

一本掌握英文聽力╳閱讀，
戰勝各大英文考試

以戰養戰，掌握「聽力」和「閱讀」，高分自然輕鬆手到擒來！

作　　者	張慈庭英語教學團隊
顧　　問	曾文旭
社　　長	王毓芳
編輯統籌	耿文國、黃璽宇
主　　編	吳靜宜、姜怡安
執行編輯	吳佳芬
美術編輯	王桂芳、張嘉容
封面設計	阿作
法律顧問	北辰著作權事務所　蕭雄淋律師、幸秋妙律師

初　　版	2020 年 09 月
出　　版	捷徑文化出版事業有限公司
電　　話	（02）2752-5618
傳　　真	（02）2752-5619

定　　價	新台幣 450 元／港幣 150 元
產品內容	1 書

總 經 銷	采舍國際有限公司
地　　址	235 新北市中和區中山路二段 366 巷 10 號 3 樓
電　　話	（02）8245-8786
傳　　真	（02）8245-8718

港澳地區總經銷	和平圖書有限公司
地　　址	香港柴灣嘉業街 12 號百樂門大廈 17 樓
電　　話	（852）2804-6687
傳　　真	（852）2804-6409

▶本書圖片由 Shutterstock圖庫、123RF圖庫提供。

捷徑 Book站

現在就上臉書（FACEBOOK）「捷徑BOOK站」並按讚加入粉絲團，
就可享每月不定期新書資訊和粉絲專享小禮物喔！

http://www.facebook.com/royalroadbooks
讀者來函：royalroadbooks@gmail.com

國家圖書館出版品預行編目資料

一本掌握英文聽力╳閱讀，戰勝各大英文考試 / 張
慈庭英語教學團隊著 . -- 初版 . -- 臺北市 : 捷徑文化，
2020.09
　　面；　公分（原來如此：E232）

ISBN 978-986-5507-41-1(平裝)

1. 英語 2. 讀本

805.18　　　　　　　　　　　　　　　　109011910